Daily Lives in

Nghsi-Altai

Robert Nichols

VP Festschrift Series:

Volume 1: Christine Brooke-Rose
Volume 2: Gilbert Adair
Volume 3: The Syllabus
Volume 4: Rikki Ducornet
Volume 5: Raymond Federman
Volume 6: The Oulipo
(Edited by G.N. Forester and M.J. Nicholls)

Reprint Titles:

The Languages of Love
The Sycamore Tree
The Dear Deceit
The Middlemen
Go When You See the Green Man Walking
Next
Xorandor/Verbivore
by Christine Brooke-Rose

Three Novels — Rosalyn Drexler
Knut — Tom Mallin
Erowina — Tom Mallin
The Greater Infortune/The Connecting Door — Rayner Heppenstall
The Penelope Shuttle Omnibus — Penelope Shuttle
Conversations with Critics — Nicolas Tredell
The Utopian — Michael Westlake
Image for Investigation: About my Father — Christoph Meckel
Meritocrats — Stuart Evans
Bartleby — Chris Scott
How to Outthink a Wall: An Anthology — Marvin Cohen
An Aesthetic of Obscenity: Five Novels — Jeff Nuttall
Imaginary Women — Michael Westlake
A Day at the Office — Robert Alan Jamieson
Caliban's Filibuster — Paul West
The Exagggerations of Peter Prince — Steve Katz
The Alan Burns Omnibus: Volume One — Alan Burns
Verbatim: A Novel — Jeff Bursey

New fiction:

Mirrors on which dust has fallen — Jeff Bursey
Balzac's Coffee, DaVinci's Ristorante — Mark Axelrod

other Verbivoracious titles @ www.verbivoraciouspress.org

Daily Lives in

Nghsi-Altai

Robert Nichols

Verbivoracious Press

Glentrees, 13 Mt Sinai Lane, Singapore

This edition published in Great Britain & Singapore

by Verbivoracious Press

www.verbivoraciouspress.org

ISBN: 978-981-11-6034-9

Printed and bound in Great Britain & Singapore

First published in the US by New Directions (1977-1979), except *Red Shift*, published by Three Penny Press (1977).

CONTENTS

Robert Brayton Nichols: A Critical Introduction

ELIZA NICHOLS & STEFFEN SILVIS

> **"Works so near us in time and produced in an environment of advanced technology and preservation modes—in other words not in the sixteenth and seventeenth century or earlier—nevertheless disappear"—Neil Heims in a letter about Robert Nichols' work.**

> **"As those lucky enough to have read *Daily Lives in Nghsi-Altai* know, Robert Nichols is one of our most profoundly original writers, his political passion, and acuteness transfigured by a visionary gleam"—Ursula K. Le Guin**

Poet Geoffrey Gardner refers to Robert Nichols as "the forgotten man"; to Peter Schumann, the founder of Bread and Puppet Theatre, Nichols, who greatly influenced Schumann's work, is "an overlooked poet and experimenter." Robert Nichols, whom a generation of artists in New York City's Greenwich Village and several generations of Vermont environmental and peace activists referred to as "Bob," was a playwright, poet, architect, and novelist. He believed that the pursuit of art was to be always experimenting and proposing new ways of seeing and doing; that art must resist the status quo and initiate meaningful change. Nichols was a committed Humanist, becoming an indispensable component in the burgeoning arts scene and antiwar movement in New York in the 1960s.

In later years he became a proponent of the environmental/sustainability and family farming movements, and of Social Ecology. Unfortunately, Nichols' work has long been overshadowed by that of his contemporaries, including his second wife, the writer Grace Paley.

As an architect who studied under the Bauhaus School's Walter Gropius, Nichols is primarily known as the lead designer on the 1969 redesign of Washington Square Park in Greenwich Village, New York. He was also well-known locally for his work on the lower east side and the south Bronx on a series of ad hoc, often guerrilla, playgrounds designed to protect the most blighted inner city neighborhoods from social breakdown. To this end, Nichols founded and ran *Avanza Construction Company and Basketball Team*, an organization that taught young men from these disadvantaged communities important job and life skills.

Nichols established his reputation as a poet with his first book of poetry, *Slow Newsreel of Man Riding Train*, which was published in the now famous Pocket Poet Series by Lawrence Ferlinghetti for City Lights Books in 1962; a work that informs his finest play, *The Wax Engine*, which premiered the following year. He was a man of the theatre who not only produced vast amounts of dramas—many circumscribed by the political and cultural situations that prompted them—but also directed and acted. A cofounder of one of the most important of the initial Off-Off-Broadway theatre groups, the Judson Poets' Theatre, Nichols left the company in 1964 to devote his time and resources to the nascent Bread and Puppet Theatre and, finally, to political, experimental fiction.

Documentation of Nichols' life and work is sparse and inadequate. In large part, this is due to Nichols' restless energy and mercurial nature, borne of anarchical convictions and an old fashioned ethic of New England self-effacement. These forces militated against him firmly establishing himself in one position long enough to make a greater impact: The famed American actor George Bartenieff describes Nichols as "more of a legend. He was one of those important persons who initiated things, and would then get suddenly swept aside when his ideas were taken up." "Bob was an instigator," Bartenieff says. "He started things happening, but then would move on to other interests." This very restiveness and shifting of interests saturate his writing, something, Ursula K. Le Guin says might have kept Nichols from being better known: "Perhaps his mix of idealism and literal-mindedness, of wild mind-leaps and factual plod, puzzles or repels many people." As for the *Daily Lives in Nghsi-Altai* tetralogy, Le Guin suggests, "the book is ignored partly because it is *genuinely* unique. Critics and others like to compare, to categorize, which with Nichols is hopeless."

Nichols fully inhabited a cultural moment in American history, one that also honed his commitment to political action. He dramatized the cultural and political tensions that obtained in mid-twentieth-century America in his plays and fiction. His work both instigated and was a part of the performative Happenings staged in New York galleries, coffee house poetry readings, new approaches to choreography and stagecraft, and the first Pop Art gestures from a generation immersed in images and rebellion against Abstract Expressionism's officially sanctioned prominence. Nichols' native, associative intelligence connects these disparate elements, creating textual collages. Indeed, one can read *Daily Lives in Nghsi-Altai* as a collage.

In his book *America in Our Time*, Godfrey Hodgson writes that the United States entered a period of trauma and crisis at the end of 1963 after a "series of shocks." The radical aesthetic in Nichols' poetry and plays is arrested by these historical shocks, giving way to a more committed political radicalism, which led some of his writing toward the tendentious and ephemeral; work fully constrained by its cultural moment. Yet in the best of his work his non-traditional framing of the human condition took art out onto the street and village greens in an attempt to establish a charged, participatory form of art as protest in response to the times. His work reflected his intellectual engagement especially with the Vietnam War, nuclear power, U.S. government policies in Latin America and Africa, and the pending doom of Global Climate Change. Whether it was with the Bread and Puppet Theatre, his radical reimagining of the Medieval morality play *Everyman* (played in the streets of Manhattan), or his later short stories about Americans grappling with their government's covert war against Central American peasants, Nichols became a vital voice of resistance.

New Directions first published *Daily Lives in Nghsi-Altai* as a tetralogy with the first book, *Arrival*, published in 1977. This was followed by *Garh City* (1978), *The Harditts in Sawna* (1979), and *Exile* (also 1979). The tetralogy was then collectively published (albeit in shortened form) as *Daily Lives in Altai* by Glad Day Books in 1999. A prequel and prompt to the series concludes Nichols' collection of short stories for Penny Each Press, *Red Shift*, which he did in collaboration with Peter Schumann whose block prints illustrate the book. It is here that the reader meets the Environmental Control Gang, a militant cell of environmentalists who have declared war on capitalism and who are sending emissaries/explorers to investigate the mysterious land of Nghsi-Altai, which they are tasked to enter and explore "in the same way as a novel." The narrator reveals two of the explorers in *Red Shift* to be the English poet and painter William Blake and the Cuban filmmaker Santiago Alvarez. In *Arrival*, the reader discovers that the narrator in *Red Shift* and the third explorer is Jack Kerouac.

These temporally displaced emissaries (each representing a different perspective from the Left: Marxism, anarcho-syndicalism, etc.) proceed "from the known to the unknown, from a terrain where everything is familiar and accepted to one that is strange, heightened and fanciful." What follows is an imaginative work of sociology, anthropology, theology, and ecology, at first recounted by the explorers often as poetic reportage, though, as the work progresses, the voices of the land's inhabitants take control of their narrative. Nichols establishes Nghsi-Altai within the borders of Tibet's Yadong region, a tongue of land bordering China, Bhutan, and Sikkim, India. As they reach the city of Gahr in the second book, Kerouac (who meets with a fatal accident) is replaced by the nineteenth-century British artist and architect William Morris, who provides a libertarian socialist perspective. Le Guin calls the *Nghsi-Altai* tetralogy "a fascinating work, badly neglected or underrated. It is one of the very few utopias that explores possibilities in the same general direction that I went with in my *Always Coming Home*."

In "A Literature of Alternatives," Robert Nichols writes that *Daily Lives* is a utopian series illustrating Murray Bookchin's idea of "decentralism and a regionally appropriate technology" and suggests how a creative and imaginative fiction, art "rooted in life," might serve as a source of hope and inspiration. "Social ecology," Nichols says, "has developed many good ideas, but not enough practice. The main concepts of social ecology, taken in isolation, tend to thin out. For their vitality they need to be connected to *practice*." One way to at least imagine that practice, he suggests, is through a politically-committed literature. "The situation is comic. We spend a week studying some abstruse book on local self-reliance and eight hours in a food co-op serving customers. Then, for entertainment, we go to a movie made by a transnational corporation for an audience of 300 million."

Nichols's tetralogy should be recognized both for its radical ideology and for the fecundity of the imagination that informs it at all moments. Like another green anarchist fiction, Graham Purchase's *My Journey with Aristotle to the Anarchist Utopia*, *Daily Lives* details the kinds of changes that would make for an ecologically sound anarchist utopia. In "The Green Anarchist Utopia of Robert Nichols's Daily Lives in Nghsi-Altai" Daniel P. Jaeckl writes:

> But unlike Purchase's short novel, *Daily Lives* remains radically open. Nichols builds challenges to utopia into the plot, plays with the conventions of utopian fiction, and maintains a sense of humor throughout. As a result, *Daily Lives in Nghsi-Altai* remains a model of how to blend instruction and delight that over forty years later political authors would do well to emulate.

The greatest of the fictional utopias are as much about evoking the deepest of our past and present experiential realities as they are about envisioning future possibilities. Thus, the most powerful utopian works are also profoundly "topian"—they create a vivid sense of place, of topos, that is grounded in deeply experienced realities. Utopianism finds its fulfillment in topianism, indeed, we might even say in hypertopianism, the most intense sense of being somewhere; in a specific place wherein reality is manifest.

In his remarkable tetralogy, Nichols envisions the nature of our communal, yet highly individualized society in which decentralized democracy, ecological sensibility, bioregional principles, and liberatory technologies are integrated into a traditional culture. It is a vision of Utopia emerging out of the rich particularity of history and lived experience. While *Daily Lives* has never gained the recognition it deserves it is, in fact, an extraordinary contribution to both literary and theoretical utopianism.

Nichols creatively incorporates concepts of utopian anarchist and decentralist writers and imagines what they would mean in a rich cultural embodiment. In Nghsi-Altai they are realized not in a utopia of static perfection, but rather in a peaceful but still mildly chaotic world in which people live the good but still slightly messy life, and achieve an expansive yet communally bounded freedom. What is so compelling about this work is its extraordinary synthesis of utopianism with an acute sense of both the universals of the human condition and the specificity and particularity of culture. Nichols brilliantly creates a sense of the utopian "ethos." It is not surprising that Le Guin has recognized the importance of Nichols' influence in her development of a utopian project that culminates in a social anthropology of Utopia.

According to scholar Taylor Stoer, Nichols' *Daily Lives in Nghsi-Altai* avoided the trouble with most utopian novels which has been that they cannot escape the present, the platform on which the imagination must stand. Some authors have solved the problem by embracing the past—such as William Morris' *News from Nowhere* and Austin Wright''s *Islandia*—but Nichols, whose ecological anarchosyndicalism has much in common with these agrarian visions, has discovered a new way to see into not-quite-the-future, but the possibilities of the present ("It was meant as current events," Nichols has said). His technique is montage, many glimpses of familiar and unfamiliar sights, drawn from daily experience, from cultural anthropology, from modern technology, history, and literature. This crowded world comes to life in its juxtapositions: monorails and wooden plows, shamanism side by side with progressive education, participatory democracy merged with popular sporting events held in huge stadiums to suggest what a parliament of 80,000 might be like. Nichols invents wildly, but nothing is that impossible, or even very unusual. The surprises come in the connections he makes, the improvisations. This is his formal method, and it is also his utopian message: the mixture is plausible both as civilization and as novel. The structure of neither is "realistic," that is, grounded in systematic verisimilitude, a mesh of cause and effect organized according to conventional expectations. That is what weighs most utopian novels down and makes us dread their coming true. Here we feel the rush of life itself, as full of complexity and obscurity as ordinary awareness.

From Kropotkin to Goodman, the one great virtue of anarchist thought is to accept confusion and human fallibility as a given and make room for it. Nichols' art does the same thing, using his improvisational technique. It was this method that author and friend George Dennison praised when he reviewed *Daily Lives in Nghsi-Altai*: "It is overtly imaginative, overtly a product of mind, classical in spirit, but drawing freely on the broad repertory of modernism, especially the collage in time of modern poetry, which is handled here with great verve." But even more than modern poetry, the freedom of imagination displayed in *Daily Lives* has its analog in Nichols' early experimental and protest theatre.

Social ecology proclaims the ideal of local self-reliance and dependence on indigenous resources and talents to the greatest extent possible. Self-reliance recognizes and encourages interdependence among communities. It emphasizes an ecologically sustainable ethos in the realms of production and consumption, decentralization in the political sphere, and a healthy respect for diversity. The development of healthy communities requires a rebalancing of town and country, a reintroduction of the organic world into the largely synthetic environment of the city. Such an action may initially be rooted in the purely material realm, as in the introduction, through community initiatives, of green spaces, neighborhood gardens, food parks, permacultures, etc. This transformation of the physical environment and the introduction of the skills of nurturance and husbandry needed to transform the physical environment will contribute to the development of a new sense of community, which will reflect these skills as social values. Nichols involvement in Loisaida, the Puerto Rican section of New York's Lower East Side where residents attempted to actualize elements of this approach in the mid-1970s, is where he began to enact these theories. The community's problems were turned into a community resource. In Loisaida, there were over one hundred vacant lots. They were rubble-strewn dump heaps, breeding grounds for rats and an eyesore and health hazard. These lots often served as a dangerous "playground" for neighborhood children and constituted a blight on the community. Viewed from the perspective of social ecology, however, these lots represented a precious community resource: open space.

In an environment of concrete and decaying tenements, these lots, a substantial percentage of the land of the neighborhood, offered valuable sites for recreation, education, economic development, and community cultural activity. Nichols, together with other local activists, recognized this potential and began the development process at the grass roots, organizing residents to clean up the lots and put them to constructive use. Most of the lots belonged to the city of New York, which had done nothing to improve them. The people of Loisaida combined a critical analysis of their problem with direct action. They protested to the city, and they cleaned the lots themselves and began to use them. They converted some to "vest-pocket parks," a concept introduced by Nichols, outfitting them with benches and planting green spaces. Others were turned into playgrounds, utilizing recycled material for equipment. Swings were made from discarded lumber and old tires, and Jungle Gyms were built from recycled beams. Other lots were turned into community gardens, which became a focal point for intergenerational contact. One large lot was transformed into an outdoor cultural center, La Plaza Cultural, where community poets, theater groups, and local musicians all performed. Several lots were adopted by local schools for use as teaching centers where area youths were introduced to lessons in agriculture and ecology. The transformation of the lots helped to reintroduce the natural world into this underserved community.

The results were profound. People reconstructed their environment without the official sanction of the city; in fact, in some cases, it was in the face of opposition from the city. This direct action illustrates community empowerment. The initiative came from local people. They did not look to the city for a solution; they created their own. They gained either legal leases to the lots for token amounts of money or outright title. Several community land trusts were created to remove particular lots from the real estate market forever, and to guarantee their continued use as a community resource. Teenagers were involved in the movement, and their experience in constructive social action helped to bring them off the street. A cooperative was formed to manufacture playground equipment from recycled items, creating jobs and income for the people involved.

Daily Lives in Nghsi-Altai should be considered in the canon of utopian literature, as it shares much with Sir Francis Bacon's *New Atlantis*, Edward Bellamy's *Looking Backward*, and Morris' *News from Nowhere.*[*] But it also must be considered as a work of environmental literature, with Nichols' Environmental Control Gang being a possible nod to Edward Abbey's *The Monkey Wrench Gang*, which was published two years before *Arrival.* And while Nichols' gang members are ecological saboteurs in *Red Shift*, the explorers they dispatch to Nghsi-Altai are sent out to peacefully learn

* 'Utopia and Liberty: Some Contemporary Issues Within Their Intellectual Traditions', Kingsley Widmer, in Leonard P. Liggio, *Literature of Liberty: A Review of Contemporary Liberal Thought*, San Diego State University. *http://oll.libertyfund.org/pages/utopia-and-liberty-a-bibliographical-essay-by-kingsley-widmer*

'The Green Anarchist Utopia of Robert Nichols's *Daily Lives in Nghsi-Altai'*, Daniel P. Jaeckle, *Utopian Studies*, Vol. 24, No. 2 (2013), pp. 264-282, Penn State University Press. http://www.jstor.org/stable/10.5325/utopianstudies.24.2.0264

about the country's success with alternative energy. Nichols' descriptions of wind, solar and geothermal power are not only fully informed by the science contemporary with his writing, but are often prescient in their utilization and advancement. There is a system of ecological universities throughout Nghsi-Altai, a country that is divided into "biomes." As a term to distinguish distinct ecosystems, biome had only recently become established after its adoption within the International Biological Program (1964-1974). Nichols obviously aims to popularize the word through *Daily Lives.* But Nichols is also interested in economics, an interest he takes up most fully in his last and as yet unpublished novel, *Simple Gifts*, written in the 2000s and finished before Nichols' death in 2010. In his tetralogy, Nichols both uses and is in tension with E.F. Schumacher's ideas of "intermediate technology" (which Nichols' even references in *Arrival*) and particularly with Schumacher's 1973 book *Small Is Beautiful: A Study of Economics as If People Mattered*. Nichols' blueprint for a sustainable future seems even more urgent and necessary forty years later. As Nichols writes, "it is through the new man that a new rhetoric becomes established." His tetralogy is an attempt to help establish both the new human and new thinking. It is significant that the travelers in Nghsi-Altai choose never to return home. The work also benefits from Nichols' varied artistic interests. He brings a trained architect's eye to his descriptions of Nghsi-Altai's cities and their structures, occasionally achieving arresting, fantastical images that are reminiscent of Italo Calvino's *Invisible Cities.* Also, Nichols' the playwright and director laces his narrative with theatrical events, such as a shamans' caravan performing in masked processions just like in the Bread and Puppet Theater, complete with one of Nichols' and Schumann's archetypal stock puppet villains, the bloated capitalist Uncle Fatso. As an added bit of avant-garde theatrics, the surviving emissaries from the West, Blake, Alvarez, and Morris, become an exhibit in the shamans' caravan: they are "freaks" of individuality.

Nichols' career in the late 1960s as a playwright with Theatre for the New City; his later poetry (*Address to the Smaller Animals*); his radical work as an urban architect, and his abandonment of the theatre and New York for novel-writing and environmental political action in Vermont, all demand more critical analysis, while *Daily Lives in Nghsi-Altai* itself warrants discovery. "I'd say that in the limited circle I move in, he is totally unknown," Le Guin says. "I am forever being disappointed when even knowledgeable writers on utopia don't mention him."

Robert Nichols was an American writer fully engaged in the culture and politics surrounding him, which prompted a transformation in both his writing and philosophy on theatre, literature and the arts. To analyze the substantial store of Nichols' writing is to move closer to a greater understanding of the mid-twentieth-century American empire: they each serve as the other's contextualization.

In this introduction, we hope we have shown how the tetralogy, *Daily Lives in Nghsi-Altai*, is part of a diverse and varied body of artistic work and political activism that, viewed all together, shows how Robert Nichols' art and politics were shaped by daily life, meetings with other people and the era in which he lived. True artists transcend their historic periods while shaping and being shaped by them. We contend that Robert Nichols' utopian series is an expression of the author's many interests and projects whether they be literary, political or personal.

for novel writing and an [illegible] political system [illegible], all [illegible] more critical analysis, while they give [illegible]. After their [illegible] discovery, [illegible] say that to the limited [illegible] he is totally [illegible]. [illegible] says, "and forever being disappointed when [illegible]."

[illegible] novels with a [illegible] writer fully integrated in the culture and [illegible] surrounding him, which he [illegible] to both [illegible] and politics by [illegible]. To analyze the [illegible] to a greater understanding of [illegible] the country and [illegible], they each serve [illegible] other [illegible].

In [illegible] we have shown how [illegible] of literary work and political [illegible] [illegible] [illegible] [illegible] [illegible] what [illegible] political [illegible].

RED SHIFT

drawings by Peter Schumann

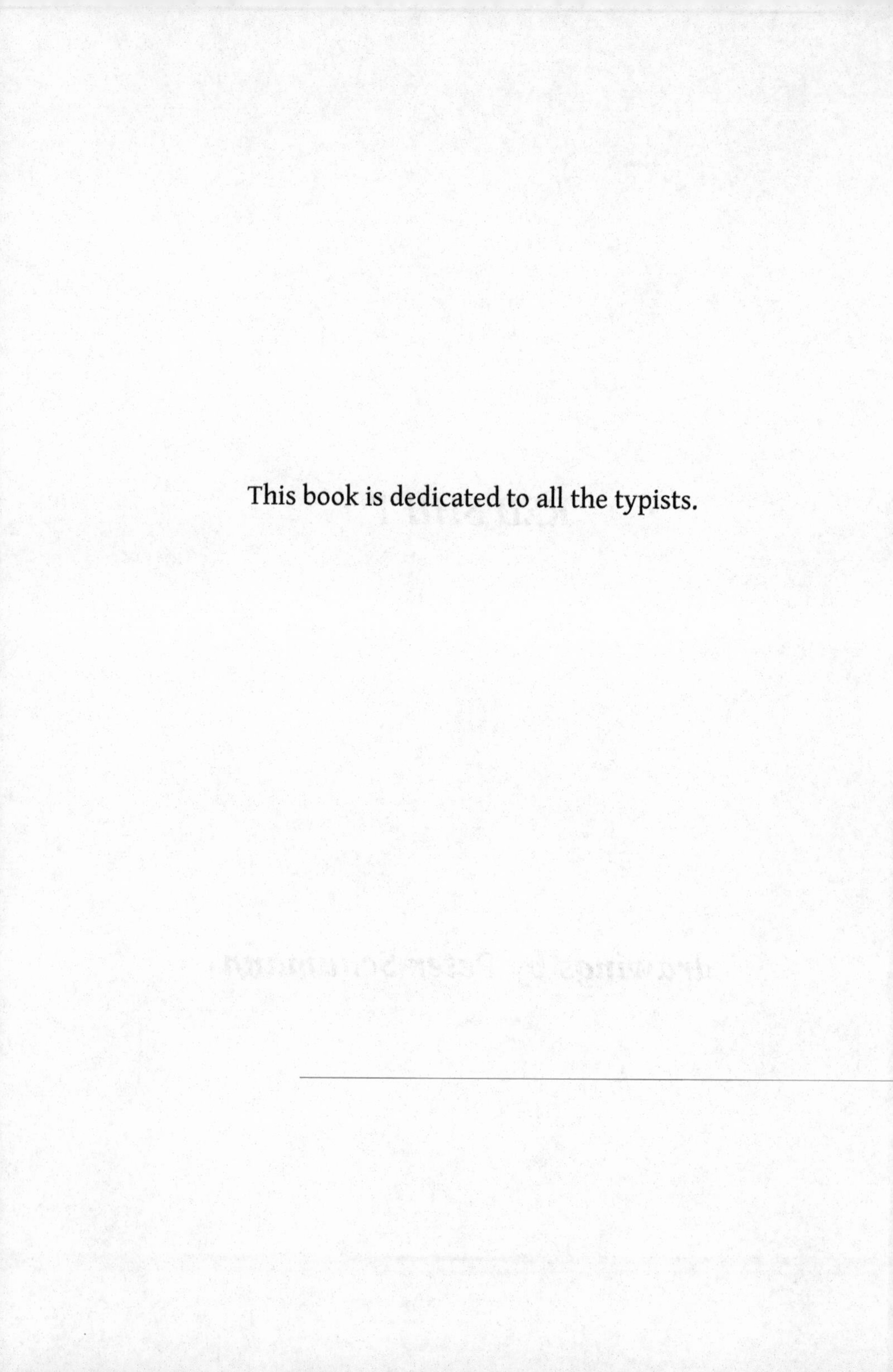

This book is dedicated to all the typists.

Cleaning Up The Hudson and Other Stories

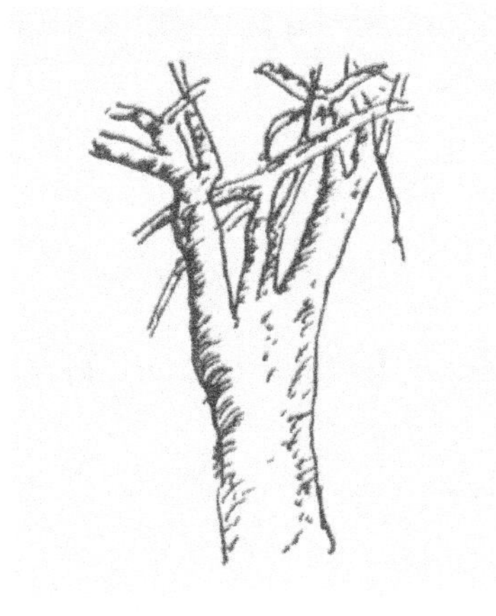

*   *

Lost
The bees' engines hemmed him in
He was lost in the fields of Thel
and Thel is everywhere

Begin now to look around for moorings
The delicatest branch is a ballast
Don't let the old men give you advice
The bass fiddles of Being
    pick up the drone of the grasshopper's existence

Blake went through the roof of the sky
    like a balloon
But I am lost here
    with the bees cannonading
inside and outside the screen

* *

A rotten nite not very much sleep. Shouldna jacked off no fun in it this year. The blankets in knots not enough air but too sleepy to get up and open a window. Which one of the kids will wake me up first? Sonofabitch, my last chance to recover

MY STRENGTH

before tomorrow.

The "I" is smoothed out in the folds and wrinkles of the bedclothes.

* *

Bands of color
the primary colors are red blue green yellow violet
By grinding the lens and placing the prisms at the correct angles thus
light can be bent and decomposed into its various wavelengths
the wavelength blue is calibrated on the scale .48 microns
the wavelength yellow is calibrated on the scale .57 microns
the wavelength green is calibrated on the scale .53 microns
the wavelength violet is calibrated on the scale .62 microns
the wavelength red is calibrated on the scale .76 microns

(a chromopoem)

Below the zone Infra-red
    I wandered

threatened by a vague sense of
fear
from an unidentified source

* *

We were passing one of those mild country ponds that lie unobtrusively around Lancaster when the weeds parted and an enormous frog jumped in, making a deep "plop." I explained to her how the frogs do it: the female frog lays the eggs—that green slimy mass over there by the bank. Then the male frog comes along later and fertilizes them.

"Oh," Barbie said, her eyes sparkling, "that would be a much better way." She was twelve years old then.

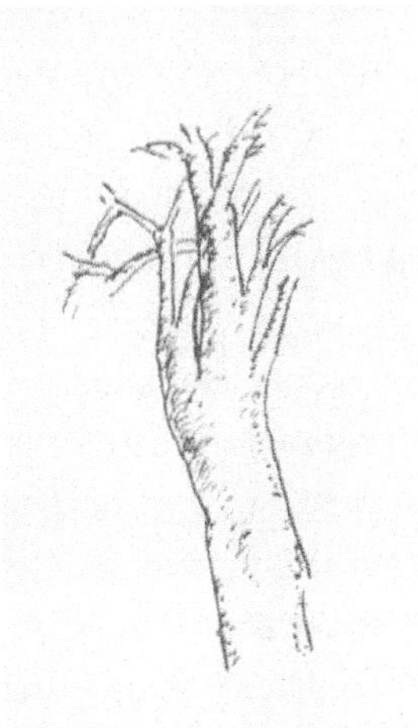

A DIFFICULT JOURNEY

Our ascent to the Monastery was by basket up the cliff. All the implements of scholarship had been carefully prepared: maps, references to the place in the ancient manuscripts, pottery and vases depicting various life scenes, and finally the Anachronistic Codes by which we had deciphered the actual reference to the woman's name in Linear B. It was or had been the Goddess Alma from the Sanskrit "O — mha." Or could it be "Ahhii — kwaa," in which case our trail would lead through the Hittites. All indications pointed to the latter, a thesis moreover supported by Professor Duntzer after fifteen years of the most painstaking researches among the Grundzinge Excavations. How lucky we had been that this article had been published in *Les Annales des Sciences des Antiquités*, Bulletin 4, pp. 153ff. shortly before our expedition emplaned from Idlewild.

But now the Ethiopian desert lay behind us. The ramparts rose above, virtually impossible to scale except by the most elaborate means. Even with the aid of the monks, the surmounting of this obstacle took up the better part of the first week. Our anchorites had rigged up an elaborate system of winches supported at the top by a cantilevered bar.

The bales into which had been trussed up the tenting and clothing were hauled up fairly easily. So were the packing crates containing the scientific instruments, and the large panniers of food, medicine and trading supplies. But how to hoist up the donkey engine, an Allis-Chalmers 600, contributed by the Carnegie Foundation? This was to be the key to our excavations.

But what if excavations were not called for when we reached the top? Might there not be a less arduous method than the one we had calculated on at the base camp? But everything pointed to a long haul.

It will be helpful to you at this point if I give some indication of the terrain. To the left of us the escarpment, running down ultimately to the plain on which had been built in their successive centuries the outer fortifications IV, X and XIb (Chadwick: *Akademie der Wissenschaften, philhist.* Diagram appended end of chapter). Beyond XIb the shepherds still tended their flocks. To the right rose the butte proper, even more precipitous than we had guessed from the aerial photographs. The formation of rock angled to the north and east where the watch towers had been, and finally completed the circle which was the base of this inscrutable citadel. At our own assault point, the cliff face actually overhung the base, the supply shaft disappearing through a hole in the upper floor. The diameter of this hole was some 20 feet. It was directly overhead. Fortunate for us that the monks, our co-workers on the upper levels, were friendly, though as yet we had had no communication with them except by hand signals.

However, it was the rock itself, a mixture of dolomite and volcanic pumice, that proved to be the most treacherous element. A single concussion or jar against this friable material would have caused the whole mountainside and probably the city as well to come tumbling around our heads. I can tell you, there were moments in which everything in the entire expedition literally hung on the balance of a thread.

At last we were hauled through the hole to the top. There we were guided to the side by rough hands, and found ourselves on the rock floor. This floor proved to be tipped, and inclined at an angle of some 15 degrees towards the highest point. The few huts and stone storage bins could hardly be called a village and what we had taken—because of their triangular shapes in the photographs—to be the earthworks of the ancient fortifications were simply olive groves ascending the plane in tiers. Here the shade was very pleasant. On one of the furthest terraces we found the girl Alma. She was seated under one of the trees. When we appeared she looked up at us with the frankest and liveliest expression. Her breasts were milky. Her dress, which was of blue wool, was stained from menstruating. Or was it from the shadows of the leaves, the sun filtering through the cool criss-cross of olives?

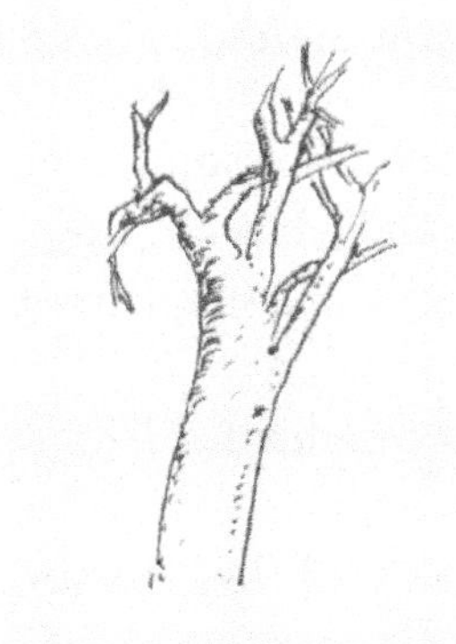

Miguel Aguerra ran into the street.
An agile fighter against his wife
he was not so brave against Carrabinieri's Band.
Carrabinieri's Band was composed of horns, banjos and drums.
It could blast you off your dum-dum.
When Aguerra heard all that wild music
    the blood rushed to his eyes.
He felt like he wanted to commit murder
or start a new revolutionary party on the Lower East Side
or open a small supermarket or something

An Article of Faith

I believe ALMA will come
with her suns
and waken me where I lie sleeping
and waken me where I lie
be-shit with myself
She will explode over me
in great buckets of sea water
running down my thighs buttocks knees
back into the sea

Notes on the Commissioner's Memo Pad

How to set up a remedial reading program:
First obtain books and a blackboard
reading stalls (they can be simple room-dividing screens
                                        if necessary)
a school or church basement will do: sufficiently dry and
                                        well lighted
Use ordinary residents of the community
ordinary 'para-professional' teachers

from the block preferably
ordinary kids.
But in some
OTHER AMERICA
In this one all the words turn out to spell LIES!

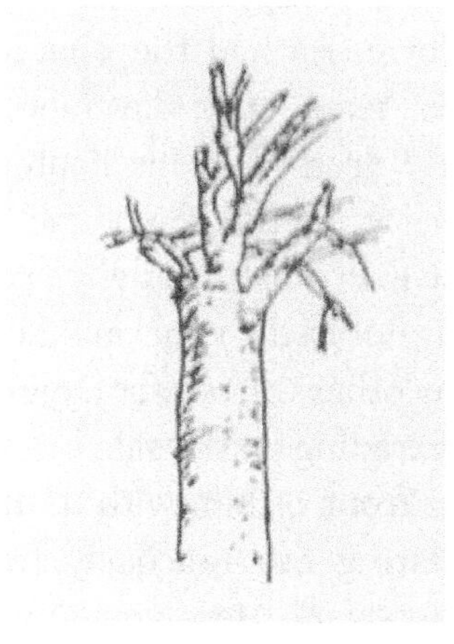

* *

To move through the twilight world. It was like being in the realm Infra-red. Dick Turpin had been assigned to the Pentagon from one of the nation's top chemical laboratories. His specialty was the eye and how it sees, and how it distorts what it sees. And how this distortion is effected by the "inter-tones," areas of low-intensity light diffusion.

Now at last Dick was to test his ideas on the Black Market! It seemed that for years he had been working in the Pentagon basement, surrounded by his micro-chemistry equipment: light refractors and diffusers, oscillators, mass spectography apparatus and, of course, the statistical and tabulating Machines that aided and abetted all this. The analysis had been exhaustive. There was not one corner of the eye that Dick's team had not gone into. But the work had left Dick drained. He was glad to be out in the open air again, walking down Ginza Street at a fast clip in the direction of the Mulmein Pagoda.

Yes. It was true, he realized with a shock: he had not been outside the lab for two years. He wondered how it was on the Main Street in Fayetteville, North Carolina, at this hour of the night. He had been born and raised there. But this was Bandung, in the heart of East Asia and the seat of Allied Military Operations. Walking down this street one could never be sure what dangerous antagonists one might meet up with.

Dick checked his uniform. He had the photo-cell in his pocket, the device that he and his team had developed for detecting Black Marketeers. He was neatly dressed in his lieutenant-colonel's uniform, the first time he had worn it off the compound. The top pocket bulged somewhat, over where the micro-batteries were concealed, the actual eye of the "pickup" cell being located in the middle of a row of campaign ribbons. He looked like any other G.I. out for a night on the town, with the possibility of doing a little trading on the side.

The Ginza stretched in front of him with its half-mile of dirty shops, and its canned music blaring out raucously from loudspeakers hung under the crumbling lattice-work. Here you could buy anything, from a pocket watch to a whole emergency field hospital.

But Dick decided first to visit a whorehouse. He did not have to wait long. A dried, elderly woman, wrapped up like a mummy, that the other customers called "Mamma-san," led him down the corridor to a narrow cubicle with walls of screened paper. He went in and was greeted by a brief kiss and then there was nothing to do but fumble with the girl's long sash or "obi." But once down on the bed, Dick's photocell began to act up and he realized he was in the presence of a black marketeer. For a while he had forgotten where he was. His pants were off. He himself was naked below the waist and he had the curious feeling that the lower part of his body was giving off a smell of ammonia, probably from the photo-developing equipment back at the Lab. In that case the girl had probably tagged him the minute he came in as being from the Pentagon. So the response that the "bug," or micro-cell was picking up from her would not be an altogether typical one.

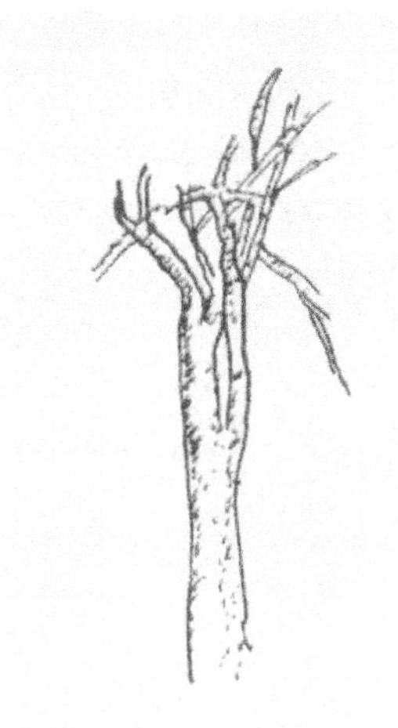

WHITE COLLAR PORTRAIT

I remember Ben Lyric
Ben was a draftsman
worked same place I worked
BB&Z Engineers for 28 years
Ho hum

He had a large nose
aggravated by colds
and a fine hand
for laying out ink titles.
After the first five years
they wouldn't allow him to do anything
but ink
Ho hum

Why sure, Mr. BBZ
everybody's an expert

in this here highway Engineering Office
In that section they make maps
in that section they compute angles
in that section they design bridges
and Ben's a ink specialist
Ho hum

One time it snowed   none of the bosses showed
Through the blurred windows
the tops of the city disappeared
only a few of us there
sitting around that big empty office
twiddling our thumbs
Ho hum

That day we laid out the centerline
of the whole State Thruway
from Tarrytown
to a point just below Buffalo
snaking it out
in long loose looping curves over the hills
Ben drawing with the "spline"
his feet sprawled over three tables
me running the computer.
330 miles of hi-speed road in one afternoon!

Course we didn't have no degree
That evening, we tore up all the drawings
before we left
so no one would find out about it
Ho hum

Ben and me we always walked a kind of thin line

between being liked by everybody
and not being noticed
by hardly anybody
You last longest that way
Ho hum
Ho ho ho hum

INSECTS IN DOWNTOWN NEW YORK

Two dragon flies were seen on a day in June 1959. They were on my fence railing. The fence is of iron, Victorian design, paint flaking. Each sat upright, tail out on the horizontal holding onto the picket with its six feet, head up and looking around airily.

The body (thorax) is a compact bulb located astride the upper section of the tail, like a cabin on a tiny helicopter. The head of the dragonfly is round. Two yellow spots are the simple eyes placed within the larger compound eye, which is simply a bulge or large segmented swelling. At the top two little black tufts constitute the rudimentary flight antennae, the whole head being tight and specialized like an instrument package.

But now my dragon fly is quiet. The tail (abdomen) breathes. In. Out. It pulsates like a bellows.

The body must be incalculably strong for its minute size. Fitted into the bottom are the six segmented feet with their complicated movements; while stitched across the back as an anchor are the wing ligaments. From here the double wings are swept forward in the most graceful way: the heavier members in front stiffen the edge, the lighter catenaries to the rear compose the surface (for the air to lift) the whole wing being an elaborate thin net, very complex, ellipses within ellipses.

I lean down and speaking softly as I can I ask the dragonfly in its own language where it comes from. Its answer: "From a pond."

(second chromopoem)

* *

"Where did you get her?"

"They brought her in. The body from Plieku. The head from Dalat. The feet and ankles from Can Tho and Nha Trang. The arms and fingers from Tu Bong. Because of all the fighting it is hard for them to get through by helicopter to the Base Hospital. The eyes were brought in a couple of days ago from Tourane. It is a child."

"It *is* a child," the reporter agreed, "and a beautiful one. When do you expect to begin feeding her?"

"Well, we just put her together. We hope to start feeding her in a few months."

* *

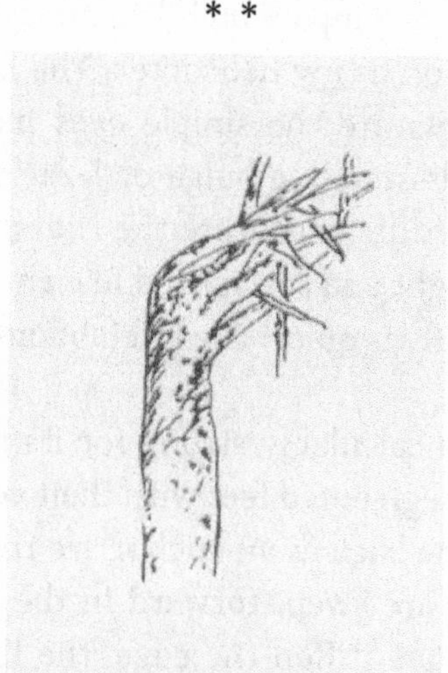

CLEANING UP THE HUDSON

A group of men were standing at the end of a pier looking out over the river. They were: Errico Malatesta, nicknamed "Rags." Takaati Yashimoto and his pal Micky. "Powerhouse" Bill Haywood from Nebraska, who had formerly been a railroad detective. A man simply named Warren. A man named Nechaev. Lund Schimmelpennick. Sandy Berkman, the secretary of the group. And three cousins of Malatesta: Costa, Giuseppe Fanelli and Cafiero. Except for Berkman, all men were in their middle fifties, and some carried briefcases.

Below them and out into the middle distance, the river slipped by colorlessly, bearing out into the sea bits and splotches of the city's waste. The water stirred softly among the underpinnings. Occasionally a squat tug would pass by and the pilings rocked. Three kids were playing cards miserably nearby in their underpants, smoking reefers.

Malatesta broke the silence. Shaking his head, he said, "When I first came here, from Peoria, this was a great river. Now look at it."

"It was a bee-oot-i-ful river," the middle-aged Haywood agreed. "There ain't nothing like it in the whole country, except maybe the Sacramento dropping into Puget Sound. Sure is dirty as an old muff now, though."

"Cleaning up the river is not going to be easy," Luud Schimmelpennick averred. "Because of the politics involved, you'd have to do it through Albany. And you know how rotten that is."

"It's got to be done, though." Rags looked gravely at the two little boys. "And fast. So these little glue-sniffers can swim."

"I believe State Senator Fine is the key," Micky Osawa said, and the others nodded in agreement.

The party turned and headed for two large black cars parked at the head of the wharf. The water slogged by. Nechaev flicked his cigar into it.

"I'd look into that Fine," he said to Berkman. "Might as well start here as anywhere."

The secretary nodded, crisply. "Yes. I intend to."

The Oriskany Caper

As it proved, the first move of the Gang was not against State Senator Fine, but against the Rome Metals Company of Oriskany, New York, one of the main sources of industrial water pollution on the upper river. Oriskany had a small newspaper with a column for personal announcements under the title "The Cryer." The following appeared:

> A picnic will be held for the dead on Sunday afternoon May 20 at the Saint Mary's Wood Cemetery near Peach Street north of the Town Line on Route 5. Those planning to attend should bring lunch for two. Swimming off Corlear's Ledge.

This item was curious because there had been no swimming off Corlear's Ledge for almost a century, that environs of the river being completely polluted by the factory wastes. Saint Mary's Wood Cemetery was not widely known. It was pointed out by one of the customers in the town barbershop that May 20 was the date of the burning of Oriskany in 1780, when occupied by the British—an event still mourned.

May 20th arrived. It was evident that large numbers had responded to the announcement—whether out of curiosity and a literal reading of the text of the newspaper account, or simply because of the fine weather, it was difficult to tell. Residents who came in larger families brought food for extra guests. Blankets were spread under the trees and among the stones. The children played catch.

Saint Mary's Cemetery was on a high bluff over the river directly above a section of the city known as Claverack which had, up to the 1850's, been a fishing village. Around 1:30, the first contingent of the dead arrived. They were several families from a marshy district further up the river, Amityville, which had been abandoned after the New York Central Railroad had been put through. Other dead followed. By late afternoon all the living and dead of the whole region were assembled. As the early population of Oriskany had been small, and had grown rapidly only in the last decade, there were about equal numbers of each. Among the dead were some Indians.

The location of the Rome Plant was on the bank opposite, a distance across the river of about a half mile. The plant was located high up, and from the cemetery could be clearly seen, with its great ducts and flumes discharging into the river. Below there floated numbers of bloated fish. At exactly 5:30 the dead began to move out towards their destination, considerably strengthened by the picnic lunch. The steep bluff was an obstacle to all save the Indians, who moved down deftly through the brambles and tangled honeysuckle vines, checking themselves at a slim birch in the slipping gravel.

After a time the company reached the bottom and straggled up onto the railway embankment. Here they collected around one of their number, a bearded fisherman in a red-checked shirt. Some of the older picnickers recognized this big man as Tyson, the last Claverack man to catch a sturgeon. Several of the other men wore deerskin. A child cradled a dog.

Once on the embankment, the route was clear. The picnickers on the bluff watched as the whole party of the dead made its way towards the opposite bank: the younger and hardier ones swimming, though with some effort, against the floodtide which was coming in (and which carried them upstream). Some negotiated the stretch by propelling themselves half in, half out of the water, as if crawling or dragging themselves along. And the remainder simply walked directly across the surface, as if it were mid-winter and the river had frozen from bank to bank.

When the whole crowd had reached the opposite shore they started immediately up into the ducts. These led directly above to the pickling vats where the metal was treated. The conduits were so large that two or three could walk abreast. Once inside, the dead were lost to view. Nobody saw them, and the watchers from the opposite side were not able to follow the course of climbers as they went up, through the conduits up into the vats, then through die mixers and re-circulators, finally issuing wet and livid through the main pumps into the control room.

It was learned later that only three employees of Rome Metals were on duty, a senior engineer and two helpers. The whole plant was shut down and did not reopen again for some months, and then under greatly reduced volume.

The Symposium

Errico Malatesta's office was located on the 80th floor of the Empire State Building. This was the headquarters of ADD-RITE, a small distributing firm dealing in office machines which was the cover agency for the Environment Control Gang.

The administrative officers' suite was furnished in contemporary style and had a bar in one corner. Rags was drinking No-Cal. The other members of the gang sat in a circle around Malatesta's desk, except for Warren, who stood at the window examining newsclippings.

"The Oriskany Adventure," Luud Schimmelpennick mused aloud. "Well, that was quite a caper, even if I say so myself." He had been in charge of the invasion of Rome Metals. "Where do we intend to strike next?"

"It ought to be a breeze from now on," Joe Warren volunteered enthusiastically. "It looks like on this boatride everything's running our way."

Malatesta nodded thoughtfully. "But before we move on to the more difficult sections of the river, I wonder if we shouldn't examine our plans and ask ourselves if we are using the right methods."

"Our objectives are simple enough," Tacks Yashimoto said. "Man has lost control of his environment. And no ordinary political means—no matter how conscientiously pursued —will return it to him."

"Hear, hear," concurred Schimmelpennick loudly, still elated over the clippings, and rattled his glass of bourbon as the others laughed.

"On the other hand," Tacks continued, "I'm ready to admit that people don't always know they have lost out. And they don't always understand or agree with the methods by which we propose to regain environmental control. The State, not human nature, rules. Crass power has established its legitimacy—over the minds of men. That's the reason we are an underground organization."

"You have raised some interesting points," Malatesta acknowledged, smiling. "But we are all hungry. May I suggest that we postpone this discussion until after dinner."

Supper had been sent up from Schrafft's. It was served buffet style by Emma, who presided over these monthly conviviums. When the meal was over, Rags passed around a mahogany box of cigars. He selected his own, clipped it with a silver cutter, then looked at the secretary sharply.

"Well now, Sandy, why don't you be our first catechumen? Do you mind if we interrogate you on some of the questions that Tacks has raised? Perhaps you can provide us with satisfactory answers."

"Well, if I can't answer them I'm sure Emma can. A bright woman." He winked at her. "Go ahead, shoot," the secretary said.

"There is one point that has always puzzled me," Rags pursued. "I realize that we are engaged in activities that are, broadly speaking, of a conservationist nature, and that they benefit the general public. We have benefitted them. Why can't we carry out our work openly? For instance"—Malatesta waved towards the door—"why couldn't that be our real name up there in frosted glass, the ENVIRONMENT CONTROL GANG, instead of this silly cover, the ADD-RITE Corporation?"

"It's perfectly true," Fanelli broke in. "We are conservationists—as harmless and innocuous a breed as there is in these United States. How can anyone be intimidated, either by us or by our motto: No Man Is An Island?"

"Then why do we have to hide?"

"That's easy," answered Sandy. "In America normal social relations have been skewed. They are no longer direct and natural, as in the past, but have become perverted by our contemporary institutions. In a world poisoned by competition, ordinary sociable acts have come to appear criminal. It is the public that is confused, not we."

"I should like to put in a word for Sandy," Andrea Costa said, leaning forward in his chair and touching Berkman's knee. "And perhaps also for history. It is true that history abounds in instances of the most ruthless struggle, and of class and inhuman competition. But it abounds also in instances of the opposite: willing cooperation between men and of mutual aid. Otherwise little would have flourished during the last millenium, from the smallest craft up to our greatest industrial combines. One only has to look at it with some degree of heart."

"I'm afraid your heart is leading your eyes away from the plain facts," Luud Schimmelpennick remarked, "unless up to this point the writing of history has been false."

"It has. It has," Sandy cried. "And worse still—morbid! Don't misunderstand me, Luud," the secretary continued, "I'm not for universal love and sympathy and all that. I have always felt that such sentiments narrowed, rather than widened, the field of moral action. It is simply that when I see my neighbor's house is on fire, I run towards it with a pail. Not because I like him. I may not even know him. It is an act of human solidarity."

"I think Alex has put his finger on a most important distinction," Rags said, "and one we should do well to keep in mind during our discussions. This faculty of simple sociability in human beings, which Sandy has so wisely discovered for us, is crucial, and is the basis for our whole action and strategy in the field of conservation. It is, in fact, the particular stress of our group—over against the competitive individual. And for this reason we call ourselves MUTUALISTS.

"Now I see that Emma has made coffee. Would any of you care for some? Or for some sweets?"

The Symposium (Continued)

This stimulant was served and a new round of cigars lighted. Afterwards, Powerhouse Bill Haywood leaned back in his chair. He looked at Warren quizzically. "We have found our way through certain complications but perhaps have only entangled ourselves in others. There is one matter that has disquieted me particularly and I should be disappointed if it were omitted from this discussion. That is the question of power. Josie, would you care to comment on that?"

The latter who had been about to pop a piece of chocolate into his mouth looked around at the company uncertainly. Warren's two upper front teeth were missing. He said: "I suppose you are referring to police power?"

"No. I was referring to all forms of state power," Haywood explained.

"That would be only one manifestation of it. We should also include the law generally: courts, judges, legislators, etc., and all agencies formulated to enforce order and maintain privilege."

"Doesn't that include commercial privilege?" Micky Osawa spoke up. "I don't think we should exempt from our inquiry merchants and businessmen, brokers or real estate operators. They also exercise power because they control property."

"We should add to the list banks," Nechaev offered with some relish, "and the regulators of money. As everyone knows, banks are here theoretically to extend credit, but as often as not they stifle it and so close off free initiative."

"And what about the Army? Certainly we ought to include the Selective Service System," Tacks Yashimoto suggested.

"We are aggregating a long list." Powerhouse Bill smiled. "After all, we can't expect to cover everything in one symposium. Though I can see, wits are sharp this evening. I move we accept the agenda as it stands. Now to my question, put in a nutshell: Is Power moral or immoral?"

"It is immoral," emphatically stated Warren.

"In all its forms?" Powerhouse Bill asked.

"In all species of government," Warren said. "By which I mean tyranny outright, fascism, social imperialism, etc. Or in its disguised forms: parliamentarianism, so-called mixed socialism, oligarchy, and the like."

"And so the leaders of these types of government are all bad?"

"Undoubtedly."

"Then aren't you leaving us in a position," Bill Haywood continued, "where there can be no leaders whatever or any form of social organization?"

"Not at all," Warren countered. "Of course, there is what we would call the natural leader: that is the man who has a greater understanding and ability to carry out a certain task, succeeds more easily in having his views accepted, and so acts as a guide to others. But he can never coerce others."

"What if he did coerce others—for their own good? I mean, if his aim were a Mutualist society?"

"No, that is a contradiction in terms." Schimmelpennick laughed. "There must be voluntary assent at all times. Otherwise nothing beneficial will happen. The people have to be prepared, no matter what transformation occurs, even a so-called popular revolution. Or afterwards all the old forms of tyranny will creep back."

"Including the police," Warren said.

"Including all merchants, lawyers," Costa joined in, "property owners, bankers and the military. And we are right back where we started from."

"I see," Haywood said thoughtfully. "Then the operating word here is 'consent.' It doesn't matter what the goals are?"

"No. No. You are putting the question in the wrong terms," Warren objected. "It is a question of process, not formal ends, and the process has to be evolutionary and experimental. Experiment is the key word. The aims of men are always obscure, especially groups and congregations of men. They have to be made plain by a process of working things out in common, over a long period by testing multiple solutions.

"That is why we insist on the democratic system. Not because it is the richest and gives the most room to individual caprice, but because it is the most flexible and experimental."

"I think Josie has expressed this very succinctly," Malatesta broke in. "And also he has thrown light on the character of our gang. That is, we are not ideologues or shapers of some comprehensive program. We are day-to-day activists, agitators within a given political tradition. It is for this reason that in addition to being MUTUALISTS, we also call ourselves DEMOCRATS."

The Conclusion of the Symposium

"Would anyone care for a brandy or liqueur? We have several kinds," offered Emma.

"Yes. Let's pause and drink a toast to Emma," Tacks Yashimoto suggested. "And to the Spirit of these gatherings."

"Anyway we need a quiet moment—to settle all this loud talk," said Nechaev. And, having gotten to the bar first, he was quick to seal his own lips with a glass of neat Armagnac.

The diversion did not last long. Cafiero resumed:

"We have spoken of the sociable as opposed to the aggressive man, and of various kinds of power." The gang members settled themselves again in a friendly circle. "So far we have piloted ourselves bravely, between one reef of argument and another. Now I should like to ask a very practical question—what about work in our Mutualist society? I presume there will be work? We are not so cold-blooded as to envision complete automation, are we?"

"Such a world would be fatal," Costa said.

"So in this world of ours there would continue to be labor and exchange, industrial and farm workers, distributors and managers and so forth?"

"Of course."

"And these workers would, I take it, own their own means of production and distribution?"

"You're getting too abstract already," Andy Costa protested. "That economist's jargon will get us nowhere. Obviously, there will be as wide a variety in the types of distribution and production as there are types of workers; and there are diversified technologies. For instance, in one sector of our commune we might have heavy and expensive tools, harvesting combines, cranes, drill presses and the like, while another sector—say watch-makers—would use very light tools. Job styles would differ."

"And these various types of tools and temperaments would affect structure, you mean? They would alter ways of bargaining and the exchange of services between one sector and another?"

"Yes. Confederations would differ depending on each case. And there would be also a wide range of regional and geographic confederations molded according to interest."

"There are also historical differences," Cafiero broke in. "And advantages accruing to certain classes—or even to whole exploiting countries—who have industrialized first and so satellized the others. One century plunders another."

"But still, our goal as Mutualists would be to level all these advantages and disadvantages, would it not?" Fanelli suggested. "In the interests of solidarity?"

"Naturally."

"And you said before this always had to be achieved by means of consent, isn't that correct?"

"That is correct."

"And in each of these categories that we've mentioned—that is, in terms of labor and tools, of geographical locations, and of historical groups—there are people with superior powers and privileges. You'll admit that?"

"Yes."

"Well, they will hardly surrender this power voluntarily. Wouldn't you say your theory has landed you up against a stone wall at this point?"

"No, no. That's too logical. Of course we have a strategy that comprehends all that," Cafiero maintained boldly. "Peaceable agitation and anarchy up to a certain point. Beyond that point, we know perfectly well that the rulers will find it no longer possible to make concessions and they will fight. Then we'll take over, naturally: the workers will occupy the factories, the small farmers and sharecroppers will seize the land, and the private businesses and corporations will be expropriated. In this way we will rid ourselves finally of the exploiting classes."

"By armed force?"

"By armed force, certainly: otherwise it would be them that would get rid of us."

"In other words, in addition to being MUTUALISTS and DEMOCRATS, our group must also call ourselves INSURRECTIONISTS?"

"In this regard, certainly. Cafiero is absolutely correct," Rags commented.

"More brandy, anyone?" Emma asked.

"I'd like to bring up one further point—while we're on the subject of violence," Micky Osawa said. "We have decided, I take it, that violence, by itself, like power, is neither moral nor immoral; it depends on the circumstances in which it is used?"

"That's a fair statement," Rags said.

"Would that include criminal violence? I'm thinking here of specific acts which are thought legally to be crimes: robbery, for instance."

"Law is the criminal. Expropriation by law is robbery," Cafiero said.

"So theft is OK. How about sabotage? Would that also be justified?"

"In certain cases, yes."

"How about murder? Might there be a case of justifiable political assassination?"

"That is a tricky question, Masamichi," Rags countered. "Here you touch on some deeply sensitive points within human nature. It is true that political assassinations and acts of violence generally have had in the past a bad smell about them. They have derailed anarchism. Often they have been carried out by selfish or crazy persons. I myself favor collective, rather than,individual action, and preferably action that has some wider educational effect on the general public. So it depends on the particular circumstances."

"But you can conceive of such a situation?"

"Of course."

"We have had an excellent symposium," Bill Haywood averred. "I think we can all agree this discussion has been useful, and carried out under the pleasantest and most convivial circumstances."

The Albany Pool Gambit

The next place the gang struck was Albany. Ten miles to the North was the manufacturing city of Troy. A short distance to the South was Rensselaer. The river flowing by these points formed what was called the Albany Pool. Due to the heavy concentration of raw sewage and other wastes, the surface of the Hudson was here a metallic dead black. The water was septic. There was no oxygen. Up from the sludgy bottom, bubbles of hydrogen sulphide and methane gas broke languidly under the bridges.

It was from here also that the three city area, known as the Capitol District, took its water supply.

The task of carrying out the Albany operation fell to Nechaev, for reasons which will become clear. In laying the groundwork he was assisted by the whole Gang, particularly Yashimoto and the secretary, Sandy Berkman, who were good at research. The principal object of their research was Terrence Soakerseller, owner of the Intercontinental Bank and also head of the Hudson Valley Clear Water Commission.

It was Soakerseller's custom to commute by boat upriver from his estate at Rheinbeck to his Albany offices, conveniently around the corner from the State Capitol. Numerous aides accompanied him on these trips, which began each morning at seven from the estate landing. On a certain day the party arrived to find a tug tied up. The captain explained that he had a passenger on board, a frogman bound for a certain industrial job in Troy. However, the tug had received a radio message from the company to turn back. Would it be possible for the frogman to continue on the banker's yacht? The new passenger was made welcome and the daily commuting trip began.

With a shudder along its teak deck and a discreet chafing of the canvas fenders against the sides, the boat migrated out into midstream and turned north. The diver's bulky gear had been stowed below deck. Coffee was served under the awning aft. Soakerseller, interested in all varieties of the industrial arts, plied his surprise passenger with questions, to which the frogman responded capably.

A half-hour passed with the yacht progressing nicely upstream. Soakerseller sighed.

"It is curious," the banker remarked, giving the diver an appraising look, "your trade lies *under* the river; mine is over it. Oh, I don't mean banking. That's a bore, frankly. My interests in that area are looked after by others."

"I know you are the head of the Hudson Clear Water Commission," the frogman acknowledged.

"You've read about that, have you?" The banker smiled, pleased. "Yes, that is my real life. The river fascinates me. It is like a beautiful woman that one wants to protect from the most vicious abuse." Soakerseller looked across the unruffled surface to the riverbank, where there was a used-car dump.

"Yes, it's fallen into a bad state," his passenger agreed.

"Tragic," Soakerseller murmured, and went on to explain the plans of the Commission for salvaging the beleaguered valley, and in particular the ten-mile strip of the river which was considered the most polluted: the notorious Capitol District Pool. Here the water would be purified by treatment plants. They were now passing Saugerties.

The frogman was of course Nechaev. Soakerseller had been chosen as the Gang's recent target precisely because of this interest just expressed in water purification.

Soakerseller owned most of the river industries. At the same time, as head of the Clear Water Commission he was able to pose as a principal conservationist.

It was a sparkling clear day. Abeam lay Roon's Hook, an arc of pasture and wild gooseberry land bending into the main channel. Over a hedgerow of willows the spire of the State Capitol building could be just seen. At this point the surface of the Hudson became mottled—olive and matte-greys, occasionally thickened by a blotch of brown. Soakerseller, a handsome figure, leaned over the rail, watching the first condoms float by.

"What impresses me," Nechaev was saying at his elbow, "is the extraordinary chemical action of this stretch of the river, which is, of course, tidal. The whole basin is like a huge chemical sump with an almost limitless number of ingredients pouring in. In some cases these act on each other powerfully, and combine into new elements."

"New elements?" Soakerseller asked.

"As yet unanalyzed in the laboratory."

"Yes, I suppose there's a catalytic action," one of the banker's aides who had been attending them remarked. "The bacteria from the raw sewage attacking the rest of it: fibers, oils, acids, metallic oxides and the like. A real stew pot."

"Would any of these elements be valuable?" Soakerseller inquired.

In answer the Frogman produced a small bottle from his pocket. He handed this to the banker, who examined it, then passed it on to his aide.

"Bismuth," the latter said. "Highly concentrated, I'd almost call it bismuth Extract."

"It's completely unprocessed. In its natural state," Nechaev countered, "just as it was taken from the river bottom."

"Interesting you should bring up bismuth," Soakerseller remarked with a smile. "I don't know if you know, our organization has extensive dealings in this particular element in one of the Latin American countries, where we own some mines . . ."

The Frogman's eyes narrowed. He said slowly, staring at Soakerseller, "There is more high-grade bismuth in this section of the Hudson River from Troy to Saugerties than in all your holdings in the country of Paraguay."

"Well, I own Paraguay," Soakerseller confirmed. "But it's a lot of trouble." He stared at the thick water dreamily. "Imagine, right under our noses."

"Under our noses in more ways than one," the aide joked. "Oh, by the way," he turned to Beeves casually, "I don't suppose there's any one particular source for this catalyst? I imagine there are several?"

"One source. The North Troy Sewer," the Frogman replied. "As a matter of fact, that's where I'm headed now."

The yacht had passed under Dunn Memorial Bridge linking the town of Rensselaer with South Albany, and pulled into the Soakerseller private landing. Above this surmounting an abandoned railroad station, a wide area of parking lots, and a hillside of dilapidated faded tenements, stood the State Capitol, an impressive building. The greater part of the Soakerseller group debarked, but Soakerseller himself, with a section of his staff devoted to industrial chemicals, remained on board. The lines slacked, the waters roiled under the backing props, and again the party found itself chugging upriver, enveloped in an abominable stench. With the exception of their frogman passenger, none of them had been on this stretch of the river before.

During the trip Nechaev had been favorably impressed by Soakerseller. The financier turned out to be more enterprising than he had been led to expect. A man of forceful character, yet he had an easy congenial way with his inferiors. In fact the Troy boatride had seemed very much of a lark.

What was most pleasing was the banker's flaming red hair and freckles. Nechaev guessed that there was some scotch blood in the family.

After a short time the frogman called for his gear. In addition to protective clothes, it consisted of some chemical testing apparatus, sampling tubes and a jimmy. Nechaev stripped to his underwear on deck, a paunchy man, and pulled on the tight skin-diver's outfit of black neoprene. Over this he added a reinforcement of heavy leather pants and arm gauntlets.

"Eels," he volunteered. "There'll be a mess of them around the sewer outlet where we go in. They're rapacious devils. I wouldn't want one of them fastened onto my leg."

He then explained that their destination was a meat-packing plant. This was located about a half mile up on the trunk sewer line. If the tide was right they would reach there around noon.

"I suspected that blood had something to do with it, from the color of your bottled bismuth," one of the Soakerseller aides remarked.

"When are we due to reach this outlet?" Soakerseller enquired.

"It should be around one of these bends."

They had now left Albany and were at the boundary of Troy, but this was a matter of names only. The cities merged into one district. The abutments of the river were a solid wall of small manufacturing plants, oil depots, body and fender shops, iron works, interspersed with poorer tenements hanging over the bank. The bank was punctured every few yards by sewers. Somewhere behind all this the business and residential districts sprawled. The party had lost all sense of smell. Occasionally the channel regurgitated from below, releasing a bloom of raw feces, grease and soiled beer cans.

"Thank God for chlorine, or whatever they put into it around here. If it weren't for science the whole population of the Capital would be dead. But I imagine the legislators would go on talking. We have some scotch and soda on board, though, if anybody would like some." Soakerseller was jovial.

"I believe we're here," Nechaev announced. The engines slowed. The Frogman pointed. "If I'm not mistaken, that should be the meat-packing plant over there, in that direction." Somewhere over the roofs a vast chimney gave off smoke. The party fell silent.

They approached the sewer outfall, edging in sideways. The river level was a foot below the lip. The brick main, about ten feet in breadth, was dry except for a slight trickle. Below this, the water was alive with eels. As they watched, the sewer filled suddenly and discharged with a rush, a reddish stream. Then it died down, leaving behind on the brick gobbets of grey meat and chicken feathers. After this the eels came, swarming up into the pipe, writhing and scavenging over one another, their jaws wide. Then they fell back all at once in turmoil.

"Greedy sons of bitches." Nechaev grinned. The eels were as big as Nechaev's arm. He continued: "We're in luck. The tide's ebbing now, and in another half-hour, they won't be able to get in. We'll have the whole approach to ourselves, until the next tide. Look carefully, please. I have here an underground map of Troy. Interesting old piece of engineering, somewhat antiquated now. This main services all the processing plants in the area. From here it runs up about a quarter of a mile to a central manhole; we should be able to pick up our trail there. It's a fairly complicated system, because at each break, that is at each change of direction, there's a grate."

"How thick would the bars be? A half inch?" an engineer asked. "And rusty?"

"Right you are. Easily pried open." Nechaev waved his crowbar.

"Are you sure there's no danger of getting lost?" another aide asked. He was studying the faded map. Made in the late 19th century it was embellished with engraver's wiggles.

The frogman reassured him that although there were a good many changes of direction, and hence a good number of grates, they could easily manage to get through them before the next tide.

"So you think we'll have plenty of time for our investigation?"

"No doubt about. The ebb tide still has a little to go. Then it will be at least three to four hours, after that, before we should have an appreciable flooding of the underground system."

The banker said: "Well this should be quite an education." He raised his glass. "Here's to Bismuth-Plus."

The party, was in an elated mood. The starboard bow of the yacht rested against the sewer outfall, rocking gently. Soakerseller's band began to jump lightly across, assisted by a sailor. They were mostly in light summer business suits, seersucker, and some of them carried straw boaters. Soakerseller himself had on a bright blue blazer with an insignia that he had earned on the crew at boarding school.

With a spring he leaped unaided onto the slimy brick, trickling along the center, and began to walk jauntily towards the head of the column into the darkness.

The impromptu mining exploration under the Troy meatpacking plant had already taken on a sporting style.

"Bismuth-Plus," one aide remarked to another admiringly. He had written the quote down in a notebook. "We already have the title of the product! But what a stink."

"We are following the scent of liquid assets," his companion shot back.

One of the last in line asked Nechaev if he could take his briefcase, explaining that he had important papers of the firm, legal and confidential, that he would not like to leave behind.

"Oh sure, you can take them with you," Nechaev assured him. Then the accountant stepped in. The frogman followed at the end of the line.

In the offices of the ADD-RITE Corporation the members of the Environment Control Gang were gathered around Nechaev. The mood was festive. Powerhouse Bill Haywood read the headlines:

> TERRENCE SOAKERSELLER DEAD
> PROMINENT BANKER DEVOURED IN SEWER
> EXPLORATION UNDER TROY ENDS IN TRAGEDY FOR BANKER'S PARTY. LOSS OF 20 FEARED IN ATTACK BY EELS
> BISMUTH HUNTER'S FATE SEALED BY MYSTERIOUS STRANGER, SURVIVING MEMBERS SAY GLUCKENHEIM APPOINTED NEW HEAD OF HUDSON CLEAR WATER COMMISSION

He remarked thoughtfully: "Gluckenheim. Well, I doubt if the second commissioner will be any less ineffectual than the first. We seem to have stirred up everybody, though."

"It was a terrorist act," Malatesta observed, "which any anarchist should deplore. In fact we do deplore it."

"But what other field of action was there?"

"At this point in history, none," Malatesta agreed. "They have all been preempted. I hope this will not hold true for the future—when we may follow a more rational course."

Schimmelpennick raised his glass. "Here's to propaganda of the deed."

"And to a future without bankers," Nechaev said grinning.

"I'd say our whole Hudson River clean-up has been carried through brilliantly," Berkman said. He looked at Luud. "Particularly the Oriskany adventure."

"It is not often one can use the dead in such a creative way," Schimmelpennick admitted. "But I agree with Sandy. The Albany gambit was wonderfully educational. Public opinion will be very sensitive to the ecology establishment from now on."

"Yes, I doubt if they'll get away with as much as they have."

"To Nechaev," Warren raised his whiskey glass.

"We have accomplished some of our purpose, possibly the most difficult part," Malatesta admonished the Environment Control Gang. "But we still have to move on and see what we can do about the lower half of the river. So I do not think we should be overconfident at this point."

"All the rivers of America," Bill Haywood added, his eyes misty.

GREEN SONG

Oak leaves are the last to go
they stand green   green
against the yellow of the brown park

The chill ground is covered with yellow linden leaves
the first to fall
A motorcycle goes by

Oh you quiet dogs
everything in your park is brown brown
except the flames of the two yellow mulberry trees
and the chanting green oak

She asked me why?   and I said
"there must be a spring welling up underneath
from April"

LITTLE SONG FOR LILLY

She's left   Her touch is like my fine oak floor
all glow
When Lilly goes
she leaves my arms burning
No boat
foundering/wallowing on a wave
aches for port
as I ache for her
She is my boat
all on fire with love fuel

When Lilly leaves
she leaves

my walls/floor/windows all burning/spinning

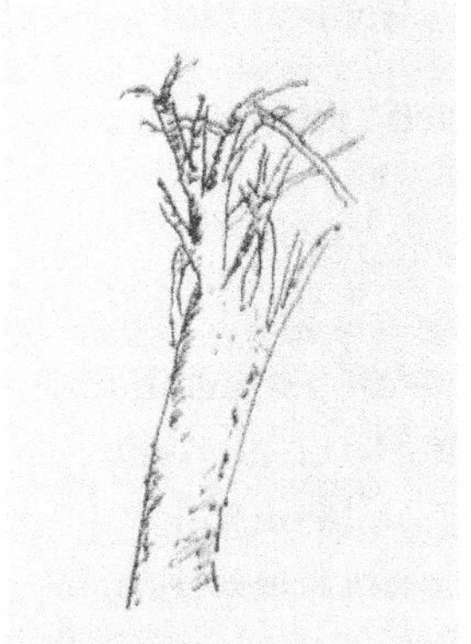

POPULAR SONG SNATCH

Jacked off again last nite
                    that was bad
jacked off again last nite
                    oh bad bad
I swore I wouldn't do it till next February
or january at the earliest
                                        Hold on Bill!
What made it worse Mable walked in
                    that was bad
what made it worse Mable walked in
                    oh bad bad
After breakfast Mable walked in. She was supposed to
be away that whole month with her aunt in Wisconsin
                                        Hold on Bill!

Done wasted all my fine strength
                    oh bad bad
I done wasted all my fine strength
                    oh bad bad
I never felt less like a man

and more like a wet dishrag than I did this morning
Hold on Bill!

We made love on the kitchen table
like always
we made love on the kitchen table
like always
The minute I started to take off her nylon underpants
I knew everything was going to be all right
Hold on Bill
Hold on tight!

A DEFEAT

The nastiness of it. His disposition has got worse and worse. It used to be the sweetest but now that he's grown so fat he can hardly open his mouth without some toad of spite coming out directed at his younger sister. Disgusting. Not that he dares hurt her openly it's all done in the manner of "good natured kidding," his chubby boy's face stretched in a grin as the hatefullest observations come out.

Will he grow up that way? What a thought. How often have I seen this exact quality in so-called "grown men." No more than thugs or hooligans, crowding around some guy with a knife or maybe a bottle behind their backs—at the same time talking to him "good-humoredly" with a kind of bland smile. All this hostility, and most of it comes from plain envy.

I know Mike is suffering and is deeply ashamed of his obesity. The other day I had the camera out at the beach and was going to snap his picture. He actually pleaded with me: "Just take my face. Please. I— I don't want to show my—you know."

He couldn't bring himself to say the word "stomach."

*   *

"EXUBERANCE IS BEAUTY," William Blake

*   *

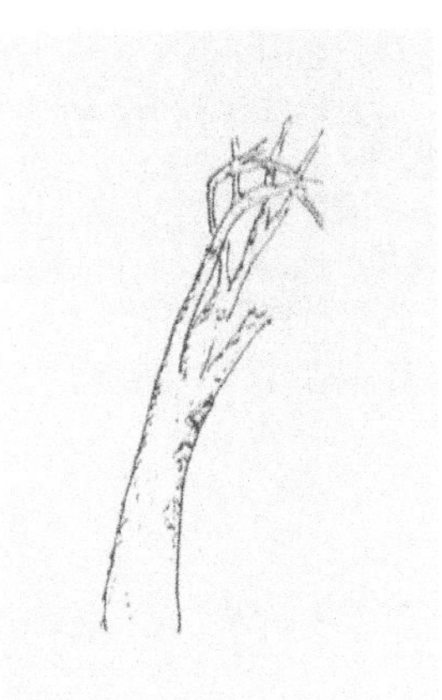

SECOND SONG FOR ALMA

I believe Alma will come
when the lake is green
and all the dogs are quiet

Then shall the pelican clear his lungs
of his rabid squawk
and float in the sky

All the midges vibrating at the lake's edge
will be still
They are still anyway

Then will I
                    then will I
                                        then will I
and the lovely mole
throw our   skins at each other
in wild play

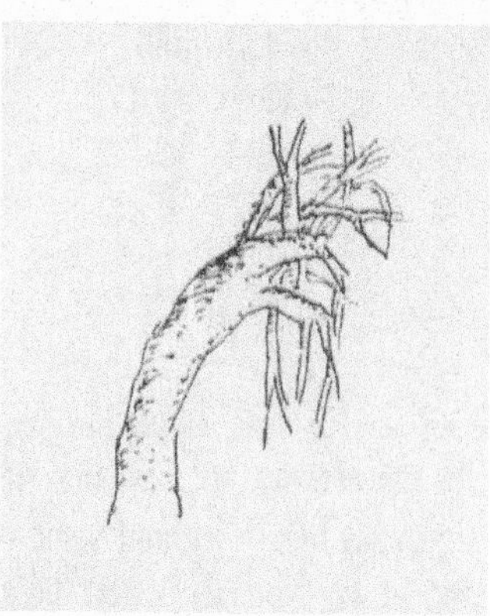

MORPHOLOGY OF THE EYE *(third chromopoem)*

The eye "organizes itself" (Stechel)
It opens wide to let in the light
light   light
floods in like sound
into a silent room
like the sound of Carribinieri's Brass Band
like the waves from a steamship flood the beach
setting bathers awash
like waves of color
washing into the empty room of the eye

* *

"ENERGY IS ETERNAL DELIGHT," Tom Paine

* *

One day two travellers landed at the Saigon Airport. They were William Blake and Tom Paine, accredited war correspondents to the British Commonwealth. Blake had been nursing a meat sandwich wrapped in heavy butcher's paper, which he kept conveying in and out of his pocket, to the annoyance of the other passengers. There was trouble at Customs—as Blake declared that his camera had been given to him the day before by his dead brother. Paine had a large tuft in his ear, the size of a pig's bristle, which was deemed possibly infectious. But they were let through.

They wandered through the streets of Saigon for one week. On their way back, I had the good fortune to interview them at Kennedy (formerly Idlewild) Airport. Blake said:

"ONE LAW FOR THE LION AND THE OX IS OPPRESSION."

* *

THIRD ARTICLE OF FAITH
I believe Ahma will come
with Carrabinieri's band
and nipples of red strawberries
a bear rattling a tamborine
another bear jangling a pair of maraccas
an ape beating a drum
                    dum dum
the "Queen of Mab" attended by her maids

                    Glorianna   in the green park

from April!

Letters Censored and Uncensored

A LETTER FROM AUSONIUS

Lugo
Iberia
October 401

Dear Ben Lyric

I'm so glad to hear you have moved with your engineering company to Haiphong. As you remark in your letter it's lucky the Americans won the war!

Are BBZ Engineers doing highways and bridges exclusively? You mention the Canton-Hanoi-Vientianne-Cau Mau highway. Or has your firm moved into other products? Petro-chemicals, possibly with a Japanese partner? I understand the conglommerate is the big thing nowadays (a thoroughly roman conception).

Sorry about your divorce.

I will try to describe Nota to you. It is a complete backwater. Vulpa's Army is operating to the North, between Cairns and Jutland. In Africa everything is pretty well stabilized with General Belisarius at Minim Here everything decays. The Vandals on the whole are nice people, even though they do smear their hair with bear grease, and many of the landgraves have become rich (in olive oil, goatskins, etc.).

You couldn't by any chance send me a cask of good wine, trans-maritime? I hear your Tonkinese Ju-ke is excellent. I can give you in exchange a crate of chickens or a barrel of our best (staple export) Imperial Gokl Medal Olive Oil. I also need paints, particularly sulphur and vermillion pigments, as I have been amusing myself lately with illustrating some of Ovid's stories. The light blue (from cobalt) and the dark green-blue (from malachite rock) are available in the stores here. I grind up a supply weekly which I keep at my elbow in a dry pot. Consequently, everything I paint has a blue tint — blue, blue. Which accords with my mood, though I would rather be merry and paint bright.

The other day a wolf was seen walking down our main street. Can you imagine? Not three blocks from where I live. And this city has been the capital of Serbonitt for three centuries!

But we still have our old grandeur. And in many respects are quite modern as well. The main boulevards are straight and lined with giant oaks and palms at regular intervals, and well lighted up to ten o'clock at night. The apartment blocks are some 800 x 400 feet square, six stories high with excellent exterior staircases and good plumbing, the drinking water comes 100 miles by aqueduct, from Basta. I forgot to say that the main streets have paved gutters. The black market flourishes.

My dear nephew, you have no idea what it's like to go to the Common Baths. (I'd forgotten—you have those where you are too—but much smaller.) But here our baths are extraordinary. Can you imagine paddling around in the same pool of hot water with two dozen or so Romans, Vandals and Numeans? The Numeans are black, the Romans pink to light brown, the Vandals yellow. It is a dizzying experience, which is enhanced by the marble columns of the gymnasium being purple, lake, carmine, beige and scum-green—the barbarity of taste in public buildings! There is always a considerable amount of activity: knee-bending, weight-lifting, and light sparring—with the slaves who are as many colors as we are. I must say that the Vandals are good conversationalists. They take well to letters, compose songs in Provencal and Latin, and some even have been to the University. There is no more execrable musician than a Roman, his ears are made of lead. I manage to play a game of draughts daily with my friend Golgo (in our bathrobes), then we spar a little to round off the afternoon and take a plunge in the pool—which is now filthy with gobbets of hair grease. But such is life among Serbonii! All centers around business, and talk is constantly about the price of hides, chicken diseases, trucking charges to Syracuse, and import duties.

The other day I transplanted my Paestum Roses. Of course they are not hardy here, but can be saved through the winter with careful housekeeping, and some luck in the weather. I have them against the south wall, as in my old garden apartment at Osta. I also have my little stone god there, with water running out of his mouth. The large Paestums have a drowsy sweet smell (with a trace of cinnamon in it). When I put my nose in them I am reminded of my old mistress Sylvia, a chapter in my life I am not liable to tell you about.

Beyond the wall are 531 hectares of market gardens under cultivation by the Expeditionary Army Quartermaster Corps. Here there is nothing but cabbages laid out in regular flat rows. But beautiful in their own way. When the first frost comes, they will all turn white, like a sea of salt. There has been no snow yet this year, though everything is already dreary and the mountains in the distance are the color of charcoal.

How I am looking forward to getting out of this place. My rotation is coming up soon. How I long to be sent home—or at least somewhere near home, under the same sky would do. Have you any idea what a roman sky looks like? Ah, the tedium, the tedium.

War news: Hasdrubal has defeated the Nervii. That makes the fifth time at least. I doubt if they will ever break out of their Vosz dugouts, where they subsist on moles and radishes. (By the way, I am also bothered by moles, under my roses.) The captives are now part of our Army. Last winter the Adamantii were a worse threat. Vercingetorix (who was once a Captain in the Praetorian guard!) had them raiding the whole Lucca Valley. Vulpa marched on them and smashed them. They regrouped somewhere in the woods, appeared a day later at Ambiox, where he smashed them again, this time for good. Now there was a rumor that the Tencteri had crossed the Garonne and were marauding our hamlets. Vulpa force-marched his army fifty miles in one night (from Ambiox), fell upon the Tencteri at Bith and smashed them. A dashing general, Vulpa! But even stupider, they say, than Dumnorix, who had the Prefecture last year.

The Franks are giving Childeric a hard time. They have been on our side for ages—after Antwerp was burned—and even shared in the administration. Though there was that little trouble in ‘05 when

[2 LINES CENSORED]

had been constructing a huge bridge over the Meuse, under the direction of their own engineers, who are said to be experts in iron truss construction. It was learned that they had been treating secretly with the Helvetii and were planning an October uprising—on the date the bridge was due to be dedicated by the Empress Theodosia. To forestall this, Childeric had them advance the bridge opening several months, and under the pretext of helping them speed this up, moved several of the Legions in and slaughtered them all. And Antwerp was burned again.

I still think your Roman Legionnaire is the best in the world. Is it the catapaults? Though there are some, even without our borders, that say the Abyssinians are braver.

Our province here is ridiculously safe. There was a little fighting twenty miles from here around the town of *[CENSORED]* and a number of small skirmishes that Kulprix took part in last

[FIVE LINES CENSORED: OFFICIAL MILITARY CENSOR CIS-MARITIME REGION, THIRD DEPARTMENT]

Otherwise everything remains quiet, and will so long as Gaiseric is Proconsul. (By the way they have just made Gaiseric's mother, who used to be a scrubwoman, Duchess of Malta.) *[CENSORED]*

I have re-read your letter. So sorry to hear your outfit is having trouble getting parts from West Germany.

My dear boy, I am worried about my nephew (also a cousin of yours), who is in school at Constantinople. Also, have I written you about Paulinus? I am sure I have mentioned him. He has always been my best friend, and we were at Old Hundred University together, in the same fraternity. He was a very accomplished boxer—An fact, he looked a little like the famous Celtic boxer O'Reilly, whose statue you see up at the Olympics. He was a favorite of Vespasian. Both had cauliflower ears—I mean O'Reilly and Paulinus, not the emperor. He later became Prefect of Thuringia. We were in close touch and sympathy our whole lives—until about ten years ago, when I lost track of him completely. I learned later that he had been transferred to Nepos, which actually is not far from here. All of my pressing letters to him were unanswered. He had become a priest in the Christian religion. My dear boy, by the staff of Neptune, that man was a complete Roman: by that I mean an utter stoic, and physically as dense and phlegmatic as a hippopotamus. What hit him, and brainwashed him in this way, I can't imagine. In any case, as I understand it, a great number of prisoners and refugees were taken through Nepos --after that same battle of Brith. Paulinus exchanged himself for several of them, so they could return free. He was sold with the rest of the contingent and taken along with them to Africa. I have heard that he is working in a quarry. He was a man of my age.

My dear Ben, write me when you can and tell me more about your new place in Haiphong. I'm glad that your oldest boy is coming over to visit you after the school semester. At least that will take him away from Beebie, and give him an idea of the world outside Long Island. I apologize for this melancholy letter.

Affectionately,

Your devoted uncle,
Ausonius

May 1985
Haiphong

Dear Garvey,

You'd hardly believe it if you saw this town. It's just like Cleveland and I have a little place (a duplex apartment) just a coupla subway stops away from downtown, so I go in to the BBZ office every morning.

Well the old firm is going great guns and I'm glad I transferred out here, after my divorce. It isn't only the pay. They give you a chance to do a lot and I have quite a lot of responsibility (we are running a ten-lane thru-way along the old Ho Chi Min trail and I do all the layouts). Not like the old inking routine.

The firm has also gone into herbicides, opticals, oil drilling (off the beach of the old capital city of Touranne) and cement, and is now called "Trans-Asian Conglommerates."

How's the old computer section these days? I sure miss the old gang. How's the bridge game that we used to have every lunch hour on Burke's desk? And who's sitting in for me, that Kibbisher Rashevski?

Cheers.

Ben Lyric

P.S. But there's nothing to do for entertainment in this hole, and the mosquitoes are bad.

May 20, 1985
Haiphong

Dear Mom,

Who do you think I ran into the other day? Aguerra, the guy that used to be the super in my old apartment. He's working as a longshoreman.

There is a rumor the outfit may get transferred to Brazil.

The weather here has been better. I have a terrific view outside my window—over the harbor and A-Long bay. It's one of the scenic spots of Asia—endless azure water dotted by volcanic islands. They rise up black and sharp. "Drowned mountains," they're called.

Mom, you were wonderful to send me the grand piano. It arrived via Railway Express San Francisco. I got it installed in a corner of the apartment now and it looks great. A little out of tune though. Also the winter underwear, that's a great help. You wouldn't believe it, how cold the rainy season is here. And the winds are bad too.

When should I expect Junior to come, for his summer vacation?

Love,

Your devoted son,

Ben

October 1985
Haiphong
S.F. Asia Quartermaster Corps

My Darling Rosa:

Do you know who's living over here on Itchy Street—Ben, the fellow who was upstairs in Apt. 414. But he's moving to Capetown soon.

Rosa, it's very cold here at night. Send me por favor the red blanket? These army blankets scratch my skin. They issue them to everyone here, even the civilians. Also, it's a small bed. Rosa, I miss you every minute.

I am putting money away every day for the supermercado we will own one of these days, you and me. Am also buying a second hand chevvy which I will bring back with me. It's in good condition it has a rebuilt engine. I can just see us and all the children driving up to the Pentecostal Church on week-ends in our best ropas. I still do not swear or drink. But I confess to you, Rosa, I have not been able to break my habit of putting up Playboy pictures. There is one over the washbowl. Now I, I have only to look at it and I get a *[CENSORED]*.

I am so happy Teresa is home with you, and also that she helps you taking care of Moises and little Raphael. When I get home (with all this money) I hope we can get all the kids back. These orphanages stink.

Rosa, don't strain yourself or take any chances going out in the New York cold and fog. Here they play music on something like a guitar, a flat box with the strings across. They tinkle, tinkle, nothing like the big church noise we make with all the trombones, trumpets and tambourines. Bai-ya!

I smashed my hand on the docks but it's OK. There are four other Puerto Ricans on the unloading crew.

It gets dark here quite late, around 10 o'clock at night. Rosa how I miss you at night. Rosa, Rosa, the bed is too small. My wife, my pajarita, I kiss your lips. My sweet pussy with the hair running all the way up *[CENSORED]* I'm getting wild. How I would like to grab you around both knees and put my

[CENSORED: U.S. QUARTERMASTER CORPS THIRD UNIT. MILITARY ASSISTANCE COMMAND FOR CIVIL OPERATIONS AND RURAL DEVELOPMENT.]

Bye bye for now

Signed

Miguel Aguerra

Haiphong, 1985

P.S. Enclose photo of Chevvy.

Journey Overland Through Quang Binh

Quan Dao Fa Tsi Long
La Baie d'Along
the Blue Bay of A – Long

brims the peaks

in the stillness
 an oar creaks
he bends his back
 the fisherman Tra Huu Quan
As the oar dips in and out
 it scatters drops
like spit   from the mouth of   a water buffalo

plows

the Bay of A – Long
the blue Bay of A – Long

"my wife at the stern   hooked to a big fish"
(hopefully)

the mackerel dives under the mountain roots
of the infinitely blue bay
CRR - EAK
the handle of the long sweep into the pivot
he bends his back
in the soaked paddy the farmer thrusts his legs
Trang Tich struggles behind his water buffalo knee deep in mud

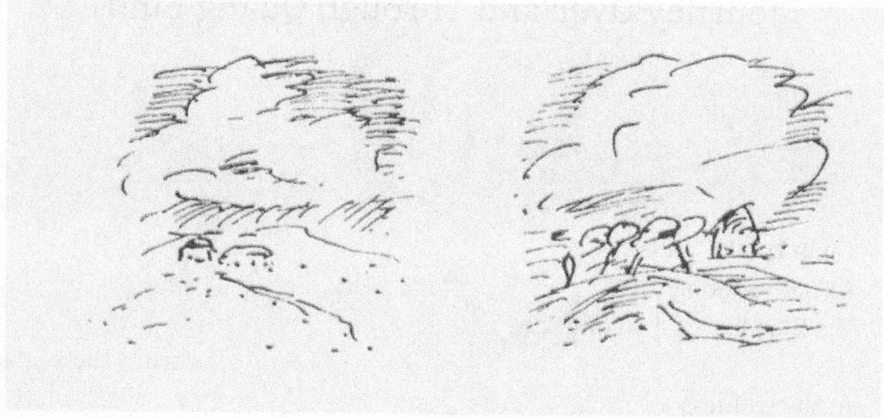

the rice terraces!
Descend
one by one
to the Bay
drenched in sweat
CRR - EAK
CRR - EAK into the pivot
at the edge of the deck
the sampan rower steadies himself with each stroke
with each stroke
leans forward and recovers
leans forward and recovers
ankles flexed

one foot balanced before the other along, the gunwale
suspended over
turquoise

We call the mud red because of the rich silts
collected from the highlands
and the river red
because of the dragon that sleeps
below its mouth underneath the islands
with their weird shapes

The noon whistle!
Nuygen Son Doc stretches
coal grime heavy on his arms
Smoothing the newspaper
he spreads his lunch out on the jetty
that runs from the bay
into the coal mining town of Hon Gai

"my brother out there catching fish"

La Baie d' Along

The blue bay

* *

In Mesopotamia and the Ionian cities of Asia Minor there were irrigation works of marvellous ingenuity on a truly vast scale. Among the world's wonders. It is commonly supposed that these were destroyed in the twelfth century by the Mongols, thus bringing to an end these great empires. On the contrary, they had begun to fail hundreds of years before, because of the lack of a sound water works policy. Over the previous five or six centuries, there had been floods, droughts, the irrigation ditches gradually filling up with silt from the upland pastures, all this due to over-grazing by goats.

How fortunate we are that our people were farmers from a very early date, that is, after rice cultivation had been discovered and brought down into this peninsula. We have always hated goats and shepherds, and have been painstakingly careful in our own land practises always to contour the land and to protect the rice terraces, which are subject to violent rainstorms.

That is why in mid-summer when you go through one of our Vietnamese villages and you hear a drum beating, that is the sign of a real crisis. One of the dykes has broken, probably because of the ratholes. Then you will see the whole village turn out and rush to the trouble source, where they shore up the ruptured earth wall with bamboo poles then fill in the holes, stuffing them with straw and even thatch and pieces of mat from their houses.

(Hydrology Studies I)

* *

Rain
from May on   thru June to end of July
                    steadily and solidly
sky plug pulled out   sluiceway open
 pouring water
                    straight

down

a grey wash
erasing the outline of trees

At the Dong Bang Flood Station

water level at the	+ 12.80 meter mark
at Yen Tap	12.95 meters
Lenh Kahn	13.25 meters
Yen Bay	14 meters
Doan Hung	13.70 meters
Ngoc Thi	17 meters

(telephoned into this newspaper from the Dong Bang Station at the junction of the Song Ngan and Song Cai Rivers)

THE RAMPAGING RED RIVER

* *

Rain
life-bringing rain
on the forehead cheeks mouth
into the open mouth
the first drops

of the first   rain
then the succeeding rains
regularly every month
skin soaked with it
Everywhere
rain drumming

into the pocked bay
into the rice paddy
into the open pit coal mine

DROUGHT YEAR

beady-eyed gull   observes hunger
close-mouth gull   surveys the signs the indications
of hunger without comment

Item   low water in Song Ngan River
Item   almost white sky enormous sun
standing directly overhead

With flick wingtips   gull elevates   glides past
Trau Huu Quan's boat   floats over the dyke

Item   to the horizon red hard-baked soil
with cracks in it every few feet
Item   a man lies on the ground with his mouth open
a beetle crawling out of it

Thirst   during the malaria fever!
Thirst   of the cracked soil during the dry months!

Hunger

FARMERS' HOLIDAY

The gong summoned everyone to the Dinh. The Sorcerer had come. He would perform a few tricks then go out with his helpers on all the roads, beating on the orange drum, all of them shouting at the top of their lungs to exorcize the cholera spirit. No harm in it.

At the entrance to the Dinh stood M. Pontebry, the French visitor, in a tropical white suit chatting with the Chief Notable. Yes, wasn't it a nice day? Already the children had crowded into the public section where they were waiting for the show to begin. Their eyes bright, they munched moon cakes. A band played in the corner. I was standing at the back next to two other laborers, Xuan Da and Kim Dong Bac who kept scratching himself.

Loud banging on the big drum hanging from the ceiling, measured strokes on the small drums, and a frenzied medley from the other musicians. Everyone stops talking about fertilizer.

The ritual begins under the supervision of Cung Bao Phach, the rites master. First, the Highest and Oldest Venerable scoots in, presents his food offering and kowtows, bending at the waist and holding out his hands at chest level, his hands trembling and his eyes watering slightly. He is followed by the other High Venerables, who also make offerings and kowtow. Then the Village Notables and the other members of the Cult Committee make their offerings and kowtow, in order of rank and by twos. These are followed again by the Police Agent and by the Village Recording Secretary. The French visitor in his white suit also kowtows. All this is done politely and smoothly.

During the first festival meal I had a nice talk with Cung Bao Phach, the Ritual Master, to whom I owe $800 VN. He gave me some good advice about planting. Last year the bottom dropped out of the Yellow Grain rice market, but Cung Bao advises me to plant it again this year, there's bound to be some demand for it. He's going to plant a half hectare of Yellow Grain and also 7 hectares of Nanh Dran rice, the best. But that would be too costly for me in fertilizer. He also advised me to plant part of my field in Fox's Fang. A smart fellow.

More ceremonies. The town soccer game against Nho Lam. Then the second food serving at five.

We ate it with relish, also drank a good deal of rice alcohol to celebrate the general good feeling. So by the end of it, Xuan Da, Kim Dong and I were potted. We were then stood up and packed up against the wall of the Dinh for the night ceremony. The musicians were all in the corner, on the wood bed.

It had been a very nice Cao An—that is for Peace and Prosperity at the end of the dry season. We hope. By May 1, the seed beds will be prepared; a month after that the fields harrowed and plowed, and the transplanting operations finished. All this with good luck, and enough rain of course. If so, we'll be through the worst danger by the middle of August; by then the plants will be grown and the first sweet smell of the ripe grains in everyone's nostrils.

Soon the Sorcerer and his party would return for the Spirit Boat Ceremony. The Dinh would vibrate with the shouting and drum beating. The Spirits would he invited to enter the toy boat and eat, just as we had been doing. Then politely but very firmly and deliberately the spirit boat would be escorted down to the stream bank and shoved off. Goodbye, evil spirits! The stem-borers had been terrible the last few years. The pesticides didn't touch them, only good against the leaf-chewing insects (because of the copper-sulphate solution). Still, it might be a good year in spite of everything. If it were, if the rains came, I was thinking, and everything worked out all right and the market prices held, then I'd be able to pay back Cung Bao, the money lender. If not, I'd be in even deeper.

Xuan Dao was wedged up next to me as if we were glued, the skin of his arm hot. I whispered to him: "How much do you owe Cung Bao, on next year's crop?"

"I owe him a half," he whispered back.

"And you, how much do you owe him?" I asked Kim Dong.

"Three quarters."

Wild drumming, a frenzied explosion from the band members. Several of them had fallen off the bed. The Sorcerer swept in.

* *

In the last twenty years (since the introduction of fertilizer) three things have happened. First the rice grains have grown larger. Second, there are more bugs. Third, the rice-planting girls have stopped singing their song.

(from: An Old Man Remembers)

* *

and that poem who was it by?
about "all the windows going up
and everybody laughed
to see an old man coming home drunk

with flowers in his hair"
Something like that

8 SONGS FOR TRANG TICH'S WATER BUFFALO

Trang Tich's water buffalo
circles around the spindly palmetto tree all day
trying to keep in the shade

In the farmyards the wives are winnowing rice.
Trang Tich's water buffalo
wanders around the lanes of the village
eating goldenrod heads

Motherfucking black buffalo!
you lie up to your eyes in mud
in the wallow hole
while the farmer does all the work

Buffalo at his best: sweeping horn
steak black coat picked clean of leeches
by the white heron
perched on his back

One little boy fishes for minnows
off the low dike where the rice stalks once grew
the other
bullies the big water buffalo

The pagoda measures the village
with its mauve shadow
On the ocean of flooded paddies
                                        off somewhere
the ploughman cuts a watery straight line

Grey skies. The only sound   rain
drumming into the field
and Trang Tich's water buffalo slogging
head down

HOG FEED PRODUCTION

Last year hog feed production improved measurably, particularly in Lang Son Province where pioneer work in agronomy has been undertaken. However, all provinces surveyed showed net gains over previous periods.

Standard feed used was a mixture of rice bran and banana tree pulp dehydrated (first column) and processed fish supplement (second column). Figures in 1000 gias:

LONG SON PROVINCE	88	320
BAC KAN	68	*
CAO BANG	62	none
THAI NGUYEN	68	240
LAO KAY	*	*
PHU THO	45	*
LAI CHAU	*	*
QUAN YEN	82	200
THAI BINH	74+	none
QUAN BINH	65+	80+
THANK HOA	30+	40+

**no figures reported for these provinces*

+ *quotas inadequate; should be revised upwards.*

OVERLAND FROM QUANG BINH

Tra Huu Quan, Trang Tich and Nuygen Son Doc went on a four months journey. They left in a dry wind. The main road to the south lay on top of the dykes. It was heavily travelled in this district. Hardly ten minutes went by without some truck rumbling past covering them and their bicycles with dust. When this happened they would stop and all shout loudly at the driver, brandishing their fists. Trang Tich making an obscene gesture and shooting his tongue out between the gap in his front teeth. Then roaring with laughter the three brothers would beat the dust off each other's clothes and continue on.

After four days travelling in this manner they came to a village at the junction of two rivers. Here a hydro-electric plant was in the process of being built. Everyone in the whole village was at work moving dirt. The women carried loads of earth and sand in two baskets hanging from a yoke slung across their backs. The men transported the heavier gravel, stone rubble and cement sacks in bullock wagons and sledges which were hauled uphill. The dam was going up directly above the town and was not far advanced.

After a supper of fish soup the travellers asked one of the foremen about the construction schedule. They received the following account: the dam was one of a series that was being planned that would eventually cover the entire valley with a flood control and power network. There would be additional benefits, such as irrigation, water purification, etc. The community had been at work steadily at this site for ten years. The project had been going along well and last year the dam was almost completed, when it collapsed, wrecking a large portion of the village and burying many people. The engineering had been sound (the foreman assured them), but the officials in charge of the project had not understood how to mix cement. Now work had started over again and this time it was going along excellently.

The travellers reached the province of Quang Binh, where the road over the mountains begins. At Ding Hoi they traded their bicycles in at a store, for camping supplies. Up to this point the brothers had worn only their black shorts and had gone barefoot. Tran and Tra Huu had on the traditional straw hats, but Nuygen Doc (for ideological reasons) insisted on wearing his blue and grey striped miner's cap with the merit worker's badge.

They walked towards the border of Quang Binh and were soon in the forest. The trail kept going up and up. As it did so the air became cooler.

The trees were very large and covered with vines spiralling up to the leafy roof through which chinks of sky glinted. The ground below was fairly open, the trail keeping to the ridges.

Towards late afternoon they stopped by a waterfall and had tea. The noise of the birds and monkeys was almost as deafening as that of the water. The land fell away precipitously. Through an opening in the trees they could see the ocean, which they had left days before.

The next night was spent at a woodcutter's hut. The moon came through the roof. On the following nights they slept with their noses directly to the moon, lying on their padded coats to keep out the dew. For a number of days they hiked towards the Annamite plateau. Tra Huu Quan, the fisherman, who was thinnest and tallest, took the longest strides. Tran Tich, the farmer, had the sturdiest legs. Nuygen Doc was in poor shape but he was the most spirited and the youngest. All were cheerful. The path began to descend. Scrambling around a boulder they saw below them a wide clearing which was ringed with fires. They were approaching a Moi tribal settlement.

Among the fires everything was wild confusion. Immediately Quan, Tich and Nuygen became lost in smoke. Naked figures appeared, and disappeared ink, the smoke smudge and among tree trunks. The savages jumped up and down beating the ground with sticks, or shouting at each other across the wide clearing in the middle of which logs smoldered. At the edges of this open space the flames ate into the underbrush, sometimes climbing up the woody stem of a vine, sometimes where the grass was dry rushing ahead quickly or exploding in fiery tufts. In the cooled ashes the spring crops would be planted.

The staples of the Moi tribesmen are corn, cotton, barley-maize and dry rice. The fields (so the brothers learned from the Moi tribesmen) are traditionally cleared in this way. The soil is fertile from the ashes and if it rains the plants grow very quickly. However, so do the weeds. The next year of course the soil is exhausted and a patch in the jungle has to be cleared somewhere else. Also, the tribesmen are much troubled by animals, which feed on the young shoots. Everyone is on guard: they are continually banging sticks, jumping around and hollering like madmen, beating on drums and rattling bamboo in order to scare away the birds, monkeys, wild boar, snakes and rats waiting at the edge of the clearing. It's a hard life. The year before, the travellers were told, the fires had stampeded a herd of elephants which had run through the village and flattened it.

The 'Montagnard' people are very good natured. Some of the men are unbelievably ugly. But they are also passionate, and the Moi lover has a great reputation for bravery and originality. Here is a Moi love song:

(the girl sings)

I look out at you between the fronds of the banana tree
I look out at you between the areca leaves
Out of the deepest shade

I am always looking at you Boy-boy.
But when you pass me in the sunny clearing
my eyes are down by my heels
inside the corn-grinding pot.

(the man sings)

Pou-ki Pou-ki why don't you notice me?
I know I'm ugly but I want you to feel my pole
I want to lay my fire-beating stick in your reed basket
Little Miss Stuck-up
If I climbed the highest tree on Voi Map
and brought back a bees' nest in my teeth
Would that make any difference?

(both sing)

Soft wind sweet wind
sifts through the tops of trees.
In her shame
she would like to hide her head under the pine needles
but after he has penetrated her
she looks at him with a wife's thanks

(Song translated by Trang Tich)

The 2 weeks spent by the brothers in this hill village passed pleasantly and instructively. Finally they left, after first paying their respects to the Guardian Spirit.

From the jungles of the plateau the road descends to the Coast quickly, hardly more than a day's walk. Soon the travellers found themselves on the dyke road running between prosperous paddy farms. That evening they were parading down the main street of Hue.

They spent three days sightseeing in Hue, then went twenty miles down the coast to the ancient city of Tourane. Tourane had been the capital of the Emperor Thieu Tri, during the magnificent but decadent Nuygen Dynasty. It was here that the Imperial fleet suffered a humiliation at the hands of the French in March 1858.

On the morning of March 23rd
when the harbor was spotlighted
by the sun coming out from under a cloud
and the harbor-side street was swarming
with whores, customs inspectors and
merchants selling dried squid—
suddenly the Fleet's sails were stripped.

One moment
the air over the harbor was cluttered
with hundreds of pink, plum, crimson
viridian and chocolate-colored sails . . .
the next
a forest of bare sticks

(Poem written by Tra Quan)

Now they were on the beach outside Tourane. The sea stretched for miles. If it had been night, Tra Quan's eyes would have gleamed in the phosphorescent light. Standing with his ankles in the waves, like a thin crane, the fisherman had grown taller and wirier. A hump had appeared on his back, from the pull of invisible tides.

When the brothers had started out four months ago, there had been a cold dry wind cutting down from the North and the Hymalayas. Now it had shifted to a Southwesterly, coming from the direction of Ceylon and Madagascar, carrying rain from the Indian Ocean. The monsoon wind. Time to return. Time to get back to work.

Tra Hutt Quan and Nuygen Doc hiked North along the beach, the ocean at their right hand, on their left the tree-tangled mountains at first, then the farms. They reached the Bay of A-Long. At a village on the shore as white as a bone, with the boats pulled up, Tra Quan remained. Nuygen Son Doc went a little further on, to the Hon Gai mines, whistling as he went. Beside him the open seams of coal shone in the rain, like wet silk.

Trang Tich had decided to visit his wife's uncle's family on their farm at the Southern tip of Vietnam near the Ca Mau peninsula (then occupied territory). He took the main highway south. After Saigon he took Route 4 over the Delta. Shortly before he arrived at Ap Nohn he heard over the radio the town had been evacuated because of a cholera epidemic. When he got there, the uncle's family was missing. He could find no trace of them.

AN OLD MAN REMEMBERS

Stumbling up Thung Hiep road
the rain and the sea at my back
half drunk from drinking rot gut while fishing
my fingers frozen
I remember how we used to gather salt
in this meadow
in this meadow I am passing
without paying a tax.

Without paying a tax / without paying a tax!
(or so my grandfather said)
oh rain
soggy old village road

Usury/War/Flood/Fire/& Pestilence
An old man remembers stumbling up
Thung Hiep road from the sea
in winter

FAMINE SONG

The milk wouldn't come
the mother is too undernourished to give milk
dried up breasts
the baby cradled in her thin arms
its fists flailing face crimson and pinched
                                        against the nipple
                                        because there is no milk
there's not enough food in the mother's body to make it
there's not enough food in the earth for her this year
Earth Earth
why have you run out of food?
No No there's enough it's all there
                                        the earth said:
stored in the landlord Bao Phach's barn

CAM PHAO COAL MINE PRODUCTION
DURING THE YEARS 1890 – 1990
(figures in 10,000 gross tons)

YEAR	TONNAGE
1890	50
1910	112

1925	300
1938	725
1941-3	*(figs. unavailable these years)*
1944	290 *(value Jap. Yen)*
1950	111 *(val. French piastres)*
1955	800
	(Note: this fig. unreliable, prob. plan fig.)
1958	290
1960	650+
	340*
1965	500+
	390*
1967	none
1970	290
1980	650
	800
1990	*(figs. unreported)*

(Note: + equals plan figure
** equals actual figure)*

A FOREST MADE OF RAIN

a forest made   of rain
the eucalyptus — Eucalyptus marginala
mahogany the teak tree
made of rain

made one half of rain

Downpour   Rainflood must exceed 3 or 4 feet in a year
and the wind be not dry   but   moist
water-laden   the wood-weight

The dense rainforest of the Pacific
                put together drop by drop
the Northeastern hardwood-hemlock configuratipn
In the mist   the Tropical rainforest
                                rises out of thin air

The soil profile is displaced   upwards
molecules of quartz   feldspar prised loose
                                pulled into the capillaries
stone   moving into the atmosphere of rain
the dead porcupine   is   raised   through   the   earth   layers
by its own quills

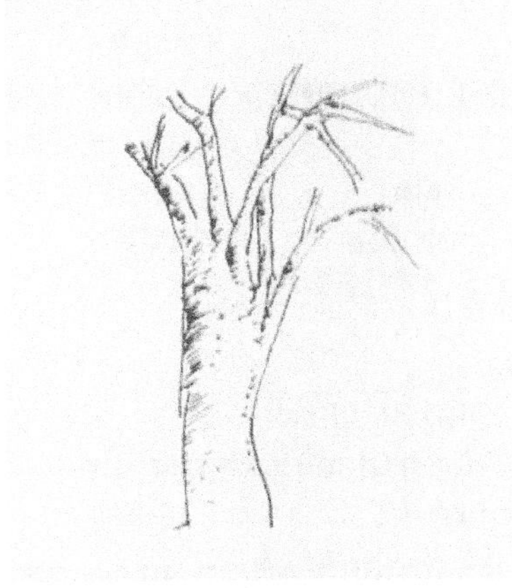

The leaf streams   Sun-engine drives   fluttering
splitting the carbon atom out from the air
binding it into the water molecule
Fat body

of the Teak Tree

radiates green green

(Fourth chromopoem)

RITUAL SONG

(composed by Ho Chi Minh for the 2000th year Congress of Wheat Farmers—Wichita)

IN THE EYE OF MY LORD BUDDHA
CARBON IS OXYDIZED
IN THE EYE OF MY LORD BUDDHA
(gong)
IN THE EYE OF MY LORD BUDDHA
(gong)
& SEA GIVES UP ITS COLD IONS
WHICH ARE DISCHARGED AS RAIN
(gong)
IN THE EYE OF MY LORD BUDDHA
(gong)
IN THE EYE OF MY LORD BUDDHA
(gong)
NITRATES ARE FORMED
(gong)
IN THE EYE OF MY LORD BUDDHA
THE WORM BURROWS
TO MAKE A PASSAGE &
THE WILD CUCUMBER APPEARS

(the participants gather. Filling the vessel with water they intone)

THE POND IS CONSTANT
UNDER MY LORD BUDDHA'S EYE

(gong)
IT FILLS & REFILLS
(gong)
THE POND REFRESHES ITSELF BY OVERTURNING
AUTUMN & SPRING
MORNING & EVENING
THE FISH DIES
& IS TRANSFORMED INTO WEEDS
INTO ROOTS & TUBERS
IN THE EYE OF MY LORD BUDDHA
(gong)
IN THE EYE OF MY LORD BUDDHA
(gong)

(the participants fill the vessel with earth & intone to the gong sounds)

THE PRAIRIE STRETCHES ITSELF
A SINGLE ORGANISM
UNDER THE YELLOW MOON
(gong gong)
IT NOURISHES ITSELF FROM THE DEPTHS
(gong)
IN THE EYE OF BUDDHA
THE FLOOR OF THE OCEAN RISES
TO BECOME BLUEGRASS
THE DEER THE BUFFALO THE CAT
GO FROM THE SALT LICK
(gong)
& THUS PHOSPHORUS IS DISTRIBUTED
IN THE EYE OF MY LORD BUDDHA
(gong)
THE WILD PUMA GOES OUT
IN THE EYE OF MY LORD BUDDHA

(An egg is placed on top of the vessel of earth and water. The participants join hands & say)

ALL IS MAINTAINED
ALL IS MAINTAINED
ALL IS MAINTAINED
IN AN OPEN STEADY STATE
IN THE FLEXED ELBOW OF BUDDHA
(gong)
HE SHOOTS LIGHT THROUGH THE GASSY ENVELOPE
(gong)
WE LIVE IN THE LIMIT BETWEEN TWO BURNS
OF THE WAVE FREQUENCY
(gong)
THE CELL IS A NEGATIVE ENTROPY
FOR MY LORD BUDDHA
(gong)
FOR MY LORD BUDDHA
(gong)
HE REGULATES THE HEAT GRADIENT
THE PETROLEUM LAKE *(gong)*

LIES A FOSSIL *(gong)*

OF STORED SUNLIGHT *(gong)*

THE WHOLE OF BLUE IS CONTAINED
IN THE COBALT OF MY LORD BUDDHA
THE WHOLE OF RED IS CONTAINED
IN THE MANGANESE OF LORD BUDDHA
THE WHOLE OF YELLOW IS CONTAINED
IN THE SULPHUR OF MY LORD BUDDHA

THE AMERICAN SOLDIER'S FUNERAL

A group of farmers were returning to Ap Nohn hamlet along National Highway 1. The road ran alongside Xuan Da's field. As they approached they saw the body of an American soldier lying across the paddy field. The earth was a powdery ochre with the stubble of last summer's rice crop glimmering a faint yellow.

The body was enormous. It stretched from one edge of the field to the other. At the north boundary the fronds of a clump of latania palms had been torn slightly. The feet rested at the south end, not far from the water paddle-wheel. A hand sprawled across a dyke.

These farmers (and their families) had been away for several weeks, at one of the Government's "New Life" hamlets. They carried bundles slung over bamboo sticks. It was a crisp day. They examined the corpse carefully, walking around it at some length, touching the big pack which was strapped on the soldier's back with their sticks and occasionally prodding the pockets of which there were a great number. Then they sat down to wait under the palm clump. Xuan Da's boy was sent on ahead to the village to inform the Chief Notable. It was around noon.

By the middle of the afternoon the entire village had come out to Xuan Da's field (except the Chief Notable who was shopping in Saigon). The villagers walked around the corpse in groups, discussing the fine points. The children cracked nuts. Luckily the middle harvest was in. The ground was dry and had not been rutted. The dykes were packed hard and were undamaged except where the hand had breached a wall next to the irrigation stream. At the bottom of the ditch the water purled softly.

What is the difference between the death of a soldier in battle and the death of an ordinary person? My friend, that's a hard question. In the death of an ordinary person the body is washed and dressed ceremonially, and the burial service has to be performed in just the right way. Then the spirit will be permitted to take its place safely with the revered ancestors. Even when the family lives far away (as in the case of the chinese merchants on Cholon) the body is simply shipped back in a box, and the ghost with it, to the ancestral village. There—you can count on it—the authorized rituals will be performed by the proper persons. But when a soldier dies, obviously this is a very serious matter.

There is also the problem of size. True, ghosts don't have an actual physical size and shape. Still, they are determined by what they were. This is particularly true of animals. For instance, in the smaller animals—the pig, the dog and the cat—the ghosts are considered relatively harmless though sometimes troublesome. These are the "Little Ma" that one stubs one's toe on or stumbles over while crossing a field at night. But the "Big Ma"—that is the large animal ghosts: the ghosts of the horse, oxen and water buffalo—these can be extremely dangerous. How much more dangerous then, spirit of this huge soldier? If it should wander around unburied, it could cause a lot of damage.

There were no relatives. Who would give it the proper cult so it could rest quiet? How could it be dressed correctly for the funeral? How could it even be washed properly?

That evening nothing was decided. The Chief Notable arrived soon after supper in his Renault, along with the Buddhist priest. But they could not agree on what to do. Under the Notable's direction the minimum precautionary measures were undertaken, to keep the corpse safe. The whole company went back to the hamlet to sleep.

Vigil During the First Night

Everyone has left Xuan Da's paddy field except three boys who had been assigned to remain behind and scare away the rats. Every so often they run around the corpse clapping sticks and setting off fire crackers. A ladder leads up about 20 feet to the soldier's stomach. On top of this several large bunches of bananas have been placed under the priest's direction. This is to divert the Celestial Dog, so he will not be tempted to gobble up the soldier's entrails.

2nd Day Occurrences

In the morning a rigging crew arrives from the provincial highway department at Soc Trang. They are accompanied by officials of the Agricultural Department. The owner of Xuan Da's land has got wind of it, and has telephoned the administration insisting that the corpse be moved off the paddy onto the asphalt paved highway. Otherwise the soil might be permanently damaged. Although it is now the dry season, rains will begin in a few months and impurities accumulate.

The A.M. passes. Everyone is here, but now the post-hole digging machine has to arrive. It is the plan of the rigging crew to drive in concrete posts on the far side of the highway. Block and tackle will be attached to these, and the corpse pulled by winch to the asphalt road. Pulling the body across the dykes will be the tricky part.

P.M. The rigging crew has driven in the concrete stakes. However the priest and the Highest Venerable return shortly after lunch and insist that the body not be moved until some time after it had been washed. None of the villagers volunteer to do this.

2nd Night

My neighbor's son, Nuygen Li, and several other teenage boys, are assigned as guardians of the field for the 2nd night, also a girl cousin of Nuygen's. Few firecrackers are set off. A thatched hut has been built temporarily in the latania grove, very comfortable. Luckily the body has not begun to smell yet and the air is still fresh, especially in the night breeze. And all the stars are shining.

The 3rd Day

A flock of beach plovers and many white cranes have perched on the body. There is danger that the soldier's eyes might be pecked out by the smaller birds, but they are protected by the bony eyesockets and heavy eyebrows which cast a shadow over the face. The cranes rummage among the uniform for fleas. An official plan has now been drawn up. The State Highway Department in cooperation with the Agricultural Administration will winch the body onto the road. The earth dykes must be levelled to accomplish this and the irrigation stream filled in. The canal has to be diverted upstream. A digging crew is already working on this. Boundaries must be changed, at least temporarily, and certain landowners will have to be compensated. The plan is to lift the corpse up onto two flatcars. It will then be transported to the estuary where it will be set adrift on the flatcars. It is hoped at this stage the body will be picked up by the U.S. Seventh Fleet and given the correct burial services.

Everyone ready to get started. However, the Fortune Teller just arrived from Can Tho. He says the day is not auspicious for moving anything (because of the star conjunctions). It might bring very bad luck. The day after tomorrow will be more auspicious.

5th Day

We move down the main road in the direction of Ap Nohn hamlet. Low tide. On either side the streams drain, rivulets of blue in the black mud. Through the paddy flats which stretch endlessly, the river loops back and forth and finally disappears behind the tall clump of palms that mark the village. This is situated on high ground, like an island in the ocean of ricefields. The palms swivel in the breeze. The procession is now about three-quarters of a mile away, strung out along the road. Birds swoop overhead.

The Hamlet of Ap Nohn

The hamlet of Ap Nohn consists of a small store selling fish sauce and canned goods, the Dinh, a primary school, two cemeteries and the town soccer field. About 50 houses are scattered at varying intervals. Each house has its boat landing in back where a sampan or pirogue is tied up, in the shade of banana trees. As the procession crosses the town line over a bridge with the planks clattering, we are almost run over by a boy driving a flock of ducks.

We parade down the main street.

The procession has been organized in this way: two villagers have been chosen to represent the mother and father of the deceased; also a group to impersonate the rest of the kin—brothers, patrilineal grandparents, the soldier's widow, etc. These march behind the hearse looking very wild. The women wear mourning shawls of white gauze sloppily put on, and the men rough turbans wrapped around their heads hastily, as if they had just gotten out of bed or were running from a fire. The male mourners pretend to be part blind. They totter on bamboo sticks making tapping noises, while the women and birds shriek.

A band heads the procession. Then the priest and the fortune teller supported on hammocks. Then come the paper prayer scrolls and flags lifted high and the lavish displays of ceremonial food held over the heads of the young men, most of whom are shouting and drunk on rice wine. Along the sides of the road children, who have recently been burned, give away paper money. At the end of the village street is the boat landing.

We are now passing Cung Bao Phach, the moneylender's house. Unfortunately the wheels get caught in the sand and the whole hearse tips over, sending the immense body sprawling against Bao Phach's barn. The impact of the fall has split the corpse open. Birds descend, the beaks of the sandpipers and cranes puncture the rotten fabric and the dry skin. In the pack that the soldier has been wearing strapped to his back, it is discovered that there is another dead soldier. There are also others inside each of the pockets, they spill out onto the ground as the clothing is ripped. The birds' beaks rip at the holes and cracks, and inside all the dead soldiers there are others. They are piled against the barn.

The air is black with birds and with souls. How many ghosts? Thousands. We will suffer forever. The land will always be damaged by them.

24 Ragas for Ahma

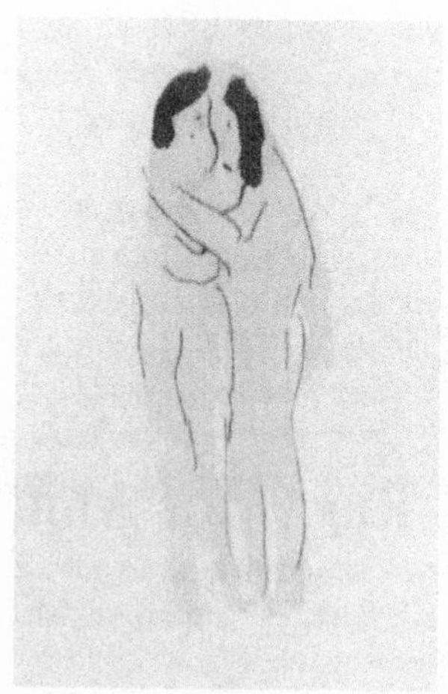

ALAP *the invocation*

Ahma   I'm inside you.   I'm in deep.
And when we wake   you sit up   and shake me out
of your hair
and prepare in the cold light

to return to the Frost King.
I have to say: Ahma   doesn't it matter who cares for you?
Doesn't love count?

Then it is that the pond in the park
fills with black leaves.
She has lost one of her earrings.
She looks at me with eyes that are not hers.

*   *

The heaviness.   The grave weight of the flesh
which she shares with her husband
like the heaviness   of a lake lying in repose.

I stroll beside it and see nothing but one serene eye
of blue under the sky

She's pulled two ways   up/down.   Molecules of water
in turbulence   motes agitated by the sun.

Ahma bitten.   Winter the kiss of the lover is like ice
the cold bites   sinks into the bottom layers
into the zones   still warm from the haze   of summer.

The heat transfer.   Soon
the whole reservoir will turn over.

* *

Pay attention. Everything depends on what she said.
Out of quicksand I have to reconstruct her in the mind's eye.

What did she *say*?   I've lost
whole areas of her towns on the map which have disappeared
and been swallowed up in drifts.

The tide welters under the cliffs.   On the beach
bones of wreckage I have put together some part of the puzzle

Her face in fragments against the wall of the restaurant
            A harsh void. Holes in the conversation
I have to go through to find her
backed into the sand caves.

* *

Absence.   Like a bolt of grey gauze
Absence spreads out in waves over the streets   which are
    deserted
nobody coming back home after work   today
they're all staying there   walled up in factories

The ferry boat they used to call "Zenith" has been
    disconnected.

Absence
has a long   dulled   thinly drawn out   quiet note
        before it begins to vibrate freneticly.
It is the color of the flatlands   before the wind hits it

and kicks up all that dust.

* *

Will she come?   Oh yea   just maybe she might

Ahma's been boycotting me for three weeks!   Famine.
I'm wasting away   starved while Ahma's off attending
        the Socialist Party World Hunger Conference.

SAVE THE CALCUTTA HOMELESS!
WOMEN IN SUPPORT OF BIAFRAN SEPARATISM!

Remorselessly she's been at it. Yak Yak. Maybe tonight . . .
she'll drop in on me between meetings
and just remember to bring her diaphragm.

*   *

Her step on the stair.   Will never come near
Still   I'm greedy for her just the same.
The bucket is being filled elsewhere   and in the kitchen
the plate scraped into the paper bag   as the cat
wreathes around the table leg. Domestic Felicity.
Well   that's shot to hell.   Here as elsewhere.

Still I'm greedy for her. Memories. The scratch on the door:
I let her in.   And undress her down to the naked skin.
After that dinner.   I devour her: every hour of the flux
the continuum. "How *were* you today?"

"I did such and such."

"Lovely Ahma   how gracefully you take all those hurdles. And the children?"

"Oh they're fine. And well."

And mine?   Oh fine fine.

Her footfall on the stair
is a habit I shall never get rid of

* *

The Andaman Island Dead.   He's gone but he's not gone.
He's here   a presence above the ground
like the wind shimmering among the leaves the mist rising

above the swamp.   The pale moon is an emanation of a former life
that reaches us in the vague signals among the fireflies
the banging of cooking utensils. The night spills and decays.
The old order.

He will speak to us as long as the bones still carry flesh.
As long as the body is covered with its frail shroud of
coconut cloth   fibers eaten by the moon.

Let him call the tune for a while.
The dead man   rotting in our midst
with the power

* *

I don't know what's happening in this city anymore
a shift a weird screech in the cars shearing off different ways
The day slides   the sky's turquoise
veering to cobalt   to   rose   madder   under   the   mercury

vapor lamps

Fire in the sky
Time going by
And on the other side of the river what? Summer maybe
After the ice break-up.
And on the other side of night my woman changed
And brought hack to me!

Smoke ravels from the stack high up over the Lehigh Freight terminal
Gloom under the expressway All the trucks have gone West
Duluth Oshkosh Minneapolis
vacancy in the metropolis

Night night
Oh well. Hello winter. I've lost her.

JOR *(fast movement)*

Oh I ache Everything is a blank
Emptiness down to my bones
I walk the room
without her

"The lover's I in a fine frenzy rolling"

The mind swollen   balls heavy as lead

like a dog playing dead   waiting for his master's
                                                quick word

RELEASE ME!
Ahma   I'll jump up and lick your face
and cover your ears with kisses

The poet as a dog
barking at the Man in the Moon

OK I'll wait   using this absence
Absence from you Ahma!   to make poems

No other women!
The hermit thrush   carolling in the swamp
until   my balls drop off.

EEEEE — Y-EE OWWW

*   *

Soft night   air in the airshalt
a radio off somewhere   cool   cool
at the bottom of a pool   the shadows of the leaves

brush my eyelids. Deep at the edge of sleep.
Then   the cattle prod jabs me awake
and I think

where is she?   that sweet mouth on his skin
Is she doing for him now   what she did for me?

The goad.

*   *

A beast walks out of the mind   with iron shoes

his breath heavy with frost   horns
hang his head down   all tubed and straggled like the musk ox
the bell of a blue flower   protrudes from his teeth
CRUNCH   CRUNCH

skin covered with warts
the leaden dewlap hangs from his throat
tiny rhinoceros eyes   hooded
against the red mist of betrayal

But he sees you   Ahma   clear
as you step out of the bath

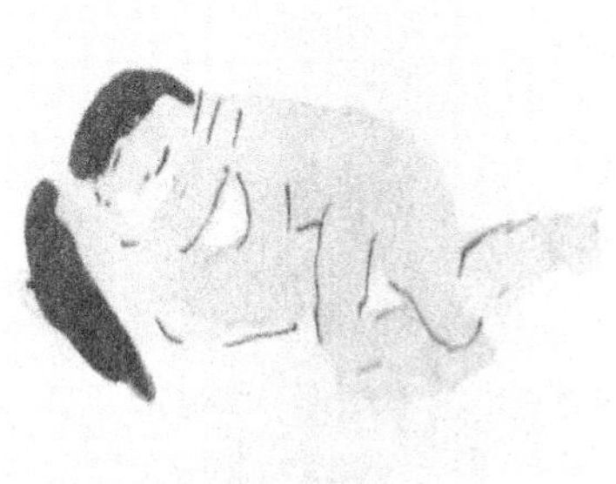

*   *

Breakfast.   And Ahma possessed.

Out of habit   the children locked in the closet

Shades drawn shutting out the sea
There's no breeze   among   the   salt   and   pepper   shakers
a piece of hard crockery sticks in his teeth.

He wrenches it loose
& throws it at Ahma's head.

From his nostrils frost flares

*   *

Awkk.   Flies around eyes.   "I'm hurt.
Nothing can pull me back into love's circle again."
A stinging under the eyes   burns upon the skin
The bear dances in a ring of headlights

Ahma   you bitch
Look what you've turned him into
GAWP

GAT *(Woman's voice. Extended movement with cross drumming)*

After the ice break-up.   Blues and purples askew
a crisscrossing of slate greens   slide over the

divide spouts of froth smack and leap up
Blocks jam the rock's lip fir tree shoots out
tearing its roots with it signalling "goodbye"
"sweet year" Summer beyond the logjam. Foam
chokes the falls pouring and thundering rocks
raked pebbles of grey green *scour the bottom*
tearing along twigs leaves muck sand the body of
a dead muskrat spins over and over under the
splintering shredding hurtling forward *Ice Smash*
through Spitting Devil's jaws. The throat opens
and the great blue cakes levelling seethe and
jostle towards the lake

honeycombed in the spring fog. A softening

A shutter bangs open and the first newspaper
hits the street. A brake screeches Oh I'm too
weak for it this new day!

Cars move in slow lanes. From the Brooklyn side.
Traffic. Moving then stopping then moving forward
again tentatively The bicyclist is carried along
inch by inch towards the bridge entrance

as the ice melts all around me
Oh you releasing Spring Thaw

The cake of ice eaten
seethes towards the lake
drilled with airholes
honeycombed

The air's still
only the whisper of the current as the floes drift

the blue crystals pulled apart
in the heat

Mud in the bog
the twigs drip
haze hangs
as the lake steams

The wind's south
Block's weakening
insides all opened up
        ducts   passages
for sweet weather's mouth

After the dynamiting of the Ice Jam

* *

Ahma walks in the park   her dress stiff against the cold
distressdistress
Past's dead. No place to go but ahead. The trajectory
of asphalt opens out. Needled by the light   the pond
stretches its eye.

The first paleness.   Over the rooftops   washes of milk
                                        and charcoal
    Gold   gold
        the hard oriole of the trees
stamped against dawn.

Oh   I'm too weak for it!

* *

At midblock a shutter rattles to the side and the hodega opens for the morning   Bunches of green and purple bananas glisten   Boxes of toys cut-rate cigars housewares are wheeled out on the sidewalk as the radio blares.

SHUTTER: *Ahma   Where are you going this blue day*
this green day?

I'm going where my feet take me   past this candy
store and past others

What speed will you go fast/slow as the day
opens out?

Under the striped awnings the street fills with
shadows and shallow pools

What will you look for Ahma as the day begins?

I'll see the smoke rising from the stacks and hear
my heels click

What do you intend to do?

I will go where my feet lead me   past the cops and fighting kids   past the catalpa trees and the empty lots   where the rubbish fires are burning   past the shiny cars and appliance stores and the scrubbed bakers where the smell of bread is coming out.   And sweeten my life.

*   *

In the glare of morning
The children with their shiny red buckets dig in the sand.
The sandpipers dip their wings in the foam.
The children's eyes are pained with light their drawn faces

are blurred.
Why? Why? cry the sandpipers as their wings dip.
The sandpipers are racing at the sandy edge their legs
yellow.
Foam fills the children's pails and washes them out to sea.

POET: *Sandpipers what are you signalling*
with your wings
this blue day/this green day?

We are signalling the children who lie buried in
the sand

What are you telling them?

We are showing them how lightly we skip

Will the wind hurt your wings?

Our bodies light as air are buffeted by the wind
We dip and fly up again racing the waves

Do you fly through the roof
of the ruined building?

We fly through holes in the roof
and in and out of the rafters
where Ahma's children lie pinned
crying the house is down!
the house is down!

Will you lift the rafters from their legs seabirds?

YES YES We will lift them up.

All sunday afternoon at the shiny edge of the foam
The birds skim over the beach and the great green combers
build higher.
The waves knock the sandcastles down and the children
stand up.
In the glare of the morning.

*   *

Begin again: Winter remembered
By the side of the expresswaya rough stalk of mullein
sticks up
Ahma walks over the cobbles her dress stiff
In the hard light the pond stretches its eye

Winter remembered: the skyline of the city sealed in rime
What's this blood coming out of me? I can't staunch it
Icicles
hung from the roof like an abortionist's knife
On the table beside the bed flowers and my lover
holding my hand
weak as paper

Love you have cut me in two pieces
Needles of the light
pain my eye

Begin again: under the ice jag
the body of the dead muskrat spins over and over metal
I've outlasted you I've outlasted you too
Winter
Between the cobbles a stem of milkweed thrusts up
its rusty pod curled

Oh you melting spring thaw
the pain of it!

* *

Ahma passes by the empty lot. Behind her the shutter of a bodega rattles back. From the factory smoke drifts.

What's that burning in the rubbish pile?
the fire asks

It is my past life that is burningit is the
husks and connections to my old love that is
burning
It's the hollow of his legs
It's the beams and rafters from the wrecked house

What's that burning in the blue flames?
the fire asks

It's shadow of his hands burning
It's the splinters of the rafters burning
the windows torn from the frame

What's that burning in the rubbish pile?
the smoke asks
in the bottles and tin cans?

It's the shape of his mouth.

In the middle of the empty lot the catalpa tree flames
The sun glazes its leaves
At the edge of the ground the rubbish fires lick
and the whole lot is filled with broken glass.

*   *

IN THE GLARE OF MORNING the peasants walked down the road. We had buried our rifles and uniforms. The sun lighted up the caves. On top of them a man was plowing millet. Hua Tsu Nan's army had come back and the whole countryside was deserted. That summer they mixed chaff and elm leaves and made bread out of it. The gate opened through the wall. The peasants marched down the road. The carrier escaped by pretending to shit in a kaolang field. The landlords said 'for every goat stolen a head will be cut off and for each ear of corn stolen a whole family will pay for it." The gate opened through the wall onto the town square. Beside the road the river tumbled down from the loess hills rattling its stones. The body of the muskrat spun over and over. We had been issued wood spears by the Brigade and had covered them with tinfoil so they'd look like bayonettes but it was all fake. I took the chairman aside and whispered to him "look, here's the secret   we have rifles but nothing to shoot them with can you give us a few bullets?" The sun shone on the town square and on the temple. We stood with our backs to it. The gate opened through the wall. When the soldiers and grain requisitioners came in we fired at them. Some of the soldiers fell and one of the carriers and after that   they all ran away.

After that we went up into the hills.   That autumn
we were able to plant seed.

In the glare of morning.

*   *

IN THE GLARE OF MORNING
MY LOVER COVERS ME   THERE'S NO PART
THAT ESCAPES
HE WILL BECOME MY HUSBAND IN TIME
AS CLOSE TO ME
AS THE LIGHT UNDER MY EYELID

HE WILL BECOME MY HUSBAND IN TIME
    AS CLOSE TO ME
AS MY OWN THIGHS
I'M PLUGGED. NOTHING LEFT THAT CAN SEEP
    OUT OF ME
ONLY A RADIANCE LIKE THE MOON'S EDGE
    DURING AN ECLIPSE
HE ECLIPSES ME

MY LOVER COVERS ME
HE WILL BECOME MY HUSBAND IN TIME
IN THE GLARE OF MORNING

Oh   I'm too weak for it   this new day

*   *

In the glare of morning
smoke drifts over the river
as the sarod player weeps.

Oh winter winter   inside of me.

In the middle of the empty lot
the catalpa tree stretches in the sun.

Catalpa tree stiff
in the june sun
your blossoms stand up on spikes
    from the vivid green leaves

In the summer
the leaves lean and stretch.
In the winter   from the stripped branches

pods hang down.

The rain slants through the catalpa branches
across the streaming fat leaves
across the   icy twigs.

Forgive me for the violence I've committed.

Questions on Method

We are about to go on a journey to an undiscovered country. What is an undiscovered country? A country is closely familiar to its inhabitants in every aspect, although it is as yet undiscovered to the explorers. Then how to describe this undiscovered country—in the language of the inhabitants or in the language of the explorers? And who is this "one that describes"? Is he an inhabitant of the country or is he an explorer? Through what eyes does he see?

We have been having a discussion on this point: myself, William Blake the poet, and the Cuban documentary film maker Santiago Alvarez. The three of us are about to undertake this journey. Our gear is packed, we have made all necessary preparations. We are now sitting having a cup of coffee in the Mutualist Workers Study Club. It is here we have pursued our geographical researches and obtained maps. Our sponsor and the chief fundraiser for this expedition has been the Environment Control Gang.

I give this information. How deceptively simple it all seems. Yet it raises some real questions. What kind of expedition is this to be? How should it be organized? What mode of operation are we to pursue on the way? My own view, which I argue persuasively, is that we are involved in an act of creation. Because the country is utterly unknown, our journey to it is like a work of art. Therefore we should proceed in the same way as in a novel.

Blake looks at me sharply and asks, "What do you mean, 'as in a novel'?" Since the Saigon press trip his face has grown purplish and we fear he may be suffering from dysentery. He has picked up the habit of chewing betel nut.

"I mean," I say, "Making the connections. The essential thing in a novel is just this: proceeding from the known to the unknown, from a terrain where everything is familiar and accepted to one that is strange, heightened and fanciful—at the same time making the necessary connections in order that the reader may follow. Therefore, my suggestion is to bring along a television crew on our expedition and record every aspect of the journey and our own reactions to it. In this way our 'readers' (that is, our viewers) will understand it and see it through our own eyes."

Alvarez remarked, "That's a good idea about film, particularly as we'll have no interpreter and won't know the language, so we won't be able to conduct interviews. But don't you think there's a danger of our information being superficial?"

"That's right. We'll capture the surface image only," Blake objected.

"That's exactly what I mean," the author replied, "by the journey being like a novel. One starts with the surface image and proceeds deeper and deeper. In the beginning what is important to the reader is not where I am taking him, but my credentials as a guide and whether he can trust me. For this he wants to know certain things about me."

"What does he want to know?"

"In a sense I represent the reader's flesh, his own body. In the words of Merleau-Ponte: modern literature is an 'unwearying report on the body. It is confirmed, consulted, listened to like a person. The intermittencies of its desire, its fervors are spied on.' It is this that is interesting to the reader, and leads forward in the wild flight like the astronaut's heartbeat recorded on TV or his very sweat in the space capsule."

"I suppose that is the significance," Blake remarked contemptuously, "of the 'jerking-off poems' that you regaled us with in the first section?"

"Merely decadent," said the Cuban film-maker. "And unproductive. With all that ejaculation you end up in the same plane. The rocket has no escape velocity from your real world."

I continued: "Then there are other items which are simply humanistic and have the same purpose of relating the reader to a common experience. For instance, the sequence of love poems just completed which tell my own story and the story of my own involvement with Alma.

There are also the anecdotes about my own children—the 12-year-old girl's sexual anxiety at the frog pond; the boy's obesity problems, etc. These are interspersed with light lyrics, such as the 'Green Song' about the park; and simple character sketches of the draftsman Ben Lyric, and the Puertorican Aguerra. These are contemporary American portraits that everyone can recognize. Finally, there are the 'chromopoems.' "

"What do you see as the function of those?" Alvarez asked.

"I see the function of those as using the language of science, of making it available to the reader in an artistic way. For instance, in the first chromopoem, which is about color wavelengths, I make use of simple repetitions to achieve an effect, and also give a certain emotional content —the feeling provoked by the term 'infra-red.' The description of the Dragon-fly is also in this vein. I eliminated the third chromopoem because it had to carry too much scientific weight—i.e., it became divorced from its emotional content."

"Which one was that? You provoke my curiosity," Blake asked.

"It was a little one about light energy quanta, it goes as follows:

SOLAR RADIATION

One of the most interesting observations in philosophy is Spinoza's remark that God has an infinite number of attributes but that we know only two: Extension (the material universe) and Thought.

A striking scientific analogy illustrating this idea is the radiation from our own Sun. In the process of converting hydrogen to helium, energy is released at the rate of 8×10^{18} (8 sextillions) kilocalories per second. But only a minute fraction of this falls on our Earth. Imagine what happens to the rest of it? Where does it go and in what form or shape does it reach and interact with other stellar bodies — that is, if it reaches anything at all?

> Of the tiny fragment of energy intercepted by our own planet, only 3% of it actually penetrates to ground level and is made available to green plants. But the process is extraordinarily efficient. It is estimated that it takes only 4 quanta of red light to yield sufficient energy to fix one molecule of carbon dioxide, by photosynthesis.

"I can see why you left it out," Blake observed severely. "It has too many kilocalories and too much carbon dioxide in it. However, it does have a poetic core: the idea of the immensity of the infinite—like an enormous void, a blackness which one peers into holding up a flashlight. Yes, it does give the nerves something of a 'frisson.'"

Alvarez said soberly: "You were wrong to leave that one out. I don't go along with Blake's reason, but it should stay simply because it conveys important information. One could well ask, as a matter of objective fact about our own world, is any information more essential? As for the fact that it doesn't work, who cares? What does it matter whether that information is assimilable to literature? Science is science and facts are facts. It is the ground and over the years it will become the humus of literature."

"I agree," Blake said. "You are too influenced by your contemporaries. Contemporary literature is simply an insane asylum in which the writers are not the inmates—as is commonly supposed—but the keepers. As I remarked on a notable occasion:

> Prisons are made of bricks of the law
> Brothels by bricks of religion
> And straightjackets by authors.

"Well certainly by the authors' publishers," Alvarez added laughing.

"As for your own book, you've got it all wrong," Blake insisted. "If it's permissible to disagree with you. Here we are at the 100th page. You've made a brave attempt to interpret it—but like all authors, you're doomed to failure." He leaned back in his chair, his ale glass empty, and scratched inside an elbow.

"Well, what's your interpretation?" I asked him.

"First of all, this demand on the author for 'self-revelation' as you call it—that's rubbish. If anything, you attempt to wipe out the author, to erase him. What else can be the meaning of the line on the second page 'The I is smoothed out in the folds and wrinkles of the bedclothes.'? You explode personal biography."

"Explode it in favor of what?" the author asked Blake.

"In favor of Direct Comprehension, of Vision," Blake went on to explain. "I mean to say, what is interesting to the reader is not the person of the author or even the subject matter, but the process of seeing and perceiving per se. And what's interesting about this process is not that one sees correctly but one sees incorrectly. You make this clear in the Dick Turpin episode on page 17, which begins:

> Dick Turpin had been assigned to the Pentagon from one of the nation's top chemical laboratories. His specialty was the eye and how it sees, and how it distorts what it sees. And how this distortion is affected by the 'inter-tones,' areas of low intensity light diffusion."

"I remember," Alvarez broke in. "Turpin operates with a photo-cell to detect marketeers, but when he gets in the whorehouse and his pants are down, the photocell doesn't work."

" 'Because his own body is giving off a smell of ammonia, probably from the photo equipment back at the lab.' " Blake quoted. "Which is as neat a description as I've ever met of the problem of epistemology."

Alvarez asked him what that was. The visionary explained: "It is this, that we authors are always at the limits of language. It dissolves downward into the flux, into raw fact, which is uncommunicable. And it dissolves upward into mystical apprehension that is revelation. I expressed it as 'the door of perception.' Wittgenstein puts it cleverly another way when he says that the Seer 'crawls up into the attic and pulls the ladder of language up after him.' The important thing is this leap, a somersault into the unknown. This has always been the true method of the Prophets. It has been my own method, and additionally, it has been the method of Swedenborg, Bunyan, Dante and Saint Augustine. The method is to extend Vision and Perception by using supernatural agents. For instance, I am very fond of invoking the prophets of Isaiah and Ezekiel. Also 'devils hovering with black wings'; 'dragon men who operate the printing presses of hell,' and the like. And you, the author of this particular work, do the same thing when you have the dead Indians in the Oriskany Adventure walk across the river to the Rome Metals Plant and go up the pipes and shut down the pumping system."

"I felt myself that was a good piece of writing and worked," the author agreed, "though I can't say why."

"It is because you are using the dead creatively, in the manner of all visionaries. That is the purpose of transcendence, to penetrate Beyond Time," Blake continued. "You employed the same effect with Ausonlus, the 4th Century Iberian administrator, writing the letter to his nephew in Haiphong. And again on page when the fisherman Tra Huu Quan makes this quantum jump, if you will allow me to quote your admirable paragraph:

> If it had been night, Tra Quan's eyes would have gleamed in the phosphorescent light. Standing with his ankles in the waves, like a thin crane, the fisherman had grown taller and wirier. A hump had appeared on his back from the pull of invisible tides.

"I say bravo to that," the author exclaimed and clapped, because Blake had recited it with feeling. The latter continued. "Yes. Admirable. You see, a writer always is in high gear when he is in this mode. The bones give a shudder. That is because time is compressed, it is condensed into legend like a drop of amber. Drugs will do it but not so efficaciously as this—jump. Jaspers, the Dutch Existentialist, says that it is the function of Art to produce these fragmentary marks, these 'scratchings on the cave wall.' One makes the Leap and glimpses Other world—whole—friend. As you yourself have done in your concluding Vietnamese section with the body of the soldier."

"No. No," the author objected. "I cannot include myself in the company of Swedenborg. But occasionally a force seizes my pen."

"What about the American Infantryman lying in the rice paddy, 'his corpse stretching from one end of the field to the other; the head in a clump of latania palms, and his feet breeching a dyke?"

"A slight exaggeration of the body count, meant only to be descriptive."

"Not at all. The Man is Legendary. What else, when they try to transport him up the road 'across a number of wagons,' the corpse tumbles out in his knapsack, and from the holesin this other dead soldiers?"

"You exaggerate the number of holes. But what do you conclude from all this?"

"My conclusion is that we should simply go to this Undiscovered Country by any means possible. We should abandon all these attempts at interpreters, interviews, travel diaries, and coverage by television crewmen, and put ourselves in the hands of the local shamans. This will enable us to see mystically and to Penetrate the Threshold. And when we return we will speak in tongues. We will reveal all that we have seen with the True Authority."

At this point the prophet called for more beer, which was brought by a Mutualist attendant. Blake qualified it, then gave us a wide grin showing stumps of teeth. From the manner of his speech he seemed to have gotten "high" on betel nut. The Club was beginning to fill up, evidently with workers from the day shift who had come to our clandestine study. We listened to the noises of the City, in a relaxed mood.

As for the Cuban film-maker, he sat sober, even frowning. He had been doodling on a paper napkin. I noticed that he had scribbled the little poem of Jacques Prevert: 'The Old are pointing out the way to the Young/with gestures of reinforced concrete.' I asked him for his opinion.

"I have listened. I think you're both wrong," Santiago Alvarez stated. "The key to the novel (and to this journey) is neither a fervor of the flesh;

nor is it an act of extended madness. It is something else. But it's not surprising we should disagree, by temperament. The book is self-indulgent. It is without form and full of wilful contradictions. In this you remind me of Montaigne who confesses in one of his essays: that 'from birth he was given over to his own inclinations, and brought up to please no one but himself.' "

"That's the trouble, there are too many themes," Blake opined. "It's like a stew where the cook can't decide on a particular flavor but keeps vacillating as he tastes, switching one ingredient for another."

"That's right," the film-maker said. "You have just made the case for exploiting the dead in order to give the transcendental view. On the other hand the author has presented us with half a dozen or so little biographies which are contemporary and stuck in the present like so many flies on flypaper. That in itself is a contradiction. There are the so-called scientific poems which you have attempted to justify. Then there are the political sequences."

Blake said, "Yes, those spoil it. The thing is going along nicely within a recognized literary frame—the Travel Essay. Then politics comes as a shock and causes a needless anxiety in the reader."

"Carramba! There I disagree with you. Isn't that anxiety and shock, as you call it, the real key?" Alvarez went on to develop his thesis. "What I take to be the theme of the book so far is neither the personal nor the prophetic. Both strike me equally as mystifications. The real theme is different: it is the making of the New Man. To pursue our metaphor, we have likened the book, have we not, to this journey where the destination is unknown? What I maintain is that in course of their travels it is the traveler himself who will be discovered. This implies a hard transformation. It involves the smashing of conventional forms. The process will be necessarily shocking and painful first of all to the author. Let me ask you a simple question: You've written this book for the present-day North American reader?"

"Obviously it's not written in Tagalog or Russian." "Okay. Let me ask you. What American is interested in hunger?"

"None. Least of all the people who read books."

"What about the other things you have touched on:

Usury, War, Flood, Pestilence.
An old man remembers stumbling up
Thung Hiep road from the sea.

I'm quoting your own words."

"Of no interest whatever," the author agreed.

Blake said: "Then we must conclude that the book is unpublishable."

"No. No. You exaggerate the difficulty," the author protested. "Isn't it the business of the artist, simply through his skill, by a touch of his pen or brush, to make the subject present no matter how unfamiliar it is? For instance, the fisherman Tra Huu Quan on his skiff on the Bay of Along, I describe as:

. . . bending his hack
one foot balanced before the other along the gunwale

and give the creak of the oar in the oarlock. And in Famine Song what american or european woman no matter what her background or affluence would not respond to the opening line:

The milk wouldn't come. . .

"But the end is wrong. It destroys the feeling," Blake objected. He quoted:

> No, there's enough, it's all there the earth said
> stored in the landlord Bao Phach's barn.

"You would prefer to omit that? When you say 'destroys feeling' what you mean is the mixing of images—that of the nursing mother and the landlord—within the convention of the lyric poem?"

"Precisely," Blake agreed.

"But this convention is unacceptable. What it means is," the Cuban insisted, "that you straightjacket yourself. Feelings, experience (in this case of hunger) are the special province of the writer. The circumstances that produce hunger are left to the political economist or agronomist."

The author said, "I agree with Blake. Art has its conventions. It is unfortunate that they make it saleable."

"Then you don't understand what you've done. For instance in the story, Farmers' Holiday, you describe South Vietnam in its feudal and colonialist aspect. The two farmers are in debt are they not? Are they not superstitious: they kow tow to the police, go through the exorcism ritual, there are parades, banners. Among us this anthropological claptrap passes conventionally for literature. In fact for the underdevelopment of a third of the globe there is no other solution but socialist planning. This has to be faced up to directly, with a new rhetoric. This you've succeeded in very nicely in your descriptions of North Vietnam. For instance, the figure of Nygen Son Doc, the socialist coal miner, also in the agricultural and industrial poems."

Blake groaned, "Those doleful lists: on Hog Feed and on 'Cam Phao Coal Mine Production during the years 1890-1990.' They're worse than the chromopoems."

"It's true that they are a literary failure, these 'econopoems,' as written. That's because the author hasn't pushed himself far enough, with enough conviction. All that was needed was to have found the right voice, or persona. This you could have done by developing the character of some political commissar, local party functionary or 'ganbu.' "

The author asked, "What then are your conclusions about all this?"

The film-maker replied: "I should like to suggest forcefully, that in this journey we are about to undertake, we find such a person. Our efforts should not be to provide a television crew to dramatize the expedition, nor at going to the Shamans, but at finding the right officials of the country who can explain its workings to us correctly. It is through the new man that a new rhetoric becomes established—and it is the face and character of this new man we are seeking.

It may not be a familiar face, perhaps someone extraordinary; but we must seek him in ordinary surroundings, in his everyday world. It is this conjunction that interests the artist. For it is at this point—the intersection of the objective social conditions, and individual biography—that the truth lies."

* *

(Author's note: I want to make plain to the reader that none of the above interpretations are correct, including the statements by the personnage referred to as 'the author.' All interpretations leave out vital points- in particular the Dismemberment and Reconstruction of the Child, described on page 13, which is my own secret, the meaning of which may not be revealed here.

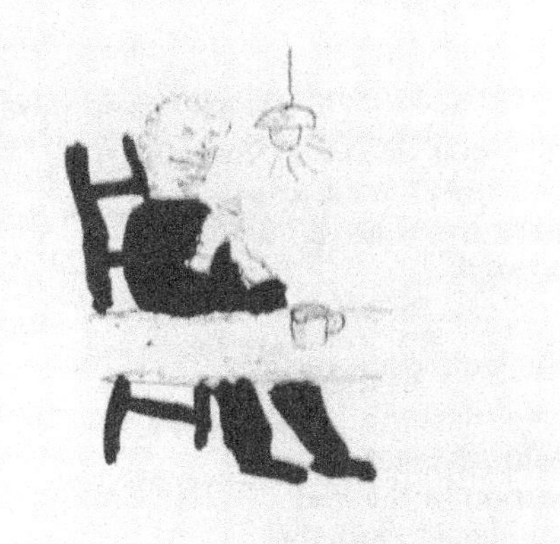

In any case, is it proper to discuss the author's methods? Rather, are not these trade secrets, the more resistant to analysis the better? On their mystery and evasiveness the effect depends. However, I will say this as to working methods: that the book to date has been nothing more than an extended improvisation, with no forethought whatever. I started out, as did Flaubert, with 'a blank piece of paper, like sawdust in a circus ring before the performance unfolds.'

Has there been any law governing the performance? Only to proceed at top speed, to digest and assimilate the facts as they unrolled, like an ox putting on meat; to exhaust each point mentally as it came up and then move on as rapidly as possible to the next, the only limit being the author's strength and stamina. In this my method is like that of the quick tree, the sumac in spring, which I described once in a poem (and which described without my knowing it, and ten years in advance of this novel, my exact method of composition).

FLEX

No pace like that of Sumac unfolding
planes don't travel at such speed

wind and sky travel as fast as planes
light even faster

wind/sky/ and light
are the locale
in which plane
is loosely buoyed

But the tight squeeze!
the combustion in the bud
of sumac unfolding

Small galls and midges wintering in the fruit
don't know what it's about

OLD SUMAC SPIRE

rusty old red velvet house
that has survived winter

but won't survive the spring

burst!
and burgeoning
of sumac unfolding

When the sheath rips it sends out 2 or 3 extra feet
of leaf and stem in a few weeks!
the increase of sumac
the speed at which it accelerates
and the old stem still downy and soft
barely solidified from the liquid
of last year's spurt

the flash
and quick
of sumac unfolding!

And the year's growth before that
not yet congealed into bark
skin still rippled and scarred with
motion
showing which way the drive went
and stretched
the flex of it!
the quick spring
and the unfolding!

See it
with eyes on the inside
all you spiders/ midges/ and small bugs
covered with the red velvet dust
in the old WINTER PALACE
AS THE TREE BREAKS
AND EXCEEDS ITSELF
UNWINDING AT SUCH A PACE

AT SUCH GREAT SPEEDS

* *

After Alvarez' remarks, the discussion broke off and we were joined for supper by our sponsors, the members of the Environment Control Gang. The meal was served in the club lounge.

After dinner the discussion came back to travelling arrangements. Blake had been going over maps with the gang leader. The Seer turned to Malatesta, remarking that the "location of the place was still not clear." Could he give them some better idea of where they were going?

All the leader would say was that it was located somewhere in Central Asia, in a country "Between the borders of the North Punjab and China," and was in "another century."

"What century—forward or back?" Alvarez asked him with interest.

Malatesta only closed his eyes and drew on his cigar. He would not say, but suggested that it was the traveller's job to find this out and report back to them.

"Couldn't you give us some idea of the character of the country? What inhabitants and institutions we should expect to find there—so we can make some preparations?"

"I can, but only by analogy," the chief replied. "And by invoking a phrase famous in the storybooks, the phrase 'As if'. The country is simple but paradoxical; it is the skin of history turned inside out. When you arrive you will find it *as if* the industrial revolution had come first to India in the 14th or even the 9th Century. And *as if* in our own time the anarchists of Catalonia had won the Spanish Civil War."

"Both excellent conjectures. I am all eagerness to go," Alvarez said. And the others nodded.

"Your plane leaves at midnight."

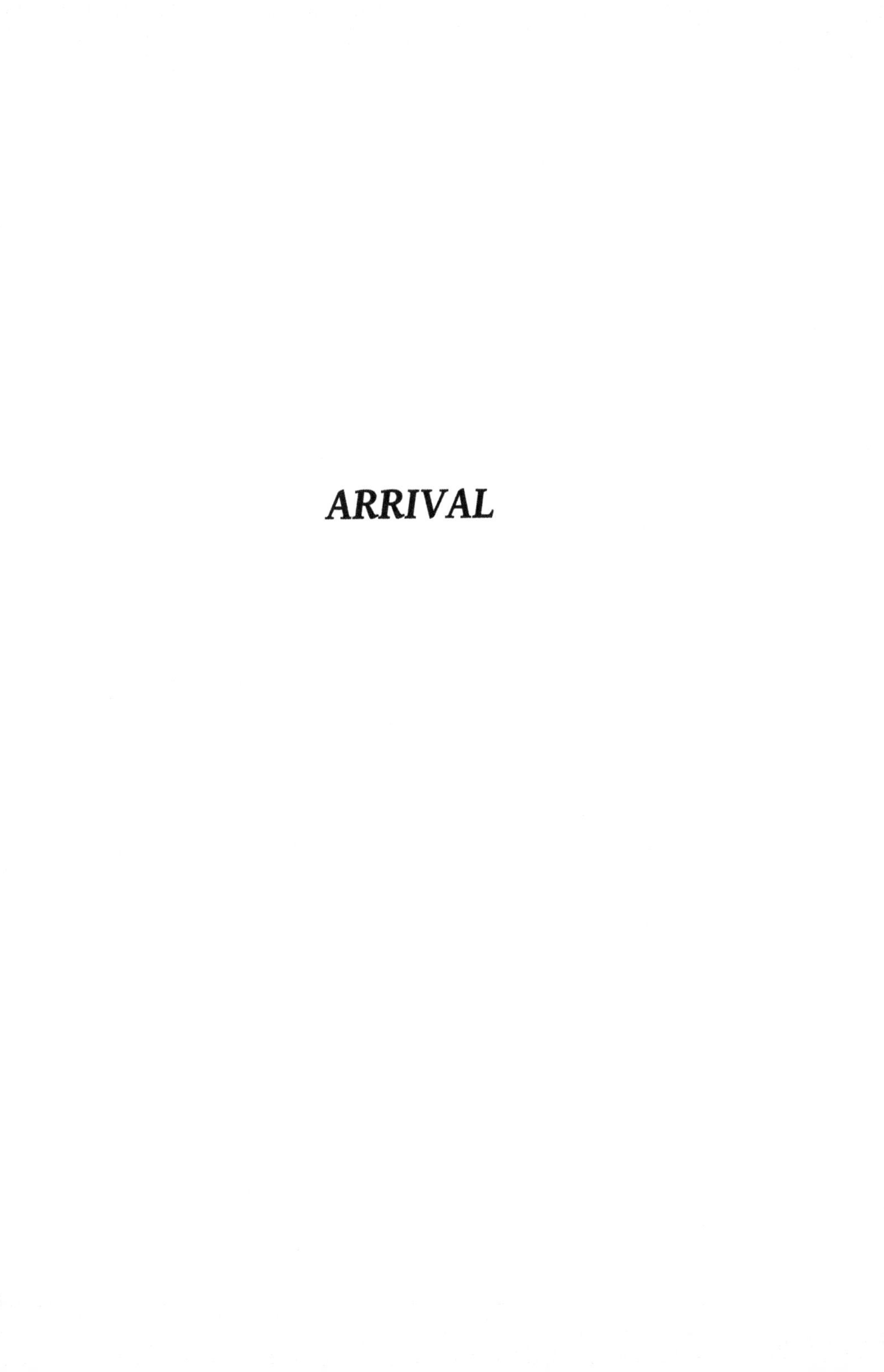

ARRIVAL

To Grace

ARRIVAL IN SAWNA

The rice terraces!

Blake, Alvarez, and Kerouac have just awakened. A veil has been drawn across the range of mountains at their backs. A squadron of geese coasts high up. From under clouds the rays of the pale sun slant onto the Nghsi-Altai landscape below, picking out clearly the specks of the villages distributed at intervals over the plain, and the shine of the Point Towns.

The helicopter has departed, bearing with it the crew of TV cameramen. Jack Kerouac is burdened with a hi-frequency transmitter which may be beamed to the United States. They have agreed not to make any reports for some days.

Alvarez rubs his eyes heavily against his coat sleeve, and Kerouac finds himself doing the same. All are dog-tired, exhaustion—or is it the altitude?—affecting them like a drug, which they are determined to shake off. They prepare to descend.

The distance from the ridge down to the Great Plain is almost a mile vertical. To traverse this the party has to descend by steps across the cultivated terraces, clambering down the steep banks which form the dikes, then striking across the strips of flooded earth. In these the sky is reflected. To the right, to the left, as far as the eye can see, run these luminous sky-mirroring terraces, a few yards at the narrowest, following the contour of the hills.

"We had better take off our shoes," Alvarez suggests. "We'll navigate more easily."

The thick oozy mud is up to their knees. Occasionally a plow team passes indifferently, both the plodding ox and the peasant bent down, intent only on the line of furrow traced in the water, and noticing them not at all. Evidently they are still invisible to them.

"Well—we've been invited here by the shamans," Blake says with a grunt. "When the time comes, I imagine they'll take the wraps off us."

Nightfall. Arrival at the first village, called Sawna. No square of "public space" within these Jat villages of Kansu-Hardan. However, a gong has sounded their approach, spreading out hollowly over the orchards and the outlying fields as they pass by, like some dye diffusing through the night. A crowd of villagers has gathered under a white wall, brightly lit by a street lamp around which insects buzz. They are led into the friendly glare by the shamans.

This evening there are only brief words of greeting by the elders and the presentation of flowers. The discoverers are allowed to retire early to the rest house, as the following day, the beginning of the Festival of Basora, promises to be a busy one.

THEIR LANGUAGE

This is how the official records are compiled in Nghsi-Altai. Writing is outlawed and has been for some centuries. However, computers are in general use for purposes of planning. All village panchayats, or common councils, have them, small consoles being set up among the hookah, or smoking, groups. In computer programing only the "stiff" language is permitted, composed largely of archaicisms and algebraic symbols; the common or "fresh" language is reserved for speech. (The above information furnished by the panchayat.)

Here is an example of a typical village computer-programed production plan, projected for the year 3670 for the village of Sawna in the Kansu-Hardan district:

Crops: dry season rotation (rabbi) pulse 50 hemp
or cotton 80 millet 210 hectares
wet season rotation (kharif) sugar 120
legumes 140 fallow 140 hectares

Industrial: cotton 1500 bales (T_c) light metals and
plastics 120 tons (M_{as})

$$(1)\ \Sigma\ (PP(2000) + Q(130) + MG_0) = 20510gk\ /\ L4000$$

$$(2)\ P_c - M_{as}\ \surd\ T_c\ (L_{ca}) = 1.00734$$

Where: PP, Q, MG are resource — productivity constants and gk and L are transformation functions. The second formula refers to a work input/population growth integral. It should be noted that the words "sugar," "hemp," "cotton," etc. are in the archaic or "stiff" script and vary considerably from their equivalents in everyday use.

Kerouac wonders how he can use the above material in his radio broadcast. He decides that he cannot. What he is after is the "fresh" speech. The ear registers the color, the flash of the spoken language. But how to convey this when to reproduce it is illegal?

What follows is an example of the spoken language, a story of an eleven-year-old girl, which the novelist was able to tape. The tape remained hidden in his rucksack for some time, and was later smuggled out of the country with the aid of a shaman.

A YOUNG GIRL'S STORY

My name is Sathan. I'm eleven. I am waiting for my husband to come. I have never seen him. I heard from my aunt, yesterday, that my mother has selected him, and tied the "red holding string" around his wrist, in the village of Chadar Bhat.

How long will I have to wait until I touch him? It'll be a year till I see him, at the wedding ceremony, then three years after that when we perform Gaur together and he comes home with me to live in my village. In the meantime, I'll have to grow lots of black pubic hair.

In a month from now we'll have the first of the fifteen wedding ceremonies: Sagai. In this I shall send all of his brothers and sisters coconuts, his mother Venetian glass, and his father a pair of bast shoes. After my messenger has left, we'll all sit down and eat sweetmeats.

After that, let's see (counting the months on her fingers) —after that comes Balandbat, when the engagement is announced, in his village, and in my village. On that day, hand marks will be made on the walls with red henna dye, from the gate of the village, all along the walls to my house. And from his village gate to his house.

He will have his hair handsomely cut, and the red nylon thread taken from his wrist and tied around his left ankle, and I will have my copper armbands struck off, and put on a necklace of jade beads. Then we'll both be given ceremonial oil baths, and rubbed until our skin glows. In his village, and in my village!

Once we went to Chadar Bhat. It was during Ghantal, on the way to the big fair at Garh. That was when we saw the shadow players. Chadar Bhat has groves of bay and almonds planted around it, and I guess beyond those, their millet fields merge with ours—somewhere. A monorail runs by there.

One day I was making chapati cakes in the courtyard of our house, with my cousins. Two of the American gypsy children came by, on their way to the well. They were carrying plastic buckets. "George," the freckled one, is fifteen, and his brother's nine. George was carrying two cocks.

"Won't you come with us to the well?"

"We can't go, because we're making chapati cakes, for tomorrow's supper."

"Come with us to the well. We'll go down the main street. We have grains of rice—we'll sell them to buy roasted rice candy."

"No, we can't go because we're making chapati cakes."

I looked down at my dusty feet and rubbed one toe over the other, and he screwed up his eyes. He held one of the white cocks over my head, pretending to be a shaman. The cock fluttered and closed one eye. He said:

"Someday you'll be married. But you won't stay here."

A prediction.

They say, "Tij comes and sows the seeds of festivals. Holi comes and takes away festivals in her shawl." Tomorrow Holi starts, and I have a shawl woven of scarlet thread, with red henna daisies hand-painted on it, which covers up my whole head. But in the crowd I can peek out of it, with my brilliant eyes.

Here in Nghsi-Altai men share the housework with the women and switch-roles. It is supposed to be same for field work. How I should love to drive a tractor. But the fields are all filled up, people say. "There are too many of us."

After the Deir Festival, the weather changes and food has to be taken out of the house and put back in the refrigerator. That's why we eat ice cream on Deir. The festival Devi-Ki-Karalis is dedicated to good marriages and keeping children healthy.

Kanagat is the time when ghosts come back, and also the time of the shamans' freak shows.

The festival of Siv Rati is to celebrate electricity and when people replaster houses.

And so the year passes . . .

A BOY'S STORY: THE FACTORY YEAR

Here is another story, a fifteen-year-old boy's:

In the old days boys used to do all kinds of real work in the fields. Now we're not allowed to. Now it is limited to tending cows, sheep sometimes. I'm in the fourth Age Grade, but below that all you're allowed to do is play and take part in festivals. And that's boring. What I used to like to do best was swing swings from the high trees—and sometimes make double swings—and skip flat stones on the pond.

When a boy is fourteen he goes off to serve his factory apprentice year. I served mine last year at Garh. Some of the boys live in dormitories there, but most live in the apartment blocks with branches of their families. From the apartment block you can see the whole Drybeds section, all the way from one cliff to another.

I lived in our family's apartment, that is, my mother's relations. It's thirty stories high. They have no kitchen, only a hot plate and small refrigerator, and meals are sent up by dumbwaiter from the common kitchen. Also living there was my mother's brother's wife, who is my tatti, and their four children.

There are lots of steam trolleys in Garh. And almost as many chickens and ducks as we have at home. When my relatives came to visit me from Chadar Bhat, they brought poultry. People often have gardens on the roofs of the apartment blocks. One Jat even kept a cow up there. You see everything at Garh.

There are also lots of fairs: every week end, and also on certain festival days. Everybody from the region comes. There are girls from our own twenty-village cauga, or county. We apprentices were always following them, trying to guess who they were under their shawls.

My cousins were all brats, but my tatti was nice. It was pretty crowded in the apartment.

I liked going to work in the factory. For the apprentices, the classes run between five and seven a.m., after that there's breakfast. Then we do our factory apprenticeship until two. In the first couple of months the apprentices are taught chemistry, particularly about clay and glazes. Then we have machines for another three months, and learn how to wire generators, and all that. In the last six months you actually work in the kilns along with the regular workmen from the syndicate. The plant makes firebrick and ceramic insulators.

I enjoyed the electrical part the best. Though I'll probably never use any of it, because I'm going to be a farmer.

During harvest time, at Cait, of course everybody leaves the city to go back to help with the dry harvest, and the same way at Davana, for the wet harvest.

One weekend at Cait my uncle was away and I stayed behind with my tatti. She had complained she had a headache. That night I slept with her in my uncle's bed. When my uncle came back, he pretended to be very angry, but he wasn't really. That's the custom among us Jats, for a boy's first time with his auntie. When the kids were in bed, the three of us sat down at the table and ate initiation halvah. It's very sweet, and at the touch of your tongue it crumbles and dissolves into a sweet spit. With it you have a glass of peach brandy. That's why they say: "In the village it's black bread. But come to town to eat halvah."

THE GEOGRAPHY OF NGHSI-ALTAI

The discoverers have been given space of their own in the village resthouse, not spotlessly clean. William Blake, Santiago Alvarez the Cuban filmmaker, and the American novelist share a room with bunks. The sun in the morning, slanting under a latania palm, strikes a rose plaster wall.

What is one to make of this country which their travel researches have only identified as "the other"? Other Country, then. But how to approach it and experience it? The three keep closely in touch with In-tourist, the regional agency that runs this chain of travelers' resthouses. Blake and Alvarez have obtained some maps and a brief description of the geography of Altai.

Looking out over the nine territories. To the north, home of the Yang-shao, Lung-shan, and Jat tribes, lie the Great Plains: featureless, almost treeless, a flat yellow-brown mat stretching to the mountain rim interrupted only by the gleam of an irrigation ditch, and the thin spikes of windmills. In the Jat section the villages are closely spaced, from one to one and a half miles apart, each with a population of three to four thousand. The ancient villages are sunk below the surface of the land for wind protection. The plains soil, fertile for farming though dry, is a tawny ocher most of the year. With the sudden advent of the monsoon when the moisture-laden winds sweep in from the east and from the Indian Ocean, the plateau is transformed overnight into a vivid green.

To the south of this lies the second biome. This is dense forest with a climate somewhat colder and more moist than the rest of the country. The Drune is sparsely populated. There are two tribes: the Mois, who make their living from silviculture, and the Deodars, or Bluefaces. Dwelling places are by the woodland lakes and consist of longhouses built on stilts over the water. Every opening in the forest has its settlement or cantonment around the lake, which shines at dusk like an eye in the prevailing dark green. Here the great ecological universities of the Deodars are located.

At the center lies the Rift, or Drybeds, bisecting the other two biomes. It is formed by a grand canyon and lies at a level some fifteen hundred feet below the plains. Entirely urbanized by the Karsts, this area runs in a sinuous line varying in width with the canyon walls, at the narrowest only a mile or two across, at the widest—fifteen miles. The base is desert with geologic formations typical of this sunken landscape: mesas, buttes, dolomites sculptured by wind; and also volcanic beaks, geysers, petrified forests, hot springs, and "paint pots." Among these, the mines and factories of the energetic Karsts have been constructed, and their linear cities under the bluffs.

Patterns of Nghsi-Altai. See the three biomes, its distinct landscapes of Rift, Great Plains, and Drune forest: a triad. And superimposed upon this another triad dividing it again, at right angles. Thus three autonomous regions are formed, each with the whole landscape. Each one having also the whole people, the Six Tribes.

Thus the pattern of Altai: a double triad. One superimposed over the other. A hexagram.

The areas are linked together by a transportation grid. Running from west to east through the brown fields are the irrigation canals. A barge is being pulled by a water buffalo led by a ragged child. It is carrying a load of sugar cane. Forty feet overhead, and rushing away at right angles to it in the direction of the Rift, the steel track of the monorail.

The Unity of Nghsi-Altai. As of a great bowl. On three sides the foothills of the Altai range, their flanks tamed into rice terraces. In the gray distances beyond, over a thousand miles of tundra and frozen steppe, lies Tibet. To the west and south the Indian upper provinces. And to the southeast the independent border state of Bhutan. Eastward of the hanging plateau, the dry bed of the Rift thins and flattens over a basalt ledge. The thin river of Nghsi slows, combed out by cypress roots, then disappears over the Great Falls. Nothing visible but the sky. The white mist, billowing and hovering, shreds and drifts downward over the Chinese province of Kwangtung.

MAKING A PIN

A number of old men not occupied as agriculturalists are the makers, or village craftsmen, of Sawna. One might say they occupy a privileged place in the sun. A wall shelters them from the wind; they sit on their haunches peacefully when not working, smoking their hookahs, yet enjoy the excitement of being at the center of things. The women of the village are always passing on their way to the well or communal freeze locker, or stop in to have some appliance repaired. A gang of children and dogs continually surrounds the old men, as their bazaar is next to the sweet shop.

In these sunken villages this craftsmen's bazaar is located at the bottom of a ramp leading down from the fields. These lie overhead, and extend out from the village on every side, devoted generally to vegetable plots and orchards. Beyond are the common fields. The village lies in a depression, scooped out of the soft red sandstone.

The travelers pay a visit to these old men. Blake, in particular, is interested in blacksmithing. They find this outdoor shop equipped with an excellent array of modern metalworking tools, including a small solar smelter. The stock, packaged in standard bar sizes, offers a wide range of alloys, all manufactured in the Rift. A nearby shop is equipped for woodworking and tinsmithing, and has a kiln for pottery making.

The art is demonstrated by one of the makers, a brusque fellow who has a harelip. A customer appears as the band stands talking to him. This is a Jat farmer who has come to have a ploughshare repaired. He stands at the edge of the field over their heads, halloos at Magor, and hurls down a piece of metal, which lands with a clatter at the blacksmith's feet.

It is the iron pin, or kus, which is used to secure the wood share of the plough to the curved wood handle.

"What am I supposed to do with this?" Magor holds up the bent kus, shaking his head in disgust, then passes it around to the other makers.

"Why, give it a few blows, you old fart."

"It's not worth fixing. We'll have to make you another. Just wait a bit."

And with this the farmer sits down, his back to a corn row, his legs dangling over the embankment, and begins to chew grass . . .

"Here, uncle, find me the right mold." While another of the old men does this, Magor goes to prepare the jig, first kicking aside a chicken.

The other makers continue to squat around their hookah pipes, listening to a transistor radio and exchanging insults with Magor. Meanwhile the blacksmith has wheeled out from under a shed the solar furnace. This consists of an iron frame about the size of a barbeque grille, lined with small mirrors, the facets focusing the sun's rays. At the center is a crucible. Squinting, the harelip adjusts the focus and drops in one of the manufacturer's steel bars. In a short time the color of the bar lightens, turning first a dull mauve, then pink, then a blue flame pencils from it. From the crucible, the molten steel is poured into the ceramic mold. The maker shatters this after a few seconds. Holding it with a pair of tongs, he bangs the kus on an anvil to knock off the scale, then plunges it into a pail of water as the steam rises in clouds.

By this time the farmer has fallen asleep in his vegetable patch.

"No use waking him," Magor remarks. "Might as well wait a bit, and finish it up proper." The smelting process has taken only about ten minutes.

But now—as Blake, Alvarez, and Kerouac stand by watching—the work continues. The blacksmith devotes the next hour or so to elaborating his artifact, or as he says, "finishing it." This he does by reworking the back end of the kus (which sticks out beyond the shaft), reheating it in the flame, and hammering it. At the same time with the brazing torch he drops little copper beads on it until he has shaped it, very beautifully, into an ear of corn.

[FROM KEROUAC'S NOTEBOOK]

"Well, we begin by making a pin"—a witticism of Blake's. What is the next step?

Our Cuban filmmaker is worried about malaria. Before his siesta he climbs on his bunk on all fours and beats the corners of the net for mosquitoes. Is it mosquitoes they have here?

Magor talking to us the other day spoke of the holiday "Ghantal Deo"—has a nice ring. And perhaps we've celebrated it already. The other day Blake and I watched a colorful procession pass by on its way to a market town, and the pilgrims stopped at the village pond to bathe ritually.

When I described this to Alvarez, he asked, how did we know they weren't washing their shirt?"

Blake and myself have become adepts at smoking the hookah: with some of the old men who were on hand to welcome us. Thus far we have followed no program. We are all dulled and wearied by the sights . . . the new sounds . . .

For instance: a bullock cart creaks over the cobbles, and the boy driving it is calling up to someone in a window . . .

We wonder how to proceed. I insist we shouldn't make schedules, and say to the others: "Let's just sit. Life passes before us."

A COUNTY MACHINE BANK

The visitors, because of Alvarez' technical interests, have obtained permission to inspect one of the general-purpose machinery pools operated by the cauga, or county, and have left this nearby village of Dhabar Jat escorted by officials of the panchayat. A ramp leads up from the bazaar into a zone of private gardens and orchards (each extended family is allowed several hectares). Beyond this they come to the common fields, where laborers are ploughing behind buffaloes. Alvarez asks the guides with surprise why there are no tractors.

"There were tractors in the old times. But a tractor is unproductive—not like an animal; it returns nothing to the soil by way of fertilizer. And in tractors the blade pulls too deep. It is not suitable for the soil here."

"You mean you follow the so-called 'Japanese' system: labor-intensive and not capital-intensive?" Alvarez asks. It is obvious the old farmer does not understand him.

"How many bushels do you get per hectare here?"

"Twenty-five hundred."

"That's not bad. Not at all bad," comments our Cuban expert in agronomy.

They come to an irrigation canal flanked by a bicycle path. A monorail truck appears overhead, stops briefly at a freight siding, then shoots off.

The machine banks, a regular feature of the plains counties, are protected by windbreaks of cottonwood, in front of which are several windmills. Beyond are buildings surrounded by huge piles of manure, some of them up to thirty feet high, of alternating dark and light bands, the tops sprouting weeds.

"Where does all this manure come from?" inquires Blake in astonishment.

They are informed by the guide that it is collected each night in the city, by a brigade known as the honey bucket men, and transported here where it is stockpiled. The manure is contracted for by the Farmers' Co-operative, which buys it from the city brigades at the exchange rate of one cubic yard manure to five sers of grain. The stockpiled material is analyzed by the laboratory, and chemical fertilizers and other nutrients added in accordance with local soil requirements.

Beside the manure piles is a large pond. It is rectangular and appears to have been dug artificially. Alvarez inquires if it is for recreation.

There was some difficulty in the translation of this word. "But what is recreation?" When it was finally understood, our guides roared with laughter.

"No. It is a solar pond."

"What do you mean, a solar pond?"

Incredulity that the discoverers do not know what these are. It is explained that the ponds are for the purpose of trapping solar radiation and are dug shallow and sealed with a black polyethylene liner. From the soil layer below this, heat is conducted through a series of exchangers to the bank's industrial plant, where it provides steam to the electric turbines. This is in the summer, the dry monsoon season. During the rest of the year, the energy comes from the windmills.

As with many banks, this one is run by a Karst. The trio is introduced to the Karst manager. He takes them on a brief tour of inspection and explains the operation.

These banks service all co-operative heavy machinery used in the cauga. In addition, they serve most of the light industry needs. Unlike our own machine tools, these are not developed to make a single product only (thus being rendered obsolete when the product is no longer marketable). On the contrary, they consist of "banks" of highly adjustable, multipurpose tools: presses, brakes, milling machines, etc. Of these the manager is very proud. He shows off, for instance, the drill for the extrusion dies, which is equipped with a photometric scanner and is adjustable from .0008 microns up to a diameter of 2 inches. Now this extraordinary tool is being set up to make aluminum irrigation pipe. The pipe is to be followed the next week by a run of electric wire and after that of lipstick tubes (a popular item among the Dhabar Jat women). This system is completely automated and computerized, equipped with a feedback scanner, and may be set up to make a number of runs, then switched over to another set of products, depending on the tastes of the regional consumer.

The tour ends. The visitors walk away slowly through the windbreak of poplars toward the village, assaulted by the twin smells of ammonia from the manure piles and of the heated plastic radiation liner. A strange combination.

* *

It has been very hot. The house to which the explorers have been assigned is called a baithak, made of pakka or glazed brick. The walls absorb the daytime sun and give off a radiance. In the evenings—a welcome relief—the three sit out on their earth court, the light from the street obscured by banana leaves.

Santiago Alvarez sweats profusely. His ears are red. When he stands against the sun these appendages of his head flare, like translucent tomatoes.

Blake is listless, and the villagers marvel at his height—when he is not lying down. On the other hand Kerouac is all energy, a hard vigor. He plays soccer with the young men. They wear long trousers tied at the ankles and turbans. This gives the American an advantage over them, when lofting the ball with his head. And so he has become a specialist in lofting. He is much admired.

The pressure from the great numbers of people exhausts the explorers. They are not used to such numbers, crowding the lane on their way to market, filling Makers' Square.

Kerouac has made the acquaintance of some of the women—not easy in a country where the purdah shawl is worn. But the older women are less formal, and less cautious with strangers.

One of the families of the tholla, or neighborhood, has become friendly with the author. And so the party has received an invitation to dinner in a Jat household.

INSIDE A JAT HOUSEHOLD: AN EYEWITNESS ACCOUNT

The children greet us at the gate. We are led through the dirt compound where a buffalo is tethered, up the steps to the house. In the kitchen we are taken before the matriarch. Saraswathi Bai Harditt is suffering from phlebitis and sits on her stool, her feet in a pan of water. In front of her is a two-way radio-television transmitter. One of the younger women is bathing her feet, head bent forward and long hair spread glossy over the back.

Our band kowtows before the matriarch self-consciously.

An older woman, the matriarch's sister, tells us that supper will be late. She explains that the fieldworkers have signaled in that a drag harrow has broken down. Saraswathi Bai has just dispatched one of the makers to fix it. It is this operation that the old lady has been attending to on the communications screen.

The talk which had died down when we entered is now resumed. Soon a girl sitting on a high stool recites in cadence. This is a worksong, so it turns out. The large common room is full of people doing a multiplicity of chores. There is a huge stove and food processing area in the center and a section of the room devoted to light machines. One group is making shoes, another busy with a mixer and roller. We are told they are manufacturing pills for the pharmacy.

Two young girls are playing on the floor with dolls. A boy sits against the wall. The floor is cold; his bare feet are tucked under a sheepskin. One of the young girls is Sathan. We are to see her fiance later.

"Hey, hey, where is Gerta?" The sister of the matriarch shouts boisterously. From behind others a small girl is produced and pushed forward by her mother. "Darling we have to have some milk. Do you think you can fetch it? Run now." The old woman claps her hands, and the child runs off into the courtyard, looking frightened. "And don't spill it!"

The matriarch's sister, a terrifying woman, is named Helvetia Harditt. She is about sixty and has a heavy black mustache. Again at her command, we are handed a glass of sendi wine and told to be comfortable.

"Don't stand around like sticks." This from one of the aunts. "And don't expect anything fancy, just ordinary fare, like the rest of us. We're poor people and can't afford wheat cakes every day." None of the younger women so much as look at us during this interchange.

Regular fare among the Jats consists chiefly of black grain millet or barley. This, fried and served with a vegetable curry, is called bajra roti. Another common seasoning is catni, made of onions, salt, and chili. With millet cakes people drink sit, made from buffalo or goat's milk.

By the stove, a cook in trousers stirs a huge frying pan of rice. Helpers are cutting up onions, the tears running down their cheeks.

Over the rest of the worktables heads are down and hands are flying.

Over a glass of sendi we converse with the aunties. We are told about the lam no custom of clan apprenticeship. Both young men and women are bound at an early age to work for these communal families. The service is harder for the men because of the practice of exogamy. A man must marry outside the village. He is working for his in-laws.

We suppose the burden lightens as the apprentices get older and they gain status by marrying and producing children.

Most of the housekeepers are women, but there are men standing by occupied with domestic tasks. We are told by the matriarchs that these are switch-roles.

As we talk, children run in and out. In this household they are served whenever they are hungry. The small ones are bare-bottomed, a smock just below the knee. The child holds out a grimy fist, and the mother or auntie, smiling, gives her a ghi cake.

In spite of the hard work all the Jats dress attractively. The standard dress, even for house chores, consists of a wide skirt (ghargki) spotted or striped in red, yellow, or white. There is the shirt (khurta) and the usual plaid shawl, obliged to be worn when there are men present. Then there are the low half-jackets worn by unmarried women, these often sparkling with rhinestones and little mirrors which are sewn in. Women also wear arm and ankle rings.

The switch-roles' clothes are more practical, though they have their own allure. They consist of baggy pyjamalike trousers (silva) and a long collarless blouse called a kamiz.

Suddenly the singsong story stops. A wail from outside brings some of the younger housekeepers to the window. They begin to laugh.

"What is it?" shouts Helvetia Harditt. "Now what's the matter?"

"It's Gerta, the one you sent with the pail. The buffalo won't let itself be milked. Instead it's pissing on her."

And now the fieldworkers have arrived. As is the custom among these plains people, they are served separately. The sober meal is taken in silence, there is no small talk. A housekeeper stands behind each agriculturalist's chair with a straw fan which she waves to brush away the flies.

At the end most of the family go out in the courtyard to play with the children. Later we all take coffee together, that is with the male members of the clan and the older women.

Generally by nine the men retire to their own baithaks.

I have been paying particular attention to the young women. From the time the men had arrived, we noticed, the heads of the younger women had been veiled in the deep shawls. It is not usual in this company for a husband and wife even to address each other, except in the third person.

Occasionally I try to catch the eye of the child bride, Sathan. She continues playing on the floor. The young man who is her fiance has recently arrived from another village. His name is Venu.

We are introduced to Nanda, Sathan's older married sister. Can there be some drama here? This union will make Sathan's husband her deva—a special relationship in Nghsi. Older sister and the prospective bridegroom talk easily together. They laugh often. Nanda leans over the young man, her hand resting on his shoulder. Sathan, still playing with her doll on the floor, glares at them both.

FIRST STRUCTURAL ANALYSIS AND SELF-CRITICISM SESSION

The explorers have decided to hold periodic self-criticism sessions. Only Blake voices objections. What will it accomplish?

Alvarez reminds him they are on a voyage of discovery in South Central Asia. All three plan to send reports home to their separate sponsors in order to justify the trip, and each sponsor has his own expectation. Should they therefore not make an effort to co-ordinate the material? Disciplined self-criticism would serve to monitor the flow of information, evaluate its accuracy, and give a more balanced view.

"Bah! Balance!" is Blake's comment. Though he denies interest in "sending back any reports," he does not exclude the possibility of writing a poem or so at some future time.

The first session is held in their baithak. Blake sits smoking his pipe peacefully. Alvarez is cleaning his boots.

The novelist has adopted native dress, consisting of a tunic, or kamiz, and long baggy billowing white trousers fastened at the ankles. Kerouac's feet are bare. Recently he has taken to wearing a turban, but this is giving some problems. The difficulty is that the headpiece is not ready-made. It has to be wound around the wearer's head, and the band of cloth often gets tangled.

Before broadcasting the typescript of the foregoing visit, Kerouac has consented to submit it to his two colleagues.

The evening air is muggy. Mosquito netting drapes the windows.

Alvarez, scraping the mud from his heavy workboots, begins the discussion. There are many things about the piece he likes, that are skillfully done. But it tends to be superficial. The novelist has got the surface only.

Blake observes, "Yes. All those sights and smells."

"Naturally, an eye-witness account has to make it real. The scene has to be fresh, vivid," Kerouac explains.

"The buffalo pissing in the yard."

Kerouac picked up on this. “And the wail from Gerta. And the glare of the girl Sathan, directed at her sister.”

Blake confessed he had seen no child bride at all playing on the floor with dolls or otherwise. “And is it necessary to deck them out in costume?”

The novelist said he was after a viva-voce description, some coloring was helpful.

“What you mean, I suppose,” Alvarez said, “is Local Color. I see the tale is wound up with primitive and folklorist elements: the matriarchy, exogamous marriage, the custom of clan apprenticeship.”

“What you are giving us in your proposed radio broadcast,” Blake suggested, “is fictionalized anthropology.”

The author confessed he had made some slight use of anthropology—a study on Jat customs in northern India—which had been one of his source books for the expedition.

Alvarez asked, “Isn’t all anthropology a fiction—by the mere fact there is an observer, who represents an outside culture? What is observed becomes an artifact. And it is the interest of the anthropologist to preserve the artifact, to bottle it and serve it up to the sponsors of his expedition.”

He added that there might be some uses for anthropology. “But we must identify the sources in order that we may be put on guard.”

* *

Kerouac has re-examined his “Inside a Jat Household” in the light of Blake’s and the Cuban filmmaker’s criticism. He feels he may be guilty of the charge: “fictionalizing anthropology.” He concludes that he has done it out of vanity and to appear original.

He decides to make use of the sources all the same, properly identified. The book is Oscar Lewis and Victor Barnow’s study *Village Life in Northern India*, published by Vintage in 1965.

But was it possible, as Alvarez had suggested, that this source might be tainted? The introduction to the work—which describes the village of Rampur—states that “the expedition was financed by the Ford

Foundation, with the consulting anthropologists Oscar Lewis and Dr. O. C. Karin, head of 'Program Evolution' for the Indian Planning Commission—a department also financed by the Ford Foundation."

It is true that the stress is on the reactionary elements: traditional modes of behavior, caste relationships, etc. Probably one should be wary of this.

And to go deeper, one may well ask: who *are* these local students that helped the expedition collect much of its material? For instance the songs were collected by a G. A. Bansal, a graduate student and undoubtedly an Anglicized Indian. Doubtless his rendering of them, his translations, are not untainted either—being marred by certain "folkloristic attitudes"—and possibly a repressed sexual emphasis.

But can one say that the art itself is adulterated? The ballads do give important information. There stands the unadorned lyric, going back over thousands of years, and the naive narrative and dramatic form, improvised by the performers to fit an occasion of the heart. One hears the authentic voice.

Beside these songs Kerouac decides to place his own poems and stories of Nghsi-Altai—in the spirit of frankness that Alvarez commends and in addition to give new factual information. Thus the listener to the proposed broadcast may compare the two versions as he likes and make his own evaluations.

BALLADS FROM THE MARRIAGE CYCLE

GIRL'S SONG: GOING AWAY FROM THE VILLAGE

(*Sung on Bida: Sixteenth Ceremonial Step*)

O Sathan! you are going away!
My eyes are brimming with tears.
I would sew a shirt for my own Sathan.
I would place two lines of buttons on either side.

O Sathan! you are going away!
My eyes are brimming with tears.
I would stitch a skirt for my own Sathan.
I would place two lines of lace on either side.

O Sathan! you are going away!
My eyes are brimming with tears.
I would escort my Sathan to her palanquin.
I would send my brother along.

O Sathan! you are going away!
My eyes are brimming with tears.
I will soon send for my Sathan
by sending her younger brother.

O Sathan! you are going away!
My eyes are brimming with tears.

IN-LAWS

(*Sung after Gaur: Twentieth Ceremonial Step*)

O my friend! My in-laws' house is a wretched place
My mother-in-law is a very bad woman.
She always struts about full of anger.

O my friend! My in-laws' house is a wretched place.

My husband's elder brother is a very bad man
He always slips off to the threshing at his hayrack.

O my friend! My in-laws' house is a wretched place.
My husband's sister is a very bad girl.
She takes her doll and runs to her playmates, jeering at me.

O my friend! My in-laws' house is a wretched place.
My husband's younger brother is a very bad boy.
He takes his stick and slips off to the men's quarters,
joking at me.

O my friend! My in-laws' house is a wretched place.
The she-buffalo of that house is very bad.
When I milk it, it urinates, but when Father-in-law
milks it, it gives milk . . .

SWING SONG

Daughter-in-law:

Mother-in-law, the month of Savan has come.
Get me strings of yellow thread for my swing.
Mother-in-law the month of Savan has come.
Get me a plank of sweet sandalwood.

Mother-in-law:

Daughter-in-law, let it come let it come
The plank and strings are ready at home.

Daughter-in-law:

To others, your own, you have already given them.
Before me you have placed corn to grind.
I shall break the grindstone in eighteen pieces.
I will spread this pisma [grain] throughout the bazaar
Let the hali-pali people come
Let them pick it up from the floor and eat it

Mother-in-law:

Listen, son, how this foolish girl talks.

BRIDE'S COMPLAINT: A HUSBAND TOO YOUNG

There is a banana tree in the courtyard of my home.
I feed it milk and curd.
I go to my neighbor, sad at heart
My husband's sister knows the secret of my heart
She asks, "Why do you stand so sad and still?"
I say, "Your brother is young and still a babe.
He doesn't know the longing of my heart."
She says: "Take a bath and adorn yourself.
Make a wish from your heart and come with me.
I will make my brother meet you.
Even doors of stones would fall open
and iron bolts fall
Before your beauty, love and charm."

LONELY WOMAN

(Note: a love affair is permissible in this culture between the wife and her devar, husband's younger brother. Jeth is husband's older brother.)

O Mother-in-law, where should I sleep?
It is so cold.
My man has gone away to the army.
He is guardian of the country.
O Mother-in-law, where should I sleep?
It is so cold.
My devar is very young and innocent.
O Mother-in-law, where should I sleep?
It is so cold.
My jeth has gone to the fields.

He is the guardian of the fields.
Mother-in-law, where should I sleep?
It is so cold.

UNTITLED

(*Song about a rape [?] by the bride's jeth*)

O sister's husband I die of shame because of you.
My sister's husband said he would work at our plough.
and I was to bring him food to the fields.
O sister's husband, I die with shame because of you.

My sister's husband said that I should come quietly.
with no one seeing me.
I said that big thorns would prick my feet.
O sister's husband, I die with shame because of you.

They worked at the plough on one side.
The cattle grazed at the other side.
I was lain prostrate between two bullocks.
O sister's husband! I die with shame because of you.

I came home weeping and crying.
I told her my sister that her husband had brought about
my death.
She asked what had happened, and whether I had been beaten
with plough wood or plough iron.
I said I had been beaten with neither.
O sister's husband, I die with shame because of you.

I was lain prostrate between the two bullocks.
They worked at the plough on either side.
The cattle grazed on the other side.
O sister's husband, I die with shame because of you.

KEROUAC'S SONGS AND STORIES OF NGHSI-ALTAI

THE HOUSES OF SAWNA (1)

Kakka houses   of the poor   made of mud brick
Pakka houses   of the wealthy   made of baked brick
  fired and brilliantly glazed
All are jumbled together   there are no separate houses
The town anchors itself into the rock   Like a lichen
  it has grown in layers   from the ground up   through
the centuries

HOUSES OF SAWNA (2)

Staring at each other across the lane   the houses of Sawna
  form
two continuous planes at odd angles
    white stucco walls
  stained in the rain   henna   lime green   and ocher
A rough cobblestone street
  just wide enough to admit
a bullock cart   At the end of this story
  Sathan's youngest boy
Dhillon   will be driving it

HOUSES OF SAWNA (3)

I have said   that the Redwillow section
is a beehive of dwellings
Four communes or collections of families
    forming a tholla
these are the Harditt, Teka, Dhobi and Nai communes
under the leadership of the Harditts
As we approach

over the great stretches of country
we can see nothing   only the windbreak
A cloud passes   the plain darkens for a moment
the heat shimmers

HOUSES OF SAWNA (4)

They are tunneled into the loess   the roofs baked
a drainage ditch full of nettles
Swings hang from the trees
left over from the Tij Festival
it is hot   hot   nothing travels but the clouds
From the gate
a bridegroom sets out on a motorcycle
bells jangling from his cap

FACTORIES IN THE FIELDS

The grass moves to a sound
it is the footsteps of Rajpal and Harelip
as they go to the canning factory
through the tall grass

The stone moves to a sound
It's the factory manager   Tzu Tzu
kicking a pebble out of his way
Can he kick a man like that?

On high grass
On stony baked road
Factories planted in the fields
of the Yellow Sheaves Agricultural Commune
the brushes of the dynamo   go   wwhisssh   wwhisssh

I have made a necklace of grains of black millet
alternating with checkerberry

it is threaded over my heart

SATHAN'S SONG OF EVERYDAY CHORES

"Sathan   Sathan!
time to fetch water from the well."
The courtyard is dark   the streets are deserted
As I go carrying two pots on my head
the cold strikes through the folds of my dress
even the mirrors on my blouse shiver

"Sathan!   the laborers have to be brought lunch."
The path to the field is rocky and steep
in the heat   the oxcarts are drawn up
their backs gleaming   with sweat   the men of the commune
lean on their hoes   joking with one another

"Sathan, now the clothes. Laundry has to be scrubbed."
After work the village girls stand hip deep in the pond
the cotton of their ghargkis   sticks to their brown skin

A line of field laborers come through the grove
Sathan stands watching them
    soaping herself under the dress
one hand on her crotch   the other cupping her small breast

Oh my young flesh
my arms and legs   like sticks
My body
    Venu!   when will it grow
            full and seductive as Nanda's?

NAMING OF PRODUCE

There are three categories of grains and vegetables in Nghsi-Altai, depending on use. Thus with tomatoes: those consumed by the commune for food, and also used for ceremonial and festival purposes are called frooz—a fresh speech word signifying sacred. Tomatoes allocated to the State Buying Co-operatives are called kijh—meaning tax tomatoes. The third category is kumbaj, meaning market tomato. Only the market tomatoes may be priced and sold.

The grading and sorting of produce is called naming. It is done by one of the village men's societies, the Squirrels. This operation is a privilege of the society, and appropriate regalia is worn. The Squirrels also serve as a special police force and give out fines to those caught selling sacred or tax vegetables. This is black marketeering and the crime is: mixing up names.

MATRIARCH'S SONG

Men are good for nothing
The young are good for nothing
Children and animals are practically no good

Without us   society would fall apart
The men would only make politics and smoke
The young paint their faces
        and dream of the next age-grade society
The children and animals wander around and piss

It takes an old woman to plan for the commune:
to run the data-processors   to buy grain
five years ahead   Everything harnessed and trussed up
the water squeezed from the socks
the veal pounded with mallets
the pie crust punched and rolled flat

Is it any wonder   we have hair
like wire growing out of our noses?

COUNTY WORKS PROJECT

The huge dam above the village
    rises higher and higher each day
Rubble and earth dike
People are toiling   hauling stone up in baskets
winching up concrete blocks.

What a great Public Works!
Nothing to equal it since China in the eleventh century
When the great rice terraces were made
under Chou.

I am lying in a bank of huckleberry
    watching it grow.

A HARD DAY

The herdsman marched head down. The wind had come up and he had gone back to the village to get his padded coat.

The animals were not where he had left them. He spotted them at some distance over in the pasture that adjoined the Nai commune. The electric power line ran in that direction. He walked below and to the side of it, looking up at the steel trusses supported on the great pylons. Some of them were still covered with red turmeric paste where they had been "worshipped" during Siv Rati.

The pasture was treeless. On the ground were the buffalo wallow holes, now empty. Ice was in some of them. Near the herd he tried to catch some of the calves, but they cantered away from him up on the slope, their hooves drumming.

The cowherd made a fire and took his clarinette out of its felt bag. When his fingers were thawed he began to fool with it. The sound made him feel: What a pity! It's a hard life.

Some Nai people came over the slope. They were men of his age, they herded for the clan owning the adjacent pasture.

With the music from the clarinette the weather seemed to grow lighter. They sat down with him and brewed tea on the exile's fire.

They talked of home.

SONG

Our eyes at water level
the woods reflected   green   green
          We have been
swimming through stalks of pond lilies
          New England
My daughter hangs on my neck
    while I try to write poems
        of Other Country

SONG

Venu the Bridegroom stops by the shrine
        on his motorcycle
I stick this waterlily in his cap

UNDER THE HARDITT LEADERSHIP

My name is Jagivan Sanjivaran Gopal Harditt
sixty years old   ganbu of the Red Willow Commune
                     for twenty years
Come smoke a pipe with me and we will discuss facts

Beyond the lighted porch   there is a clump of banana fronds
At the edge of the smoking group
                     dominated by graybeards
the young men stand   giving us black looks

They are muttering: how long will you rule?
they whisper: you made such and such mistakes:

for instance: why did you trade soap for salt?
why did you refuse
to sell the commune's eighth part ownership
in the Nai waterbuffalo
in exchange for a tractor?

Who is a revisionist?
Who is taking the "capitalist road"?

The street lamp comes on   and throws a purple glow
over the faces of these quarreling young men
        of the Kharab faction/   of the Dabas faction
I tell you the road's slippery
            an old man has to keep his wits
and stay five jumps ahead

MARKET DAY AT PUTH MAJRA

One day some of the clansmen were chosen to go to market at Puth Majra. This the young men considered a lucky break, a relief from village chores. The communes sell their kumbaj produce at the seasonal markets, and several members from each are assigned to transport it by truck steamer.

When the Harditts arrived at the village Dri-Freeze, the men of the Squirrel Society were grading and sorting vegetables. There were three huge piles of tomatoes. One of the Squirrels was "Harelip." He was high up on the hydraulic lift, balancing a long bamboo pole at the end of which was a reed cup, or divider.

"So you're going to town today," Harelip shouted.

"That's right, today and tomorrow, we'll be there two days."

"You're in luck."

The clansmen packed the kumbaj into circular woven reed baskets, called boats. It took six men to lift a boat. There were also boats of cabbages, chilis, and melons. These were loaded onto the steamer truck. The Harditts were joined by two Nais and three Singhs, then they were off to Puth Majra.

The road ran along the top of the canal dike. On the other side there were the commune fields. They passed a young wife on her way to take the laborers' lunch, a baby strapped to her back. The men on the road yelled at her. The Stanley truck steamer went off huff-puffing at a fast clip, blowing out steam from its rear and raising a cloud of red dust. They lost view of the village. Everyone was exhilarated.

"The old bus is really making time."

"Brother, don't run over that chicken."

They reached the market town in about an hour.

In Puth Majra, the government Buying Co-operative is located on the north end, along the flats. They dropped off one of the tomato boats, signed the papers, and drove on to the section of the town called Freemarket. As they approached the market the truck had to inch its way through a dense crowd of pedicabs, bicycles, and pedestrians.

"What a racket," one of the Singh men said. "And watch out for thieves."

"Look at them tall buildings!"

Inside, buyers crowded around the stalls. A wall of pumpkins gleamed beside a Jat truck. Pigeons wheeled. A barker shouted in front of a fortuneteller's booth. The thick air of the market was drenched by the smell of leather and kerosene. The stalls offered Drune medicines and liquors; Jat produce, melons, cabbages, pumpkins, and other vegetables brought by the trading communes, and cattle. Under a striped tent Karst factory representatives demonstrated harvesting machinery.

The crowd pushed against them on all sides. Along one side of the square they could see the large concrete building of the Conservation Ministry. The crowd surged, parted for a moment. A massed band of "Bluefaces," Sensor Cadets in green and gold braided uniforms, swept through playing a Sousa march, followed by a trained bear.

The Sawna men set up a booth and unloaded their produce. It was a hot day. The sun beat into the straw baskets. Flies buzzed in close. Some of the communards did the selling and keeping accounts. Others stood off unobtrusively in the crowd, to guard against thieves. The three Singhs were to be off duty the first day and "on the town." Toward the end of the afternoon, the best tomatoes had been sold. The rest were bruised from handling and being picked over. There would be enough for the next day, though the prices would drop.

The square began to empty. The stall next to them shut down. A loudspeaker from the Syndicate Hall announced a soccer match to be played that evening.

The three Singh men returned in high spirits. They had been shopping. One of them had bought a portable phonograph and records in the Foreign Quarter. After supper the villagers sent over to a restaurant for coffee, then they squatted together on the cobblestone pavement. One of the Singhs took coins from his pocket. He made four little piles on the ground, sorting the coins of the same sizes together. He squinted.

"Don't you understand money?" he was asked.

"He hasn't been to the city since his factory year," another Singh explained.

But the man liked to use it. He swept the coins together into his palms. He jingled them, and then smelled them. The others laughed.

"Tonight, man, we're going to have ourselves a time,"

One of them said that they were going to Paradise—the American gypsy section.

One of the salesmen had begun to play his harmonica.

The square was relatively deserted now. An old lady with a shopping bag bent over the straw boat picking over the tomatoes, the rim against her waist. She was one of the poor Karsts. There would be more of them that evening.

A Nai took out his paint pot and began to decorate himself. Holding up a small mirror he drew sketches on his face carefully. He was followed by the others.

The decorations were geometrical: straight blue lines over the body, in fine arabesques, starting at the lips, dividing the face into quadrants. Some of the men had brought guitars and a bagpipe. The Sawna men played riffs back and forth. Then they turned on the phonograph and improvised along with it. The record was a Coleman Hawkins piece. They played against it, the instruments weaving in and out of it, now in counterpoint to the tune, now drifting along with it. So that people around them in the square waited or moved softly.

The square was empty and dark now. From a distance over the city roofs, an aura of lights and shouts beckoned them, but nobody paid any attention. The painted clansmen played softly, and all around them people sat listening wrapped in their blankets, or lay asleep under their booths on the stones . . . In the big city . . . on the great square of Puth Majra . . .

SECOND STRUCTURAL ANALYSIS AND SELF-CRITICISM: ALVAREZ' REPORT

Blake has taken up a musical instrument, the gusle. The trio first heard the native product at the Harditt household accompanying a dance during one of the festivals.

Blake plays but he does not sing. What words, what language, would he use? But he does chant and growl when practicing his gusle.

A friend from the Weather and Soils Station has been teaching him. Bomba, one of the so-called Blue Deodars.

Santiago Alvarez has become popular with the ganbus, leaders of the village production teams. They have given him a merit badge for his enthusiasm cutting sugar cane. In fact the Cuban is an outstanding filmmaker but a poor cane cutter. During the first weeks he suffered agony from blisters. Now he wears gloves when wielding the machete. But he vows that someday he will cut cane barehanded.

Tonight Blake has brought his Deodar friend to the bathaik—accompanied by the latter's tame puma. The two are inseparable. Blake, Bomba, and the puma sprawl on one of the bunks yawning.

Alvarez has invited several guests of his own. They are members of the panchayat, and seem to be the oldest and most doddering of these village notables. Alvarez' purpose is to enlarge the range of the group's "self-criticism." He will read his report on Sawna. By including some of the native population, he hopes to get a more comprehensive view.

Alvarez begins to read his report, but after a few minutes Bomba, the soils and weather technician, gets up to leave, excusing himself. The puma follows him.

Blake lingers on the porch with his friend. They converse softly, looking up at the sky. A warm wind has come from the east, which, they say, will "push the peach blossoms."

Alvarez resumes. The report, on the economics of Nghsi-Altai, is addressed to Alvarez' sponsor, a publishing organization.

> To: The People's Voice
> Cuban-American Friendship Society
> 9 Rockefeller Plaza, New York, N. Y.
>
> This will be my first full-scale report. Recently I have been engaged in detailed discussions with the Regional Planning Office, Kansu-Hardan district. Their chief planner, a Mr. J. P. Naroyan, has been very helpful to me in going over the general picture. He has also suggested that I look into two of his own pamphlets, "Socialism to Sarvodoy," Madras, 1956 (written when he was with the Indian Congress Party), and "Village Republics: Swaraj for the People," Benares, 1961. Unfortunately neither is available in the U.S.
>
> J.P., the chief planner, also gave me useful historical background (which has not been forthcoming from the shamans contacted by Blake, and is of course beyond the scope of Kerouac's glosses).

Alvarez paused in his reading to give a look of apology at his colleagues.

> We are concerned with how this system (of political economy) works. And of course we must look for the answer through the method of dialectical materialism, i.e. in the modes of production and property relations which lie below the superstructure.
>
> We must place our observations within the proper ideological framework. But at the outset I am puzzled. But which model are we to follow?

Marxist-Leninist?
The Frankfurt school?
Rosa Luxemburg?
Gramsci?

None of the orthodox models exactly fits. However, I *resist* going the road of anarchosyndicalism (Bakunin and Co. after their expulsion from First International).

Here is the preliminary scheme:

FIRST THESIS (FOR A DESCRIPTION OF NGHSI-ALTAI): MODES OF PRODUCTION DETERMINE HISTORICAL DEVELOPMENT

We Marxists understand the relation between technological development and fundamental property relations. The great technological inventions (wind, steam, water power) that came to Europe from the ninth to the twelfth centuries were grafted on the base of feudalism. This stage passed rapidly into capitalism producing its appropriate energy forms—an immense steel-coal aggregation organized around the nation-state. (And later petroleum and worldwide monopoly capitalism.)

In Nghsi-Altai this stage has been by-passed. Apparently, the Industrial Revolution came several centuries earlier. With no base for heavy capital-formation, the system has gone directly into an open, intermediate-scale technology. This technology is highly sophisticated. It is based not on extractive fuels, but on other free energy sources. These are wind, solar, and geothermal energy. Compared with our own, these are low-yield energy systems. They imply decentralization and must be tied in closely to a regional economy.

Possibly we must look for answers on a plane somewhere below state socialism and national planning. Unfortunately in Nghsi there is no State. I am loathe to descend to the level of regionalism, with its "populist" ideology. But again this is most emphatically not the regionalism of Godwin and Proudhon, the Italian anarchist Malatesta, Murray Bookchin, et al.

SECOND THESIS: NO URBAN-RURAL DICHOTOMY, UNIFIED SYSTEM VS. SATELLIZATION

In the West the rural economy has been satellized by the city, not only under capitalism but regrettably under socialism as well. However in the Nghsi-Altai the operating unit is the confederation (see the early Russian revolutionary soviets). The city itself has been broken up, so that its subdivisions (or sections) relate directly to the surrounding countryside in the same way as the Paris sections of the 1790s related to their rural departments, and relied on them for food supply. I am told there is virtually no central municipal administration. Naroyan suggests another example in our own day would be twentieth-century Calcutta, which is hardly a city at all but an agglomeration of practically self-governing birlahs, each with its own nationality groups and even its own language.

(Note: The above is clearly not Kropotkin's romanticized "countrification," viz. his Conquest of Bread. You will agree that my analysis of the failure of the Paris Commune differs from Kropotkin's radically.)

One can say that the city has been dis-urbanized. At the same time the countryside has been allowed to develop hegemony, through the means of its own production and industry sectors. For instance the market sector of Puth Majra produces tractors and railway carriages. Each county has its own light industry complex, the "machine banks."

THIRD THESIS: HIGH LABOR VALUE VS. CAPITAL RATIO

The key here is population differences between Asia and United States/Europe. Population density in Nghsi-Altai is at a maximum of 3,000-4,000 persons/sq. mi. (similar to present-day Ceylon; and at a level predicted for the West not until the year 2800). Under the circumstances one would not expect to find a value system which sets a premium on machines as laborsaving devices. On the contrary the Nghsi-Altai system maximizes labor power, i.e. it is labor- rather than capital-intensive. The only machines developed are those which increase productivity but do not penalize employment. There may be some exceptions here (telecommunications?).

Thus in Nghsi socialism has not "succeeded the last stage of capitalism," or been built on mature capitalist modes of production. In this country it has by-passed them. Does this mean that capitalism lies in the future here? Possibly.

I know of only one school of economics in the West which advocates smaller production units and denies the efficiencies of scale associated with both capitalism and communism. This is a

> minor tendency—the so-called Middle Technology Development Group, whose most noted proponent is E. F. Schumacher. See his *Small Is Beautiful*, *Buddhist Economics*, and other works of petty-bourgeois romanticism.
>
> I am also disturbed that the authorities here have permitted a limited Free Market sector. Probably this is transitional—not a permanent feature (as the unfortunate aberration in Yugoslavia)."

The filmmaker had finished. He turned to the others. But the local notables had left—including it seems Naroyan himself, whose works the Cuban had alluded to. Blake had fallen asleep. Alvarez dropped his report heavily on the bed and asked Kerouac: "What do you think of it?"

"I really dig all your negations. That's an art form in itself."

* *

Blake has been absent from Sawna a good deal of the time.

Where has he been? He goes off cheerfully with his rucksack and walking stick into the landscape. Blake is detached from the explorer's party, and his mind is hardly engaged in the business of making reports.

On the other hand Blake is something of an embarrassment to Alvarez and Kerouac. They have found that he has made several trips to the Drune Forest in the company of Bomba. Possibly they have set up a hut there in the woods and are enjoying nature, with the puma.

But Blake returns at intervals. Then he is all affability. He goes to considerable trouble to keep abreast of Alvarez' researches. The progress of Kerouac's narrative interests him less.

THIRD SELF-CRITICISM SESSION: BLAKE ON THE PLAYFUL

Blake in one of his rare good moods. In the past he has been unenthusiastic about the form "mutual self-criticism" (as being inappropriate to genius). However today he is willing to indulge his colleagues. Would they care to have his views?

"Yes. Let's get into it."

As for Kerouac, Blake suggests, the novelist has been following a tried and true literary formula: the subject presented as personal, and to some extent, sexual biography. "The ardors of the flesh have been spied upon . . . a tireless indexing of the body in all its modes" (the sage quotes from a well-known existentialist).

On the other hand Alvarez has given the material base, and by extension the social context. Blake feels that the approaches worked together. "No artist can convey the whole. But between you, you get the Nghsi-Altai character pretty well. But you have left out something essential."

They ask him what was that?

"It is simply: worship. The element of the marvelous. And the lives of the people of Altai are organically connected to it." Therefore Blake would prefer to recast their joint account. He would like to arrange it as a chronology of the various Year Festivals, the sacred holidays.

Alvarez' reaction: this would be "mere obscurantism."

"The obscure . . . the obscure," the poet muttered. "How do you suggest we penetrate the veil?"

Kerouac's difficulty with this approach: that it might be accurate but would be unbelievable to the folks back home. "We have a secular audience."

Blake: "But this country is permeated by the sacred. It's what gives it its aura. Not to take account of it in your exploration would be like going to the moon and bringing back only rocks."

"And that brings me to the next point: style. You'll pardon my saying so, but you are both too literal, each in your own way, and therefore somewhat mechanistic. The universe of the miraculous calls forth the mode of Play. One's style should be playful, vis-a-vis the reader or listener, and it should be obvious that one is playing."

Blake recommends a number of stylistic tricks: the fictional narrator, the plot within the plot, etc. As an example he offers Cervantes: this author was usually credited with giving the world Don Quixote, but in fact had assumed a whole gallery of disguises. He had interrupted his tale with pastoral romances, taken from who knows where, and insisted that a large part of the text was from an ancient Arabic manuscript written by the scribe Sid Hemmete Bennegeli.

"And now I'm going to tell you a story. I'm curious to know what you think of it."

Blake tells the following story, called "The Insect Pilgrimage," which he claims has been related to him by Bomba.

THE INSECT PILGRIMAGE: FIRST PART

After ten years of marriage it is traditional for couples in Nghsi-Altai to go on their "insect pilgrimage." It is called that because it is done in the wet month, Asauj, when the insects swarm in the fields. The pilgrimage is to the Drune, to one of the forest universities.

Venu and Sathan had departed from Sawna with their three children. They had left by monorail around noon and by five were in the Garh station in the Drybeds. They had spent the night at a cousin's apartment, in one of the quarters inhabited by Chandpur people. The next day they set out again, by trolley across town. At the base of the cliff they transferred to cable car.

As they approached the top of the cliff face, they could see the layers and striations of soil, could almost touch the birds' nests. They wore their ceremonial face and body ornaments. Their dress denoted that they were passing into another age group.

Below them, filling the grand canyon, lay the familiar city of Garh. They were at a level with the roofs of the point houses and the antennae of wireless stations. Across the flats was the great steel mill complex powered through its steam ducts. The chalk face of the cliff stood opposite them. Beyond they could see the beginning of the plains, and in the distance, the windmills that stood over their own familiar fields.

Here is the point, crucial in the life of every Nghsi-Altai citizen, where one says good-by to the old life and turns to the new, not without some pain. At the edge of the precipice, Venu took out a carton he had brought with him which contained the "four souls": bread, water, earth, and a sample in a bottle of the air of their native Sawna neighborhood. These he loosed into the Rift, for the Place Spirits. Then he and his wife turned. From a perforated locket around her neck, Sathan drew out a striped caterpillar. With a prayer she placed this on a forest leaf. Now it would go into its resting stage, and break from its chrysalis in a few weeks to become a monarch butterfly. This ceremony marked the start of their pilgrimage.

Beyond the canyon rim the Drune forest begins. For the first day the road ran in a cutting between the trees following a railroad bed. At intervals there are intersections of railroads, and trading settlements. Here one began to see the Mois. On the road also they met Thays, the children in furs bound on the travois sledges. As they passed, the Harditt children saluted them.

The last railroads had gone. After the small forest cantonment of Oodagoodooga, the road became a trail. The leaf cover of the great trees came together over their heads. But here the trees were primeval, and there were spaces in between every so often where the sun filtered through and there were flowers. It was their first trip away from the commune. At night they pitched camp, the children sleeping in a tent, and Sathan and Venu on the ground in a sleeping bag.

They had never made love to each other alone before. Venu had slept with other women in the fields. But with his clan wife, with Sathan when he had the urge, he had come to the common quarters from the men's club, found her among the sleeping forms, and made love to her briefly before orgasm.

Here they were alone under the sleeping leaves. Their sex play lasted a long time, and it was tender. The massiveness of her response excited him. They slept in each other's embrace. And in the morning when they awoke and looked into each other's eyes, the novelty of this struck them, they were almost ashamed.

The children brought them gifts from the woods. Maddi and Dhillon brought snails. Srikant, the oldest boy, was now six. Everything he found in the wood delighted him. He was up at dawn, and arrived each breakfast with a new kind of shining beetle or berry. They proceeded farther into the drune.

Gradually the ground ascended, and the hardwood forest gave way to conifers. They met fewer Thays and more Deodars on the trail. By the fifth day they had arrived at the Drune cantonment of Egwegnu.

At this point the narrator paused to fill the pipe with bang, a habit he had picked up from the shamans. "What is Egwegnu?" Alvarez asked.

Blake replied: "It is a lake city, the seat of the great ecological university."

"And what is that?" Jack Kerouac asked. "The tale is fascinating—and improbable."

But the seer had had enough of storytelling for the evening. They relapsed into smoking their hookah. Blake and the novelist pulled alternately on the ivory stem attached through a long tube to the transparent chamber, and watched the water bubble.

AN ACCIDENT ON THE HIGHWAY

The travelers have learned of the death of Kerouac. This misfortune occurred several days after Blake's recounting of the second half of his "Insect Pilgrimage" story.

The event, totally unexpected, has cast a shadow over the expedition.

The two were informed by the authorities of the regional panchayat that their friend had been "the victim of a highway accident" and that this had involved a bullock cart. But could Kerouac's death have been merely accidental, as it was claimed?

In the interview at the panchayat headquarters they had been given a good many circumstantial facts, without conclusions. Unfortunately there had been no eyewitnesses on the road that day, which was normally well traveled.

From the details furnished, the two men were able to reconstruct what had happened—or what had probably happened—piecing the story together with their own assessment of the novelist's character and inclinations.

Kerouac was traveling by himself along the route leading from Dhabar Jat to Sawna when he came upon a cart pulled up at the side of the road with a lone driver. This struck him as strange because in Nghsi such a cart would usually have a crew to do the unloading.

The wagon was full of grain sacks. Kerouac struck up a conversation with the driver. The man appeared distraught and kept looking back at his load, which increased the novelist's suspicions.

Then it occurred to Kerouac that he had seen the man some months before at a wedding in Rampur. It had been in a courtyard with a canopy overhead. Around the fire the bride circled the prescribed seven times. In fact the man had been the bridegroom. The face of the child bride was unseen, and as she went around, hidden by the thick veil, Kerouac had noticed the man and been struck by his look of heavy sensuality. The man, who was middle-aged, had been somewhat drunk.

Somehow this look had increased Kerouac's own erotic feelings.

This was the fourteenth stage of the marriage cycle, in between the steps of Bida and Gaur. Therefore the man would already have spent some months living in the bride's house.

Now on the highway, the man did not want to talk with Kerouac and in fact lashed the bullock so it would go on.

Kerouac leaped on the back of the cart and began rummaging through the sacks. Sometime later he was found dead by people in a procession passing that way to market. The body had been crushed. It appeared that the cart had been driven over it.

Blake and the filmmaker discussed at some length this possible scenario. They had been present with Kerouac at the wedding, and had also noticed the behavior of the middle-aged bridegroom.

It occurred to them to wonder to what extent the death was unavoidable, or was simply the result of the novelist's curiosity.

The man was later apprehended for the murder of his wife. They had learned he had been on his way to dispose of the body, hidden under the grain sacks.

Only a week before this tragedy Kerouac had been sitting with Blake and Alvarez in the baithak, watching the pipe smoke coil as he listened to Blake's story.

It is unlikely that he had any premonition. And to what extent for the citizens of Altai, that is for the inhabitants of the country, was this death "real"?

The two remember him as he leaned against the post of the bunk, his head tangled in the mosquito netting.

BLAKE'S STORY CONTINUED: THE LIGHTS FESTIVAL

Egwegnu is the largest of the great Drune ecological universities. The period of study, initiated by what is called the "insect pilgrimage," lasts for six months. Tuition is subsidized by the confederacy, and couples come from all over the country of Nghsi-Altai. As the pilgrimage is made traditionally on the tenth year of marriage, the age range of the students is from about twenty-three to thirty years.

Again Venu and Sathan found themselves among people from the plains, and among city people as well. The couple was assigned to a point house. These combine dormitory apartments for the married students with laboratories and study rooms. The cluster of tall buildings of black metal and glass covered a promontory jutting out into the lake. Across the shine of water, they looked down on roofs of Egwegnu town obscured under dark trees.

Each apartment is equipped with a small kitchen where supper and breakfast are prepared. Or meals may be sent up by elevator from the dorm kitchen. The children of the students are taken care of by the cantonment, and are "adopted" by a Drune family during the day, returning to the apartment only in the evenings or on week ends.

Thus during this interval the young couples are free of cares, much as the university students in the West. No hard labor in the fields. No child-rearing duties. Solitude, quiet. The university means a break in the lives of these individual couples, a resting period and a relaxation from the pressures of tight communal living. As a matter of fact there is even a clinic in the dormitory where psychiatric counseling is offered to individuals suffering from the stresses of "overcommunalization." An interesting idea.

During the first months at Egwegnu students are required to take general courses. These, which are held in the open, are called Meditations and are the same for everyone. After that the student is expected to concentrate on some aspect of an environmental study having to do with his own geographic area.

The lecturers are the Deodars, the great "blue" shamans of Nghsi-Altai. It is said that they were the original people when the land was covered by forests, and that they invented the first musical and scientific instruments—in particular the sensor devices used in the weather and soils laboratories.

"Could you tell us what one of these meditations is like?" Alvarez had asked.

Blake gave the following account:

A LECTURE UNDER THE TREES

We are in a forest university, in a "lecture hall" under the trees listening to the famous Deodar lecturer, Totuola. An exceedingly tall man, with protruding shoulder blades. He is in his own flesh, the mark of priesthood.

The subject of this particular series of lectures has been "City Weather" and certain aspects of the recycling process. Totuola's talk is accompanied by slides. The slides, from a carousel or control console at the back behind the crowd, are projected simultaneously on ten screens hanging from the branches of trees.

Sun slants into the clearing. There is a slight rise toward the back (where the projector is located). The students sit at the lecturer's feet on the ground covered with pine needles.

The Deodar shows the slides. In one hand he holds a South Asian oboe which he uses as a pointer. From time to time—at the end of some difficult passage—he will blow on it, a long drawn-out dreamy single note, or several staccato jabs of varying pitches. This is to "dispel logical thought sequences" and "to concentrate the spirit" of the listener.

The following are some of Totuola's "thought sparks" (or koans) jotted down by one of the listeners at random.

1. Every breath out is heavier than the breath taken in. What is the exchange?

*

2. The water cycle: Ocean ———→ to water vapor ———→ to windy rain ———→ to the rivulet feeding the Rampaging Red River.

*

3. Don't ask the atom smasher to recycle life.

*

4. If you want to comprehend the oyster you have to study salt water.

*

5. No individual without a commune.

*

6. The sovereign territory of Nghsi-Altai:
4 x 10^{13} quanta Energy (solar radiation)/sq. ft./sec.
The wealth of Nghsi-Altai:
79.11% Nitrogen—20.96% Oxygen—.003% CO^2/cu. ft.
of fresh air
The frontiers of Nghsi-Altai:
below 0° ice/above 100° steam

*

7. The holy man subjugates himself to the natural.

*

8. Learn to wind the clock before you take it apart.

*

9. Lake Erie died, January 1955—April 1968.

*

10. Man is not a geological force.

*

11. The soil cycle: Weathering of minerals ——→ Tunneling of the earth by earth worms ——→ Decay of butterflies ——→ men/giant lycopods (from the Mesozoic) —→ Potassium and phosphorus deposits
At the end of each tiny root hair colonies of nitrogen-fixing bacteria

*

12. The hawk is the scavenger.

*

13. The earth is 5 billion years old: inhabit it. Life is 1 billion years old: revere it. A strong sneeze will blow away 40,000 years of topsoil.

*

14. The louse travels in the feathers of birds.

*

15. A good astronomer collects ants.

*

16. If you come on a one-dimensional system look for decadence.

*

17. The carbon (breath) cycle:

plants (in the presence of light)

$6CO_2 + 5\ H_2 \longrightarrow C_6H_{10}0_5 + 6\ 0_2$

$\longleftarrow$

animals

*

18. Four carbon bonds allow infinite complexity.

*

19. Go naked / walk with the leopard / carry a transistor radio.

*

20. Remake the prairie soil twice a century (lightning, fires, etc.).

*

21. The cell maintains an open steady state.
The city maintains an open steady state.

*

22. If all the world were a supermarket the study of limits would be unnecessary.

*

23. A sweet soil is the result of many cataclysms.

*

24. The three great earth cycles: circulation of water/ formation of soil/purification of air

The two great Festival Cycles: Savanni (dry)Sarhi (wet)

*

25. Gas penetrates / water dissolves / the membrane holds

*

26. Which of these two is the more complex:

an LCM (landing craft module)?

a milkweed pod?

i.e. has more operating parts?

*

27. The dry dandelion will float to the moon.

*

28. Express all natural resources as constants, including the population constant.

*

29. It is dangerous to interfere with spontaneous arrangements.

*

30. Power within nature: ecology

Power outside of nature: the shamans

"Those are beautiful," Kerouac had said. "And I see what you mean by the miraculous—as a quality of experience. Or of *possible* experience."

Alvarez asked: "What happened to our students? Did they graduate? Did Sathan and Venu return home?"

The story continued:

A week before graduation the two students were sitting in their guardian's study atop the Point House. Tattattatha, the young Deodar who had been assigned to them, was standing at the window. He was describing the coming Lights Festival. It would be celebrated on the lake at night. From the shore people would watch the "spirit boats."

The walls of the apartment were bare white without the woven prayer mandalas which one often finds in the cantonments. Here and there were sprigs of bamboo. A bunch of wheat stalks in a fired pot. The bright day, reflected from the surface of the lake, flooded through the open windows and made the white of the walls more intense.

The young tutor sat naked. In the light, the blue of his skin was intensified. An enormous thatch of kinky black hair crowned his face, in which a bow was tied. A leopard slept at his feet.

"So now you will go back to the old life," Tattattatha addressed them. "And I will go to the new." Their tutor would return to the plains with them to serve for the next year as the sensor at the Sawna Weather and Soils Station.

He asked them what they had learned during their "free" period.

Venu wondered whether they should not have come earlier, when they had been in their teens. Would it not have been better then? He felt his brain had been dulled by hard work and that he would have made a better student before the years of working as a cowherd and farmer, and before the cares of bringing up a family.

Sathan said, "We must obey the cycles."

Tattattatha sat at rest. The light wavered on the ceiling.

The guardian gazed at Venu.

"Wind Brother," he said, "your clan and phratry are guided by the weather. The atmosphere in all its aspects has been your study here. You have mastered the sky currents."

He turned to Sathan, whom he called "Moon Sister." "And your tribe's part among the Six Tendencies of Altai is mathematics and planning. So you have mastered cybernetics and have made a computer model of Venu's patch of sky. You have taken your insect wings together in this life phase."

"Now I must ask you: the sky and a region of the earth make a habitat, a biome. A biome is a living organism that exists within certain limits. Outside those it is dead, isn't that so?"

"Life is fragile."

"Well, ecology is the study of the web of life. And history, in a sense, is the study of breakdown—of the errors and diseases disintegrating the web. Civilizations have died of their mistakes. Now, would you say there is any such thing as a sentimental education?"

"No," Venu answered. "It has to be about truth."

"And the truth is, you have come here to be useful and good citizens. Not for individual development and expansion of consciousness. You have discovered your individuality. And with it an increased spirituality. But it's best not to overrate these things. Remember what the lecturer says: 'No individual without the commune.' "

"What do you mean, civilizations have died of their mistakes?" Sathan asked him.

"Through good, they have exceeded themselves and gone in the wrong direction. In the same way there are misdirections of love. During this Insect Pilgrimage, you have discovered sexual love; and you must not abuse it, but return it to the Commune. In the same way your studies must be directed back to the commune . . ."

That evening they went to the cantonment park. It was by the lake. Sathan and Venu strolled through it, along with many couples, walking arm in arm. On the benches under the lamplight a few of the students were reading books, and in the shadows couples embraced or laughed softly. Venu could feel the movement of Sathan's hips under her kurtah. On the lawn a quartet was playing Mozart. At the entrance to the park was a statue, an angel with a sword. On this was inscribed: "The Fruit of This Garden Is Forbidden. Taste It."

Inscribed on the opposite gate was: "Your Paradise Has Been Lost."

* *

At the end of each term period there is what is called the Lights Festival. Students take samples of whatever they have been working on in the lab—leaves, grains, soils, etc.—plus strands of their own hair and photographs of themselves. This is mixed with clay and formed into pots. Broken old pottery of former students, found on the shore, is also used. On the evening of the Lights Festival, these vessels are launched. When the moon rises, each couple places its boat on the lake, and floats it out, with a paper lantern burning in it. The lights drift out over the surface. And the children are allowed to throw stones at them and sink them. This is called: chrysalis-breaking. It is the end of the first life phase.

With the others at Egwegnu, Venu, Sathan, and the three children—Srikant, Maddi, and Dhillon—did this, participating in the rites. The next day they left the Drune cantonment for Sawna, their native village, accompanied by the young sensor.

END OF BOOK I

GAHR CITY

To Mary Perot Nichols, Stanley Isaacs,
Stanley Tankels, and Jane Jacobs

IN THE DOLDRUMS

We have been here a year. The time hangs heavy. But there is no time. A wheel of seasons.

We have a new member of our Explorers' Party.

Jack Kerouac's death was extremely painful to us. But we have learned to do without him.

The people expressed their regrets. But soon after they seemed to abandon us to the chores of housekeeping in our baithak. Which is none too comfortable.

Alvarez is the active one. He manages a kind of official contact with the ganbus and is sent off on agricultural duties with one of the work sections.

One day we ran—quite by accident—into our third companion, William Morris. A rucksack on his back he stood in the Makers' Square with a guidebook. He had been examining the solar furnace in the blacksmith's shop and was much taken with it.

Regrettably Morris (another associate of The People's Voice), who had been scheduled to be sent with the original team, was blackballed by Alvarez. On the flimsy ground that Morris was a utopian and his naive brand of Christian socialism might prove a political liability.

We have abandoned our criticism/self-criticism sessions.

Meanwhile we have slipped into the habit of using the word "we" in the journal that is kept jointly. Is it that we are any less individuals? Perhaps not. On the other hand there is a common wave band, a range of vibrations, through which "Western eyes" see Nghsi-Altai.

So it is the local inhabitants who have defined the explorers.

• •

We have learned only one of the languages of Altai. But there are so many.

Sometimes the children come to visit us. It is easy to attract them with candy. On the other hand they prefer their own sweets—millet grains roasted in brown sugar. However, they are permitted this only on holidays.

Our expedition has been based here on the plains. That is limiting. We have been excluded from the other biomes—for what reason it is unclear. Long ago we applied for passports, but these were denied. Only Blake has made a short trip to the Drune forest. The Drybeds we have not seen, though this area is reputed to be the most advanced. Alvarez in particular is anxious to inspect the anarcho-syndicalist unions there.

It is mostly Morris who enjoys playing with the children. A knack. There was a time when the matriarchs tutored us (in Jat), encouraging us to open up, then laughing at our mistakes. Now we no longer make mistakes. Or they have other things to do than listen to us—notably refining and storing sugar.

Alvarez gives out proudly that he has been assigned to a county works project, after "meritorious service" cutting cane. Yet he is not as close to the ganbus as he would like. And he is beginning to sour on them. They are not as progressive as he first thought.

Blake has improved his playing the gusle. Joking, he says "it goes with the beard." But he has been drinking.

The meteorology station predicts that the rains are coming.

• •

Assauj (Sept.-Oct.)

A dreary day. Monsoon season is full upon us. The world is soaked. At four o'clock every afternoon the skies open as in a sluice, roads and landmarks are obliterated, the village becomes a sea of mud. Rain drums on the roof tiles. But our baithak is tight, though dark. No light through the straw shutters, and we sit huddled on the bamboo floor smarting from the flies that swarm up from below, from the cattle stalls.

Where has the time gone? We have spent several years here; can we say we have come any closer to an understanding of these people? They remain opaque to us, as is the landscape fogged by rain. They *resist* comprehension.

The original goal of our expedition: Discovering Nghsi-Altai. What a mockery the words seem. The deeper one goes into it, the more mysterious it becomes.

For a time we have seen little of Blake. He has been away visiting the sensor at the Soils and Weather Station. He returns at night, sometimes followed by Tattattatha's black leopard, which curls up on the bunk.

But today Blake is with us: the monsoon has confined him. He seems extremely lethargic . . . too much pulque . . . or can he have gotten a touch of malaria?

• •

Blake has been practicing solemnly on his gusle. He strikes the strings mournfully as if to resonate them against the rain, and he asks us if we'd like to hear a composition.

"By all means, sing it," Morris encourages him. "What is it called?"

"It's called 'The World of Nowhere.' "

Blake sings:

"No matter where you start
This world remains a place apart
Nothing to find here after your own heart.

"Everywhere your foreign eye,
Your foreign ear, no matter how they try

Catch no familiar gestures in reply.

"The people here pursue,
Even if its miracles you do,
A close serenity that puzzles you.

"As for the countryside,
So many trees brush your glance aside
Your greedy heart must go unsatisfied.

"Only, perhaps, across an opening lake
Some traveled echo of the search you make
Will send you homeward for perfection's sake.

"Be sure, this world of nowhere will expel
All who seek here a chance outlandish spell
That any place could offer just as well"

"A sad song, but appropriate. When did you compose it?"

"It's by a colleague of mine on Parnassus. Allan Hodges, English, twentieth-century."

"I don't like it all; it's too negative," Alvarez comments. Lacing up his boots, he stalks out.

"Of course the rhyme is a drawback. After the seventeenth-century nothing was quite right," Blake confided. "Would you like to hear another? This one is not mine either. It's called 'Europe,' by a Polish contemporary. Alas, I have forgotten his name."

Strumming the gusle, Blake sings a second song.

O EUROPE

O Europe is so many borders,
on every border, murderers.
Don't let me weep for the girl
who'll give birth two years from now.

Don't let me be sad because
I was born a European.
I, a brother of wild bears,
wasting away without my freedom.

I write poems to amuse you.
The sea has risen to the cliffs,
and a table, fully laid,
floats on foam among the clouds.

"So there you are," Morris agrees. "We are *between* worlds, the old and the new. And the borders of the one are as closed to us as the other."

The tonic of rhyme seems to have revived Blake. He adds lightheartedly, "But though the past is gone, we are still writing poems, and offer you still: A table fully laid/floating among the clouds . . ."

Alvarez returns with good news. He has been to the panchayat headquarters and has come to tell us our passports for the "closed biome" have finally come through. Our itinerary has been approved, and we are to leave for Garh City in three days.

So perhaps this signals a break in the weather.

ENTRY INTO GARH CITY

At the invitation of the Planning Ministry we have come to visit Garh. After a short trip across the plains, we arrived last night at the transportation node. Descending by skip (electric cable car) into the Rift canyon, we were plunged at once into the excitement and fervor of the big city.

The glare. A barrage of noise. Buildings of unexpected structure and function crowding the narrow area between the cliffs, connected by raised passageways. Everything compact, enormously compressed, "miniaturized." Yet they say this is a city of three million. An expanse of water in a canal is illuminated under a neon sign, lights flash on and off, the metabolism of urban movement, traffic. As the skip glided over the submerged rooftops, a tower loomed on our right. Within the steel frame was a cylinder of shifting, multicolored light, like a giant cathode tube.

Our guide informed us it was a "synerg" or public art object. "It registers the energy state of the city at a given moment—traffic flow, heat, number of telephone calls, air composition index, even demographic information. The data comes in from the stations, is absorbed cybernetically, and emitted as light signals."

There are no streets, no automobiles in Garh. Pedestrian and bicycle paths, called "meanders," wind through this inexplicable city. Rapid transit is by canals, which form the right of way for three kinds of traffic: boat, rail, and the ubiquitous air taxis.

We were taken with our luggage in one of these and soon reached a small hostel which is run by Intourist. It is to be our headquarters during our stay here.

A SWIM WITH ANARCHO-SYNDICALISTS

This morning we visited an anarcho-syndicalist club in the Third Ward. It is housed in a large building which contains a meeting hall, libraries, and data bank, and also health and recreation facilities. Here we were introduced to a number of Karst foremen. Unlike the Jat ganbus, who are inclined to be stiff, these talked to us readily.

Alvarez had been delighted to learn that the motto of the syndicalist unions here is "BEYOND SOCIALISM."

We were invited to take a swim in the pool before lunch.

"Do you swim well?" one of them asked. Alvarez, the activist, assented. Morris looked at him skeptically.

"Don't worry. We'll take good care of him in the water."

We were taken to the lockers, where we gave our clothes to a club attendant and started for the pool. One of our hosts stopped us.

"Wait. You've given him your money."

"I don't see how I'm going to take it with me," Blake growled. "Unless I'm to stick it up my arse."

"No, you'll be issued a pouch." We returned to the screened counter.

"Never trust a Karst. We Karsts make it a point of honor never to trust each other," we were told with a wink. In this way we were ushered naked toward the pool, with nothing on but our money belts like the rest of them.

The atrium of this workingmens' club is an airy space, under a high plexiglass dome. Forest trees in enormous pots cool and freshen the air. We were told the balconies cantilevered out from the sides contained restaurants and small sports arenas.

The pool was situated at the center of the space. On one side was the gymnasium. Here sweating Karsts were lifting weights, wrestling, and boxing. A group in toweled bathrobes sat in wicker chairs ranged in front of what appeared to be a teletype screen. "They are following the frontón game upstairs. Those are betting figures."

We were told that the insignia on the bathrobes indicated these were "Construction and Wrecking" workers.

Against the walls of the baths of veined and striated marble, the skin of the bathers glistened. There were only a few Deodars and Jats, the hue of their skins a cold blue and a warm chocolate respectively. The Karsts were a glaring white and somewhat translucent. All Karsts are albinos and have an unpigmented skin and startlingly pink eyes. They are of medium stature and have a curious barrel-like physique without extremities. No ankles or neck. The head seems to protrude directly from the torso. Their hands, which have a yellow palm stain and are webbed, stick directly out of their forearms like paddles.

In contrast our own band must have presented a bizarre spectacle. We were all painfully self-conscious. Alvarez like a small pugilist was the pinkest, with flaming ears. William Morris stooped and tried to be self-effacing—like all uncommonly tall men. He has ruddy skin and fine, rather pampered hands. Blake, with a long lumpy cock, is absolutely cadaverous. He stood with all of his ribs showing. We were all heavily mustached and bearded, whereas the Karsts and Jats are hairless.

However, none of the syndicalists paid us the slightest attention.

The pool seethed with swimmers. A game of water polo was in progress, pursued with utmost ferocity.

As Blake hawked up a cough which he disposed of in the scum gutter, Alvarez began dancing up and down on his toes and jabbing as if he were shadowboxing.

"Well, brother, are you ready to take the plunge?" one of the foremen asked him. And before he was able to answer gave Alvarez a violent push into the pool.

The Cuban was engulfed in the melée.

After a second he surfaced. His head popped out but was immediately grappled by a woman player. Caught in a headlock between her knees, he was submerged again. The scrimmage passed over them both.

Blake cried: "Good lord, save him somebody. He'll drown."

"Oh that comrade will take care of himself. He's spunky."

"They're only roughing him up a little."

The two surfaced. The wave of polo players moved on again. The filmmaker was pulled from the pool and lay on the tiles panting.

Our hosts gathered around him highly pleased. They kept congratulating him, shouting down at him: "SPRECCIA! SPRECCIA!" This is the highest compliment in the city. It means "spontaneous."

HOW WASTE IS HANDLED

There are no words in the Nghsi-Altaian languages for "waste," "rubbish"—everything is included under various aspects of recycling. Thus the system of waste disposal is called "urban mining," or alternatively "urban farming." In large measure this furnishes the basic materials for industry. Even the layout of the city into wards or geographical districts is determined by it.

We were taken to one of these wards to see the system in operation.

First we visited the superblocks—clusters of dormitories and work places. Within each of these a number of contractors handle the disposal business: that is, collect rubbish from door to door (paying a good price for it) and also heavier jobs, then conveying it to the reprocessing depots. Work here is divided into four operations:

Cannibal Shop. For worn-out appliances and machines (refrigerators, communal T.V.'s, solar cooking units, etc.). These are repaired for block consumption, or salvageable parts are removed (cannibalized) and returned to the appropriate manufacturer.

Scrap Heap. In this section bulk materials are handled, with equipment for magnetic sorting, shredding and grinding, bailing, etc. Material is compressed hydraulically into standard shapes, then encased in concrete, steel, asphalt, or plastic. These are sold to the building industry. Broken glass and crockery are also reprocessed here.

Juicing Room. Paper and textiles are treated chemically and reprocessed.

Composite Materials Lab. Here new structural materials are made from old. Various materials form the "matrix": polyethelene, glass, nickel-chromium, ceramics, lead. To these are added the "compositing elements": in the form of fibers, particles, laminae, flakes, fillers, etc. Machine parts, plywoods, honeycomb structures are produced here.

In one lab, an engineering artel was making a multidimensional "organic" composite (Thornel 50) of graphite fibers embedded in epoxy resins. This is a high-strength metal substitute used for gas pipe. Yet the process is simple: the graphite fibers are produced by carbonization of rayon filaments. To be precise, by burning discarded stockings.

Blake conversed with a group of workmen in the Juicing Room, engaged in producing paper. The rag paper struck him as of good quality. He was pleased that they knew something of the process of engraving.

We stood at the door of the Composite Materials Lab at the end of our tour. Alvarez struck up a conversation with some of these "urban miners." He complimented them on the orderliness and what he called the "rationality" of the system.

"Yes. And there seems to be considerably less waste," Morris added. "Where are all the cans and cardboard boxes?"

Alvarez hazarded the explanation that in a nonmarket, regional economy there would be less need for advertising and transportation, and that this would reduce packaging.

The workers did not respond, apparently not understanding "packaging."

The following day we were given another demonstration: in the treatment of liquid wastes. There are two recycling systems. In the first are grouped processes having to do with cleaning and oxygenating the canals. The second, the "closed" system, deals with sewerage disposal and is referred to simply as "urban farming." The following are the steps in this chain:

Every ward has its truck farms. The vegetable produce supplies the neighborhoods and is also sold commercially on the free market. In Jat neighborhoods there are also roof farms.

These products are consumed; the waste (fecal matter, urine) is pumped back to the farm area into settling lagoons. Here it is treated by bacterial action. Many types of bacteria are "raised" and in fact cultivated for specific functions.

From the lagoons the inert sludge is settled out, bagged, and used in soil conditioning. The effluent, rich in soil nutrients, is returned to the farms by a process of spray irrigation. The cycle repeats itself.

WE MEET UP WITH AN ARTEL

We are in a town square. Bands are playing. A speakers' platform from which oratory reverberates over the loudspeakers. An answering roar, armwaving and dancing by the population. Around peoples' shoes pigeons are scavenging crumbs.

In the Rift, politics seems to be a national game.

We are wedged up against the speakers' platform, the populace at our backs identified with the flags of the localities. The Syndicates and Communal Commandos are represented. They are wearing armbands of different kinds. A cheer bursts from the throats of a band of teenagers.

As the rally breaks up we merge with the crowd as it streams out by the streets leading from the square.

After a quarter of an hour we cross a bridge. We are with one group, so it appears. The surge of people at our backs carries all of us along.

"Well, what was that all about?" Blake asked an older man.

We learn that it is a "seasonal demonstration."

If there is a further question it is unanswered. A vaporetto passes under the bridge at that moment and the steam, amplified under the trestle, makes a deep puffing sound. Then the canal boat emerges, its waves gently rocking the embankment.

The paraders are passing through a different ward, consisting of lofty superblocks. The street rises to a higher level. On both sides are the stores of Karsts.

The festival crowd has thinned considerably. The streets of this section are not full. There are no longer cafes or luxury shops, only local shoppers. The seasonal demonstration is far behind us.

Our own group to which we have attached ourselves are Karsts. All are dressed alike, including the women: buff or green short-sleeved jackets, shorts, and wooden sabots. There seems to be no differentiation among them except size. They walk at the same pace. But as we go on, several engage us in conversation. Blake, however, is uncommunicative.

Our straggling band of marchers turns into a lane between concrete walls as the street lights come on. The group keeps on silently with an air of letdown.

The narrow lane of the meander passes a series of juicing depots. We walk along in the line, no one seeming to notice us, or at least paying any particular attention.

However, as the meander comes out on a brightly lighted square with shops, the animation returns—they shout slogans led by the older cadre.

Our leader is a large man by the name of Bang. We learn that they were all from the same "Big Family/Little Family" group and are heading home to their own superblock.

Finally we arrive at another square. We stop before the burghall. It has begun to rain. We are invited in to dry ourselves and to have some warm ale.

A SPEECH TO THE COMMONS

Alvarez has gone several times to the burghall, which turns out to be called Red Cats. The place is both a restaurant and a meeting hall for the neighborhood Commons.

After our meeting with the artel in the square, we were anxious to become better acquainted with them. We went to the Red Cats one evening at Alvarez' urging.

The restaurant was open to the street, and there were cafe tables on the sidewalk under an awning. Beyond on a cobbled square a small band was playing, and acrobats were performing in a desultory manner for coins.

We entered to the usual amount of noise, which we have got used to in Garh. Orders for food were being shouted over peoples' heads. There was the clatter of dominoes and the added din of wooden shoes over the sawdust floor. They do not take them off in this public area. But what area here is not public?

"Big Bang," as he is called, was surrounded by cronies. The table was covered with beer mugs and plates of blood sausage. Our friend, who had been rattling a dice-box, stood up to greet us, extending his paddlelike arms.

"Welcome, citizens. Join us."

He and Alvarez gave each other the fraternal embrace, which consists of first shaking hands, then kissing each other on both cheeks and patting each other on the back, then shaking hands again.

"Yes, sit down. Draw up chairs. We're now in closed session here at Red

Cats, but soon you'll have the treat of seeing an open session of the Commons."

We sat with them for the space of a half hour.

We were mystified as to who precisely the "Commons" were.

The room was filled with confabulating men and women, and even children. The superblock to which our artel friends belonged was having an informal meeting in preparation for the Assembly which was to be held the following week.

Big Bang was evidently a person of some importance—in a room filled with others of importance. People kept coming up to Bang and addressing him as "citizen," bending down and whispering in his ear, embracing him in an effusive salute. Or someone would approach in a more deferential manner and say, So-and-so sends respects.

For a Karst, the leader was particularly slablike. A bald head, which he seldom moved, rested on rolls of fat welling up from his shirt front. He seldom used his arms either, preferring to make a point by heaving up his chest. His eyes were kindly and his skin mottled. He looked like some old seal.

Throughout the room, other clusters of tables also had their chiefs, a number of them women. Women like the men chewed tobacco, particularly when arguing. Spittoons were placed between the tables, so that during debates these areas were in cross fire. There was a barrage of flying tobacco juice.

Bang circulated among the tables.

We heard the word "factions" repeated a number of times.

More trays of blood sausage were ordered.

A waiter squeezed by among the tables holding up a black board on which a list of items was written in chalk. At first we took it to be the menu. But it was a list of political items on the agenda for the Assembly.

The chief interest of our table appeared to be an addition to the municipal waterworks which was to come up.

Occasionally amid the rattling of dice and the clattering of dominoes, tempers flared on this question of the water works—or possibly it was some other issue. A small Karst ferociously playing darts in the corner made an impassioned challenge to the faction at our own table. We learned that this was "Short Wang," an inveterate opponent of Big Bang's.

During his attack, Wang choked with indignation, spat and clumped with his shoes on the floor.

This orator received applause. Several of the other table even threw potatoes into the air. But there were some boos. Apparently the majority of the room was with our own faction.

The debate continued. Bang, leaning over to Alvarez whispered: "I think we have them."

There appeared to be a general pleasure at our table for all the orators —even when they were opposing the Bang faction. The orators marshaled sensible arguments—at least judging from the faces of the hearers. However, some local characters when they stood up met with catcalls and guffaws, no matter what they said. Evidently, they were known—and not to be taken seriously on any point.

Curiously, these were the people who spoke most vehemently.

This part of the program appeared to be a kind of screening process. No votes were taken. Yet the citizens did not seem to be making any effort to achieve a consensus either.

The point of the closed session appeared to be to explore conflicting points of view and develop opposing speakers, the more opposed the better.

It was approaching ten. The brass and percussion band playing in the plaza subsided by slow degrees; first the trombones and tubas, then the cymbals and French horns, leaving only the drums to accompany the gyrations of the acrobats. Gradually these stopped as well. The sidewalk diners began to shift their attention to what was happening inside.

Tables were pushed together, clearing a space in the center of the hall. A crew of television men began setting up its equipment.

Bang and the citizen known as Short Wang took seats in the center, assuming a dignified manner, their position "on camera" being arranged by the T.V. men. Both wore carnations in their buttonholes, we were told, so that these Red Cats speakers could be distinguished on television. There was also some posing of the crowd itself. The folk were not to be left out of the picture. Everyone appeared excited, and somewhat self-conscious.

A communications system connected this burghall with the others in the locality, known as the Redhook section. There were about ten neighborhoods or superblocks represented by the diners in the restaurants. Together and connected by T.V., these made up what was known as the Commons—now in session.

A screen had been set up from floor to ceiling. This was at first blank, then showed the synerg winking over the city skyline, evidently a signal. Around the main screen was a border of smaller screens. Framed in these appeared the gatherings in the other burghalls. Faction chiefs also were seated among their supporters, prominent with their boutonieres. As neighbors appeared and as familiar figures were recognized by the Red Cats, these elicited amusement and ridicule.

Our own group appeared in one of the side frames. When the light was on over this, Red Cats was on camera; that is, occupied the center screen throughout the whole system. (The system is called a "multicom.")

What followed was a wide-ranging exploration, and cross-discussion, of the issues that were to be on the agenda for the forthcoming Assembly. Differences on the items were ventilated. But here again we noticed they were in no particular hurry to press on to conclusions. For our own burghall, Bang appeared to represent the majority point of view, and Wang the minority; but both speakers behaved with more dignity than before. During the course of the debate—after the major speaker had made a point with especial eloquence—there was prolonged applause throughout all the Commons. Bang was presented with an umbrella, which he accepted but did not open.

Naturally, the times when our own speakers were on proved most interesting to the Red Cats. There was a period open to the floor. Much to our enjoyment a number of children spoke, and also one of the street acrobats. In fact, any speaker was welcomed. We were not a little surprised, at one point, to see Alvarez on his feet telling of his own experience as a cameraman in Cuba "when popular communications technology was not so highly developed" and complimenting the assembly on "escaping from capitalist atomization and on their revolutionary leap forward."

A DIRECT ASSEMBLY: MORRIS' NOTES

Approach to the stadium. Crowds. A holiday atmosphere. The meatpie peddlers. Our friends have brought along a keg of beer.

The stadium of the Fourth Ward dominates this section of the city. A huge berm rises over the hustling and approaching crowds. Pennants wave over heads, balloons float in the clusters held by the hawkers. The earth berm is about a hundred meters high and covered with grass; an occasional blotch of heather. At the base are the escalator entrances. A press here. The throng crowds to get in. Cards are being punched: the folk hand their cards over to half a dozen or so uniformed young men, who I am told are members of the Dog Society.

To vote is obligatory for every citizen in this direct Assembly. If one doesn't attend, one pays a fine.

• •

Once on top of the berm we find outselves on a wide promenade where the crowd circulates in two directions, observing each other. The crowd has thinned out here somewhat. Excellent view over the rim. The city drops away in a jumble of roofs and construction derricks. At the skyline one can see the stadiums of the other wards.

Sandwichmen move among the crowd. I see an old face, bleary eyes without interest. Yet the sign proclaims the Calendar of Events with the principal speakers in attractive block lettering. One can also buy printed digests—they are called "guides," giving a tabulation of the preliminary voting on the agenda items by neighborhoods.

• •

Our friends from Red Cats have come prepared for a long stay. They have great quantities of food in wicker hampers and even a portable refrigerator, cookstove, wet weather gear in case it rains, sleeping bags. (Alvarez has already picked up our sleeping bags at Intourist.) When we ask them jokingly where they intend to pitch camp, they motion down below among the tiers of seats. In fact there are already tents pitched down below there.

• •

Below us on the inside lies the great bowl of the stadium. It is a quarter mile across at the top. Not oval as I had first thought but circular. It is divided into sections by ramps. The seat tiers descend sharply to a center forum. The space around this is grassed.

I would say the stadium seats upwards of eighty thousand.

The rows of seats do not rise uniformly from the center but are terraced. About every twentieth or thirtieth row there is a wider platform. Here at intervals there are structures whose domes shine like onionskins.

There are about a dozen of these within the stadium, which we learn later are "city halls." There is an open plaza around each; that is, the promenade widens here. Directly below the tiers of seats rise more sharply. Thus the terracing in the stadium is not uniform but contoured.

A feeling of the basic architecture here: is it derived perhaps from the rice terraces?

Groups of citizens in front of the domes are spreading out their sleeping bags. Elsewhere large sections of the bowl are empty.

• •

Bang's niece has brought us to see one of the information kiosks. A crowd is around it asking questions. The clerks are at a counter, like a railway station. The kiosk is octagonal in shape with screens on top which I at first took to be advertisements.

But the citizens' questions are of a technical nature. Kikan (the name of Bang's niece) explains the kiosk is a data bank. There is an index of subjects. With the help of the clerk one punches out one's question on the computer, and the answer appears up above on one of the screens.

We stand around Kikan—an attractive woman if somewhat self-assertive. To demonstrate the machine, she says: "What do you want to know? Ask it anything you like."

Blake says facetiously: "Tell me where is Fancy bred/or in heart, or in head?"

"No, it only has to do with subjects related to those coming up before the Assembly," Kikan replies sternly. "That kind of question isn't in the data retrieval system. You'll have to ask it something else."

The kiosks are surrounded by disputatious Karsts, arguing among themselves and pressing buttons.

• •

Alvarez has attached himself to Short Wang, who is prepared to address the Assembly. Wang will go down to the arena to join the long line of Commons' representatives who wish to argue some point or other. But first he must put his name on the waiting list and be given a number—his place on the speaker's calendar.

Meanwhile he struts around carrying a wicker hamper with a chicken in it which he will sacrifice to the Spirit of the Ward when his turn comes.

• •

Sporadic activity down in the arena, which we see far below. Acrobatic troupes of various neighborhoods are on display. Later in the day will come the principal teams of acrobats, those of the boroughs.

There have already been several votes, on the first items on the agenda presumably. These have elicited little interest among our own commoners. When a vote is announced, there is a call over the loudspeaker, which booms hollowly over the promenades. Then people go down and take their seats.

The voting procedure is as follows: If you wish to vote yes on a question, you stand up, wearing a green hat. When opposed—red. A simple and sensible method of mass counting.

Voting tabulation is done by sections; however, the sections don't vote as a block but by individuals. Thus one says, "The Firth was carried by one thousand hats."

• •

What is happening down there on the field? Considerable hoopla. The forum is filled, while below on the packed grass waits the line of prospective speakers.

It seems each faction chief has brought along his claque, consisting of private musicians and acrobats. Whenever a speaker is introduced a formation of drum majorettes wheels below the rostrum. Confetti is thrown up.

Can the band be playing Sousa? Squalls of applause drift up to us over the loudspeaker, but we hardly bother to watch these extravaganzas.

At night the public dances occur, performed by choruses of masked officials. But I have slept through two of these dance series already (in my Intourist sleeping bag) sufficiently exhausted by the day's excitement!

Politics as a tribal rite?

• •

A vote has been announced. Only a few moments afterward the tally is shown on the T.V. screens above the information kiosks. People applaud, munching hot dogs, a rucksack slung over the shoulder. And for some reason I am reminded of Aristophanes' description in *The Frogs* of the Athenian citizens coming to the Assembly with their "bottle of wine and three herrings."

Alvarez is contemptuous of the Athenian analogy. He suggests: Barcelona.

• •

In fact, the main action is not happening down there on the field—but up here, among the promenaders who are meeting, discussing, greeting old friends, etc.

Big Bang, as the Red Cats faction chief, seems to be at the center of this. The umbrella is unfurled at a certain point, which calls attention to him as one of Redhook's pre-selected floor leaders. One of the claque suspends the umbrella over Bang, while another holds the telephone by which he communicates with other chiefs. Both phone and umbrella are badges of office here. The telephone is used only for political purposes, there being strict penalties for private use.

• •

I note in these animated gatherings of people a general air of release, of expansiveness—everybody having been cooped up perhaps in their superblock apartments. I do not remember having seen any sizable parks or plazas throughout this city—in fact no public monuments.

So that possibly this stadium functions as THE public city space.

What is my purpose in being here? Why am I setting down these notes? My eye is for the surface; I have perhaps some talent for noting similarities, metaphors. But should an artist be interested in politics?

I think so. What politics stands in need of now is metaphor.

Images of the city? The scene vibrates between contradictions. *Can* there be such a thing as a direct Assembly in a city of upwards of four million people?

At the same time I feel delighted to be a part of all this. But am I a part?

• •

Observations on city size.

Garh made up of ten wards, each ward of three hundred and fifty thousand. A total of three and a half million. But it is hard to see much beyond this ward. It may be the stadium that gives this impression of a self-contained process. The whole city is concentrated here, as under a lens. This impression is false perhaps.

Below the ward level are the boroughs and the neighborhood Commons. The smallest unit the neighborhood: about six to eight thousand people; meets at the burghall.

Singly, the neighborhood political organization is "a commons." When several meet together as during the open T.V. session—they become "the Commons." We are from the Red Hook Commons, or borough. Perhaps the section of the stadium we are sitting in is the Red Hook section.

In fact this is the case. We are told we are sitting in the Red Hook section and are shown its insignia. In this stadium ten boroughs are represented, each of approximately fifty thousand people. Ten boroughs together make up a ward. It is the Assembly of the ward which meets in this stadium.

It is clear to us that the neighborhood authority meets in the burghall. But is there some political unit or intermediate governmental body corresponding to the borough? I have not heard of any. If this is so, why aren't the neighborhoods and their chiefs—small fish like Bang and Wang —submerged in the ocean of the Assembly?

With all this—in order to govern a city of three and a half million— there does not seem to be any system of popular representatives. Everything is by direct vote, and I must confess this is incomprehensible to me.

• •

Third day. Alvarez sticks close to Wang, the orator. I am more interested in Big Bang, who is cast in the role of clubhouse organizer or boss. Bang is at the center of everything, but says little. Most often he is at his seat in our section of the bleachers, on the telephone.

At all times he is surrounded by a crowd of vocal Red Cats—a permanent distraction. In the middle of a phone conversation he will look down at the floor and scrape his shoe, as if trying to collect his thoughts.

Suddenly he gets up and announces he is going to speak with another community chief personally. Or is he going to "city hall?" He starts out and makes his way slowly around the promenade. But in the space of a hundred steps he is interrupted a dozen times. Finally he gives up and returns to his seat.

The ceremonies which take place down in the arena dominate the action at times. They appear to bore Bang. He plays dominoes.

Blake is fascinated by the stage happenings. These are on the wooden stage or forum, called for some reason the "congress." He enjoys particularly the choric dance rehearsals, which he goes down to attend. He has come back this time with a ceremonial mask. Also an article of dress which he claims is "a senator's." But the senators operate mostly at night, so it seems. At the same time Blake complains of the crowds. "They are stiffling him."

• •

Oratory is highly prized in the Drybeds. People keep coming up to Short Wang and encouraging him. "Give 'em hell, Wang."

His time to speak has finally come. As he prepares himself, throwing his cloak around him, the chicken's head sticks out between the ribs of the hamper with fierce unblinking eyes. Then we watch the three of them go down—Wang, Alvarez, and the rooster—descending from tier to tier of the immense stadium—through the binoculars we have purchased at one of the kiosks.

But soon we lose them.

I am surprised to learn that Wang will speak in favor of the waterworks (which he previously opposed). The reason for this being, we are told: "discipline of the Commons."

• •

Some metaphors:

1. Contours of the stadium—the rice terraces

2. Political activities here—the Athenian Assembly (doesn't 2 contradict 1?)

A possible analogy between engineering system (one of recycling) and the political system: This stadium is like a wheel with its numerous groupings, sections, etc. I.e., power is not a structure, but a set of relations between groups which rotates. In fact we are told that the senators "are the senators of the Rotary Club."

Power rotates. With each issue, a different set of officials?

• •

Another vote has been called. This is announced over the loudspeaker, where we happen to be on the promenade gathered around Bang. Our cluster immediately breaks, and people rush to their seating section.

• •

The politics of water. In this semiarid metropolis there are certain interests to be balanced. In Garh energy demand (which is local) conflicts with transportation, a citywide requirement. Must this be resolved by the faction chiefs?

Because of the canals being tied in with the energy-generating system, there are so many uses of water—for cooling, electricity, reservoirs, etc. The element water itself seems to be altered—because it is something the citizens determine specifically as to use. I suppose if I were a citizen of Garh I would actually *see* "a glass of water" in a different way.

• •

Faces: In the Plains I was struck by the faces of some matriarchs. Here too in Garh certain citizens have a great air of authority about them—not only the cadre but ordinary commoners. Where does it come from I wonder?

The expression on these faces as if to say: "Nothing is delegated."

On the other hand are not these people—standing and palavering, and who are continually donning and taking off their green and red caps and munching sandwiches—somewhat ridiculous?

• •

I have now had a closer look at the city halls, those globe-like structures where the terraces widen. Each is about twenty meters high. My first guess had been that these were inflatable structures, the dome being covered by a light membrane. But no, they are permanent features of the stadium, and each contains a fully equipped amphitheater.

However, these are only in use during the day. At night the membrane retracts below the stadium surface.

• •

There appear to be television personalities in Garh. They are not stars of the entertainment world. Bang is in contact with one right now. Her name is Mrs. Zowie of the Flatbush borough. The face seen below an umbrella is sober. A wide, straight mouth gives the impression of frankness. Penetrating pink eyes, the white hair constrained under the peaked fatigue cap which is the ubiquitous insignia of the faction chief here. Suddenly after making a point Mrs. Zowie grins at us over the portable T.V. screen that Alvarez and I have clamped onto our seat. She comes in clear and inspires confidence—though I am told that Flatbush is pushing a proposal counter to ours.

• •

The fourth day.

We are told that the waterworks measure is coming up for a vote today. Bang is in an emotional state. He has spent half the night at the Redhook city hall whipping his borough supporters into line. From his seat command post he is in feverish communication with a score or so of his "fatigue caps" (community floor chiefs) in other parts of the stadium.

During each call he is surrounded by the local Red Cats gang, who keep giving him pointers. There is no letup. He appears exhausted.

• •

Apparently in the tangle of issues before the direct Assembly our own proposal is in difficulty. Our plan is for using the new canal to generate electricity (Bang and some of the Syndicate leaders want this for a processing plant). But this has run smack into another proposal: that of using the additional water for municipal swimming pools. Industrial growth is opposed to recreation. The health of the children is a charged issue. Mrs. Zowie has emerged as the children's champion.

• •

I have followed Bang into the Red Hook city hall. In the dark I make my way toward the back. The small amphitheater rises sharply on three sides. The stage is filled with shirt-sleeved men and women. I recognize some chiefs from the television debate and others who have conferred in the bleachers with Bang.

Cigar smoke hangs in the air. On stage are the inevitable spittoons.

Excellent acoustics, voices carry easily from the platform, one doesn't have to strain to listen inside this structure. Hence its popular name—the "speak chamber." The amphitheater seats about eight hundred.

Our chieftains are deep in formulating strategy—apparently to counter crippling amendments that have been added to the waterworks proposal. Bang, having disposed of a number of points, has now left the stage and taken a seat in the front row with some cronies.

A cry is raised: "Point of information. Point of information"—and a formal motion is made and passed for a film showing. This film is projected onto the stage so that it may be seen and debated in a manner similar to that of the Red Cats screening. Here the emphasis is less on personal style, and more technical. In fact every projection and statistic bearing on the waterworks alternatives may be laid out graphically. And with cybernetic controls, repeated at will. This is the same material available to the public at the kiosks. By now it has become boring.

Bang with his walrus hulk is on stage again, along with other figures from the Commons television debate. I am beginning to recognize a number of them. All wear their regalia. Each faction chief has pulled into the amphitheater several of his personal claque, though the musicians are without instruments. Colorful as they are, these floor managers will disappear into the crowd when other issues are up for debate, their rank abolished as they set aside their umbrellas.

I realize with a shock that there are *no* elected officials in Garh. At least not in this ward.

• •

The design of the structure of the city hall is interesting. On three sides the seats rise toward the back. At this point the supporting beams curve back in a sharp parabola and return to form the roof, where the trusses come together at the center. Here, in a kind of architectural feature or "boss," is suspended the communications control booth. The setup is similar to the multicom of the burghalls. The control projects the information and also brings onto the center screen, or onto those along the side frames, scenes of what is occurring in other parts of the stadium.

• •

The Red Hook chiefs on the stage are conferring with those of another borough on the multicom. Their counterparts are down in another amphitheater, one of the city halls across the stadium.

Evidently we are in for a surprise. The word is we are to receive a visit of state. Mrs. Zowie is making a personal appearance, coming over from the Flatbush speak chamber on the other side of the stadium. I am told that such visits are unusual, though not extraordinary.

Mrs. Zowie arrives and is welcomed onto the speaker's platform with applause—which seems strange, considering the Flatbush stand on the canals.

But Mrs. Zowie's speech is conciliatory. A deal has been made apparently. Both Bang's plant and the children are to be taken care of.

• •

Now the vote is in. We watch the official counting on the center T.V. screen. The boroughs were fairly evenly divided. But with the help from Flatbush the amended Redhook proposal has carried by "three thousand hats."

• •

Night time. The balance has returned in Nghsi Altai after the pandemonium of the day. The eyes of eighty thousand spectators in the stadium are concentrated on the circle of the arena which glows below.

This forum at night becomes the Congress. The ceremonial dances are held here which express, in music and pantomime, in he amplified masks of the senators of the Rotary Club, the political votes which have been ratified. On this last night what is being performed is the "Fourth Dance House."

We stand thus in the bleachers, the hundred refractory struggles and acrobatics of the day muted, and the communities hushed. The burghalls are merged. The globes of city halls, sliding on their retractable frames, have sunk into the floor. They have simply disappeared from their various levels and locations on the promenades. The stadium is now one, a single concave shape that contains the whole. It is a great bowl of darkness with the pinpoint center of the dances.

The people in conclave. But is this all?

What do the dance houses mean? Blake is down there somewhere. Alvarez and I walk along the upper promenade. By I lie edge of the grassy berm we look out over this City of the Ten Wards—where the lights of the other stadiums glow over the rooftops. Are assemblies being held there also?

BLAKE MOVES TO A REST HOUSE

During Asauj, Blake moved out of Intourist. He has been living at a rest house sponsored by a sect of the Deodar priesthood. "It's quiet at least. What a relief to get away from all those guides," Blake tells us. Here is an account of the Ekwensi rest house:

The Ekwensi priesthood, a branch of the Wilderness Society, operates in all city wards. Because of the fast pace in Garh and the tendency of its citizens to hysteria, these missions are conceived of as providing relief from urban stress. Shelters are operated in each section, generally near the business center. A small fee is charged. The patrons are businessmen, operators from small plants who come during the work break, shoppers, and even neighborhood children.

Upstairs there are a few rooms for "foreign persons," who have a privileged status in Nghsi. Below, an attendant who presides over the rest room, which is called ku-man-senu: literally, "shadow-sound bath."

They operate in this way. One enters, takes off one's shoes, and is assisted into a full-length burlap sheathe which fits over the head like a potato sack. The senu is a raised stage about the size of a boxing ring enclosed on four sides by walls also of burlap. Once inside the enclosure one simply sits or lies on the mat. A changing light pattern is thrown onto the screened walls from outside. The pattern is abstract, though occasionally there may be projected a phrase or specific word MILK AMETHYST). Simultaneously there is a sound projection from speakers mounted at the corners, the circular loop repeating itself. The sounds are also abstract: mysterious, persistent—like a frog pond at night.

The effect is quieting, Blake says. One can see out of these burlap sheathes, though the vision is misted. But one cannot be seen. There are generally not more than six or eight persons admitted at the same time. One feels physically in contact with them, yet at the same time invisible. In Blake's words: "I have rested here often. Closeted within my hood, I had the feeling I have had so often in Nghsi-Altai, of being anonymous—of having *lost my own individuality* and being immersed in some deeper and mystical community."

Talking is forbidden. Then, when people come out of the ku-man-senu and take off their sheathes, they will smile at each other, touch each other on the shoulder, and go their own ways. Blake will go up to his own room and play the gusle or do some engraving on a plate.

But he is always being interrupted. Curiously enough there is no word in the Karst language for "privacy."

ALVAREZ' DESCRIPTION OF THE BANG COLLECTIVE

HIS FIRST LETTER: ON DORMITORIES

Dawn-Is-Red Superblock
Eighth Ward, Garh
Redhook Commune
5 Baisakh

The People's Voice
9 Rockefeller Plaza
New York, N. Y.

Saludos Compañeros:

Since I last wrote I have moved out of Intourist. I'm living in a workers' collective on the opposite side of town. During the last months I have seen little of Blake and Morris. Frankly, that's a relief.

I am now a full-fledged member of a working peoples' artel, live with them in one of their dormitories. See above address at which you can write me. And have even been assigned a wife.

Would anyone have imagined this a year ago? It's like shedding your own skin. No more foreign observer role for me. I have thrust myself forward full speed into the life here. I hope I have become that *new man in the making*. "In the making" is the operative word here. There is still some distance to go.

First, let me tell you how all this happened. I wrote about our meeting with Bang's group. We joined them one day on a parade, and followed them back to their neighborhood. Well, I soon became friends with the old man—I guess he's some kind of political boss, or ganbu. And politics is everything here: It's like baseball back home.

In any case it was not hard to become accepted. People here pride themselves on getting along with foreigners (we are made pets of). And Bang is naturally gregarious. It wasn't long before I became a member of his band of cronies. When I arrived at the commons, there was always a place for me at the table and a mug of beer.

Well, I can see you fellows asking, what's it like to have a native wife? You can get that idea out of your head immediately: These people are very sophisticated. Typical city dwellers. As for the women's looks, they're not that bad either. On the streets they wear one thing, at home another. At home they like to dress up, put on make-up. The first thing a Karst woman does when she gets through the door is put on bright lipstick and cheek rouge.

With their white skin and hair sticking up out of their head like bristles, they look like dolls. They also like frilly things. I bought her a pair of nylon panties at the American gypsy quarter. She was wild about them.

Life in a dormitory. First of all we're all crammed together in what is called a "sixteens": That means sixteen "pairs." But also there are a good many children and older people. We share the same space: eating, sleeping, socializing—and also work. This is the meaning of an "artel." Am I correct in thinking that *this* is the fundamental unit of communism?

I have just learned another name for the dormitory: "Big family/Little family unit." The "Big family" refers to the room where the common activities are. This is two stories high. Around it on a second level are the cubicles occupied by the pairs. These are pretty damned small. In Kikan's and mine—only enough space for a bed and bureau. Luckily the children aren't here during the week; they're off at a "child center." When they do come on week ends they sleep on the floor of the balcony on mats outside the cubicles. I hear it's noisy: pillow fights, throwing spitballs across the balcony, etc. Not something I look forward to.

(resumed later 10 Baisakh)

This week end Kikan's children came for a visit. I had been apprehensive: You know how children are—my not being an albino and speaking with what must seem to them an outlandish accent. But they were delighted with my pink skin, pulled my mustache, and even called me "Father." As they do with a male members of our "sixteens." They make no distinction it seems.

I must sign off now—the bell for an exercise period.

(resumed 12 Baisakh)

I'd say the big experience here, living in the Dawn-Is-Red Superblock, is going up and down elevators. I may have mentioned, the city is on multiple levels—not just the apartment and business buildings, even the parks. One is always whizzing from one level to another on an express elevator.

Our apartment building is typical of those in the Eighth Ward (one of the older wards). It's about thirty stories high (but on the fifth "city level"). The building is a central spine or mast (with elevator and utility core inside), around which the dwelling units wind in a helix. The apartments are globular like pumpkins and hang from the structure from a single stem. They are called "pods."

Within ours, the divisions in the upper story dormitories are formed by the pumpkin ribs. Below is the common space. From the commons there is a companionway leading to the elevator. Another leads outside to the "terrace."

But these terraces are huge—they are more like hanging lawns. Each artel has one, suspended in air. So as one looks outside, this is a major feature of the cityscape. From our window one sees literally hundreds of these hanging outdoor terraces, almost always full of people.

I have already started my training sessions with the artel. But of this more later, in a following letter.

Till my next, fraternalmente,

Santiago

THE SECOND LETTER

Dawn-Is-Red Superblock
Eighth Ward, Garh
15th Jaith

The People's Voice
9 Rockefeller Plaza
New York, N. Y.

Saludos:

I have decided to work hard eradicating individualism. This must be my number one priority here if I am to become a real member of the collective. I had thought with my socialist background I had come a long way. But I still have some antisocial habits apparently, so my "wife" tells me.

For instance, Kikan has been complaining of my smoking in bed. And she's right. Our cubicle is not designed to accommodate my corona-corona cigar. It smokes up the whole balcony, and soon all the other "pairs" are coughing. But the tither artel members' habit of chewing tobacco communally is repulsive to me.

I have promised Kikan I will reform.

You ask in your last letter what the Bang Artel does during he day? Here is the daily schedule (brief outline):

Up at dawn to the sound of a sonar gong (which wakes the whole superblock).

Immediate assembly on "the nets" (outside parks). The spectacle of the entire borough doing mass calesthenics. Following this we break up into small groups for self-criticism sessions. Delegates are elected to the public works organizing committee. Then we descend to our commons.

At breakfast, sitting around the table, members of the artel tell each other their last night's dreams. These are commented on.

A work-study session is called after this. Economic exercises. We "simulate" class and production relations to be anticipated in that morning's business with the Syndicates.

Group calisthenics.

Second and Third Age Groups go to a superblock Maintenance Center and to the Spray Farm. Exhortation by "veteran workers." Assignment of the afternoon tasks by delegates who have returned from the public works organizing committee of the superblock.

Then our artel goes off to its places of work, generally by vaporetto, carrying box lunches and with much talking and shoving. The artel goes as a body, men, women, and veteran workers, and some children who have been designated "observers."

In the afternoon the public work of the municipality is done. I am not clear as yet as to the distinction between "public " and "private."

I've been getting on fairly well with Kikan—though we have ideological arguments and disagree on certain points. She loves to argue (she is Bang's niece). But affably. I sometimes wonder whether these Karsts take their duties as a revolutionary vanguard seriously.

In the evenings—exhausted from training—I relax in the common room and play "go" or six-handed cribbage with my "children." I've become their favorite father. The name of my eldest son: Kao. A strapping boy—a hellion.

And I have a daughter called Peach Blossom. I am going to school with Peach Blossom.

And by the way, "school" here seems to mean "child labor"! Is this possible? After leaving our pod we go to the superblock Maintenance Center and simply perform chores.

This brings me to the subject of artel training here in the Drybeds. The subject is mystifying—if one can use this word in a socialist society which is supposed to be clear and rational. Perhaps it is rational for the Karsts.

They are a food-producing artel. What techniques, what training does this entail? On this they will not enlighten me, saying I "must learn the general things first" and "perform the exercises." The exercises are as follows: We all climb out the window onto the terrace and throw ourselves into it—men, women and children, grandfathers and grandmothers! All are very agile and coordinated. There are dances in the style of folk opera, "Cutting Maize," "Planting Rice Shoots," etc., accompanied by songs. Then, there are the "body economy" exercises. These are slow, similar to tai-chi. But what is the relation to food production?

As for the "general things" I suppose they are inculcated at the Maintenance Center school: labor discipline, working with others in common tasks (praxis). This alternates with classroom studies on an abstract level. Certain "earth sciences" are taught, biology, plant physiology, nutrition, the mathematics of growth, Newtonian physics, etc. The Karsts breathe in the sciences like air.

I was touched the other day to find out that my daughter, age eleven, is memorizing for her language studies stanzas from Calderón. The teacher has a wretched Portuguese accent. Fortunately I was able to help her, and she helped me with the Second Law of Thermodynamics. We are in the same class—both being Third Set Apprentices.

All the age sets in the artel are studying heat. The method of advancement is bizarre. In the Drybeds "ideas" are considered property, at least as a kind of group privilege to be taken over by one group from another—like medicine bundles among the American Indians. Thus, when I reach the Fours, my son Kao (who is now fourteen, a grade ahead) will confer on me the Third Law of Thermodynamics.

(continued 15 Bhadon)

I am advancing rapidly. Have already passed through Grades Three and Four. In fact the whole artel praises my enthusiasm. Bang predicts that I will soon be in the Fifth and a mature proletarian.

And then I shall go off to work with the artel, after breakfast.

I am told a curious thing about the Fives. They operate "space and technology lab": that is, machines are studied not for their mechanical functions but as they affect work space and the emotions of the operator. How people can reach and stretch, pass things on to each other pleasantly, communicate instructions directly, etc.

So—rapidly I advance. But I am sorry to say that Kikan is less encouraging of my progress than some of the others. She warns that I should not be overcurious and push myself into mastering the applied sciences too fast, before I have learned "correct attitudes."

Does she resent my advancement? As for correct attitudes, I am sure I cannot be faulted on this score!

Fraternalmente, your compañero,

Santiago

THE ZIMBABWE STEEL MILLS

We have been taken to visit Zimbabwe, the great steelworks on the city's outskirts. But there are two "Zimbabwes."

The plant is in a section of the Rift called the Dolomites. How pleasant the trip there by canal, almost like one of those enchanted rides of childhood. The scenes changed as we passed through the various city sections, which revealed themselves to us afresh in shifting perspectives. Our vaporetto chugged placidly along the embankment, past rows of point houses, the images of trees and strollers reflected in the water below agitated by our own waves.

"Old" Zimbabwe used to be the principal steel mill in Nghsi-Altai in the days of the National Industrial System (before the economy was regionalized). Now there is a new, smaller, and more efficient mill nearby —a so-called "natural energy" plant. The old rolling mill, now become an antiquity, has been preserved as an industrial park and is used for cultural and recreational purposes.

Like a moon landscape this dolomitic area seems to the beholder a proper setting for steel-making. The bare walls of the canyon tower above, where birds scream. The surface is composed of beaks and volcanic craters, with every once in a while a geyser shooting up. The color of the earth is salt. Curious domes, fossil trees are the only architecture.

We passed through this and came to the old park. Here we glided along the shore for several miles, the steam from our funnel drifting over the ancient works now interlaced with trees. the old blast furnace was a skeleton, girders and roofs twisted and surrounded by slag heaps. A pitted slab. Some remnants of the original cranes and rolling presses. Occasionally we came upon a group of sightseers gathered around a cultural exhibit. The bulk of the site of the obsolete rolling mill, which used to be it mile long, has been converted into a soccer field.

"We don't have anything this big any more, and it's not the custom these days to build with permanent materials. It's really a museum piece," our guide informed us during a brief lecture

A hawser was thrown ashore. We were winched into the dock with much shouting.

• •

Here on the opposite bank of the canal is the new steelworks. We visited it next. This is a geothermal plant; that is, run by the earth's steam, which is tapped from a lower layer where the heated rock acts upon subterranean water. This "geotherm" lies everywhere under the Rift and is tapped through boreholes. These pressure points are capped, and the power is led through ducts to the plant.

As we came up from the landing, these ducts ran everywhere over our heads. The steam is led into the superheaters where it is "boosted" from a temperature of four hundred degrees centigrade at five atmospheres to the temperature an pressure required by the turbines. The turbines, which we were told were "single-reheat turbosets," power a generator developing a hundred megawatts of electricity.

"Now would you like to see the furnaces?" Blake said he was interested, so these were exhibited next. The small electric smelter, a standard item, is first charged with scrap, then molten iron, then carried along and subjected to a process called "the blow." Pure liquid hydrogen is injected and the impurities are oxydized. Then the poured steel is batched: carbon, manganese, and other elements added to produce the required alloys.

Another feature is the elimination of the long continuous hot-strip rolling mill and its replacement by a smaller planetary mill. In this the plate is pulled under pressure in opposite directions through a series of rotary gears, and thus rolled to size and tempered. This type of mill is in general use throughout the many regions of Altai.

A meeting with the management had been scheduled for us. However, we were first taken on a tour of the plant vegetable farm, which is operated in conjunction with the mill. Mostly cabbages are grown here in the mineral-rich irrigated soil running along the canal bank. The crop about to be harvested, and the green, placid rows surrounded the steel factory like an inland sea.

It is mostly Jat in-city immigrants who work on the farm. The plant also runs a professional sports league, staffed for some reason by Thays from the Drune. Together these three enterprises make up the Zimbabwe Association.

• •

We had been granted an interview with the two officials who head the Supreme Committee or Committee of Commitees that runs the steel plant. But they were at a meeting, so we waited. Finally the two men arrived together followed by a crowd of associates, stenographers, and what seemed like a press corps with video crew. All were talking at once. Liu Shao-shi, the manager, had a top hat and was dressed in a striped swallow-tailed coat. He was introduced to us and nodded in an exhausted manner, at the same time mopping his face with a red handkerchief. The second official, introduced as Lin Piao, wore a full field marshall's uniform.

"Be with you in a minute. We have to sign some decrees."

"We've just come from a conference with the Planning Committee."

The video crew completed its business. Liu posed at his desk with Lin Piao a respectful distance behind. The decrees, signed, were carried by cable T.V. throughout the branches of the Association, we were told, in a simultaneous translation into three languages. Finally everyone left except one of the secretaries. Liu Shao-shi stripped off his jacket with relief and grinned at us. Lin Piao had already taken off his, revealing underneath a rather dirty woolen undershirt. They broke out a bottle of whisky and the interview began.

"So you are the syndicalist group from the United States. You're interested in how we operate here? Go ahead. Shoot. Ask anything you want."

"We are not all syndicalists," Blake remarked. Morris complimented him on what they had seen of Zimbabwe. Alvarez asked about the Association, "Was it large?"

"About twenty thousand workers," was the reply.

"Your committee manages this enterprise; it is under your and Mr. Lin Piao's direction. Yet you have these positions only temporarily, as I understand it?" Alvarez pursued.

"Yes. The leadership is rotated. Everyone has a crack at it for a time. I have another term to go. Then thank God I'll be rid of it."

"So, after that you'll be back at your regular trade in one of the departments. What is that?"

Liu was a welder. He rolled up his sleeve and showed us his heavily spotted upper forearm. He told us this was caused by the sparks from the welding torch getting inside his leather protection gear.

Lin Piao's trade was "metallurgical chemist." He also expressed a desire to get back to the shop and complained that "management was an awful headache."

Alvarez complimented them on their trades, then gave them both the fraternal salute he had learned at the swimming pool.

Morris said: "I'm intrigued at this rotation business. With us, we have trained people, managers, to run the day-to-day operations of our plants —which after all are pretty complex. You don't think that a specialist is required?"

The word "specialist" drew a blank. Lin Piao merely stared at us, while Liu scratched his behind.

"You're speaking of a class of people who do nothing but manage the whole time?"

Liu seemed nonplussed by the idea. He acknowledged the advantages of brains. After all, one didn't make steel with a bunch of dumbbells. Every worker had to be trained, and promoted according to his skills—but that was the business, wasn't it, of the departments?

Lin Piao, who appeared the theoretician of the two, asked us whether it didn't seem to them "risky"—a permanent management. Work was work; but running things and "the management of one group of men by another—well, wasn't that a political question?" As such it was better handled by rotation.

"So it would be fair to say that you have a hierarchy of skills, but not of power?" This formulation seemed to please Alvarez.

Blake asked how the heads of the Committee were chosen. Liu said they were chosen by lot, or "by the bean."

"By the bean?" the engraver asked, his eyebrows raised.

The manager explained. There was a jar of beans. The Committee members were led up blindfolded. If they picked a colored bean, they were chosen.

This applied only to the Supreme, or Executive Committee, called the "Prytaneia," which was rotated every six months among the principal groups of artels. In the other committees—chosen for a one year term—the officers were nominated and selected by a show of hands.

Together all of the committees made up what was called the "Boule" or "Syndicate" which ran the plant.

"What are the duties of the executive?"

The manager described them: seeing to it that production schedules were met, labor discipline, and the making of "short-ranged decisions—subject to ratification by the assembly."

Blake asked what was meant by labor discipline.

"Well, mostly imposing fines—for absenteeism, carelessness in handling equipment, etc. In some cases an employee is beaten . . ."

"Beaten!" Morris interjected. "How barbarous"

Liu hastened to reassure them on this point. If he felt wronged, the worker could petition for redress of grievances of the next General Assembly of Workers—which met every ninety days. If the managers were upheld that was the end of it. If not, they were fined or themselves beaten.

Alvarez, approving this procedure, said it was harsh but fair. He went on to ask about the other committees.

Lin Piao ran through these. They were: the Planning Committee, in a way the most important, as of course "everything had to follow the production plan," the Committee on the Agenda, the Committee on Industrial Relations (meeting with the shop stewards in the departments), and the committees on Finance, Statistics, Sports, Farming, Research and Development, and on Municipal Affairs. There were a few others were not great. The steel plant "pretty much ran itself," and the members of the Boule were merely delegates. Ultimately they were responsible to the General Assembly of Workers, which met every three months in the sports stadium.

"The sports stadium—ah," Alvarez remarked. "And there every worker has a voice?" The manager nodded. Blake said, "It must be pure bedlam."

To Morris this seemed a rather unwieldy arrangement. He asked how it worked. Wasn't it difficult to make decisions?

Lin Piao acknowledged this. However, he insisted there were certain customary rules and procedures according to which the Assembly, or "Ecclesia," as it was called, functioned. He explained as follows:

The Assembly met, and the first order of business was a vote of confidence in the executive officers.

After that there were reports by the committees, the Finance and Sports committees being generally of the most interest.

Then there was new business—all proposals having been first submitted to the Committee on the Agenda and then posted for a week previously on the shop bulletin boards. Lin Piao explained that any workman could make a proposal and speak for it. This was called "right of initiative." The proposal carried the workman's name, and he had to be responsible for it. In other words it had to be positive—for a capricious or sectarian proposal an initiator could be fined or beaten.

There was also the "right of amendment"; that is, to offer a counter proposal and argue for it.

After these popular debates, the motion was referred to the Prytaneia, the chief officer of which (in this case Liu Shi-shao) would be presiding. But the Supreme Committee had no right of veto. It could either approve or offer the motion to the floor "without conclusion."

The Assembly thus decided each proposal by vote.

This account delighted Alvarez, though he had been apprehensive in the beginning. He clapped his hands and shouted: "Bravo! Bravo!"

Morris also was pleased. He said he would like to see a plant Assembly in action.

Liu answered, "I can tell you, it's something!"

• •

After lunch at the Zimbabwe sports club (the welder and the metallurgist had donned uniforms again) Blake said to Lin Piao, "So you feel you have achieved workers' self-management? And by God, everything is managed isn't it? One swims in the canals; the ruins of blast furnaces are parks; even the city air is clean."

Alvarez asked him if he missed "the dark satanic mills?"

Pensively the seer had been looking out the window at the cabbages. "I do not think we have arrived yet at the New Jerusalem."

• •

Alvarez and Morris engaged each other in argument. It was clear there had been Karst improvements in metallurgy, but what about the ownership of the means of production? Morris explained his views:

"For instance, I myself had a small textile plant, in which we wove fabrics. We had, I like to think, an advanced attitude; the workers were trained in a creative and craftsmanly approach; we encouraged participation, group discussion, etc. But still: it was I who owned the plant and the looms. I don't think it would have occurred to any of us that it could be otherwise."

Alvarez: "And you call yourself a socialist?"

Morris thought the question of ownership was probably irrelevant in the Drybeds. Property would be a resource, as among the Jats. Even the property of a steelworks and the improvements made on it through capital investment would be like an agricultural plot with its improved soils: it would be considered to be held in common.

Blake asked: "Who owns Zimbabwe?" Still looking out the window he replied with a poem extemporized:

"Who owns Zimbabwe?
The sky. The sky owns Zimbabwe
through its smoke.

Who owns Zimbabwe?
The lake. The lake underground owns Zimbabwe
through its steam.

Who owns Zimbabwe?
Who owns Zimbabwe?
The slag heaped on the earth owns Zimbabwe.

The fires inside the smelter own it.
But not the hands that set the fires.
Nobody owns it.
Nobody owns Zimbabwe."

Morris returned to his own defense. "Yes, I called myself a socialist, but there cannot be only one socialist enterprise." He went on to say that that solution was not feasible unless general. His mill had been after all located in England, and when a weaver left for one reason or another and went to work in some textile plant elsewhere, he was penalized. Being nourished in a co-operative attitude, the poor man was even more alienated from his machinery. He was even worse off than before.

Lin Piao, who had been listening, asked in surprise, "You mean an individual worker can hire himself out to a plant?"

The idea struck him as entirely novel. Liu explained that in Nghsi it was the artel as a whole that was employed. The idea of an "individual employee" was unthinkable.

"Unthinkable?" cried Morris. "Then who is it that is hired?"

Piao offered his own case. He said his own artel had first discussed "buying into" the steel plant and whether they had enough capital. Then they had made a proposal to the industry and had contracted to take over part of the operation in return for profit.

Alvarez asked, "So you bought into it. And for this you put up your own capital. But what is that?"

"But of course. The capital is our artel." He explained that they were members of the Fire and Metals Brotherhood—of which there were numerous branches. As such they possessed "certain aspects of scientific knowledge and certain skills . . . In short, we had a good deal to offer."

"How does this work practically?" Morris protested. "After all, we're not dealing with a primitive operation. Here it is not a matter of a group of laborers having a few small tools—a scythe or a pickax, or even a tractor or payloader which they can bring to the job; but of a complicated technology. Let's say your artel arrives at this steel mill and contracts, as you put it, to operate the reduction furnace. How do they know how? And this is tied to other skilled operations: operating cranes, batching mixers, crucibles, etc. In short, a production line. Does the whole assembly shut down, while they are being taught to do this?"

Liu said he saw no problem. Of course there was a brief training period. But production went on. And he added that it "was quite customary for members of the old artel, who were of course of the same brotherhood, to train the new."

"But why would the old artel be replaced? And why would they want to go elsewhere?"

"One can't go on making steel for a whole lifetime."

Lin added, "That would be boring. It would lack spreccia."

Morris rose. "But we must be taking up your time."

Both the president and the chairman of the board smiled broadly. "The plant closes in the afternoon."

COUNTRY HARDITTS IN TOWN: THE FOREIGN QUARTER

Each ward has its foreign quarter in Garh. In the Sixth Ward it was the Kansu-Hardan Quarter, named after a locality in the plains. Many of its inhabitants had come here. The Sandranapaul Harditts lived in Kansu, in the Grain of Millet Superblock overlooking one of the canals.

In the foreign quarter the buildings were of the Jat type. They were not the high cylindrical point houses with their tension masts but were of middle height and joined together in the country manner, with wide roofs for chicken or turkey runs and vegetable gardens tended by the commune.

One room in the apartment was the Shrine Room. Though for the worship of the Ancestors, it was set aside for guests—meaning Sawna relatives during the great city festivals. During much of the time the room was empty and had a sacrosanct air. On the shrine joss sticks burned in polished brass jars before photographs of the Ancestors. The family crowded into the remaining three rooms. The grandmothers, also Sandranapaul and his wife Olga, slept on planks which were put against the wall each day. The rest slept on the floor on bedrolls.

Sometimes the younger members would complain of these arrangements and point to the prevailing city customs, which they felt superior. Then either Olga or one of the matriarchs would say: "I don't care how the Karsts live. Let them be as practical as they like. We have our own obligations."

Venu and his family arrived for the Fourth of July-Ten. It was here, at Grain of Millet, that Venu had boarded during his factory year at the age of fifteen. And had been given his first sexual experience, sharing with this same Tatti Olga his initiation halvah. This was the custom in Kansu. But it was also customary to keep the seduction secret. Thus to Venu the memory of the halvah had a peculiar sweetness.

However, he found his tatti had grown fat and was much given to moralizing—like her mother.

There were a dozen or so Sawna relatives. Venu and Sathan brought their three children. There was Sathan's older sister, Nanda, with her children, but with no husband. The elderly Bai had been left behind because of her phlebitis. The matriarch's sister, Helvetia, was very much present, growling in a deep voice and shouting out instructions from the moment they arrived at the plains skip.

It was during the middle of the summer. The Bai Harditts had made the all-night trip by monorail, accompanied by a small donkey—a pet of Maddi's—and crates of chickens. These were taken up to the roof by freight elevator. The guest apartment was opened, the shrine turned to face the wall, and the joss sticks in their jars replaced by marigolds. All of a sudden the sacred room was full of bedrolls, knapsacks, and the small babies of the country Harditts, and looked like a camp.

The younger Harditt children were perched at the window. Dhillon's chin was pressed against a hair braid of his sister Maddi's.

"There's the canal. Look, to the right. There's the synerg, it's blinking. And there's a boat coming."

Maddi said: "What a racket there is. Every time you come to the city they're putting something up or tearing it down." As if to punctuate this remark the sound of riveting came at them from across the plaza.

Not only the city had changed. The Bai Harditts found the fortunes of their city relatives had bettered in recent years. They were more prosperous, for one thing. Olga's own children had grown up, and her daughters had brought back husbands into the compound—from country villages near Sawna. One was a barge pilot and made good money.

Another was a tanner.

A grandson, Bangi, was already Srikant's age. Soon Bangi would be coming to Sawna to spend his farm year working for the agricultural collective and living with the Bai Harditts, while Srikant lived at Grain of Millet and learned glass-making.

As a smaller boy Srikant had collected snakes. Now he immersed himself in a book on astrology. He was always looking up references in this to tell the favorable auspices listed for the day, which he would read off to the other children in a pedantic manner. Bangi, who remembered being taken in the village into holes and caves, and the lure of danger, considered his cousin to have become less interesting.

The Bai Harditt children did not consider themselves strangers in the Sixth Ward. But Bangi knew his way around the whole city down to the last alley. He took them to lurid districts and even showed them how to smoke "bhang." He had become a hardened street urchin.

They enjoyed taking the vaporetto. Maddi could spend all day just sitting at the rail eating popcorn. Dhillon collected Karst coins, which he jangled in his pockets.

They also explored the albino sections. Bangi had a friend, Kao, who lived in a Karst dormitory. When they went there, the Sawna children stood still and marveled at everything. Bangi's friend's mother called Maddi "Eyes-as-Big-as-Saucers."

Maddi preferred these excursions with the boys. However, mostly she accompanied her women relatives shopping. On these trips through the crowded streets the older Jat women wore purdah, putting Maddi in agonies of embarrassment. Both her mother and Helvetia wore the long woven shawls up to their noses and seemed to think it perfectly natural, and even Tatti Olga. But Maddi's Aunt Nanda did not wear it.

The family of Jat women commented shamelessly on the Karst women's clothes. Helvetia thought the standard uniform of pants and sleeveless jackets was simply ugly, while Nanda said, "They all looked middle-aged."

To Maddi the Karst women seemed attractive, with their saucy mouths and round transparent faces. She also became conscious of her own neck, which seemed overly long and fragile. She walked down the street carefully, as if balancing her head.

• •

One day the children walked by a canal. There were the three boys and Bangi's friend from the Noodlemakers, Kao. Bangi was in the lead and very much in charge. Maddi trailed, a burden.

"Hurry up, Maddi."

The sun filtered through a bright haze.

Dhillon and Srikant were throwing rocks at street signs. Each time they hit a sign it went ping . . . the steel post vibrated. It was like striking a tuning fork, Srikant said. A pleasant crowd was hanging around the dock where the swan boats came in.

Bangi vetoed the suggestion that they take a boat ride to the Spray Farm. Dhillon echoed him: "It's too far. And besides, we've been there before." Bangi and Kao had their own plans.

A Drune family from the Wilderness was having its picture taken on a wooden donkey.

The paths branched off from the embankment. They took one, Dhillon and Kao stopping to chuck stones. They tried hitting further and further signs.

They were walking beside a long fence. Through a hole some children came out carrying boards.

"They're stealing wood for the Fire Festival," Bangi told them. At the same time he held up his hand.

Kao said soberly: "We'll go in. But be careful. Watch out for cops."

On the other side of the fence were old-fashioned row houses sandwiched in between the Points. The houses had wooden back porches, stacked one above the other. At the bottom was a back garden and laundry yard.

Some smaller children stood back. They had been placed as sentinels, their eyes out for trouble on the upper porches. A gang of boys was violently attacking the lower back porch. They had the steps and the railings off already, ripping and twisting and making a ferocious cracking. Then one wrecker would hand a board to waiting helpers.

Bangi and Kao joined the wreckers. Dhillon was about to but his older brother stopped him.

Bangi shouted back: "Oh, it's allowed—the two weeks before Holi. They just pretend it isn't. But don't let anyone you."

In fact, faces were peering out from the windows of several of the row houses.

Below the wrecking continued. A line of children streamed toward the fence hole with armfuls of boards. On the street they met gangs of other children loaded in the same way, all headed for Franklin Park.

When they got there they found the great Fire Pole set up—which would be used for the Fourth of July Holi pyre. Already there were mountains of wood and rubbish stacked around the base.

ALVAREZ' THIRD LETTER: THE NOODLEMAKERS

Dawn-Is-Red Superblock
Eighth Ward,
Garh 6 Magh

The People's Voice
9 Rockefeller Plaza
New York, N. Y.

Compañeros:

Things have been going fast. I am now a full-fledged production worker in the Bang Collective. But things haven't been going so well in my domestic life. Of that, more later.

The Bang artel are noodlemakers. That is what we do. And that is where we go after we leave our communal pod after breakfast—all sixteen pairs of us, our Big Family/Little Family unit.

I'm told that in past years our artel has done a variety of jobs:

vegetable freezing, production of pork sausages, pastrymaking . . . and now noodles. Our members put their whole heart in it and go off to work with great zeal. The other day I marched with a woman seventy years old who sang work songs and strode with a sprightly step. She said: "I have been kept young by cooking."

I have been working at the noodle factory for several months. I've written you the Karst syndicalist slogan here: "Beyond Socialism." Could this represent a step backward?

Noodlemakers in Garh: a huge operation, the citizens are crazy about noodles. Our pasta plant is operated with a big flour mill and food producers' co-operative. Very active and aggressive outfit: but can you imagine, they shut down every afternoon! There are about four to five hundred people in our brigade at Checkered Foods, with daily noodle production of about eighty tons. The various jobs are broken down by sections, as follows:

Egg gathering detail brings in four hundred dozen eggs by trolley from the Spray Farm.

Warehousing. In a warehouse near the mill bags of flour are stored, and brought over by fork-lift.

The "cooks." This detail does mixing and batching, then rolling out the dough. Then the noodles are cut.

Finally the pasta is hung out on racks to dry. After drying it is put into baskets and taken directly to the ward free markets.

It didn't take me long on the job to understand that production is targeted extremely low. Obviously because the operations are too broken up . . . everything on the scale of a half dozen to a dozen people. Production is all dispersed. It was not hard to see for instance that the warehousing could be combined with the mixing and batching operation —by having a conveyor belt bring the flour directly from the mill and having it come through the dryers and mixers to the vats.

The production plan—arrived at by such an admirable process of democratic centralism in the plant assembly—could be *doubled*!

Of course we have our own self-criticism and work-study sessions in the artel. I was quick to point out the deficiencies of the plan and that with streamlining and efficiency, production could be enormously increased: They only said: "But why?"

However, I have persisted, against resistance. Rebuffed at home, I continue to agitate in my own work section (the warehouse). We have a small nucleus of like-minded persons, call ourselves the Output Group, and distribute handbills.

Unfortunately Kikan, who operates a fork-lift, would be displaced under these reforms.

The older day a "big character poster" attacking us was pasted on the warehouse wall and discussed all day by excited workers. And at home I find myself less popular than before—despite their claims to proletarian internationalism.

But let us advance without compromise! Avanzar sin transar!

(later. 11 Magh)

I have been having trouble with Kikan. Is it the cigars? which she labels subproletarian and a retrograde nationalist fetish. I am more than ever determined *not* to give up smoking. She has also been after me—and the rest of the sixteens likewise—to bleach my mustache with peroxide.

Kikan has moved to another cubicle.

I am involved in a ferocious ideological dispute with the food producers. I can see now, this simple proposition of mine: the rearrangement of equipment along rational lines, involves serious questions. It seems that the *cooks* (who would also be eliminated under my scheme) enjoy flavoring their own noodles "to the taste": that is, adding spinach, parsley, scallions, certain herbs such as tarragon, etc. It turns out that this "taste" is not for their own palates (in which case it would be a simple issue of civil rights)—but for the marginal differentiation of the product, i.e., for commerce. Each artel *sells* its noodles on the free market to its particular customers who "like their noodles that way."

In other words, they *compete.*

I asked Kikan: Is this Socialism? In turn I am accused of Left Infantilism!

Yours in struggle,

Santiago Alvarez

ALVAREZ' FOURTH LETTER

Dawn-Is-Red Superblock
Eighth Ward, Garh
4 Phagun

Compañeros:

I have attempted during my stay here to "become the new man." I had hoped some day to give you an insider's view of a self-criticism or "struggle" session. Now I am the target of the struggle.

Positions at the plant have hardened during the last month. Big character posters have bloomed against us! Well, they do not accuse me personally . . . "an unnamed foreigner who is subverting Karst revolutionary methods . . . and leading us along the road to adventurism." A modest text is labeled "dangerous" that we circulated at our work-study group meetings. "The text is based on none other than Marx's "Critique of the Gotha Programme"!

We are now labeled the "Adventurists" (the Output Group). Kikan's faction—of which she is the head—is called sententiously the "Six-Sides-in-Balance."

Today the dispute came to a head inside our artel—in the most sinister manner, as you can judge for yourselves.

The after-breakfast meeting began with the reading of a sacred text (by Mazda), then a discussion on heat in relation to body movement within the factory. A song praising the First Law of Thermodynamics (heat conservation). It all seemed abstract, and innocent enough. But the heat was on me.

However, the discussion seemed not to be going anywhere at this point. Leaving my mug of coffee on the table, I went to the bathroom.

I returned. Something had altered in the room, violently. I did not know why. Kikan had moved to the front row of the assembled breakfasters where she was painting her nails furiously. My supporters were lined up in front.

They were being forced to give an account of themselves—and when I say forced, I mean the noodlemakers were doing it with relish. As they made their confessions my supporters shifted their feet and avoided looking at me.

Having regained my seat, I sat sipping my coffee and trying to eat my bun, but my heart wasn't in it. The crowd was hostile. At any moment I would be called upon to make my own "auto-criticism."

This would not be difficult. I could see, from the political events of the last weeks, where the land lay.

But what if I committed some *personal* crime?

Kikan looked particularly outraged. The thought occurred to me that while I was out of the room, she had accused me of certain sexual offenses. Perhaps I had not been fornicating in the national style!

I stood before them a foreigner. I looked around the room at this set of uniformly unpigmented complexions and insipid hair and felt suddenly the *blackness* of my mustache. My own face seemed *coarse*, like an overgrown strawberry.

Luckily, as it turned out, this was not to be a trial of unnatural offenses. My case was helped by Big Bang. He spoke indulgently on the subject of my ideological shortcomings. I had not "taken the correct line"—but I had tried hard to reform myself, although my background was against me.

A cook seized the floor. He shouted at me:

"You've been running around having a good time and sticking your nose in everything . . . you don't seem to realize there are crimes in Altai. I can assure you the people are quite able to decide what the crimes are in their own courts and to mete out the appropriate punishment."

The cook's reference to "nosing around" horrified me. I had heard about punishments inflicted by these peoples' courts. One comrade had gotten a hand cut off for pilfering. Another offender, for "meddling," had had his nose slit and been exiled.

I was in a state to expect something of this kind in my own case.

But Big Bang pleaded for leniency because of "special considerations," and suggested in any case this judgment should not be given by the sixteens but by a wider group of neighbors.

And so the sentencing has been postponed.

What I had been found guilty of was "Productionism"—a capital offense—and for certain grave misdemeanors which involved antisocial behavior and "going against harmony."

But I expect the worst.

Fraternally,
Santiago Alvarez

MORRIS' AFTERNOON ON THE NETS

Everything here is refreshing. In the course of my wanderings I keep noting fresh facts. The arts: there seems to be no split between what we would call "commercial arts" and "Art." Nothing is handmade (it's straight from the factory). But everything is, in some personal way, embellished. Thus, somewhat the feeling of "folk art."

• •

Have been interested in locating a small shop where I could set up weaving or chairmaking. Not that I'm eager to make chairs (a tedious business). But I am eager to experience what it's like being associated with one factory as it exists *among others*. In other words, a whole new social system. So that anarcho-syndicalism becomes, in a sense, a fresh background.

• •

A friend has referred me to the Commerce Department. They have put at my disposal an excellent gentleman by the name of Yao Wen-yuan. We have toured the city several times together.

I showed Yao a picture of my famous Morris Chair. He thought it "very pretty" and asked how it was used.

• •

It turns out that in Ngshi-Altai looking for a factory is not so much a question of real estate. Mr. Yao's first questions to me were: with what forms of energy would I want the chair produced? Solar, water power, geothermal, waste products, etc.

And on this depends what brotherhood (groups of artels) I am to seek out in order to make the chair! So already we are a far cry from just going out after available rental space and a work force. (Of course, the basics are the same.)

Looking for a suitable artel (in the solar energy field) we have toured the Eighth Ward extensively.

• •

Answers to mysteries come in a rush.

I had wondered about these small groups of Garhians working around the city. For instance, I spent an afternoon in a park pleasurably watching what I took to be a gang of municipal employees. They were laying out a bed of tulips in the approved manner that must be the same the world over. A battered truck with topsoil . . . workmen in muddy boots and with spades, and foreman . . .

In another case a gang in the streets was repairing a pipe . . . as office workers watched during the lunch break. But these were not crews of the Department of Parks nor the Department of Public Works, but ordinary (private) artels "spending the afternoon publicly."

Again distinctions break down!

On any afternoon one sees these bands of private citizens out working for the city with a certain air of festivity. Apparently this municipal work is equated with sports—another urban enthusiasm. Now it is summer; but what about the winter, with its icy blasts?

• •

Yao is amused at my notion that public work is done for sport. No, it is labor—but without pay. It is considered a direct exchange between producers, the artels of each community helping each according to need.

I ask, "Are there no wages then in Garh?"

Yao Wen-yuan replies cryptically, "Yes. Socialist in the morning. Communist in the afternoon. And capitalist at odd moments, when there is money to be made."

• •

Yao Wen-yuan has taken me to the area of the nets—the upper membrane above the city where solar energy is trapped. He thinks I might find here some artel suitable for chairmaking. But he is vague on this point.

We are going to spend the afternoon with the "moss-gatherers."

As we rise up from one of the higher levels of our own ward, the whole city comes into view.

This is not one of the ordinary passenger elevators servicing the point houses. The shaft runs vertically up beside an enormous steel tube about twenty feet in diameter—the function which I am to understand later. At certain points on this tube are "nodes" or branch stations where, Yao Wen-yuan explains, certain small industries are located. Here the passenger elevator also stops.

Apparently we are in an industrial sector.

At the top the view is quite breathtaking. Bright sun . . . whereas on the levels below there is generally a patchwork effect of light and shade—one of the drawbacks of this "miniaturized" city, one always looks up through layers, either structural parts or membrane. But issuing from the top of the mast one is struck by the bright sky. The first impulse is to shield the eyes.

But of course: on this uppermost layer solar energy is generated.

• •

The highest station. You can imagine being at the top of the pole of a giant circus tent. There is an opening around the pole . . . the wire cables stretching out . . . a walkway. Then the immense surface begins, like a shining meadow. At a further distance out, suspended on this meadow, Yao Wen-yuan points out to me a gang of moss-gatherers at work.

This field is a warped plane of hills and hollows, divided along the lines of the supporting tension cables. Along these great catenaries are the promenades. On either side stretches the surface, this *membrane* of sun-absorbing crystals. Making our way, suspended on this floating meadow, we clamber toward these Liliputians. I am introduced to them and we chat for a few moments, as the solar energy-gathering process is explained to me.

• •

Basic energy formulations for solar batteries: a constant of 1.94 calories per minute of sun's heat equals 130 milliwats per centimeter squared. At 10 per cent efficiency this yields 100 watts per square meter of solar batteries at earth's surface.

For continuous supply of energy (regardless of weather conditions) excess solar radiation is taken to energy accumulator/storage batteries.

Solar battery grid at the surface is thin film polycrystallin (silicon or other) layer which absorbs photons, acting as photo voltaic cell.

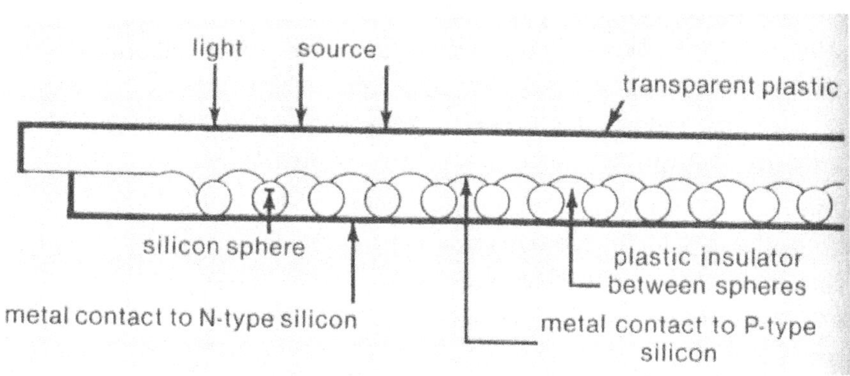

In this way light energy is converted to electrical energy and a simple circuit is set up (generating 100 watts per square meter per minute).

• •

Interesting to note that this constant (the proportion of heat to radiated area of the semiconducting film) is the same as that produced by sunlight falling on a leaf.

Both the leaf and the membrane function as photovoltaic cells: little factories where E (energy) is produced/accumulated, and from which it is taken off to serve life-support functions.

From the cathode layer (see above diagram) current goes to an accumulator and thence to an electrolyzer, where it is stored as gas.

Yao Wen-yuan had wandered off. This was all explained to me by a child.

• •

Yao Wen-yuan and I had approached the small band of thirty to forty persons. I had noticed they were making sweeping movements. Their bodies moving together in rhythm, a band of sweepers covers one section of photolenses at a time. They work downhill, one section of cells at a time. As they work they sway slightly. This process is repeated over and over. From the catenaries they reach over with a long bamboo brush to which a water hose is attached, and lightly wash down the cells (like reaching over and weeding a vegetable patch). The stream of water flushes off the soot and dust that accumulates on the surface of the cells. This is why these afternoon work gangs are called colloquially "moss-gatherers."

The soot and the dust—so they have told me—has drifted on the high air currents from "America."

• •

A dizzying feeling looking *down* through layers of these sun-trapping stratifications—at the city roofs. Still further down, city squares. Tiny figures are seen threading across a park.

• •

The moss-gathering section sways up and down gently on its scintillating net. They balance. Again the feeling of a circus performance. I am reminded for some reason of Picasso's picture *Les Saltimbanques.*

• •

Curiously enough, I am now informed by Yao that this *is* an artel of Singers and Acrobats. In fact they are the very group that we saw performing so profitably in the square before Red Cats. In the evenings they perform commercially; now they are doing their public works exercise.

The sky reflected from the photocells onto these albino faces—makes them bright blue. But the figures are cheerful. They chatter and hop around like so many sparrows, hardly bothering to look down.

I chat with the Red Cats acrobat who was sitting beside me in the speak-chamber, and she tells me her impression of the Assembly. She says that the "dancers are getting old and clumsy."

• •

From the solar membrane covering the city with its millions and millions of photocells, the electrical energy accumulates at the poles.

At the tops of each pole there is an electrolyzer station. Here water is disassociated by the solar current into its component gases. The gases (in the form of hydrogen and oxygen gas) are then stored in the pipe cylinders. These are called "tank farms."

The tank farms also function as the power-distributing system. At lower stations on the pole the electrolysis process is reversed: water is reformed and the recombination of the gases produces current for the industrial power outlets.

Here is the quantitative electrolysis formula:

1. Solar batteries———→E accumulator———→electrolyzer

2. Water disassociated to two parts (17 cu. ft.) hydrogen and one part (8.5 cu. ft.) oxygen volume, and compressed to 100 atmospheres

3. Fuel cell: reaction is reverse electrolysis

H_2 (g) + O (g) ———→H_2O

yields 56.6 kilocalorie/mole = 1.23 volts

• •

We are not dealing here with large amounts of energy. The solar energy available to the whole of the Eighth Ward would be less than that delivered by several large plants using coal or hydropower. But the method of storage and delivery of the power is novel.

Four hundred and twenty gallons of water produces one kilowatt per hour electricity for use, the tank farm delivering on the order of two to five hundred thousand gallons to each point. Thus each reverse-electrolyzer station at one of the system's nodes has clustered around it a number of small-to-medium-sized manufacturing plants.

• •

Another tree analogy: As the photocells function as the canopy of leaves, these enormous tubes rising everywhere throughout Garh are the trunks containing the transport and nutrient system (corresponding to the phloem and xylem tubes of the tree).

Perhaps this is not merely a metaphor. What a simple system: yet somehow miraculous.

Indeed, what could be more natural: that the basic design system of a city should be that of a forest?

In Garh, each borough owns, and is composed of, its "tree trunks" (direct sources of power).

• •

Another question. I've been told the city is divided into ten wards. Is the whole city then decentralized in this way, i.e. do the separate power sources (photoelectrical, steam, etc.) guarantee the political autonomy of each ward?

If so, what is the federating principle?

Possibly there may be no Garh City in the sense of a physical entity. The "city" may be merely an aesthetic impression. (I am reminded of the synerg from its great tower winking its municipal data as we arrived.)

A metropolitan illusion?

CRYSTAL GROWING/AN ANARCHIST BUREAUCRACY

Yao has found me a manufacturer. However, the product manufactured will not be chairs. As it turns out chairs are not used in

Nghsi—people squat on the floor on mats. I had gotten the wrong impression from Intourist, and Yao had been too much of a diplomat to tell me. In fact when I had shown him a picture of my Morris Chair he had not known what it was.

But the designs for fabrics and the famous Morris flower patterns on drapes and wallpapers offer distinct commercial possibilities here. And so I have made up a portfolio, including some of Blake's fanciful engravings which have an art nouveau flare.

It is this portfolio which Yao has been taking around.

So now we have a prospective client that Yao tells us is "a dynamic outfit." We have an appointment with their Research and Development section.

• •

This morning we have come for our appointment with the Crystal Growers, at the very top of one of the big office buildings. The appointment is with the chief engineer of this artel. We wait in the reception room. An exhibit showing the development of the firm is explained to us by a young technician.

Like so many of the solar industries located at the nodes the fortunes of this one have grown with technological advances in energy-gathering. The old sunlight absorption surface had been composed of millions of individual photocells, each a single silicon seed crystal one by two centimeters in diameter embedded in a matrix. The artel has developed a thin polycrystalline film which can be rolled out in a single layer. This is more flexible, and vastly more economical.

However, the absorption properties, the technician explains, are the same: depending on the material, the photons must be absorbed with enough energy to bridge the band gap.

The artel, after experimenting with a number of new materials, including a "light" silicon, Indian phosphide and silenium, finally hit upon "gallium," a workable composite which could be spun out in a continuous mat like fiberglass.

This material is melted and poured over a plate. In the process of cooling there is a deposition of dendrite crystals.

Yao and I are given the opportunity to examine one of these lovely crystals under a microscope—also a feature of this stylish exhibit.

The Crystal Growers have gone into the domestic home products market. They make a number of items: "thin film" carpeting and wallpaper, insulating material, crystal radio sets, a small solar generating panel for commune laundries—in addition to fabrics and certain applications of engraving.

Our wait for the Research and Development head turns out to be long. I begin to get impatient, but we are told this prominent official "is in the legal department" of the artel overseeing the draft of our contract and that "she is anxious to meet us."

Concentrating on the scientific exhibit I had not noticed how impressively decorated the reception room is. It is in the grand style, with oak-paneled walls and several dignified, bluff oil portraits in gold frames. Could these be of the founders?

But finally we are shown in. Vigorous words of greeting from across the room and a broad smile. We are introduced. I remember with surprise that I have seen the face on television. It is Mrs. Zowie.

However, she does not have on her fatigue cap, the badge of political authority from the stadium. She wears instead the large bonnet of the guild master decorated with plastic cherries.

• •

I wonder if I should pay Yao Wen-yuan a finder's fee? In fact there are all sorts of uncertainties having to do with getting our designs manufactured by the Crystal Growers. For instance, must Blake and I live with this artel in one of their dormitories now that we are production partners? That is the law here. But Mrs. Zowie has advised us that "we can get around it somehow."

What about patents, royalties, etc.? How is this to be managed? And what about the contract between ourselves, that is Blake and myself, and the artel—since individuals are not recognized as legal entities here? Contracts are only made between collectives.

In this regard too Yao tells us that Mrs. Zowie "has arranged everything."

• •

I had not visited Yao's office before. I found it on the second floor of the Flatbush National Bank Building, the same that houses the Crystal Growers (in the penthouse). If you will believe it, the mint, where they print their own currency, is also located here.

I had noticed the many varieties of money in use in Garh. Each ward—even each borough—has its own currency, which is exchanged somehow. Horrible thought: could they be intending to use our designs—or more exactly, Blake's engravings—to manufacture bank notes?

I decide to keep this possibility to myself.

In his office Yao is depressed, says he has a head cold and can hardly breathe. He complains of the paper work.

"In the old days it wasn't so much. Now there are carloads of it. We are strangled in red tape."

I tell him that with the elimination of printing in Nghsi I would have expected the elimination of paper work.

Yao sighs and says: "The documents have to be preserved for legal reasons." He refers to the commercial agreements between the artels, deeds of leasing, licensing of patents, etc.

Upon stepping off the elevator I had reached Yao's section down a decayed marbled corridor. A reception desk. The office occupies the entire floor, which is divided into cubicles. In each one, blurred by frosted glass, some applicant was being interviewed for a license.

Sniffling through his nose, Yao is constantly on the telephone with Mrs. Zowie.

On the wall of Yao's cubicle is a photograph of the chairman of his department.

It would seem that bureaucracies are the same the world over.

• •

We are at the Red Cats again and meet up with old friends. Lin Piao of the steelworkers' syndicate has dropped by. He is a friend of Bang's. Bang, the veteran faction chief, has recovered from his exhausting performance at the Assembly. And Yao Wen-yuan has recovered from his cold.

But Yao is habitually depressed. His head droops over the table. He has been drawing his finger listlessly through a puddle of beer.

The Commons will not meet tonight over its multicom. It is an ordinary evening at the Red Cats, of food and acrobatics.

I am wondering out loud: Are there rich and poor in Garh? I have seen no poor people—only poor sections of the city, relatively.

"Yes. Some boroughs, even whole wards are rich," Lin Piao admits. "How can one avoid it? Some artel makes an invention. Associations are formed. Inevitably this leads to the accumulation of wealth, and to power."

We discuss the Crystal Growers. Bang explains that, expanding their polycrystalline lines, they controlled numerous power outlets at the nodes. Recently they had gone into mining.

"There's plenty of gallium. In the petrified forest, near Zimbabwe. They have a complete monopoly." Lin Piao is cynical. Mrs. Zowie, he says, was now a member of the Sola Producers Board. The Crystal Growers sponsored one of the "dance houses" and several of their officers had become long term senators of the Rotary Club.

I had thought this was illegal.

"It's true. All positions in the Rotary Club are impermanent. But some are less impermanent than others."

Bang calls for more beer and sausages.

I tell them I would like to explain my "medieval theory" of capital accumulation in Garh.

Briefly, the theory is this: that Garh and presumably the other cities of the Rift—are at a precapitalist stage. That is, economic activity is generated by the guilds (the artels) and tied to a limited free market. As it was in the cities of Antwerp or Bruges in the late Middle Ages in Europe.

Of course, there are differences. For instance the improvements in solar technology by the Crystal Growers do not make them the "owners" of the technology in the same way that a group of Flemish merchants would be the owners, say, of a fulling mill.

But, somehow benefits accrue. This is due to licensing agreements, patents, etc.

There were also the religious attitudes. In Altai the stress is on the communal, on the brotherhood bonds. In the Europe of the late Middle Ages the individual was not so important either: it was the guild of artisans. But this was weakening even at that time. The character of the entrepreneur was changing.

I mention certain medieval works of art of which I am particularly fond: the biographies of adventurers by Froissart and the sharp character portraits of Holbein. In the eyes of these merchant princes and guilds craftsmen, as they sit with their tools and counting boxes around them, one can see the future history of Europe.

I felt the same thing ahead for Nghsi—I tell my companions—as I looked into Mrs. Zowie's eyes.

Yao continues drawing disconsolately in his beer puddle.

Bang denies that they are in a state of precapitalist accumulation: "No, no. That's all behind us, centuries ago. What do you think is the meaning of our slogan: 'Beyond Socialism'?"

He admits on the other hand that people did tend to backslide. There had to be "periodic rectification campaigns."

Lin Piao looks at me gravely. He says: "And it is extraordinary to look at Nghsi-Altai through *your* eyes."

Suddenly from outside the Commons there is a squawl of martial music. Yao lifts up his head. Everyone is at the window of the burghall. There is a band of bagpipers marching down the street.

"The mummers' parade," someone exclaims. "Next week will be the Fourth!"

A chain of small explosions, which they say are from gas bombs, shakes the Red Cats window. Outside a crowd of panhandlers seems to have descended on the little square. They are dressed in rags and hold out their bowls piteously.

"They are from the Tenth Ward," Yao remarks with great satisfaction.

"They are practicing begging."

PATRIOTIC PAGEANTRY/ CHILDREN'S GAMES

The Minutemen are going down the street. Long ago people have forgot what their uniforms mean. It is only known: "In a moment they were able to mobilize." Against what?

The Adversary lost in time.

The alert of the drums, the shrill of the fifes now calls us—to pleasure. Under his snapping anarchist banner, my son stands selling pretzels.

• •

We will become the Rooster Dancers, also called The Alarmists, because these roosters which sit so placidly on our shoulders were in fact once alarm clocks. There's no mistaking the roosters' colors: their fiery red and their fierce black is of—NOW. I pluck a tailfeather for decoration.

Soon all these alarm clocks will go off, calling us from sleep. And to action around the Fire Pole.

• •

Legendary heroes, a brigade of SQUATTERS marches by to struggle against the HARD HATS. Their emblem is corrugated tin. And these wire cutters, crowbars, jimmies and oxyacetylene torches are their keys of office. The old fences are down. From the tin sheets they will resurrect Resurrection City.

But this battle has been won years ago.

• •

We will join you on this, the fifth day of the festival which is to last fourteen days, to eat "fire crackers." And "gulgulas," patriotic pancakes, which were perhaps originally made with red pepper.

• •

Tangles of barbed wire. Clippers are used to cut into the currency exchanges and luxury hotels of El Centro—the international hotel section. Their bronze doorknobs are now preserved in museums.

• •

An effigy of the chairman of the board of the last historically recorded Steel Co-ordinating Committee is burned, by the so-called Blue Man.

• •

Overlays of legend, one obscuring the other.

• •

Now every low dive is emptied and from the poolrooms and sports palaces erupt whole squadrons of HARD HATS who rush in the direction of Franklin Park. They are members of the syndicates on their day off.

To the defense of the Tenth Ward! And ancient codes.

They go by with a dazzling display of technical apparel. From our shoulders the roosters taunt them.

• •

So on this day of the year only "gas" is sold.

• •

The traditional "gas dragons" one hundred feet in the air, of inflated rubber, are loose! Breathing their nostalgic fumes. The gas dragon has ten tails made out of colored paper. Cut each tail off in turn, hordes of squatters and "swamp alligators," future citizens, will erupt violently.

• •

They are called milliliters: these small bombs consisting of milliliter cans of gas which are thrown by the children of squatters under the motorcycles of the National Planners.

• •

And what do they hold up, these raiders and these revelers? Weeds flowering on the back lots.

• •

Remember your origins, you most honorary and respected of the Syndicate Leaders, in these clandestine squatters organizations. Wear rags of every color! Put on your "rooster finery."

CHILDREN'S GAMES OF THE TEN-FOURTH

Here is a song/game/dance performed with foreign word borrowings while making mud pies, supposedly on a stove. The "pies" are made and served.

Q. Children, what would you like to eat today?

A. Roast Beef. Roast Beef . . . with Pittsburg sauce.

Q. Children, children, what would you like to eat next?

A. Lamb chops, with Chicago gravy.

Q. Children, then what do you want?

A. Oysters Rockefeller.

Then all the pies are dropped and squashed up. On top of the pile is planted a stalk of joe-pye weed.

• •

Marching on to the National Capital

All children take their "automobiles." When the children arrive at the Capital, they give food to the "starving" congressmen.

(This pantomime is from the National Famine era.)

• •

Stock Villains of Puppet Shows

Stompers-Gompers, the Centralizer. The children stuff pennies into his pockets. Another: Uncle Fatso.

• •

Piñata Game

A "trailer truck" made of papier-mâché is hung up. It is filled with elaborately wrapped packages in containers, plastic bags, etc. The truck is destroyed with canes of bamboo.

BLAKE IN THE WILDERNESS

At Egwegnu University the students had departed. The lake was vacant —none of the little sanjhi boats with their fluttering candles that the children had thrown stones at on the night of the Lights Festival. The dormitories had been cleaned out and dusted. It was the term's end.

Tutuola and Blake left for a walking trip through the woods to visit some holy places.

They carried nothing but the clothes on their backs, a couple of woven straw ponchos, a Coleman stove, and a rucksack.

The forest fascinated Blake. But soon he grew tired of it. The lonely footfalls on the path went on endlessly. The monkeys chattered in the murky canopy. They waded through deep moss during the day and at night rested against trees twined with orchids.

The path was well used. Wood deer traveled that way. A family of zemboks joined the pilgrims for a stretch of the journey, the buck with his great boss and striped hide, walking with slow stride several paces ahead, the cubs frolicking to the side out in the bush. That night Blake lay down in his coat and dreamed of huge lions with the face of God.

They visited several shrines, at which both men worshipped and left bowls of meal. Blake had taken a slight chill which developed into a chest cold by morning. Tutuola kept the fire going continually, wrapped him in both ponchos, and fed him tea brewed from roots. They were by a peat bog. They talked far into the night. The blue shaman asked Blake to tell him something about his birthplace.

Blake's account of the City of London:

"London where I saw the light of day in 1757 was a city of half a million people, and grew in the next fifty years to one million. My father was a hosier. I was born above his shop on Broad Street in the parish of Marylebone.

"The first sounds in my ear were the wagons of the carters clattering over the cobbles. As a small boy I was in and out of the wheels, while the carters cursed. We oversaw with pleasure the unloading of casks and bales. In the winter I could watch the lamps being lit in the gloom. Our town London was notable in the Europe of that time for its improved streets and street services. We had covered sewers, a novelty. I can well remember a gang of men digging a sewer along Aldermaston Street. I marveled at how they threw up the gravel. We followed them a stretch each day for the five months they worked—and in that way came upon the Thames.

"I think that was the first time, also, I saw the sky.

"We were very cramped. The city had pushed out beyond us years before—to Saint Giles, Cottage Terrace, King's Crown, St. Pancras. New subdivisions, new factories as well. My whole horizon was the buildings, with our church piercing one edge of the skyline, and Big Ben another. Those bells had a dead sound. Nearby there was an alehouse; and that was full of light, talkers, and smoke on a winter's night—much more cheerful than the church.

"You may remember my lines: 'Dear mother, dear mother, the church is cold, /But the Ale-house is healthy and pleasant and warm.' "

Tutuola asked: "So the country was far away in your London?"

Blake: "I don't remember seeing a blade of grass or a weed till I was fifteen and my mother took me to St. Pancras. I couldn't have named you any bird but a cheeping sparrow though I was a great expert on market fowl and the crawfish and crabs they trundled from door to door. I could never write in the country. After a few months in the fresh air composing lyrics about sunflowers I was in a rage to get back."

Tutuola: "What was the weather like?"

Blake: "Clammy and wet. Horrible. The worst weather in the world. A grim place. The closed courts, the tenements Dickens describes. Tuberculosis. I'll tell you, the average Londoner didn't live long. It was a life-and-death matter when you sent the bucket out, and the children returned with a few lumps of soft coal."

Tutuola: "You spoke of the chimney sweeps."

Blake: "I knew several. Tom Dacre was one, whose sister was a whore. How extraordinary those poor fellows looked with their stove hats and faces covered with grime. It was a marvel to watch them climb out of a chimney. I don't wonder I was struck by it and took them in my writing as messengers from another world.

"And Tom's sister—standing on an icy corner in her finery against the stones of some bank . . . A face printed in hell.

"Scenes. Scenes. Hogarth was the painter. Rowlandson . . . Yes, yes. There it was bitter weather."

The Deodar asked him: "I suppose you've seen the notebooks of Hiroshige? The Tokyo of his time—twice as large as London and Paris combined. His sketches are fascinating."

Blake: "Yes, but I never drew from the visible world. The human figure yes, that was from life and taken directly after Michelangelo and the Greeks. But the *world* in which they moved was phantasmagoric. Good God, as if there would have been any point in *describing* London. No. The spiritual world was all my aim.

"But I am a great admirer of Hiroshige. He scribbled some verses too."

• •

They had another discussion in which Blake questioned Tutuola on the priesthood's practice of celibacy. His answer (unsatisfactory to Blake) was "the animals are in the forest, from which we draw our strength." And added that the relationship helped "restore balance."

Sexual satisfaction from animals the shaman seemed to take matter-of-factly. He was far more interested in London and returned to that subject. Tutuola asked:

"So the city was so large you say you could scarcely conceive the end of it?"

Blake: "I could scarcely. In my mind it went on forever. And beyond it another world which I called Paradise"

"The city kept growing?"

Blake: "Buildings, churches, warehouses, factories which produced as much steel and cloth as Birmingham and Manchester—a smoky pall which ate up the countryside round about as well."

Tutuola quoted the lines:

"There's the dirt and the smoke
and the millworking folk . . .
Manchester's not a bad town."

Blake laughed and explained that was the wrong "Manchester." The poem referred to another industrial city in "New" England.

Tutuola: "So England is growing continuously too? Tell me, this fascination for murk and grime. It's not conceivable to you for a city to be clean?"

Blake picked his teeth and did not reply.

"I noticed you spoke of the London of your day using the harshest imagery. Surely it was not the city of the Lamb and the Rose, and 'piping down the valleys wild.' But of something diabolical."

"But of course!" Blake cried. "The City is an infernal machine! And the principle of boundless energy."

"And man is innocent, against the bloody stones?"

"It is true there is a crime against the heart, but that is the price paid for all the power, fire, and light bursting out. The city's image is the open-hearth blast furnace. No, not the Rose . . . but the ingot turning to rose in the smelter."

"Even the furnace has to be metered," his companion suggested. "This seems a curious notion to me, this energy source which is infinite and expanding. For us the city is not an engine, but subject to organic rhythms. It is not a tree—but a forest of trees. And so should be thinned occasionally."

"Who is to thin it?"

"We have a saying here in Nghsi: 'Once in a man's lifetime he watches the city die.' That implies I suppose that the two—the man and the city—are of the same measure."

• •

The forest was still around them. They had been following a narrow track among the cliffs, unable to ascend or go down.

Tutuola had built a grass hut. They were sitting in a narrow clearing near the base of a waterfall. Crags rose above them. Spume drifted over the small island from the falls. The beads of moisture seemed to weigh dawn the bamboo. Blake's socks hung on sticks.

The fire kept sputtering from the damp wood and even the smoke appeared heavy. Blake, who had begun to suffer from cold and was wondering when he would ever get his clothes dry, was surprised to hear a whistle blast, followed by the rumble of a train. He thought they might be near one of the lines that carried freight to the forest cantonments, but Tutuola said it was a factory whistle.

There was another blast from below. The sun began to break through, and the mist cleared. In a short time they were looking down at the city of Garh.

"The city is never far away," the priest said. "Either in our imagination or in our experience. The walls of the canyon muffle it. But sometimes, when the wind is right, the noises carry almost to Egwegnu."

It was enough for Blake to look down on Garh, its canals, its towers, the steaming ducts. The wayfarers did not go down. When they broke camp and re-entered the wilderness, Blake felt refreshed.

Tutuola also seemed exhilarated and walked in front of Blake with a light step.

A yellow butterfly settled on the blue priest's beard. He cut a stick of bamboo and carried it.

Then he repeated: "No, the city is never far away. We will re-enter it soon."

THE FIRE FESTIVAL

Yao Wen-yuan heard the cock crow. The noise would be coming from the mummer's band down in the street. It was somewhat earlier than his usual waking hour.

Each dancer attired in holiday costume had a stridently crowing cock on his head. Sometimes a band would actually practice for these performances, or at least learn how to play the instruments correctly. Judging from the sound drifting up from far below, this group was very inept.

Already everyone in the bookkeeping artel was up. They were talking about the Ten-Fourth holiday and greeting each other. "Spreccia!"

"Spreccia!"

Rubbing his eyes Yao went over to the window. Below him on the street the mummers were milling around beating on tin sheets. A small crowd of kids were setting off milliliters, which exploded in ripples.

In the past few days the Eighth Ward had been invaded by mummers. There were two kinds; mummers who were dressed as Squatters, wearing rags of red and orange colors. The others called Hard Hats, wore black costumes somewhat like old fashioned policemen. They were called the Red and Black Mummers and appeared on the streets of Garh once every ten years on the Fourth of July holiday.

On that day a special breakfast is served: red cranberry muffins drenched in molasses, like pancakes. These are some times called "patriotic pancakes." And the children munch hard biscuits, "fire crackers."

Yao decided he would not go to the office right away but would make a detour along the bank of the canal to see what was happening. As Yao came out of the elevator into the lobby he was accosted by a crowd of rag bedecked squatters. There were also beggars from the Tenth Ward. He recognized some business clients.

Along the canal it was sunny and noisy. It was already jammed with boats, crowding each other and blowing their whistles. When he reached his office in the bank building a half hour later, he found everything in disorder. A young woman clerk in his section stood before a window blowing papers out into the street with an electric fan. The filing cabinet stood open behind her. She was calling gaily to other clerks to watch. Papers in four colors drifted on air and sidled down toward the pavement.

Yao Wen-yuan told her: "You mustn't do that. Those are important files." In spite of himself he was shocked.

"But it's the Fourth!" All the Karst clerks wore bright fingernail polish and their cheeks were rouged. The woman stuck her tongue out at him.

"Well, yes. I suppose so"

Elsewhere the office was a scene of cheerful confusion.

Mechanical shredders were in operation eating up files. Duplicate and triplicate papers were being consumed in burn-baskets. Already the place had taken on the air of an office party. Junior clerks were drinking from paper cups. From a cubicle a couple ran into the aisle pulling each others' hair and screaming. Windows were wide open. Yao felt a mixture of horror and relief.

As he went out into the street for the noon hour, another group of employees threw colored powder at him. "Spreccia!" "Spreccia," the head clerk answered.

• •

Balloons were rising past the Noodlemakers' apartments and catching in the solar net. Each time a balloon came by the windows of the pod, coasting and eddying, infants would scream. All were privileged to be home from the nursery for the Fire holidays.

The faces of the older children were already smeared with powders. The gang had been at work outside on the plaza all morning. Periodically Kao and Bangi, his friend, reappeared for tools. Now they had come for a soldering torch.

They were followed by four country children. The youngest Jat girl, Maddi, sucked at her fire-cracker, which she had smeared with ghi. Kao's sister Peach Blossom was also munching her cracker.

It was the morning when everyone in the superblock was constructing their "Tinguely machines."

"Be careful," Kikan's mother said, brushing aside the boy's hair. "Don't self-destruct."

But of course, that was the point of a Tinguely machine! The children rushed toward the elevator.

"Is it really dangerous?" Srikant asked Bangi as they came out into the courtyard. He did not want to ask the Karst boy.

"Well, is it?" Bangi turned blandly to Kao. But the older boy was busy examining the tip of the soldering torch. He turned the knob a fraction, and compressed air hissed out. They were accompanied by several other

Noodlemaker kids. A step or two behind Kao a Karst cousin was carrying a length of cable. Dhillon and Maddi and the smaller Noodlemakers were clutching bags of colored powder.

Each crew in the courtyard had been fabricating its own Tinguely. The large paved space, an extension of the lobbies of several point houses, was full of these enormous constructs. Groups of older onlookers gathered around them with an amused air. The constructs looked flimsy. Most of them had been fitted together with rods, wheels, and bits of sheet metal tenuously held together with wire or solder. Small motors made the parts move. In fact this was what was being tried out now.

Kao started an electric motor, and a bicycle wheel began to revolve. It was geared to a series of larger wheels by belts. A ball descended a chute, and on the top a vane swung around as if pushed by the wind.

Dhillon and Maddi watched for a while, then wandered off. The whole plaza was full of Tinguelys. Some of the models looked like giant birds with elaborate tails and wing structures covered with bright silk. Others were like industrial machines, with gears, greased tracks, and cable drums. Some were spindly and spidery, balanced like dentists' drills.

The country Harditts were wide eyed, and so even was Peach Blossom. Hopping up and down with impatience, she cried: "When does it begin? When?"

At three o'clock all these machines would begin to go off at once. Fantastic nonsense. Explosions. One level of the "self destruct" contraptions gyrating and collapsing on another level.

The prospect thrilled Dhillon.

• •

As the Grain of Millet residents passed through the Sixth Ward they ran into people with shopping carts going in the other direction. The carts were loaded with consumer items.

Olga told them, "They're from Konsum," naming a big department store in the Tenth Ward.

Occasionally the group ran into a crowd of dancers. The mummers no longer carried their roosters. They had been released—perhaps because their function of awakening the town was now over. The roosters had been allowed to fly off, like the balloons.

The country Harditts were astonished at the crowds. They were being pushed helter-skelter. Sathan had to step off the curb so as not to be bumped into by a loaded cart. But in the street they were liable to be run over.

A shopping cart cavorted by harnessed to a goat. Helvetia pointed it out with amusement to the other women. They would probably be Jats. Nanda walked beside Maddi holding her niece by the hand.

There was much throwing of colored powders. As they crossed a square a drunken woman came out of the burghall beating a man with a stick.

This feature of the Fourth was a familiar one to the Sawna women. It was the country way of celebrating.

Helvetia said, "The women are getting their own back."

"Here the women don't have to get their own back. They do what they like," Olga remarked.

Today none of the Jat women was wearing purdah.

They were on a "shopping spree"—an event that occurred not every Fourth of July, but every tenth Fourth. Hence, this festival was called the Ten-Four. They had brought several of their own carts for carrying things. Olga's mother, Sandranapaul, the matriarch of the urban clan, was with them. A woman of seventy, she insisted on pushing a cart—particularly as they passed acquaintances.

Helvetia (who was actually older) kept calling her "Grandmother," much to the other matriarch's annoyance. On this holiday Helvetia was pleased to ask:

"Grandmother, are you sure this is not stealing? Walking halfway across town, and breaking into a department store! The idea."

"It's being torn down anyway," the old woman replied.

Olga's clan took this adventure in stride. The Sawna children were apprehensive. They could hardly believe that they were bound for a "free" zone where rules regarding property were suspended. Maddi kept watching for the police.

In fact at several intersections of the Sixth Ward streets Hard Hats were on patrol. Increasingly they ran into groups of runaways from the destabilized neighborhoods. A stream of refugees passed them. From time to time they met a Drune priest jangling a bell and waving his "wilderness branches."

They were approaching the border between the Sixth and Tenth wards. The pace quickened. The crowds were more packed. They were swept faster. More carts laden with goods were returning. At the same time local people were watching them from the balconies. They kept urging them to move on.

"Not here. Not here. Across the canal!"

They laughed and threw colored powder down. From railings anarchist flags snapped. The shops below were barricaded against the raiders.

The crowd finally swept across the canal bridge into the Tenth. For the first time they could see with their eyes the condition of this ward. It was pitiful. The wreckers had preceded them. Many of the superblocks had already been torn down. Rising from the desolation was the Tenth Ward stadium, which would be the scene of the Fire Pole celebration that evening.

Near the canal bank which they had now reached the department store, Konsum, stood along an open square. It was in the process of being ransacked. Clusters of Hard Hats watched helplessly.

A packed mass of people stood on the sidewalk pressed against the building. All the show windows had been smashed. Heaps of looted furniture and broken counters were being used as steps up into the store. Over these barricades people clambered in and out, handing things down —radios, flamboyant dolls, refrigerators, curtains. These were passed over the heads of the crowd to the back and miraculously secreted in the carts. It didn't seem to matter whether the articles were whole or broken.

• •

The syndicalists had retired to a restaurant on the bank of the canal. Blake and Morris sat with them, drinking beer and watching the demolition as it proceeded. These were members of the Builders and Wreckers Syndicate. Not far from their table on the terrace of the café a steady stream of paraders were going by. Children held balloons.

Across the canal, the boom of a fantastically tall crane moved across the face of one of the point houses. This was one of the syndicate's "nibbling cranes." On a cable hung a clamshell bucket. In this, two men were suspended like balloonists in a gondola—the cutters. The building mast was constructed in modules held together by rods in tension. Long tubes of oxyacetylene gas swung in the air, hanging down in loops from the bucket. Delicately the men would lean out into the sky, cut certain of the rods, and a part of the building would fall.

The foreman was explaining to Morris and Blake that the demolition of the buildings was professional. The job was contracted out among the syndicates of the ward, bids being taken on an entire superblock. Different artels had different methods. There was a lively spirit of "mutualist competition."

The sky was filled with rigging. Puffs of steam from other cranes drifted over the work site. The foreman explained that as the inhabitants of a superblock became displaced and moved out, that section of the borough came down. That was all there was to it.

They could see across the cleared space all the way to the further canal. There the adjoining ward stood, a diminished skyline. Already several square miles of the Tenth was waste space. Only the ruins of one of the department stores was left and several of the national banks whose solid marble fronts had so far resisted being dismantled.

There was a tremendous explosion. In the near distance a section of a point house shot out sideways into space like a pile of exploding barrels. The top of the structure hung in the air an instant, with its apartments, radio towers, and the booms supporting the solar arrays—then wavered. It plunged straight down into the basement, raising a cloud of dust.

"Dynamite," the foreman remarked. He added that he thought this job —which had been done by another artel—was unnecessarily heavy-handed.

"What we are observing," Blake remarked with some awe "is a systematic destruction of one tenth of the city."

• •

"Here they come!"

"Spreccia! Destroy the Tenth!" yelled the small Dhillon, not knowing what the cry meant.

The Bang and Harditt children, separated from the Noodlemakers, were wedged onto the sidewalk behind the barricades. Everyone seemed drunk or camouflaged under streaks of holi powder.

Rooster feathers were stuck in Bangi's hair. The small fry were behind him. Bangi had picked up a pair of wire-clippers somewhere. The children were ragged, Maddi's coat was torn, and Kao's younger brother had lost one of his shoes.

Already they looked like Squatters.

They crawled under the barricade again and rejoined Kikan. After a halt Bang's artel was beginning to straggle into line. Beside them the canal was empty and lurid. There were no boats allowed beyond the Sixth Ward express stop because of danger from skyrockets and falling debris.

Because of the great crowds the marchers were continually having to stop. During these halts, an artel or even a whole section would squat on the boulevard watching the puppet shows. Some of them would go into a café and drink beer or pulque.

Following the Noodlemakers in the line of march was a foreign quarter, the Grain of Millet neighborhood. In this contingent came the other members of the Harditt family. One of Olga's brothers and Venu struggled to hold up a Sawna landscape stretched aloft on bamboo poles.

In the line of march the major syndicates were represented. Most of them had put together elaborate floats, showing the lives of the Great Decentralizers. The Zimbabwe steelworkers came by dragging a float with moving parts operated by steam. The Electrolyte-storage Operators followed. Then, the Recycling Depots. Then, the Honey-bucket Men in gleaming white coveralls accompanying a brigade from the spray farm. The paraders surged past, treading on the pavement thick with the remains of exploded milliliters.

During one of these halts, Maddi, exhausted by the day's happenings, sat down with her smaller brother on the slope of the embankment and began to cry.

The children could barely see across the canal into "Waste Land." The marchers who had already gotten in and crossed the bridges had scattered and were running back and forth under the cranes. On the mountainous piles of rubble, battles were being fought. The children watched the seesawing struggle, at the top the Hard Hats defending, from the base the Squatters surging up with their wire-cutters and blood-curdling shouts.

"Spreccia!"

"Down with the Center!"

There was a blast of bagpipes. Ahead the columns had started up again, but the Noodlemakers were still wedged. To the rear inflated figures soared up in the sky and began to plunge forward.

"The Gas Dragons are coming!"

A flotilla of Gas Dragons, villains and heroes of folk history, soared by over the Noodlemakers' heads. The great figures were held down to earth with wires, but barely. The riggers struggled with them, lurching and bucking as they went along the street straining their necks up.

• •

By nine o'clock all the banks had been dynamited. The municipal debt moratorium had been declared.

It seemed as though most of the population of Garh had been compressed into Waste Land. The rest were spectators lining the far banks of the canals.

The paraders had entered the grounds, but the parades were over. The skirmishes had been fought. Armies of the night—the black/the red—were scattered with the scattered holi powders.

Small bands from the various neighborhoods kept together, were separated in the crowd and darkness, found each other again.

"Happy Fourth!"

"Spreccia!"

Everyone was converging on the Franklin Park stadium.

In the leveled landscape that had been the Tenth Ward only a few national bank buildings still burned beside great heaps of rubble. The stolid marble walls were torn open. Gutted interiors continued to smolder. A pile of beams would ignite suddenly. Sparks which floated overhead mixed with the fallout of skyrocket comets.

Venu's arm was around Sathan's waist. She had drawn her shawl around her. Maddi clung to her mother tightly. The child's face was smudged. Her hair, wet from the heat, was plastered against her forehead.

Maddi had been given the slip by the boys, who were already up on the berm of the stadium perhaps. At ten o'clock would begin the burning of the holi pyre.

They had seen Blake move off several minutes before, with a boy (Dhillon?) on his shoulders. Or could it have been Peach Blossom? The child had one hand gripped across Blake's eyes and with the other held up a sparkler. As they waded into the dark crowd, the light from the sparkler could be seen for some time wavering and bobbing.

Then it was lost among other small fires.

A ferris wheel was turning off to the right. A line of exhausted children waited below it in the dark. The wheel went around, and the gondolas as they reached the top were lighted by a glow coming vaguely from inside the berm of the stadium.

Elsewhere in the crowd Tante Olga had been leading the older Harditt women. Helvetia refused to go a step further. The country matriarch's shawl had been trampled. And she had lost a jeweled brooch, an ancestral heirloom.

The women had come to rest along the side of the canal by the steps of a demolished bank. The Sawna matriarch had pulled up her khurtah and was bathing her feet. In the water near them mummers, dressed as "swamp alligators," were still dumping currency into the canal. The sodden notes floated off.

Helvetia, her gums purple with betel nut and her hair in a tangle, spat out:

"What hysteria. Imagine. To replace a whole section of a city like a worn out part!"

The idea struck the old woman as so comical, she promptly revived and got up. She began throwing colored powder at Nanda, shouting and guffawing.

"Energy! Spreccia!"

• •

The landscape below the stadium was like a dark sea. People floundered up through the tall grass and heather of the berm as if up the flank of a great wave.

Bangi and Dhillon were on the promenade of the stadium. The escalators were now closed and guarded. Breaches had been made in the berm by giant earth-movers colored a lime green. And since late afternoon bulldozers had moved over from the rubble heaps and were attacking the stadium structure. The traffic of wrecking artels and heavy equipment was being directed by members of the Dog Society.

From their vantage point at the top of the berm, the two boys could see far below them benches and other paraphernalia of the Assembly being carried over and piled on top of the Congress. The fire pole at the center of the stage had already been lighted. It was crackling and the debris piled up around it was also beginning to flame.

In front of the forum of the Congress, senators of the Rotary Club were dancing. There were mummers—the Minutemen and Squatters—among them. All were performing the final Dance House.

And now the wooden stage of the Congress itself caught fire.

The boys suddenly felt awe.

A moment before they had been playing and running through the crowd. Now they stood still. The core of the stadium became a giant blaze under the night sky. A flare of light seemed to move upward from the center, illuminating the entire bowl. The bare and empty bleachers glowed like a bone.

A moment before there had been only the lighted pyres in the center of the field and the masked officers dancing around them at the base. Now the arena was empty. The heat had driven the dancing officials away to take refuge on the lower tiers.

The whole pyre flamed. A funnel of sparks shot directly up as if sucked by the sky and without cause, having nothing to do with the stadium at all. The officials stood isolated, as though shipwrecked. They looked out from the lowest tiers, as from a beach onto the sea. Behind them there was nothing. A void.

The senators and the mummers stood floodlighted.

Through the breaches in the earth dike the citizens of Garh had flowed in and filled the upper third of the great bowl, looking down at the scene, themselves lighted by the glowing sky.

Now came the final event of the Ten-Fourth, the razing of the speak houses. The globes of these structures were set to the torch one by one by the wreckers. Over the tiered seats they were like bright onion skins. The fabric had already been splashed with "wilderness" marks. These marks too flamed and crumpled.

Explosions rent the air. From the six sides gusts of material seemed to be heaved up over the spectators.

Srikant shut his eyes tight, then opened them in a daze.

"Spreccia! Spreccia!"

"Holy Fourth!"

"Energy!"

The people gave a shout.

• •

The next day Blake, Morris, and Alvarez walked with the priest, Tutuola, as he went about his task of "sewing the ground." The destroyed Tenth was to be the seedbed for the new ward in Garh. The blue priesthood from throughout the Wilderness had come to conduct the ceremonies of renewal.

Evidently there was no single (and official) rite. In fact most of the residents of the city of Garh had left the burned-out quarter.

His bare feet muddy, Tutuola walked with a dignified mien through the encampment. There were long lines of tents where soup kitchens had been set up. He would stop every once in a while to speak to several of the new squatters.

To each group he would distribute his "wilderness branches." These would be planted immediately beside one of the shacks that had arisen miraculously during the night in large numbers. There seemed to have been some advance planning. Boundary lines of rudimentary streets between the rows of shacks were suggested.

In fact these new squatters who stood in shirt sleeves had been the property-owners and well-to-do burghers of the ward only a week before.

Blake and Morris carried bunches of branches.

In the lanes were puddles. The visitors noted that water from the canals had already been diverted by the engineers into the new settlement. The ground at Franklin Park had been trampled by the crowds the night before. It had been a scene of fire. The smoking mounds were now putting out their own dandelions and fireweed. The priest's weeds seemed not so much an addition to this local vegetation as its emblem.

Alvarez had fallen behind his companions; the two explorers returned to him now and again and then caught up with Tutuola. The filmmaker had had both ears cut off as a result of the judgment of the Noodlemakers. A large bandage covered these marks of the People's justice.

Still, Alvarez continued to wear his fatigue cap, slightly askew, and kept calling to his companions.

He was to be shipped off shortly to spend a year on the Sand Flats. However, as the term of exile had not yet begun, he had been allowed to attend this second episode of the Fire Festival.

The forest priest stopped to bless tools. Already a wall had been plastered, and the artel busy with this work had made certain technical drawings incised on the wet plaster, along with the "growth" mandalas.

Blake, familiar with the priest from the woods, noted in him a new potency.

The priest's gesture in blessing the production implements and planting the seed struck Blake as simple and natural. It was the Forest principle. An old stand of pine (which also had its periods of greater fecundity: "a good seed year") would reseed quickly an adjacent clearing. Probably the Deodars thought of themselves as ancient trees.

A group of squatters surrounded Tutuola. The group was discussing the new form the ward might take. They thought the building material would be predominantly ferrochemical However, it would take several years for production to get started on a large scale.

Residents wheeled up an electric generator. One of the bosses of the artel—a woman who was sending everyone scurrying—reminded Morris of Mrs. Zowie. Among the peers, an authority. He suspected the new institutions of the Ward would crystallize around such a person or group of persons. Of course the new institutions would be much the same. But what shape the new city would take he could not foresee.

In the mild afternoon the Wilderness men moved through the squatters' settlement and among the shanties. Now every roof sported its sacred weed, the Wilderness transplanted.

Beside one of the "soup" tents the American gypsies had set up a ferris wheel, and the wheeling gondolas were full of children. Underneath the machines were lines of other waiting children. They seemed to be mostly Karsts.

The Waste Land, flowering, had become a public park, Morris looked for Maddi in the line. But there were no Harditts. The Sawna people must have returned to rest in their Foreign Quarter.

Soon they too would be leaving Garh.

END OF BOOK II

THE HARDITTS IN SAWNA

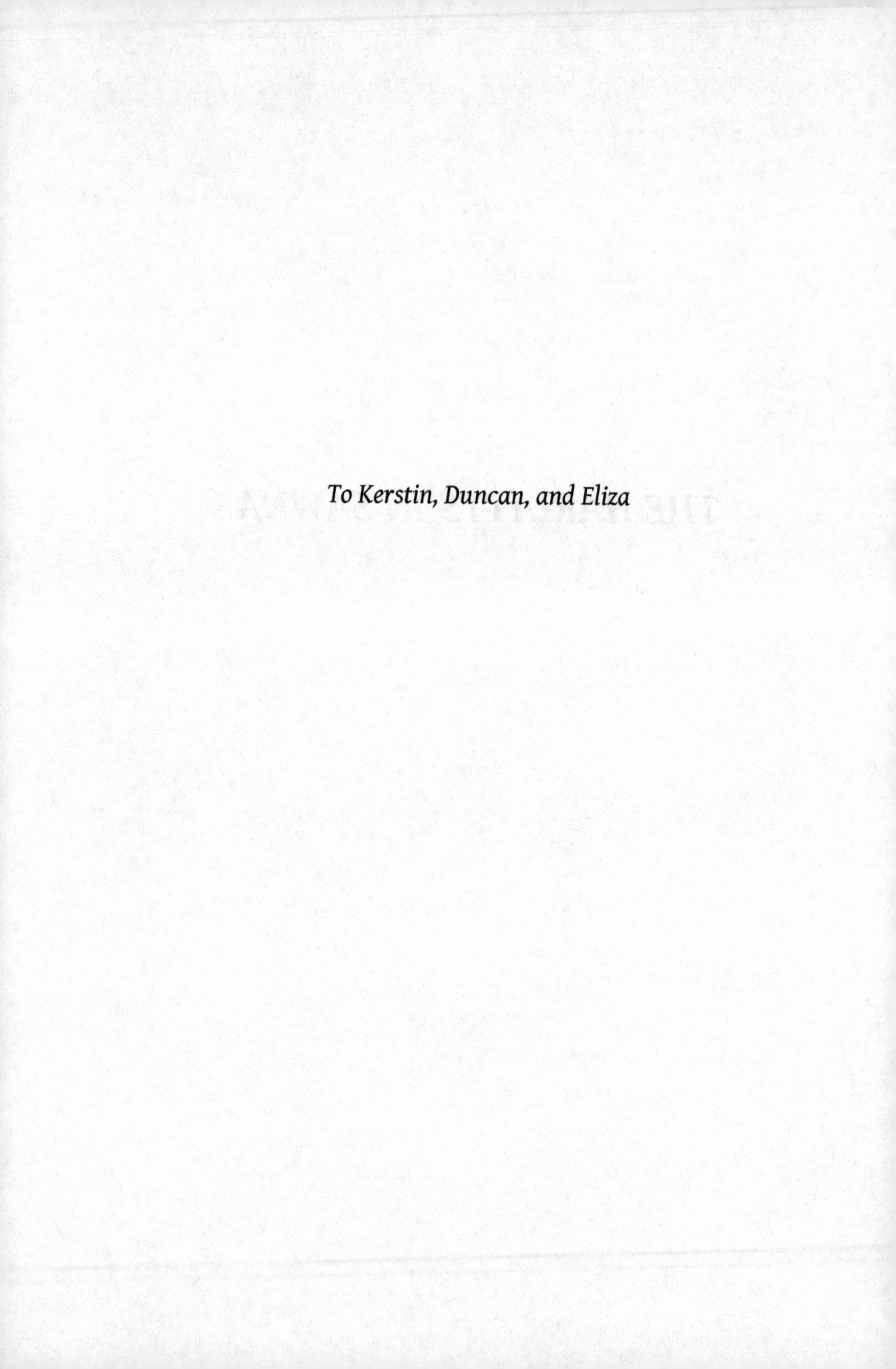

To Kerstin, Duncan, and Eliza

MADDI'S DAY

1

Maddi woke in her world. The moon was not in bed yet. But soon the sun would be up. To power the village.

Maddi from where she lay looked up through the window of the clerestory. A thin wafer of moon floated in the pale sky. My sister, Moon.

There are Six Aspects of the Region and this one is mine, my face. You may be a Water person. My father is of the aspect called Wind. They say those:

Reading the wind-rose
he learns his own name.
Dreaming under the nigh sky, his back is traced
with the brotherhood sign.

It's still dark in the sleep chamber of the Harditt compound. Around Maddi the sleepers lie scattered over the floor like sacks of grain in some big barn. In her own "grandmother's group," her two cousins sleep with their arms around each other, Azul in her blue pajamas. The baby nestles next to Great Aunt.

And Maddi's father, the blanket is off his chest. Her mother lies, her lips parted and her face dim and peaceful, breathing into his arm.

The quiet breathing of the clan.

Maddi, be careful! Don't step on wicked old Aunt Helvetia's foot. Wouldn't there be hell to pay.

In the kitchen Maddi takes down her lunch box, then goes out in the yard to feed the buffalo calf. Now the day is beginning to break. The first sounds of the household stirring behind her.

"Here, Velvet. Come to me."

The calf pricks up his ears. He nuzzles the grain proffered in Maddi's hand. The child puts her arm up around the warm matted neck and rubs her cheek against the soft muzzle.

"Oh, Velvet, how beautiful you are! . . . Now wait for me. I'll be back after school."

Then, grabbing her satchel, her pigtails flying, Maddi runs out the gate of the Harditt compound down the lane in the direction of Washhouse Square.

• •

Sawna Village in the county of Kansu Hardan . . .

The monorail going by. On the high holiday, jostling each other in the narrow lane, the cattle will have their faces painted blue, yellow, bright red oxide colors—gulal.

In the center of the village is Washhouse Square. Here the Maintenance Center is located which supplies power for the village services: the washhouse and the adjoining public baths, a communal freeze locker, the milk and food processing plant, and a light textile mill where you can hear the looms humming.

During the noon break, both the operators of the factory and schoolchildren share the cheerful space of Washhouse Square. Here Maddi will come bringing her lunch box packed by her mother or aunts the night before. Generally lunch is a thermos of sit (goat's milk) or a bottle of Nghsi-Hi soda pop and a ball of glutinous rice with a stewed plum in the middle, called a "rising sun sandwich."

• •

A list of my favorite games (Maddi's):

Pop Up
Red Rover, Red Rover
Reliev-o
Bunny-in-the-hole (marbles)
Blind Man's Buff
Singing and handclapping games
Girl Detective

People I don't like

Great-greataunt Helvetia, for one
Aunt Ranjan, because she tattles
Golgo—a bully, pulls pigtails
Almost all Desai's family—the Filtheaters

My best friends:

Reddy—my cousin from the next compound
Cousin Lucia
Velvet

• •

The children of the Second Age Set (ten to fifteen years old) are assembled on the roof of the Maintenance Plant. High stucco walls cant outward somewhat toward the street. In the center there is a steam boiler with ducts going to the generator.

If it is a sunny day, this boiler is powered by the sun, from a reflector with many-faceted mirrors that open proudly like a peacock's tail. If it is a rainy day, it is powered by agricultural wastes burned in a furnace below. On rainy days this waste is "worshipped": hymns are sung to the chaff, the straw, the corncobs, the bagasse—because all of these things come from the earth and are holy and are part of the energy cycle that charges life.

On sunny days the sun is worshiped—radiant energy pulled from the sky and reflected onto the black surface of the boiler at the rate of 600 gram calories/min/cm^2

Today it is sunny. Members of the class in a row spit on their palms, which they hold up to the sun. Then, under the school mistress's direction the class recites a canticle used for this occasion, "Poem to the Sun" by Gregory Corso. Singsong of child voices . . .

Sun hypnotic! holy ball . . .
Sun, sun-webbed heat! . . .
  hollow vial, sunbone, sunstone, iron sun, sundial.
Sun dinosaur of electric motion . . .
Sun, season of the seasun
Sun circus! tent of helion, apollo, rha, sol, sun, exult!
The sun like a blazing ship went down in Teliphicci lake.

Dreary old sun poem written by another person. Some author, Maddi is tired of it. Her mind has drifted away, wandered back to Velvet. She's lying along the soft warm-pelted back of the water buffalo, legs pressing tight and arms outstretched to the horn for balance, in her hand a switch for swatting off flies.

Look at Maddi daydreaming with her mouth open. In the dream the buffalo turns and lurches. Maddi is pitched off into the green field. Nearby Dhillon's farm crew is shouting. All around the kaoliang crop is head high.

And the sun is shining, shining on the fields.

2

Sathan, Maddi's mother, Nanda, and greataunt Helvetia are on the roof making plans. Marketing lists. What is needed for the compound today? A breeze eddies up from the fields. Nanda lies lazily in the hammock, an arm outstretched, her long hair loose and trailing on the tiles.

This is Maddi's aunt. One of the child's most joyful tasks is to comb out Aunt Nanda's shimmering black hair, pulling the comb through firmly and down.

"Nanda, how glossy and shiny it is. Like an orange!"

A wind shelter of orange trees runs across the roof along the balustrade.

A dozen or so young housekeepers are sunning themselves around the playpen. Squabbles. An infant is throwing sand into the eyes of another infant. Howls of rage and pain. General pandemonium. Sathan claps her hands sharply.

Immediate response and busy-ness among the baby sitters. A switch-role picks up the squalling victim, dandles it, and kisses it. The mother whacks the aggressor.

Lifting her skirts, the matriarch-to-be passes down the circular staircase to the sleep room. But eldest son Srikant is still asleep in his bedroll!

"Up! Up! This is disgusting." Another sharp handclap, like boards being brought together.

Sathan makes her tour of inspection through the five households. The floor has to be waxed. Sheets in the linen closets. Are the shoemakers at work? Does the pharmacist's crew have the right materials?

With Greataunt Helvetia she sweeps into the kitchen. Heads of potato-peelers turn apprehensively. A chef comes running up to the two with a long face. In the midst of bread baking, the communal oven has gone off. Another disaster.

The Maintenance Center is contacted. On the communications screen appears the face of a small boy (Reddy) who is on duty at that moment. The Harditts are informed that the gas is out for the entire village. The stand-by system has also broken down.

"It's the limit!" Sathan exclaims to greataunt. "And how is the soup to get done? We have fifty field laborers arriving for dinner!"

• •

An old man lies sleeping. He is in the compound hospital, which is on the rooftop near the play area.

Nanda enters. "Grandfather." Nanda sits at the edge of the bed.

"Would you like to sit up now? Shall I open the curtains?"

Cranking the bed she props him up, kisses him. She goes out. The old man rests there, his eyes open and his veined hands on the coverlets.

Old Harditt lies listening to the sounds from the common fields. A tractor starts up. Does it tell him anything? Outside on the roof children and nursemaids chatter around the sandbox.

3 THE VILLAGE MAINTENANCE CENTER

The Maintenance Center for Sawna serves the entire village, which is made up of residential sections or "thollas." Remember, there are four to five households (approximately two hundred persons each) per tholla.

Total energy requirements for the village break down as follows:

Work	Quantity
Cooking (electrical or gas energy)	660 kilowatts
Domestic water supply	40,000 gals. /daily
Residential and street lighting	15 kilowatts
Simple food processing	75 kilowatts plus
Pasteurizing	steam
Hot water services and refrigeration	10,000 kg. water/hr.

To accomplish this, plant operating sequence would be:

motive power of solar energy 2400 gram/cal. supplemented by stand-by fuel

↓

high-pressure steam at 22 atmospheres generates electricity for lights, pumps, etc.

↓

waste steam to waste heating and refrigeration.

(Taken from J.C. Kapur, *New Sources of Energy*, pp. 58-66; Volume I, Rome Conference of the United Nations: August 1961)

Continuous Power/Intermittent Power

Note that the above day-to-day production requirements are of a relatively small scale. Activities calling for a larger expenditure of energy —heavier food processing (such as rice milling) and textiles—can be provided on an intermittent basis, i.e., depending on the weather, calendar of holidays, and religious festivals, etc. Energy would be provided on sunny (or in winter, windy) days and would power a hundred-kilowatt generator on a roof, as we have seen.

Commune-Oriented Activities

In general the work tasks involving day-to-day maintenance activities are performed by the Second Age Grade children under the direction of the older cadres. Thus the Maintenance Center also functions as a school. The teaching advantages here are fairly obvious. Technical operations are simple and transparent (the sun's rays direct to boiler—steam to the generator, etc.) and are thus easily grasped. And the products the children make (the resulting community services) are seen as immediately useful.

The tasks are rotated, a new job being handled each week by a group of children from among the several thollas.

Typical School Calendar for Month of Asauj (by Thollas—groups of approximately forty children)

Task	Tholla
Dark Moon Week:	
laundry and bathhouse	Dohbi
light food processing	Teka
freezelocker	Nai
textiles	Singh
other (market products)	Harditt

Slim Moon Week:

laundry and bathhouse	Harditt
light food processing	Dohbi
freezelocker	Teka
textiles	Nai
other	Singh

etc.

What about Maddi and her age-mate Reddy, what are they doing? It is Tuesday of three-quarter moon week—food processing time for the Harditts.

Maddi and Reddy are making their rounds collecting bottles on the bullock wagon. Each commune has put out its used bottles at the pickup station for the tholla. From there they are carried back to the processing room, where they are washed and refilled.

The job takes them about an hour. When the wagon returns they meet Dhillon Harditt coming in on a work detail from the collective farm with a load of vegetables.

They call to him: "Dhillon, Dhillon. Hello, second brother. How is it up in the field?"

The teenage boy barely looks at them. He is busy unloading the baskets for the freeze locker with the older men, among them Harelip. He is jauntily wearing the cap of the Squirrel Society, which gives the privilege to "name" the produce.

Dhillon struts and swaggers. Little sister's question will not be answered.

Describe typical school day:

1. Returned bottles are washed, sterilized. Straining of the milk. Testing for butterfat content, etc.
2. Cooling. Pasteurizing.
3. Milk processing. Adding of vitamins. Separating into other products—cheese, yogurt, kumiss.

The teachers at the Washhouse School are generally of the Fourth Age Set. In Maddi's and Reddy's case their teacher is Amballal, whose two small children are also in class. She has just returned from the Forest University at Egwegnu, where she has received her "education"—whatever that means. It means very little to Maddi. The class is agreed that Amballal Sorabhai is a show-off and that she uses her switch, hanging up beside the blackboard, too frequently.

A History Lesson

Microbes were first discovered by the Forest Men, with their miscroscopes, in the seventh century. They also developed a method for exterminating them through heat: boil at 140° F. for thirty minutes. This process was reinvented by the Chinese in the thirteenth century, and again in France in the nineteenth—where it was called pasteurization.

Pasteur, who was Pasteur?

Can anyone spell the word pas-teur-i-za-tion? Will anyone volunteer? Maddi, are you listening? The history teacher turns from the blackboard. "Look at Maddi. She's fallen asleep."

Amballal taps sternly with her pointer. But Maddi is not asleep. Her head is down over her notebook. She is looking at the floor at a crayon drawing she had made. She pushes it over toward the boy sitting next to her. It is a big buffalo stuck in a mudhole, with a tiny man pushing. The cartoon with balloons coming out of their mouths says:

Buffalo: "Hey! Get me out of this, will ya?"

Man: "Help!"

The sexual organs of the buffalo and the man are prominent though quite inaccurately drawn. Does a buffalo's penis extend backward, like a rhino's?

If the cartoon is discovered, what will the punishment be today, Amballal Sorabhai? The birch switch? Or exile of the culprits to the roof to polish the solar mirrors?

Maddi peeks over at Reddy between her fingers and dissolves in giggles.

4

A rare occasion: Maddi had been invited to visit her cousin Lucia at her club. The dazzle of it! The day was the fifteenth of Asauj in the year of the Pine cone—which would make Lucia just three months short of being nineteen. Maddi was in braids, wound in a tight coil over each ear. She was wearing her black patent-leather shoes.

Women of the Third Age Grade, their dyed many-colored shawls open and dropped down about the neck, came and went in the lobby. Under he cousin's sponsorship, Maddi signed the guest register at the desk. They took the elevator to the tenth floor. Lucia looked tired.

This was the first time the youngest Harditt had been on an elevator since the holdiays in Garh.

And in the middle of the tenth floor lobby there was a "tinguely." The sculpture, spinning brightly, reminded her of the Ten-Fourth celebration. To the right there could be glimpsed a room with dining tables. Following her cousin, Maddi was taken through another large chamber which Lucia told her was the "quiet room and laboratory." Indeed, as they passed the great circular table with its equipment, outlets, and bubbling retorts, there were women studying and experimenting. A balcony ran around the quiet room off which opened the dormitory cubicles of the baithak residents.

Maddi found herself in a cubicle Lucia shared with another woman. The roommate, who had just showered, was wrapped in a towel, her head encompassed in a huge be-dropped shower cap. Her limbs glistening, Shusheela, dried herself. She kept chattering. Lucia showed little interest.

"The men from the machine bank are coming tonight, I heard them say so. They'll be here around ten."

Lucia asked, how was a girl supposed to get any sleep? She had her homework to do.

Two other residents came in. They were in various stages of dress. The shower caps were off. Displayed was the regulation headdress of the Third Set—an elaborate pompadour of rolls and circles, the hair wound in plastic curlers. Ranjan's were red and Chinappa's green. Chinappa's whirled around, her skirt brushing the walls of the alcove. Ranjan wore only striped silk trousers and a bra. She was carrying her garkhi.

"Oh, it's Maddi. How did you get in here?"

Maddi helped the woman button the tight bodice up the back, then stood in front to admire her. The silver mirrors and lozenges sparkled. A wave of perfume exhuded from Ranjan's hair.

The group went to the common room for supper. Women came and went, stopping by the table with trays and remarking cheerfully over Lucia's cousin. Windows along one side of the room looked out on lights far below. It *was* like being in the city, Maddi thought, in one of the point houses of the Red Willow quarter. Oh yes indeed, the baithak—with its elevators, with its laboratories and cafeterias—reminded her of Garh. It did not seem like being in the country at all. Maddi drew a breath of pure freedom.

How *restful* it is out of the compound away from all those children. How awful to have to go back.

Maddi asked aloud: "Lucia, when will I get to live here at the baithak?"

"My dear, when your age set is ready."

Another woman added, "After you have lost your pigtails," and touched Maddi's braids.

"It seems so high up, Lucia. Do you think I could have a room on the ground floor?" She would have liked to add: so I can be near Velvet, but was ashamed.

Supper was followed by an interval in the quiet room which Lucia spent doing homework. Maddi trailed, poking around the scientific apparatus and watching. Just as the Washhouse was a school under the Maintenance cadres, so the Third Set laboratory studies were connected with the routine tasks of the Weather and Soils Station. The laboratory courses rotated through the Six Tendencies, the students spending two months of the year on each. At the moment, her cousin Lucia's studies were with the Water Tendency.

Each student had a desk where she worked and a locker at the edge of the chamber. Lucia's things were in a mess.

Shusheela had come in with them. On Lucia's locker was pasted a photograph of a thin dark-skinned man with a flowing beard. He sat cross-legged under a tree, with a sweet smile, his palms extended.

"It's a photograph of the sensor," Lucia said, seeing Maddi looking up.

"I know. I've seen him at the Weather and Soils Station," Maddi answered.

"Isn't he beautiful?" Shusheela said. "Lucia's crazy about him."

"Don't listen to her. After all, he's a priest. You couldn't fall for him."

"No, because the Bluefaces only make love to animals." Both Lucia and the roommate giggled.

"Not in front of Maddi!" Shusheela clapped her hand over her mouth.

"But Lucia," Maddi asked, "what do you do there at the Weather and Soils Station?"

Lucia explained they were going out every day under the sensor's direction to take bio profiles. Now they were surveying the ponds. Each afternoon they visited a different pond and took certain measurements which were recorded in a field book. These were the nutrient count, sunlight, PH rating, temperature at different levels. At night these notes had to be transcribed and a map made.

"That's what I have to do now, Maddi," Lucia concluded. "I'll tell you what, you can help me. You can read out the figures, and I'll copy them. That's what we'll do: we'll make the map together. But then you'll have to go home."

• •

At ten the men arrived from the machine bank. There was a group of them on the pavement below in their jeep. The horn was honking. One of the youngbloods had brought along an accordion.

Where Maddi and Lucia were working quietly someone hurried by, saying, "They're here." Through the doorway they could see a group in the common room playing cards. Everyone else had drifted over excitedly to the window.

Chinappa and Shusheela came rushing by. They were in their evening dresses.

"Lucia, you're not coming?"

"No."

"Listen. They're singing." They hurried by.

Most of the Third Age Set women were by the windows now peering down into the blackness. The men's song came up, accompanied by laughter.

Oh Sheela Sheela
I see you Shasheela
Standing by the window
Jump down, into my arms.

Another voice: "Sweetheart. Come on. We'll go swimming."

"I'll bet they want to go swimming. It's all right when you're in the jeep. But the minute you step out of it, and they have you in the woods—watch out."

"There's no danger in making love."

"What a racket. Listen to them. They're crazy." Raggedly a song drifted up. A different voice improved each verse.

"Ranjan   Ranjan/we're waiting
  hurry/put on your lipstick
    and your eye makeup
We'll kiss it off."

A group of young women had moved to the elevator. The two cousins were forgotten. With the rest, Susheela, Ranjan, and Chinappa pulled on their purdah shawls and left.

Now the tenth floor of the women's baithak was deserted. Lucia sat over her desk with her T-square. There was a lined grid over it. As Maddi read out the figures in the field book, her cousin would mark down a point on the grid, with an elevation and number beside it. Then the points were connected in contours. Under Maddi's eyes—in the magic of symbols

—the map became a pond, a real pond that she recognized . . . the one by the peach orchard. Maddi had walked beside it. She had felt the wet grasses brushing against her leg.

But still—this was the area of the Water persons. Somehow the mind of Maddi could not be occupied with the mere pond—though it was interesting with its gradients of sunlight and nutrient flows. What Maddi was drawn to in an obscure way, by something deep down inside here, were the numbers themselves, the figures in their abstractness, the constellation of symbols. And one day her *work* would be those symbols. Because was she not—like her cousin Lucia—a Moon?

Her cousin was speaking to her. "Maddi, don't you think you should go home now? They'll be angry at you."

Actually Lucia was glad for the company.

"Lucia, what did she mean: when 'they have you in the woods'?"

"Oh, Maddi, you don't understand anything. Come on, read the figures. We're almost done now."

So Maddi, straight-backed on the stool, read in a clear high-pitched voice, taking care not to mix up the figures in the columns. The bio profile was almost complete now, with Maddi's help. She felt very grown up. And certainly at a great distance from the other children of the compound, particularly Reddy. But she was beginning to get sleepy. The lights shone down softly on the drawing board.

Maddi looked up at the photograph of the young priest, whom they called Tattattatha. He seemed to be smiling down at her, his eyes loving and peaceful. How wonderful to be a student of science. And what a beautiful person to have to teach you, Maddi was thinking. He *must* be because, wasn't he, as her cousin's friend had told her, so very fond of animals?

DHILLON

1

Srikant had been married and had gone off. Dhillon perched on a haystack could look across the fields to distant villages. At the edge of the plain white walls glimmered against the haze. Well, his brother would be *out there* and married. What would that be like?

Dhillon had seen the wedding ceremony which had taken place several months before. The rites were unbelievably ancient. How they receded through time.

> Shadows like winds
> Go back to a parent before thought, before speech,
> At the head of the past.

The rites had stolen his brother away. "And someday it'll be me," Dhillon thought, and looked with a pang at his own village fields. Some day he would have to leave them.

The wedding ceremony known as "phera" among the Sirhind Jats takes place in a pavilion set up in the boy's village. The relatives sit opposite each other across the fire hole. The veiled bride sits on one of the boards facing east. The fire is lit and a few mantras are recited, then the young man is escorted in by his uncle. They recite after the shaman seven vows or promises, the groom holding the bride's thumb. Then they walk around the fire seven times; the groom goes first three times, then the bride four times.

As they go around, the young man's relatives sing these lines:

Here he takes the first round
His grandmother's grandson.

Here he takes the second round
His maternal uncle's maternal nephew.

Here he takes the third round
His mother's elder brother's nephew.

Here he takes the fourth round
His mother's own son.

Here he takes the fifth round
His mother's younger brother's nephew.

Here he takes the sixth round
His sister's brother.

Here he takes the seventh round,
And lo! the dear one becomes alien.

Then the shaman removes the bride's veil and applies the tika around her neck. And the families are joined.

From the top of the haystack, his arms under his head and chewing a stem of grass, Dhillon gazed over the shimmering fields. His friends Golgo and Pindi lay beside him, smoking. The work detail labored below somewhere.

The sun soaked into them. The sweet hay was in their nostrils. But they had been spied. The ganbu came toward them waving his arms and shouting.

2

The Third Age Set young men were shooting pool in the common room. Golgo had a trick shot. The shortest and thickest of the three, he leaned a solid rump against the edge and bent backward over the table, the cue gripped under his arched back and his neck twisted like a lobster. It was a shot he rarely missed. But tonight he was missing even the easy ones. Pindi was besting him. Dhillon was no pool player.

Other young men lounged around and watched. They played a game of round robin, then teams: the Red Willows against the Nais. Golgo and Pindi tried to rattle their opponents. The air rocked with pungent insult.

Someone called to Dhillon that his maternal uncle was outside. He was wanted at home for a meeting.

The others accompanied Dhillon to the compound.

"Do you want us to split?" Golgo asked at the gate. He and Pindi lived in the same village quarter but in another tholla. "Maybe we're not allowed."

"No. Come on."

The meeting was being held in the Harditt kitchen. Old Harditt—in one of his intermittent periods of good health—presided. All the men of the producers' co-operative were present: Harditts, Singhs, Gayans, and Dhobis. The older men constituted a smokers' group at the center. As Dhillon entered he saw his father near them. Venu did not look at him.

A droll man was speaking. The little man bobbed up and down in front of the hookah smokers, waving his arms.

"In the spirit of self-criticism . . . hicch . . . I acknowledge I borrowed the commune horse . . ."

"In the spirit of self-criticism you should acknowledge you're drunk on sendi. Isn't that right uncle?" There was a laugh at the expense of the hiccupping man.

"But did you borrow the horse in order to get to the market—on commune business—or to market the horse?"

"Your honor, you understand my malady. The question is, can I even ride a horse?"

The malefactor stood before the smokers, peering into their faces with a foxy look.

Pindi whispered to Dhillon, "He's not in real trouble. He knows he can do anything he likes—because he can make them laugh."

The discussion moved to the subject of farm machinery. The leader of the cane cutters suggested that the ox, which was used for turning the grinding wheel, was inefficient. The commune should buy an electric cane grinder.

The section chief had the figures. He explained that the ox, which was old, was borrowed from an adjacent village commune under a mutual aid agreement in exchange for work on their irrigation ditches. Last year a squad of ten men had worked for sixteen days on the Dabar ditches: a total of eighty work points. But the grinding by the ox was only rated at the equivalent of sixty work points.

Someone remarked: "It looks like we're working for the ox; not the other way around."

The ganbu ran rapidly through the cost figures. Extending the electric cable at so many lakks . . . a three-horsepower engine would cost twenty lakks and be amortized over a five year period, etc.

Jeth Harditt, the chairman's brother, said, "Nobody denies that an ox is less efficient than an engine. And besides, it has to be fed all year round. But it's the Nai who is feeding the ox."

"That's right. It's his expense."

"Yes, it's an insurance. Someday we may need our neighbor. There's more mileage sticking with the Nais."

Another said, "We can't have all machines and no men or animals. Who would be in the fields?"

The argument went back and forth. Old Harditt in a rocking chair, his face drawn, listened quietly. Dhillon noticed how the veins stood out over the gnarled hands. Occasionally one of the disputants would look to him for a comment, but in general he simply listened and let the members of the collective come to an agreement among themselves.

After the meeting the three friends returned toward the baithak. Overhead the stars shone vaguely. Pindi wondered why Dhillon had been called.

"Yeah, what a waste of time," Golgo said. "We could have cleaned up on them shooting pool."

Dhillon did not know why his uncle had summoned him. Was it because he was reaching the age when he would take part in such discussions on his own? Or because the old man was sick and had wanted his grandson to be there?

Maybe Harditt would not preside over another co-operators' meeting. And the clowning man who had amused them with the story of borrowing the horse, he wouldn't be around for so many years either. The thought made Dhillon sad.

3

Dhillon, Pindi, and Golgo were waiting outside the motor pool. They were jumping from one to another of high stacks of bricks. Occasionally one of them would fall short, grab onto the bricks, and send them tumbling. Then the unfired bricks, in readiness for the kiln, would break, and the three youngbloods would look around guiltily for the watchman.

A tomcat appeared. His grizzled ear was torn. Evidently he had been on the prowl in the village. They threw stones at it.

Finally they cornered the old tom under one of the brick piles. "Let's catch him and jerk him off," Pindi suggested.

"Go ahead. I dare you to put your hand underneath there, man."

"No, you do it."

"Not me, man."

In this area called the Fire Station were gathered the various village-based enterprises having to do with the refining and processing of earths and ores: the brickworks, an industrial ceramics plant that made capacitators and transistors, and a plant that produced batteries. The area was under the jurisdiction of the Fire Phratry and was managed by one of their local clans, the Salamanders.

The young men watched the Salamanders come in to work. Carrying lunch pails they streamed through the gates and made their way toward the buildings. Outside each plant workmen stood around talking and joking. Section groups were discussing the day's tasks.

"When's our man coming?" Dhillon was referring to their ganbu. "That guy's always late."

"What are we supposed to do this morning? They never tell you anything."

"Load up the truck with the batteries, man. What do you think?"

The batteries, called "earth-energy-wafers" or "bitauras," were a special product of Sawna. They were manufactured from one of the local earths, related to lithium, which when processed made up one of three battery panels or plates. Another panel was of fixed hydrogen, with an empty section in between, the electrolyzer. When the battery was connected across the poles and there was a flow of electricity, this center section filled with an ionic compound. Each fuel cell produced a current of fifteen volts.

The batteries made at the Fire Station were also recharged at the Fire Station, using waste heat from the brick kilns which broke down the electrolyte into its original components and regenerated the plates.

Along the length of the fence between the motor pool and the brickworks stood rows of motorless trucks. The motors, which had been removed the night before and had gone through their regeneration cycle, were now ready to be reinstalled.

Traffic was beginning along the entrance road. Smoke rose from the vats where the earths excavated around the brickworks were being reduced to liquid metal broths. The youngbloods' ganbu had arrived. Golgo, Dhillon and Pindi were put to work loading the heavy three-foot-square fuel cells. These were stacked in piles on the backs of trucks and would be taken out to the various county jobs to power the farm machinery. After the backs were loaded, a fuel cell was clipped onto the front of each truck and coupled to the engine.

Other vehicles were passing, scooters and motorbikes. Many were homemade rigs run on methane. A motorcycle dashed by at top speed with a plastic bag held to the machine by guy wires floating over the driver's head, the flexible tube dangling to the carburetor. The silver balloon was decorated with the driver's clan insignia.

The work detail took off, shouting and hollering at acquaintances as they passed through town. On the country road the truck banged and rattled; the boys swayed against each other and stumbled over the pile of tools and bitauras. They were passing the collective farm. A group of gleaners was following the threshers. A flock of blackbirds screamed over their heads.

"Watch out, brother. You'll get a load on your head."

They passed the cauga machine bank, then a peach orchard. A gang of pickers swarmed over the branches.

Now they were on the plain. Ahead the road was blocked. The truck braked to a stop and everyone tumbled out.

A bridge under repair spanned a gorge. The walls were of crumbly red rock and bare of vegetation. Far down, two hundred feet below, was the dry streambed. The temporary, bridge scaffolding was of spindly sections of bamboo. It seemed to grow like a living plant up from below. Men worked suspended under the bridge.

The boys watched the repair crew with fascination. Hanging onto the bamboo, the barefoot men seemed to be levitating. A boom lowered a shiny metal strut into place. Two workmen clambered like lizards up the diagonal and bolted the strut, balanced over the abyss.

The crew knocked off for a tea break. The boys crowded around them. Squatting on solid ground, the middle-aged riggers seemed to have lost some of their magical qualities.

"Wow, you really work high up."

"Yeah, don't you ever get dizzy?"

"Dizzy? What's that?" A bragging response. The man squinted into the tea cup and spat sideways. "You boys from around here?"

Pindi explained that they were a detail of the village agricultural cooperative on their way to the fields.

"You don't say. So you're farmers?"

"Not yet. We will be."

"Work you pretty hard, do they?"

"They break your balls. Hoeing corn's no fun."

Another boy put in:

"You don't learn nothing as an apprentice. But the tractor school's O.K."

The boys watched as the men boiled their tea over a billy can. They were a mixed crew: Jats, a Karst, and two Forest Men. They had removed their belts heavy with clanking tools and wore only shorts. Their heads were shaved. All bore the tattoo mark of the Steelers.

Though they seemed friendly it was clear that a distance separated the traveled roustabouts from the territory-bound apprentices.

"Say, what do you fellers do for kicks? I bet there's plenty of pussy around here." The rigger winked at his companions.

"Yeah, if you can find it," Golgo told him. "But you have to be young and goodlooking."

The roustabouts were a curiosity around Sawna. They were all men of the Fourth Age Grade, but unlike the others they would never settle down in the village compounds and have children.

Nor could the young men, presently sharing the roustabouts' tea, have children at this stage. Upon going into the Third Set their semen tubes had been tied, and would not be untied—that is, the vasectomy operation reversed—until the next rites of passage, when they would become husbands and farmers.

But for the class of roustabouts, the vasectomy operation was permanent. They were to have no families and no home. That was the price they paid for their freedom to wander.

The bridge ahead was still blocked. There would be a further delay while the crane was being refitted. For the benefit of the repairmen the boys put on a karate exhibit: Golgo alone against Srikant and Pindi. As always Golgo got the better of it. They all stood up, puffing and grinning. To return the favor the roustabouts told travel stories. They had been everywhere in Nghsi and done everything, in the Plains, the cities, the Wilderness. The young men listened in naive wonder. Every once in a while a speaker—to illustrate a point—would wave a leathery hand toward the horizon.

4 SOME NOTES ON THE YELLOW SHEAVES AGRICULTURAL COLLECTIVE

Landscape predominantly dry steppe. The image is of endless dry plains, the heat shimmers, a haze of clouds off somewhere on the horizon. A deep friable, not heavy soil: somewhere between loam and sandy-dry loam; rich if irrigated. But then, there is the danger of salts being brought up.

And so, irrigation canals crisscross the landscape. And wind shelter belts of Acer negundo (boxelder) planted along the banks of the canals.

Crop List (Excluding Industrial)

- Wet Season Crops
  - Sugar cane
  - Millet
- Dry Season Crops (with irrigation)
  - Maize, wheat, barley
  - Groundnuts
  - Sweet potato

To this should be added fodder crops and permanent cover in pasture. Recommended varieties, alsike clover and blue panic grass.

Suggested Crop Rotation Calendar

In June the early millet (TH dwarf) is planted out. This is harvested in October, yielding three tons a hectare. Immediately after the bajra (millet) harvest, a new high-yield variety of sweet potato is planted. Maize is cultivated in December, while the sweet potato is harvested and groundnuts are cultivated. The maize is harvested in May, the groundnuts in June; and the millet sown immediately afterward. This rotational system is applied over the whole area of the collective.

Layout of Fields

Layout of fields small to medium scale and only exceptionally to meet the requirements of machines. Mostly the terrain is improvised according to crop rotations and required yields: on irrigated land, by blocking up and opening the squares formed by the earth dikes. Thus a plot is flexible and laid out in harmony with the work (as opposed to monoculture).

This the best setting also for the apprentices, who rotate from job to job (at play?) and work side by side with the real farmers—production workers.

Discipline

Are the incentives to be work points—i.e., base-rate productivity per man per job? Or some other criteria? Is temperament a factor?

In any case the work section goes out each day to a plot of ground where the size, crops, and even technology to be used have been to some extent discussed in the panchayat groups. And so it is their own "work" (work of art, possibly).

Isn't boredom perhaps the main problem—not the difficulty of farm work?

The "back-breaking" grind of labor. But worklessness equally an oppressor of the poor. The terror of the "dead season" ("los tiempos muertes" of the Puerto Rican can cutters).

So types of machines become crucial. Which machines displace agricultural labor? Which raise productivity and at the same time permit tolerable work?

5

It is midmorning. Dhillon, Golgo, and Pindi are on a work detail weeding. In the afternoon the young men will be transported to another area for tractor-driving school.

The terraced field is planted in alternate rows of maize and sweet potato. The strong stalks of maize, planted earlier in the season, shade the flowering sweet potatoes. But the sun beats down, scorching the backs and heads of the cultivators.

In the adjacent field sugar cane is being harvested. Down the hill and along some invisible line far at the bottom there is movement among the tips of the cane. They can hear the cane cutters shouting.

No doubt about it, this is hard work. Hardly space to turn your ass around between the vegetable rows. The "sweets" have shot up, their heads a tangle of scratchy tendrils and tough glossy green leaves. Spiky rotten-smelling blooms tickle Golgo's nose as he bends down.

The sky is bright blue, and the field swallows chatter and swoop, make fast dipping turns pushing their tail feathers out and banking on one wing. But you're not supposed to look . . . keep your eyes on the dirt. The ganbu is watching you.

Golgo slices through a big worm with his hoe and watches the two ends wiggle, exuding slime.

Weeds weeds weeds fill the space between the maize rows, somebody has forgot to mulch. So root them out with the hoe. Hoe hoe hoe . . . what a drag this all is! Golgo would like to heave his scrabby instrument in the air—not to hit anybody, just hurl it away in rage.

He imagines how it arches through the air, spinning and turning on itself . . . sailing . . . and falls with a clunk on the hard field.

Good. Got rid of it.

Hey Golgo, can you throw a spear? I bet I can throw mine further than you can. Pindi lifts up his hoe.

Bet you can't.

Bet I can.

All right: together . . . Whoooom! With a thrust of mighty arms the two sticks go hurtling through the air. A flock of sparrows at the other end of the field start up.

The boys run to see. Ha ha, I beat you. Ten feet further than you, Golgo.

No, you're measuring from the wrong spot. Look, I got you.

But actually Golgo is only dreaming. He continues cultivating behind Pindi's bent back. The hoe stays in his hand—and he goes on, chopping and slicing at the weeds.

Another fantasy: he, Dhillon, and Pindi are competing in a karate exhibit. This time it is not a small-scale affair. The match is on the village threshing floor after the harvest. The combatants are surrounded by crowds of people, the entire village. Lucia, Shusheela, and Chinappa are applauding wildly.

Come on, Golgo, get him! Throw him down!

Kill him, Pindi. Twist his neck!

Dhillon, Dhillon, you get the other foot. Give it to him, Dhillon!

A masked challenger has arrived from another region.

Golgo, winner of the first round, will deal with this threat. The crowd is hushed. The champion takes off his robe revealing a tremendous physique. A tough customer, Golgo will have to use all his science to beat him. Announcement of the bout over the loudspeaker. The contenders lock hands, circle. The village hero hunched down among the potato rows makes a lunge at his imaginary adversary . . . feints . . . jabs . . .

"Hey, Golgo! You gone crazy or something? . . ." Pindi yells at him in the hot field.

• •

Pindi too has been dreaming. He has passed through his Brotherhood rites and is now a full-fledged member of the Steelers. He has gone off with the band of roustabouts. They are traveling to distant parts. . . . To the lake-drowned, misted Drune Forest? To some construction job high over the Rift Canyon perhaps . . . The others call to him, the sound echoing from the cliff face. Under the bridge the rig hangs suspended in air . . . The boom of the crane swings . . . Pindi walks catlike along the beam . . .

• •

The maize field was bounded by a dense fifteen-foot-high wall of cane that seemed to compress the heat. The pale glaucous green, plumed at the top, whitened in a cat's-paw of wind. Already the line of cutters was drawing near the weeding crew.

The line of sweating and cursing men advanced against the cane, and the cane receded before them. Their shirts hung damp and loose, and the fuzz of the cane "hair" powdered their necks and arms. Keeping their footing, the men moved like soldiers, the machetes sweeping down and across the stalks, cutting them close.

Each time a blade would flicker and the plant totter. The man would lop off the leaves, cut the stalk in three pieces, and drop it behind. The stalks formed into loose piles. As the saying was, the furiously working men were "defending themselves against the cane."

After being cut, the cane was gathered by machine and loaded aboard flatcars. A rail spur ran along the far side.

The young men stood to watch the cane cutters sweep by. Now the width of the adjacent field was opened to view. On the far side was a row of trees. They could see the lunch wagon. The ox that had drawn it up from the village had been unyoked and was tethered in the shade of one of the carob trees.

In a few minutes the section would have its lunch break. But not yet. The sun blazed down on Dhillon, following Golgo and Pindi. He had fallen behind his two pals. Over in the next row a young woman was working, her arms bare. She was on her knees hauling the compost basket. As she passed Dhillon, the woman's leg brushed against him.

Dhillon's face reddened. They had been children together of the same tholla, before she had passed over into the next age set. They had wrestled in the grass behind the house, grabbing each other's hair, rolling over and over. And now Marte was married and had taken a husband from another village.

Passing by Dhillon on her knees she did not look up at him.

The ox bellowed in the shade. Some laborers who had eaten already lay asleep on the ground beside the animal.

In the wake of the cutters, the cane picker went to work. The machine was called a "spider." Powered by its triple-linked fuel cells, it moved erratically over the cane piles. The spider would stop, a grate under its belly open, and the pile of cane was scooped up and carried over to the freight cars.

It was Marte's husband—Indio—who operated the cane picker.

The young men watched the mechanic with envy. His head burned a copper red, Indio seemed part of the machine, lurching over the field with it, his knuckles bunched and his brown fingers an extension of the bank of levers.

The noon whistle blew. The operator stepped down stiffly onto the dirt, stretching his back.

Some of the cutters were already walking over to where the pots of soup had been set up. The women cultivators had stopped to rest in the shade of the maize.

Some housekeepers had come with the lunchwagon. One of them had brought Marte's baby. The peasant husband went over and took the baby in his arms covered with dust. Then he carried it over the field to Marte. She sat nursing it, while the husband tickled the baby's toes.

The woman's husband called over to Dhillon, "Come on over. Eat with us."

Some of the cane workers came over to talk to Indio. They stood talking and passing a cigarette, the husband looking down at Marte with a pleased smile.

Dhillon thought: "Well, he seems to have found a home, anyway."

Soon the sweet potato crop would be harvested; the field would be dug up, and the heaps of dried stalks and leaves plowed back. Then the maize would be harvested; by that time the groundnuts would be started. The cycle of the harvest. The wheel of growing and maturing.

And soon he would be leaving these fields. Dhillon felt a pang.

Well, that was life, wasn't it? It had to be that way. And maybe it wasn't such a terrible thing: to grow into a man, to have to leave one's mother village? To "become alien."

GETTING AHEAD WITH THE BANIYAS

1

Srikant had been dreaming of his wife all day. Images of Tulsi floated before him as he sat at his desk calculator, his fingers hardly capable of pressing the keys. His fingers should have been caressing Tulsi.

That morning he had gone into the village washhouse on a bookkeeping detail and had seen Tulsi at the public baths. He would have liked to jump in immediately, paddle around with the rest of the bathers, squirt jets of water through his teeth and splash Tulsi. Unfortunately his supervisor was accompanying him. The two of them stood at the doorway and looked in. Both carried briefcases. “How appetizing she looks,” Srikant thought. “But I’ll just have to wait till this evening.”

Some schoolchildren were playing in the pool with the factory workers. Tulsi pulled herself out dripping. Her back toward the two accountants, she bent to dry herself with a towel. Her buttocks glowed. As she stretched she showed off a little pot that swelled down under her waist like a melon. Tulsi was pregnant with their second child.

The afternoon at the Gonwanda Machine Bank crawled by. It seemed to Srikant everyone was watching the clock. He had been assigned by the family Panchayat to the bookkeeping department. The work was easy. But today the routine was deadening. Images of Tulsi on the wet duckboards floated before his eyes. The department was next to the shipping room where the crates from the bottling works were being handled. Every time a forklift rattled across the concrete, the vibration moved across the floor and sent a tingle up through his shoes to his prick, and his balls ached.

Like most of the enterprises in prosperous Gonwanda the bottling works was managed by the Baniya clan. Tulsi's Uncle Zamindar was chief of the commercial section. And it was Tulsi's Uncle Razzakar who ran the collective farm. There were brains on all sides of the Baniya family; it was said that one had to get up very early in the morning to beat the Baniyas.

Possibly this was the reason Srikant, as a member of the Moon, or mathematical, Fraternity had been selected by the clan as a bridegroom.

Srikant stared at his IBM machine and watched the flow of illuminated type and numbers thread monotonously across the screen. He pressed the keyboard again, a part of the pattern was wiped out. He was staring at another line of numbers. On the desk the pile of punch cards mounted up around him.

He was conscious of the chief standing behind him. Srikant shifted slightly. Out of the corner of his eye he observed Tulsi's uncle twirling his mustache. There was a smell of Aqua Velva.

Zamindar, nodding and smiling, remarked to no one in particular, "What talent he has. This young man will go far."

The bookkeeper worked faster.

Well, there's no harm in trying to please the Filtheaters, Srikant thought. At least for the trial period. By that time, I'll have figured things out here.

• •

Dinner at the Baniya compound was late and was served in two shifts. Field laborers kept straggling in, including members of a mutual aid team from an adjacent village. The servers moved in the back, the switch-roles in their kamiz, the women muffled deep in their purdah shawls. But Srikant had no trouble recognizing Tulsi. He caught a glimpse of her face as she bent to take away a bowl of ghi. He thought she winked at him.

After supper the five households adjourned to the veranda. Here, overlooking the private vegetable plot of the Baniyas, the sexes had coffee together. Conversation was about business or was mean gossip which descended quickly to the level of acrimonious marital disputes. But beware of helping Baniyas! When an outsider intervened, the aggrieved parties—at each others' throats the moment before—would join forces and attack the peacemaker.

The Baniya clan, united through the female bloodline, was divided according to age and rank. Indeed—Srikant had noted since the day of his arrival—age was rank. First came the matriarch, Indira Ventagiri Teka Baniya. Below her were the matriarch's daughters, Greataunt Ormolu and Greataunt Irmala and their spouses. Next came Tulsi's mother's generation. The mother's name was Veraka and her husband Naroombipad. And finally Tulsi and her numerous sisters and their families.

However, within the compound the tribe did not go by their names but by numbers. The matriarch was "One." The Great-aunts in the next generation were called "Two-One," "Two-Two" in order of birth. Tulsi's mother was "Three-Three" and so forth. The line descended finally to its lowest level, Tulsi's and Srikant's son being "Five-Six."

The male side was designated by the wife's appellation plus a subscript. Thus Razzakar, Ormolu's husband, was "Two-One-A," and Zamindar, Irmala's husband, was "Two-Two-B." Lower male in-laws were rarely named and were considered on the same level as wandering artisans and poor relations of the family.

Conversation in the compound would go like this. Indira Ventagiri would say to Razzakar:

"Two-One-A, how much did you pay the Coots for those wagon loads of grain?"

And Razzakar would reply, "Ten rupees each, One."

"Well, they pulled you by the nose."

The matriarch was a notorious skinflint.

On this particular evening the coffee hour passed as usual. The matriarch knitted, a long-stemmed clay pipe clamped in her rotten teeth. It was Naroombipad's job to clean and refill the pipe. He did this obsequiously. Veraka wound the ball of yarn as Tulsi held the skein. Every once in a while the matriarch would spit.

Again Srikant had no chance to speak to Tulsi, holding up the loops of yarn over her hands gracefully. The old woman's at the center of everything, Srikant thought. She reminded him of a spider.

Next, family prayers were held in the "gallery." They were led by Razzakar. The farm manager recited the verses to the ancestors with a stutter. The gallery was an enormous space under skylights with a raised stage on one end. The floor, the size of a gym, was used by the family for sleeping.

• •

Coffee hour and family prayers had passed and were followed by the children's hour. The singles had departed for their baithak. Now there was no one left but the marrieds. A row of disconsolate bridegrooms, Srikant among them, sat along the wall staring sullenly across at their extended family.

The gallery seethed with squawling infants. A cousin of Tulsi's bounced one up and down on her lap. To soothe it she massaged its genitals. A wet nurse was feeding another baby. She handed it back to the mother, cleansing her nipples with kamai grass. The charades continued, as everyone went on talking and interrupting each other. A circle of housekeepers stood around a brat on a pot, going "shh . . . sh . . . ," encouraging it to do its business.

Is there such a thing as privacy in Gonwanda? Apparently not. In the Baniya compound privacy is nonexistent. When the new bridegroom arrives at the "in-law" village and the young couple are joined and are assigned their place in the sleep room, they are given the protection of a screen. On the bridal night and during the honeymoon everyone is supposed to be discreet and turn their attention elsewhere. After that the screen is removed, and then what? There is only the protection of darkness. There is only the sleepiness of the others. One waits till bedtime. One waits for the sleepers to drop off one by one.

However, tonight Srikant finds this is not going to be so easy. The lights have been put out. Around them on the great floor lie the sleepers, descendants of Number One. Each household cluster sleeps together. Next to Srikant and Tulsi two nephews are snuggled up in Greatauntie Ormolu's bedroll, and the old lady is telling them a story in a wheezing voice. The story drones on and on. Tulsi's mother wakes up coughing.

Finally all is tranquil. The bright patch of moonlight falling through the clerestory across the sleepers has moved on, leaving the young couple in sweet darkness. Finally it is time.

Naroombipad stumbles over them on his way to the bathroom.

2

In the main office of the bottling works two Regional officials awaited Zamindar. One was a loan officer. He represented the People's Regional Bank, handling Development and Stabilization Operations. The other was a Deodar from the Regional Conservation Ministry.

The manager, with great deference, led his visitors on a tour through the several shops of the combine. There were few people at work. The rice husking plant was operating at a relaxed minimum. In the jute mill, the giant fiber-crusher appeared to be out of order and the machinery broken for winding the fibers into Manila rope. Several men and women were twining the long oily strands by hand as they listened to a soccer game on the radio. The conservationist asked if they could inspect the sensor laboratory.

The lab was located at the end of the main building. Little was going on; they were told that the main sensor was "away on vacation." Several minor technicians stood around in white coats; one of them was examining samples of a solid material, fly ash, through a laser microscope.

"What produces this?" the Deodar asked.

"It's from the inside of the stacks. We test it from time to time to see if it complies with the emission standards."

"Does it?"

"It's a bit heavy right now. Nitrous oxide."

Through the window of the lab could be seen the solar pond. The surface of this was ashen. A dull sludge was leaching into it through a pipe from a corrugated metal building some distance away. From here the clatter of machinery could be heard. Trucks were drawn up behind at the loading bay. On the trucks were huge ads: "GONWANDA BOTTLING WORKS. DRINK NGHSI-HI."

"At least you have some activity here," the loan official remarked.

"We make a popular soft drink, using our local mineral water. Would you care to see that department?"

A smell of sarsaparilla mash pervaded the air. The visitors were led rapidly through several office cubicles and were introduced in turn to the sales manager and several advertising and promotion men. In the main shed itself operators jostled each other around vats of the extract and carbonated mineral water compressors. The assembly line was in full swing. Cans were being stamped out, leveled off, and moved on, clamped onto rotating jigs. The mixture was injected, sealed, and packaged in a single process.

"Quite a little operation you have there," the Regional Development officer remarked after they had returned to the manager's office.

The Karst was served a glass of tea spiked with rum, while Zamindar and the Deodar drank Nghsi-Hi.

The Deodar remarked, "You know this stuff is really good." Lifting his eyebrows he brushed his beard with his sleeve.

The banker was dressed impressively in tweeds. He took a pipe out of his pocket and before lighting it polished the bowl by turning it inside the oily crease of his nose.

"So you applied for a loan from the state bank? Well, that shouldn't be too hard to arrange." An aroma filled the air from the briar. "That is, provided you fulfill all the requirements."

Zamindar assured him that the factory had met all its quotas. "I think you'd agree, we've done very well on our production norms, as they were set by the Region. In fact, on the soft drinks we've exceeded our year-end goal by eight hundred percent."

"You don't think that's a bit high? You mustn't overdo it—though I realize you are the dynamic sector." The planner looked at him quizzically.

The Deodar asked, "You don't think you're taking the capitalist road?"

The manager threw out his hands. "But how could we? We are a public corporation. The shares are held equally by all the villages in the cauga. As for the Freemarket phratry, that is the Baniya clan—we just run it—for everyone's benefit. The state takes its cut."

"Of course. Of course. I'm sure the Filtheaters don't get anything out of it . . . personally. But if I may explain . . ."

The state planner went on to explain that what he meant by the phrase "capitalist road" was not profit. After all every economic system worthy of the name yielded some advantages. Nor was the firm's expansionism in the free market sector anything less than commendable. It was an unhappy fact that money, as the medium of exchange, had an alienating effect, "tending to separate the product from the producer," but this too could be lived with. The essential thing was balance. Within the confederated system there must be a balanced exchange of surplus between neighbors.

"Neighbors! In the name of god, this is a national enterprise!" Zamindar exploded. "It's worth millions. Everyone in the whole country is drinking Nghsi!"

"But we must have a balanced growth. You do have to admit—I'm sure you won't take offense at my mentioning—that with the exception of your line of "pop," the rest of your combine is *under*developed. Practically moribund."

"You just saw it on an off day. Unfortunately, because of the soccer finals . . . I'll send you the reports."

"Do so. Do so. I'll be interested. As for the pollution problem—" The bank inspector turned sanctimoniously to the Deodar.

"Ah that. Yes. Might be a stumbling block. The solar pond is a problem. You'll have to clean up all that sludge."

"We'll have a report on that too. Of course. Within a few weeks. And where are you bound for now?" the factory manager asked. "Why don't you take a little walk? Refresh yourself. Then drop in on us afterward at the Baniya compound."

After the two inspectors left, Zamindar rang for Srikant. He asked him to bring his accounts.

The young man arrived, and kowtowed.

"Ah, nephew. We've been having a little conference here with the Confederate Inspectors. Some irregularities have been reported that have to be cleared up before we obtain our loan. And of course some of the ecology violations have to be removed. I'll see to that."

The manager examined his accounts. "Bridegroom, I congratulate you on your work. I take it the figures are complete—a wealth of detail. And the arrangement of the columns on the page, sensitive, an artistic flare. Ah, you are a true Moon! One thing, though. We'll have to add them up differently."

Srikant stood aghast. "You don't want me to falsify the accounts?"

"Oh dear, no, not that. They had their little tour and found a few faults. The faults have to be remedied, that's all . . ."

The manager, his head cocked to the side, toyed with a pencil beside the entries for rice husking and jute.

"*These* columns might be lengthened . . . don't you think? And *these* shortened . . . Just a little creative bookkeeping. 'Balance' is the key word here. So, let us make them balance."

3

The three bridegrooms have escaped from the childrens' hour onto the roof. Srikant, Arthur, and Gayan sit smoking bhang. An hour or so earlier the entire population of Gonwanda had been out at the dry creek bed at the edge of the village watching a show. The players performed on a raised stage, the spectators sitting around them on the stream-worn boulders.

These traveling shows, which went from village to village throughout Kansu, were under the auspices of the Yellow Shamans. Sometimes movies were shown as well, the screen propped up against the stream bank. That evening the movie had been *Little Caesar*." Vintage American films were generally shown by the Yellow Shamans.

Gayan was discussing the film, an old stand-by. It had been exciting. However he preferred several others—*Fort Dakota* and *The Guns of Navarrone*. He preferred cowboys and Indians to gangster films. But why, Gayan wondered, must people go outside the village for the showings? Why were they not permitted in town?

"Because of the violence," Arthur said.

Gayan conceded the subject matter was bloodthirsty. And among the audience stamping, shouting, and fisticuffs often accompanied the shamans' films. However, tempers cooled afterward. The village returned to its usual calm.

It was thought in Gonwanda that the scenes in the movies were not acted. They were performed by ghosts, and these possessed the audience as well for a brief time. It was the ghosts of violence that were summoned, and then put to rest, by the Yellow Shamans.

Gayan went on: "If the business of the shamans is exorcism, why not have the showings in one of the baithaks or in the town hall?"

Srikant was inclined to think otherwise. That it was not because of violence shown in the films, which was after all not unfamiliar in Nghsi; but that the characters were presented in such a way as to make them more interesting and attractive than Nghsi people. What a character, this Little Caesar! And his girl Flossie. And also the cinematographic effects—the speeding cars, the streets and buildings shot at different angles and with different lighting effects. A city full of wonder, Chicago. Leaning back in his chair and inhaling a lungful of bhang, Srikant said the word aloud: "Chicago."

The film showing had been followed by storytelling. That evening tales had been told by three foreigners, part of the traveling shamans' troupe. The tales were autobiographical and ended badly. Though designed to be presented as "confessions" of the foreigners, the tales actually had the opposite effect of making them seem attractive and unusually adventurous people.

These thoughts were complicated. Srikant would have liked to express them in words, but felt somehow he could not.

They sat smoking and looking out over the roof parapet. The fields where the performance had taken place had darkened. They could see the lights from the shamans' caravan winding away toward the next town.

After talking a while further the friends returned downstairs. The childrens' entertainment was in full swing. It was a shadow play. The performers, unseen by the audience, projected their shadows against a screen, in this case a sheet hung between two coat racks. Though the stories were more generally about ghosts and heros of local folklore, tonight the children were playing their own version of *Little Caesar*.

However, the characters had been somewhat altered. There were few people in the play. Instead various objects were personified—those aspects of the Chicago scene which fascinated them most. Several of the performers were automobiles or street lights. A girl cousin played the role of a downtown garage. From this, automobiles roared out firing machine guns (the performers were both cars and machine guns) and bumping into each other. In a slight mix-up of plot, Gayan's son—a heavy-chested boy of twelve considered "big for his age"—strutted around the stage as Hercules.

In front of the curtain squatted the smaller offspring, among them Srikant's "Five-Six." But the small fry were paying little attention to the play. Instead they fussed over an electric train running through a model of the Village Maintenance Center made from an Erecto set. In a corner of the gallery an all-girl band was rehearsing.

Arthur, exhausted from farm labor under Razzakar, had fallen asleep despite the din. His head nodded. Occasionally he pulled himself up with a jerk and stared at the moving shadows.

The ghost play had ended. With a climactic rush of automobiles inside, the curtain had been pushed forward and had collapsed on top of the train network.

Family prayers were about to begin. But the audience had dispersed. Though the Baniya girls were present, applauding the screeching finale of the band, the boys were nowhere in evidence.

The three fathers went looking for them and found them behind the ancestor shrine. Here there was a knot of small boys gathered around Hercules. The hero was showing them how to masturbate. The erection, beet red and already fully distended, was displayed wrapped in a black handkerchief. The onlookers were hushed, the eyes of the smaller boys large with excitement.

Gayan cried out sharply: "Hey! This is no place to do that."

By the bones of the saints—sacrilege!

However, the three fathers took a sensible line. The mysteries of sex were explained and the flow of sap at the rushing onset of puberty. Gayan concluded that it was not the act that was wrong but the timing. He told Hercules that he should "save his energies till later when he would be shooting his gun, not in the air, but in some woman's pocket."

Srikant was shocked to see the handkerchief used in this way. In the ardor of the demonstration it had been snatched from one of the photographs on the ancestor shrine.

But during the family prayers which followed, and which were intoned by Razzakar, he reflected on the idea with some amusement.

4

It was Makar-Sankrant. Quarrel patching up time in Gonwonda. The day before the women had decorated the shrine of Ong-Bap, a seedy but durable little god who resides at the edge of the village beside a tube well. Ong-Bap, the Forgiver. A minor deity—but he has a big job, considering the obduracy and general nastiness of the Gonwanda character.

At daybreak Srikant had watched the "Party of the Old" leave the Baniya compound in a hurry. They had taken refuge in a nearby field. Dressed in rags and with carpetbags slung over their shoulders, they made a pitiable and tattered group. Shortly afterward the "Party of the Young" arrived beating hand drums. The traditional exchange of insults began.

The young shouted:

P.Y. Old Ones. Old Ones. Now we've caught up with you
in the field. What are you doing, thieves,
with your packs on your backs?
P.O. Young Ones. Young Ones. Something terrible
has happened. A disaster.
We've had to run to save ourselves.
P.Y. Householders. Property owners.
You've left everything behind.
Your pots, your bedrolls, your bankrolls
the box with your silver jewelry.
You're staggering around in the wind
like a bunch of Gypsies.
P.O. Apprentices. Handymen. The tide's turned.
Yesterday we were high enjoying ourselves
at everyone's expense.
Now we're underfoot.
P.Y. That's right, Fat Cats.
You were pushing us around, exploiting the meek.
Now you're turned out in the pasture
like old mules.
P.O. Bridgegrooms. We're tired, we're cold.
Can't you see?
Our teeth are chattering.
We're suffering but we can't go back.
P.Y. Why can't you—spiteful ones?

	Why can't you—rotten-tempered ones?
P.O.	*They* kicked us out.
P.Y.	Why? Why?
P.O.	They say we quarreled with everyone: with our sons and daughters, our sons-in-law and their relatives with our grandsons, neighbors with our nephews nieces and cousins in fact with the whole world. But *we're* not to blame
P.Y	It was *their* fault. Ah. go fart out your brains, shit-britches!

So the morning of Makar passed in glorious insult. The traditional canzones were varied with personal attacks, an improvised game, the "dozens," in which the combatants squared off and went after each other. Everyone who bore a grudge against anyone else in Gonwonda got their own back on Makar-Sankrant. Then a picnic lunch followed of baked beans and apple-jack, and the traditional "fire crackers"—the same as on Fourth of July. And real firecracker strings as well, which warring members of the extended family and apprentices from the shops threw at each other in the excitement.

By this time most everyone in the Baniya tholla was drunk, the older women drunkest of all.

After lunch came the theater pieces.

A brawny young farmhand appeared in a clearing in the center of the crowd. He was costumed in the baggy uniform of one of the matriarchs. His teeth were blackened, and there was a terrible squint in his eye. The "matriarch" spat and picked up a piece of string off the ground, which she stuffed in her pocket, muttering: "Save this. Save this."

The crowd recognized the subject immediately and shouted: "It's Indira! Pinchpenny. She's got the squint."

Another character sidled into the circle. A stringy red-stained mop was on his head.

"Two-One-A. It's Razzakar! Razzakar!" the crowd shouted delightedly. "Here comes Uncle."

The Baniyas began to sweep the dirt with faggots. The audience taunted:

"What's the matter, Uncle, can't you afford a real broom?"

"That family can't even afford a real floor."

"Who are you going to cheat today, Pinchpenny?"

"Wait. You'll see what they're up to."

The two actors went around the crowd and were handed pigs' bladders. They walloped each other a couple of times, then walloped the crowd. They shouted for "the bridegroom."

Srikant's friend Arthur stepped out of the crowd. It appeared he was to play himself—the real Arthur.

The skit that followed was traditional throughout the Plains. The story was legendary among peasants. Whether it applied in this case Srikant doubted. Yet it had some points of reference to the Baniyas.

The skit is performed as follows.

The apprentice farmhand steps into the circle. The others walk up to him.

Uncle: Ah, new son-in-law, hello.

Matriarch: Now that you're a member of the family, come over here. Welcome.

(She hits him over the head with the pig's bladder.)

Son-in-law, we've provided you with a wife, to keep up the population. She's the ugliest girl we've got. She has walleyes, dumber than a chicken. That's the god's truth. So to arrange the match right, we've gone to an ugly people's village.

Uncle (*explaining to the audience*): To Rampur—where everyone has the smallpox.

(*Laughter.*)

Matriarch: And now, son, I'm going to explain your duties. You're listening?

(The old lady hits the bridgegroom with the pig's bladder. Then she hits the uncle.)

Pay attention!

(*To Razzakar.*) You explain it to him.

Uncle: Well, friend, now you've arrived at the age of a farmer. You have to work for the Collective. Remember the important thing is don't let them stick you with a high efficiency rating or a lot of work points, the lower the better.

We Baniyas don't believe in hard work, it's better to play sick all) the time.

Bridegroom (*meekly*): Yes, father.

Uncle: If you do have to work, work as little as possible, and sneak off as often as you can to our private plot. We raise the best vegetables in the village, and sell them dearest.

Matriarch: Tell him about vegetable growing, son. But first, I think his attention's wandering. Better hit him.

Voice (from the crowd): Tell it to him, Razzakar.

Uncle: The main thing about raising vegetables is to use lots of manure. Cow manure and chicken manure are OK, but the best is human manure because it comes free. And for this purpose we ask you to use this privy here in the front yard—right after breakfast.

Matriarch: Everybody in the household has to use this privy. Right here, by the front door. Do you understand that? Shit is as good as gold.

Bridegroom: Yes, mother.

Uncle: And if you are off in the collective fields and you do have to take a shit, hold it. Come back and do it in the house, so we can use it on the vegetables, got that?

(*Whistle blows.*)

Bridegroom: There goes the whistle for the collective farm. I have to go over there for the work detail.

(*He goes.*)

Matriarch (*to Razzakar*): I wouldn't trust him. You better go with him to spy on him.

(*Bridegroom walks around, Razzakar following. He works a little in the field, then obviously the need to move his bowels comes over him. He tries to hold it, walks around, finally starts taking his pants off. Razzakar runs out, brandishing his stick.*)

Uncle: Not here. You can't take a crap here. Remember what Granny said.

Bridegroom: But I can't hold it.

Uncle: Oh yes you can. Oh yes you can. Back to the family privy! (Razzakar beats the son-in-law back. Son-in-law hits him with the bladder. The old woman hits both of them. With this volley of bladder-whackings the charade is over.)

Next the accounting department had prepared a skit exposing the shortcomings of Zamindar. The factory owner was lampooned mercilessly. In fact, Srikant had written the musical skit himself and composed most of the verses. But in a spirit of caution he had decided not to be one of the performers. At dinner the previous evening he had hinted that another employee had been the author.

Why should I stick my neck out? he had reasoned. After all, I have to live with them.

The charade went off well. Srikant was not a little surprised when the manager came up at the end and, twirling his mustache and grinning, effusively congratulated the players.

The accountant had been standing with the other bridegrooms, Gayan and Arthur.

"Well, that was really clever. And you have a musical talent." The manager shook hands.

Elsewhere among the gathering presents were being exchanged, and the "Old Party" were already taking their rags off and wiping the ashes off their faces.

Veraka and Tulsi's father, Narimboopad, came up to Srikant. Tulsi's mother said rather sharply, "Well, we're square, the Baniyas and the

Harditts. Now, son-in-law, the fun's over."

"Yes, it's been a nice holiday. Everyone enjoyed themselves."

Narimboopad remarked, somewhat pompously, that there were serious aspects to the occasion, and that it was wise to air important grievances, lest they go underground and get serious. "My dear, if there have been any faults on our side, we're sorry. I'm sure, we must have tried your patience from time to time."

"You may have—and you may not," Veraka said testily. "In any case, we have been symbolically kicked out of the house. Now that's over with. It's been very trying."

Srikant said, "I'm afraid some of the skits were a little harsh."

"Oh, no, it was nothing. No more than was deserved."

It remained only to present the holiday gifts and smear the honey—the rite with which the celebration of Makar-Sankrant ended. Srikant presented a scarf to Tulsi's mother, and to his father-in-law a clay pipe.

Veraka asked, "Srikant, what's that you have in your hand?"

"It's the traditional pot of honey, Mother. My Makar-Sankrant gift to you."

"Ah, so it is."

Then, according to the tradition, he dipped his finger in it, and coming up close, smeared honey on his mother-in-law's lips "to sweeten them." As he did so he felt a wave of genuine revulsion. But he put his palms together and kowtowed.

Srikant thought: What a hypocrite I've become. And I've only been with these people a few years!

WOMEN IN MIDDLE AGE

1

There were the three women. One was that morning entering the Middles. One had passed it by. The other stood radiant and glossy-haired in her spangled garkhi.

It was Sathan who was occupying herself in the mirror. Nanda stood to the side, her eyes squinting, a needle in her teeth. Maddi was helping her mother try on the service uniform.

It made Sathan look short—doubtless the effect of the trousers. Gone were the shapely ankles. And the cut across the seat made her sister look dumpy as well, Nanda observed. Nanda preferred to avoid her own image in the mirror.

However, Sathan seemed pleased with herself. She stood before the glass, her hands to her waist, turned from side to side complacently. The pair of baggy pants of green twill had been pulled over a silk slip. Maddi helped her button on the quilted Mao jacket.

"It hardly shows off one's best points. I suppose one gets used to it."

"You never get used to it," Nanda answered with bitterness.

According to village custom the passage into the Middles took place approximately once every five to eight years, for women reaching the Fifth Age Grade. Though only two years older than her sister, Nanda had been in the previous age passage.

Maddi hummed a popular tune. "Under the stiff pocket and the matron's brown /The woman's heart still burns . . ." She asked her aunt, "I haven't seen your sweetheart around? Did he come over last night, Rathlee Golla?"

Rathlee Golla, Nanda's third husband and her private man, was a barber from an adjacent village.

"Oh that old stick. He comes whenever he can. But he barely does any good."

Maddi gave a sudden shout and stared at the uniform. "Mother, it has six buttons!"

"No!"

"Look. The prescribed number is five, isn't it?"

"How lucky we noticed it! It would have been bad luck."

The Harditt clan was waiting below for Sathan's MotherLetting-Go ceremony. This was a family affair celebrated in private households throughout the village with a minimum of fuss. But it marked one of the important turnings.

They descended to the kitchen. There the clan members were having breakfast. Sathan ate apart at a separate table. At the close of the meal the ceremonial objects were brought out—the mementos of childhood and family life: some baby pictures, a wornout rag doll, a pair of tiny gilded shoes. These were ritually burned in a brass tray. Sathan's long hair was cut.

Nanda kissed her younger sister on the shoulder and said with a wry face: "I welcome you to middle age."

Sathan's husband repeated the prescribed words. Venu said: "My wife, warmth of my bed, goodbye." The oldest Greataunt embraced her.

The mother turned to Maddi, bowing and touching her palms together. She said, not without a tremor, "Daughter, my lamp has gone out. You will be my light, Shining One."

She put on her master's cap with the red star. She was now in her complete service uniform. Members of the family accompanied them to the gate. At the gate each one kowtowed to her. Sathan had passed beyond the household. Her work belonged to the Commune.

Maddi, Sathan, and Nanda went down the lane. Except for the change of costume the day was no different than any other. The three were going to their usual jobs in the village. As they passed under the windows of the other compounds Sathan held her head high. At the turn of the lane a woman with a shopping basket, an old acquaintance, stopped to embrace Sathan. Whispering effusive congratulations into her ear, she presented her with a piece of fruit.

"Master!"

"We are all masters."

In fact the woman was middle-aged and was also wearing her service uniform.

For some reason Nanda felt irritated at Maddi. Why? Was it that while helping with the fitting, Nanda had caught her niece more than once stealing an appreciative glance at herself in the mirror?

The tholla lane ended, issuing into a larger street. A group of schoolgirls dawdled under the public notice board. A stream of bicycles was going by. Customers already filled the corner shops. Shops and warehouses stood under the earth bank beyond which the tops of apricot trees could be seen.

They passed the textile mill and metals recycling plant and came out at Washhouse Square.

In the middle of the square two men sat in the stocks surrounded by jeering children. They danced close by one of them, singing:

> "Ayubb Ayubb Ayubb Dinka
> with his ass in a sling
> and his feet in the clinker."

The urchins were more wary of the other prisoner. He was a foreigner, not known well in the district. A cardboard sign around his neck read only "Morris."

The sun blazed down on both men. Their legs were straight out and their ankles clamped into a heavy wood plank with holes like a yoke. Both were middle-aged. On Ayubb's bare pate beads of sweat glistened. This was not the first time Ayubb had been made an example of.

Sathan asked cheerfully: "Cousin I see they've got you by the legs. What are you in for this time?"

"Individualism again, Auntie." The man shrugged his shoulders.

"I suppose you'd run to the city again, where nobody can keep an eye on you. And put your name on some office door?"

It was well known that Ayubb considered himself the best lawyer in the district. The new matriarch said to him sententiously, "Well, you have plenty of chance to practice law here. Politics before professionalism."

"Among my fellow villagers? Cases of chicken stealing and wife beating? Trials before the village notables . . . those doddering old bastards."

The village lawyer occupied a minor position in Sawna working under the Village Council and attached to the rites master.

"No wonder you always end up here."

The urchins pelted the unfortunate man with gravel, which they collected from around the pump.

The three women had seen the other prisoner, an "Ameri can," in one of the traveling shamans' shows touring the villages. He had recently been apprehended for a minor infractior of the law.

A poet and a storyteller, he had been taking down the olc ballads on a tape recorder. It was against authority to reproduce "fresh" speech.

This Morris was a tall man by Nghsian standards. Wherea! the apparatus of the stocks more or less fitted the lawyer, the stranger poet was cruelly cramped by it and had to sit hunched forward over bent knees. His pale visage was ghostlike.

Nanda felt sorry for him.

The women parted, Nanda going to her Beauticians Studio, Maddi and her mother to the Studio of the Planners.

2 IN THE PLANNERS' STUDIO

The Planners' Guild occupied the top two floors of the baithak for women. From that height the eye could take in the whole space of the Commune to the furthest field: farm, factory, and pasture. And beyond in the shimmering haze pastures of other communes of Hardan.

The walls were concrete. At the corners of the hexagonal building, where the walls met, glassed-in conservatories were cantilevered out where the masters of the studio took their coffee.

A center core of the main room was the "machine room." This housed the computer banks. Within it was quiet, and there was a softened light glinting on stainless steel sides and the blue and beige instrument housings. At intervals there would be a click, as a magnetic tape spool made a half rotation. There were a dozen BPF5Y MAGNAMATRIX computers.

Outside the core were the desk terminals. Here the operators typed at the keyboards. Numbers and lines of messages winked cheerfully from screens. There was a staccato sound of typing and the turning and rustling of paper sheets being folded into the computer printout.

This section was for routine bookkeeping and data gathering. Through the computers the planners were linked to the subsection guilds. Each booth corresponded to a section of the Commune. They were labeled:

METALS AND MOTOR POOL
COLLECTIVE FARM
MACHINE BANK
MAINTENANCE CENTER AND WASHHOUSE
WEATHER AND SOILS STATION
VILLAGE GUILDS—MISC.

There was an additional terminal reserved for the Wash-house School equipped with teaching devices for the apprentices.

As Maddi on her way to her corner of the studio passed by this booth, she saw a young operator was having trouble. Maddi stopped. The computer had printed out the following in BASIC:

```
KANSU TIME-SHARE 10 SADH 35    ON AT 09.20
USER NUMBER-47778A : return : PASSWORD : return :
OLD FILE NAME YOODOO : return : READY * * LIST
10 READ N
20 LET X = O
30 PRINT X, X*X*X*
40 LET X = X + 1
50 GO TO 30
60 DATA 10
70 END
READY : return : RUN
11 12 13 14 11 12 13 14 11 12 13 14 11 12 13 14?
?WHAT? ?WHAT? ?WHAT? ?WHAT? ?WHAT?
DO YOU WANT HELP?
```

The girl was staring at the screen and seemed on the verge of tears.

Maddi, leaning over the girl's shoulder, studied the problem.

"But you're in an endless loop! Look, don't you see it's just going round again between lines fifteen and fifty. That's because you haven't programmed your IF. . . THEN statement."

Maddi typed in after line 40

```
45 IF X = N THEN 70
THAT'S ALL SORRY TO PUT YOU TO ALL THAT TROUBLE.
PRINT PLEASE: RETURN:
```

The corrected program appeared on the screen. Then Maddi typed RUN, and the machine went through its computations without further difficulties.

Maddi thought it would be fun to find out something in COBOL, "the language of inventories."

"I'll tell you what, let's see what Nanda's shop has in stock." She typed the required instructions:

```
OLD BEAUTY: return:
LIST ALL INVENTORY LIBCAT
100 FILE CONTROL
    SELECT INFILE ASSIGN TO FLOFILE
    01 selected location      pic x (6)
    01 quantity               pic 12.229
110 DISPLAY "SELECTED LIST OF INVENTORY FOR" ACCEPT SELECTED
LOCATION "HAIRDRESSES"
120 IF SELECTED LOCATION = "IRMA'S" OR "VICKIE HAIRSTYLES" OR
"GOLDENSHEARS"
OR "UNISEX" OR "PANDORA'S BOUTIQUE" GO TO ASK-FOR-LOCATION
130 READ INV FILE
IF INV-LOCATION = SELECTED LOCATION MOVE INV QUANTITY TO
QUANTITY DISPLAY "ITEM", INV-DESC, "QTY:", QUANTITY
140 END-OF-INPUT    CLOSE-IN FILE    STOP RUN
150 STOP    RUN
```

The computer replied:

```
RUN

COBOL 10 SADH 35    ON AT 09.32

SELECTIVE LIST OF INVENTORY FOR:
VICKIE          HAIRSTYLES: return:
ITEM:           MIRRORS                       QTY: 3
ITEM:           CHAIRS                        QTY: 5
ITEM:           HAIRDRYERS                    QTY: 5
ITEM:           COMBS BRUSHES                 QTY: 40
ITEM:           NO. OF CABINETS CONTAINING
                POWDERS FACEPAINTS TINTS
```

	SHAMPOOS MISC	QTY: 2
ITEM:	LIPSTICKS	QTY: 280

0.710 CRU 0.370 SEC
READY: return: BYE

Maddi and the student laughed. "If you have any trouble call me."

• •

Sathan was preparing herself to enter the Master's Studio. The door was marked simply PROGRAMMING and bore the legend of the Mathematical phratry, before which she kowtowed. This was the formula for the Fibonacci series of numbers, the "golden progression" where each number is defined as the sum of its two predecessors: 1 1 2 3 5 8 13 21 34. . . in unending sequence. Below was painted in color the cross section of a nautitus shell and the axil of an evolving leaf.

Under it was the command:

GROW!

Another legend read:

A HIERARCHY OF COMPLEXITY
IS FUNCTION, NOT POWER

Sathan had never before been inside the Master's Studio.

Two steps led up to the door, on either side of which were ranks of shoes that had been left by the occupants. Sathan removed her own shoes.

Inside the room the rows of desk chairs along the back were fully occupied. At several tables people were going over charts and figures. There were about forty women, all in their service uniforms. All were middle-aged or old.

Slipping into a chair toward the center, Sathan had misgivings. Perhaps this place was reserved for the important masters. Seated near her were two old women with a mien of stern authority. Both had soft white hair and faces the texture of battered leather. One had bristles of hair sticking out of her nostrils.

Across from them at the table sat two peasants. At least Sathan took them to be peasants because of their heavy plaid shirts and boots caked with straw and cow dung.

Although the rules of the studio obliged them to remove their boots, perhaps they had not known this. Or the matriarchs had exempted the two farmers for reasons of protocol.

On the dusty blackboards at either side matrons were chalking up diagrams. A number of discussions appeared to be going on at once. Sathan's first impression was one of disappointment. Used coffee containers and dirty ash trays were on the tables. The floor was littered with computer print-outs.

She recognized several other women from her own tholla who that day had passed into the Middles and were here for the first time. However, the masters ignored the new members. The front wall was covered by an immense green-tinted plastic screen. This was blank. Under it sat an operator at the keyboard of a Textronic desk model computer, polishing her nails.

For lack of anything better to do, Sathan began copying down a formula a matron was writing on the left-hand blackboard. It was evidently part of a productivity plan for the Collective Farm.

The formula was for expected yields per hectare of pulse, cotton, and millet—dry season crops. And for wet season—legumes and sugar cane—correlated with fertilizer inputs. The plan figures apparently were not the correct figures. After writing them up the woman erased them and substituted others. She said these were the revised figures, where plan quotas had not been met or had been exceeded.

Evidently it was the two peasants who had brought the revised data. When the matron at the blackboard finished, she returned to them a dog-eared notebook. As it lay open on the table Sathan could see messily ruled pages and some scribbled notes.

"What we have to do now is to reduce that to computer language, and then to machine language," Sathan heard the bristle-nosed master remark loudly. This was said to the woman next to her—but was evidently for the peasants' benefit.

On the blackboard across the right wall a more comprehensive plan was being elaborated. Another of the masters explained that this was the next five-year plan for the entire village. It was a flow chart. It identified by symbol the various working units of the Commune as they related to each other. They were related by arrows. Each unit and arrow had a number.

The flow chart had a harmony and elegance which pleased Sathan. She copied it down as follows:

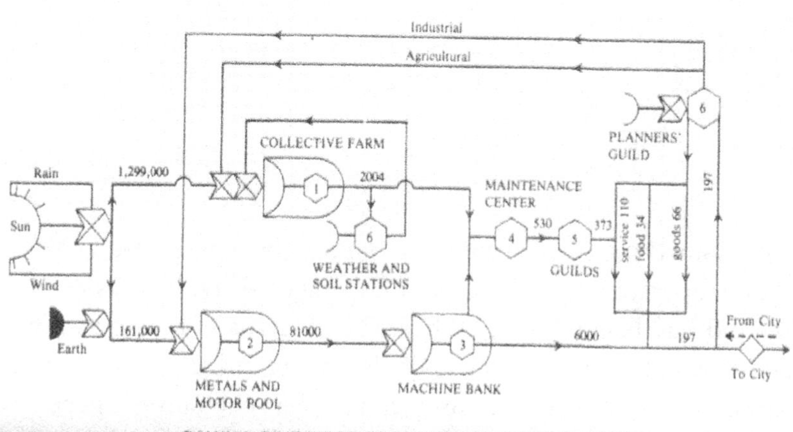

SAWNA FIVE-YEAR PLAN COMPARTMENT MODEL

The programmer labelled this diagram COMPARTMENT MODEL. Below this the MATHEMATICAL MODEL was set out, consisting of a series of differential equations. These were:

$$V_{t+1} = f(V_t, t) \quad \frac{dv_i}{dt} = \sum_j k_{ij} v_j$$

where V = value of variable at time t plus an increment of time. And Σ = sum of input-output terms of the compartment matrix (forcing function).

MATHEMATICAL MODEL

$$v_1(t) = \frac{3.0 + \cos\{3.1 + 2.0\,[\frac{\pi(t-1.0)}{365}]\}\,8.6}{1.4}$$

$$\frac{\Delta v_2}{\Delta t} = 1.0v_1 + 0.004v_3 - \{0.00027e^{0.012t} + [0.002 + 0.002\sin(2t-0.7)1.4] + 0.0014\}v_2$$

$$\frac{\Delta v_3}{\Delta t} = \begin{cases} t \leq 280 = 0.004v_2 - \{[0.0005 + 0.01\sin(t+2)]1.1 + 0.004\}v_3 \\ t > 280 = 0.004v_2 - \{[0.0005 + 0.01\sin(t+2)]1.1(\frac{365-t}{110.0}) + 0.004\}v_3 \end{cases}$$

$$\frac{\Delta v_4}{\Delta t} = 0.002v_2 - 0.001v_4$$

$$\frac{\Delta v_5}{\Delta t} = 0.00185[1.0 + \sin(2t-1.56)]v_4 - 0.002v_5$$

$$\frac{\Delta v_6}{\Delta t} = \frac{0.00185[1.0 + \sin(2t-1.56)]v_4 - 180.0 + v_5}{v_5} + 0.0014v_2 + 0.0007v_3$$

Now something was happening along the center wall. The desk computer operator at the bottom of the screen had laid aside her nail polish and had begun typing. Whereas before the immense wall with its green screen had had a melancholy air of vacancy, like an empty aquarium, now it became animated. The computer operator was “reading“ the mathematical model and developing it graphically. The final step in the programming process was called the MODEL OUTPUT.

Vertical and horizontal base lines appeared marked off in units. Within this grid a series of dots and moving broken lines of light oscillated an progressed. Within the graph the curves rose and fell, intersecting or keeping pace with one another.

A key noted that the dots were predicted data and the dashed lines observed data.

Beside Sathan the younger of the two peasants was lighting his pipe. He leaned back at ease, then absently stooped to scrape the mud off his shoes. The older peasant was looking up at the screen wonderously.

The wire-nosed matron explained to him, pointing first to the agricultural plan then to the master plan, "*Your* box has been included within *that* box. And that one will be included inside the region."

Then she added, "We've just finished doing the sunlight variables. What we are looking at now are certain intensities of rain."

• •

INVENTORY POEM
The Planners' Guild   calls to its own
    masters   apprentices
Sathan the mother   the daughter Maddi
            the Studio of the Planners
With a light step
            they enter
And from the skylight above
    lucid
The light of heaven
            falls
Onto the table where the Plan is spread out
            in marvelous symbols
    sketches of the Common Life
Illuminated
    through the glass panes of the clerestory
            "LUXE CLARTÉ VOLUPTÉ"
the full granary

The same light that falls on the "real"
    collective farm
Dhillon's work section / sweats /
            in the cane field
The buffalo slogs / rain loosens the clods
Is a feedback adequate

between the field laborer (his hands)
& the planners' mind?
the black tassels of corn dry in the sun

THE MAGICAL CATEGORIES

• •

Notes on Dress and Adornment

The Middle-aged: uniforms. No perfume. Fourth Age Set women: family clothes, the regular Jat dress around the household, full skirt, kurta, and shawl. The Third Set women the same, plus the besprangled half-jacket and hairdo of plastic curls. For their workday at the guilds the Thirds and Fourths dress up somewhat (their best clothes?).

See them bending over the computer consoles. The lovely hues—the white, the blue silk, the many-colored bright taffetas and embroideries are reflected on the polished instrument housing. An apprentice loosens her long hair and a wave of perfume floats out. It is the "perfume of planners' the young women are permitted to wear by the Village Council, the one that distinguishes them.

And Maddi's face markings? Her face decorated with the same intricate yellow-and-blue scrollwork cut by diagonals, the quadrants slightly offset—as her mother's. The line going across the eyebrows and down each cheek, to denote the Moon Sisterhood which she has joined at twenty.

3 ANCESTOR WORSHIP

Some time after the Mother-Letting-Go passage, toward the end of October, the Harditt family gathered one evening in front of the Ancestor Shrine. It was Halloween, Spook Night. The patriarch's brother, Jeth Harditt, led the prayers.

Lineage brothers and sisters. Let us worship the Ancesters.
Let us worship the oldest and the youngest dead.
There is a death/
There is a funeral/the cortege of mourners

and musicians go by carrying cartoons of the sacred fish and giving away paper money

There is a burial   that is our custom

The third day after the burial we put on our
mourner's clothes again   We return to the grave
with its bare dirt/We perform the rite
that allows the soul to leave the grave pit and
take residence in the house Now the soul will reside
there.

I am thinking now of the boy, Reddi Our newest and
youngest dead   The dirt is still fresh on the mound
the flowers unwilted
Yet he has become Ancestor

The cult of the ancestors begins   For a certain time
prayers are said at the altar of the house
                    and at the graveside
A month after the burial we have taken the boy's photograph
that his mother   our sister   carried in her purse
      We place it on the shrine
along with some of his letters from camp
   and a scratchy
   signature

Ah, the photo is beginning to fade   They fade.
From now on we must never name him   It was my fault
            to name him
   We call him "last gone" That is our custom

(At this point in the Halloween service a friend of "last gones" comes forward and places a branch before the altar in a stone jar. Other members of the family

come forward. Other photographs, hand drawings, and flowers are hung on the twig and threaded with wool thread. This is the Spirit Tree, on which all the Ancestors are represented. Jeth continues.)

We have here our own toc   all our deceased members
ascending up through the fifth generation   There is
a general. A schoolteacher. A fireman.
A woman who sold insurance and owned a motor car
                    our most ancient Ancestor.
Let us honor and feast the dead
Living Ones   beside this Spirit Tree

(A dish of rice and cup of water are set out.)

Drink revered Ancestors   Eat   all of you
    After the fifth one
    you are beginning to fade   Grandmother
    you are evaporating into the smoke of incense

(The pitcher of water is poured on the ground.)

It is night   Just as the moon's rays absorb this water
the feasting circle of the toc   suck up our prayers
The line of lineage stretches out
In life we have our own breathing circle
    In this compound
we sleep together/the new baby with her grandmother
            The line stretched into time
In the same way we are pulled   we are stretched out
beyond the wider circle with the Dead
                        The dead surround us
        like the mists of night
A cloud encompasses us   Let us draw the shawl

around us   over our shoulders
    We stand at the edge
of emptiness   Cousins the grave garments decay
    Again
we are standing here   on eve of Kanagat
    in our fraying clothes

As a new last gone is added to the toc
        the oldest/the fifth dead   fades
    she fades beyond memory

A mist   a fog of ancestors   surrounds us

Focus the light   Our lineage is in our own face
    Cousins they inhabit us
        as the light from this candle flame
    on the altar
makes the room thick
                with existence.
In the dim lens our identity is revealed
    The dead draw towards us   The flame
shows our face   We yield this room to them

    The dead feast in our house by candlelight
        And we the living
look in at the window
        Our lanterns wade through the dark

4 THE GOBARDAN FESTIVAL

Gobardan is ushered in by a week of merry-making. Bands of children go around the streets of the village begging candy. There is a display of lights. The town generator is turned up. Strings of lights glow in the window of each house at night.

And the cattle are painted. A travel account describes it: "On Amavas day the cattle are not yoked but are decorated with a reddish paste made of red oxide and oil. Spots are daubed on the animals' sides and faces; their horns are painted red, green, or blue. Peacock feathers may be attached to their heads, while their necks are hung about with beads, necklaces, and leather bands clinking with little bells."

It is Harvest Holiday.

On the morning of Gobardan the families of Red Willow thollas go out in groups to the motor pool. It is here that the fuel cells are stockpiled: the laminated battery devices called bitauras by which electrical energy is stored. Made from local deposits, it is said these are "formed by man of the earth, and on Gobardan the flow of energy is reversed." The Commune is energized.

The original bitauras were cow-dung cakes made of excrement mixed with straw, which the women of the clan used for cooking fuel. The cow-dung cakes were stored in conical-shaped mounds called boongas and covered with a protective coat of dried clay painted in diagonal colored swatches. These were a feature of the ancient village.

Now on Gobardan the modern energy packets are ceremonially heaped in the same boongas, coated with clay, and painted.

When the residents arrive at the motor pool, the farmhands are already clambering over the tops of the boongas, their legs decorated with shucks of corn. A wild scene. The shell is demolished, broken apart with blows from sticks, like a giant piriata. Pieces of caked mud splatter among the onlookers. The first bitauras are taken out and "worshipped." Then these fuel cells are transported to the Collective Farm, where they are hooked up to turn the wheels of the cane grinding mill.

The Harditt family retuned to the compound after the first ritual of Gobardan. Next came the Ganji ceremony in which the house was blessed. The compound had been swept clean. The cooking utensils shone. The machinery and locks had been oiled in each of the five interconnected households. The walls of the courtyard had been whitewashed. On the doors the flower-shaped figures had been inscribed, the sacred tantras.

The courtyard was in turmoil. Harditts, Nais, Dobbis, and Banya cousins were packed together and exchanged noisy gossip. Servers brought out food. The old matriarch Helvetia, her mustache bristling, was shouting at the top of her lungs and beating on a brass pot. Nobody paid attention.

Srikant had come from Gonwonda that morning, bringing his children to visit the family over the holidays. Their hands covered with mud, they squatted on the ground with a group constructing the Ganji figure.

Dhillon, his brother, was not here. But Golgo and Pindi were already making a nuisance of themselves, bullying and teasing.

An ox, attracted perhaps by the smell of food, had halted by the gate of the Harditt compound. The children stared at the enormous animal as they munched their rice grains roasted in brown sugar.

Facetiously Golgo urged them to invite him in. "There's plenty of room. Give him some candy."

Hanging its painted head, the beast looked at them through the bars, its horns weighted with flowers.

A game of bowls was taking place along the sidewalk between two banana clumps. Harelip headed one team and Venu the other. The latter had a modest but tricky bowling style. He would angle his own ball off the side boards. Or with a twist of his wrist he would let it go. It would roll slowly, bypassing the others, and with a breaking curve come to rest beside the marker. Harelip was known as an "aerialist." Carefully calculating his trajectory he would hurl his ball through the air, knocking away his opponent.

A crowd stood along the sidelines. Among them were Desai Patel and Rathlee Golla, a yellowish-complexioned man with a drooping mustache. A pitcher of beer was between them.

Desai yelled at Harelip, "You're gonna make it! You're gonna make it! Five says that he does it."

"Not a chance. It's too close."

"Five says Harelip can do it!"

Several other betters put their five rupees up against Desai's. Golla also matched it.

It was Harelip's turn. Desai yelled, "Come on, Uncle!"

Like a hawk the player bent over and gauged the distance, one heel dug in the ground. The aerialist kissed the steel ball and let it fly. It missed. The game was over. Players and betters joined each other.

Desai Patel put his arm around Harelip's shoulder. "Uncle, how could you do that to me? During the whole game I lost thirty rupees. You asshole, I'm wiped out.

He said this weeping into his beer. At the same time he was embracing Harelip profusely. The two of them emptied the beer pitcher and arm in arm went into the house.

Desai Patel was Nanda's second divorced husband. The aerialist had been the first. Neither had lasted long. Nanda had gotten rid of both of them. She had had several children with Desai.

In a sense Nanda's children had three fathers: two provided by the clan, and one chosen later in life by Nanda.

In Sawna at the age of forty a woman is considered free of clan obligations and is permitted to select her private man, sometimes referred to as her "bush husband." Nanda had chosen Rathlee Golla, a barber from the adjacent village.

The children had been busy on the packed earth of the courtyard constructing the Ganji figure. This was made under the supervision of the matriarchs, out of straw mixed with cow dung. It had started out being simply a pile, referred to as the Hill of Purana or Krishna's umbrella. Then gradually the Ganji was molded into a roughly human figure, a model of a man or woman sprawled in the courtyard ground. Within the stomach were the household possessions, also the residents, in miniature. From the neck four walls ran out which contained replicas of cows, buffalos, milksheds, the town water tank, the motor pool. Thus was symbolized the household extending into the Commune. The magical figure was an inventory of the family's wealth, projected in the next year through planning.

On the moist mud were the prints of hands. The children were sticking trees into the walls. These were weeds that the celebrants would thread with strips of cotton.

Helvetia's shouts were now being heard. She was calling them to circle the Ganji and to sing in chorus the "Grandmother-Cow-Dung-Wealth-Awakening Song."

Sathan was being summoned. As the latest one of the clan's Middles, it was she that was privileged to lead the ceremonial parade around the figure.

The compound's lights were switched on.

Then the smallest child applied a turmeric mark to the figure's foot. Now Ganji had a red toe. And Helvetia, the oldest matriarch, raising her pitcher, poured buttermilk into Ganji's mouth.

"The house is growing!"

"Bless us, Grandmother-Cow-Dung-Wealth!"

"Happiness and electricity!"

5

People are moving to the tables.

Nanda came up and spoke a word aside to Rathlee. The two left by the gate.

The narrow weather-stained kakka walls were purple. The clamor of other harvest gatherings spilled onto the lanes. In Makers' Square the blacksmiths' booths were closed and the shutters locked tight. A neon advertisement overhead said: Magor—Blacksmithing.

The pair walked up the ramp leading to the outskirts, Rathlee with his arm around Nanda's waist. Though it was dark now, the stone ramp worn by wheel tracks still held the heat of the day's sun.

Nanda, suffering from a headache, pressed her hands to her temples.

"A family thanksgiving. Family . . . family . . . family. A thanksgiving for what, I'd like to know."

"Those flutes . . . earsplitting. You were good to put up with it, Rathlee."

Golla had absented himself from his own Gobardan celebration. He had clan obligations of his own. But he considered he was well out of it, he told Nanda.

"Those shitty figures, disgusting. And did you see Sathan's face, when they called her to lead the awakening march? You'd think she was in charge of the whole planning operation. How she struts and gives orders."

Nanda described how the three of them, crossing the square that morning, had found the two men in stocks. "How ugly it all is! The crowd was throwing stones at them."

"And Sathan, too?" Rathlee was shocked.

"It was a little boys' gang. But she didn't try to stop them."

Nanda walked ahead briskly. Low hedges flanked the path. The gardens behind were black. The vegetables had been left matted by an early frost.

A line of windmills stood guard at the boundary of the village. Beyond stretched the common fields.

Under a black shoal of cloud the yellow moon had just risen. A cold light washed the field. Afloat for a moment between cloud and horizon the moon outlined the boonga clusters and stacks of corn and pumpkins.

Soon the processions would begin winding through the lanes to the town pond for the final celebrations of Gobardan. Here the air was still. The sails of the windmills hung limp.

Nanda released Golla's hand and kicked off her shoes. Abruptly she lay down on the stubble field. Her eyes were closed tight.

Rathlee spread his coat on the ground next to Nanda. But instead of moving over she sat upright and began vehemently pulling up the corn stubble.

"Let's make a fire."

"Well, there's plenty of fuel anyway."

"Yes, we could have a hundred fires. But we need only one. Our wedding fire."

Golla realized that Nanda was slightly drunk. At the ceremonies she had made a point of flirting with Desai Patel and Harelip and snubbing Rathlee. How perverse she is. She changes this way and that . . . like a windmill sail, Rathlee thought.

By "wedding fire" Nanda was referring to another customary rite—perhaps more ancient than that of Gobardan itself. And outside the clan structure. For the poor of the village and for those unable to afford the expenses of a ceremonial wedding, there had been the "bush wedding." The couple simply made a fire of sticks and made their first love on the ground beside it.

So the man had become a bush or free husband. And in this way it was the custom of the women of the Fifth grade to take husbands.

The flame was small on the immense field and burned low, a thick smoky yellow. Nanda stared at it, her face hard. The line of her mouth, pulled down stubbornly at the corners, gave her an ugly look.

Now what's eating her? She's angry because she's grown old, women are like that. Rathlee wanted to cheer her up, to reassure her, but couldn't think how to.

"Rathlee, my life is over. And I've made a mess of it."

"Nanda, you shouldn't say that. Out of respect for me anyway."

"That's true. I've chosen you, Rathlee." But she spoke with bitterness.

However, Nanda was not bitter against Golla. She was thinking: The blood . . . how it courses, how quickly it rises to suffuse a young woman's face. She was thinking of Maddi admiring herself in the mirror. And in Maddi she saw, she felt herself as a young woman.

What Nanda was thinking was this: What does it mean to be young? A man touches you and you respond. The laborers are asleep. He is leaning against you, pressing you against the bullock cart. You arch back, your lips open. Excitement fills the body. Yet you turn away, laugh, the pitch of your voice rises. "Oh don't *do* that to me."

The memory flooded Nanda. Her arms were clasped around her knees. Still gazing into the fire, she seized Rathlee's arm.

But what is she up to? What a woman. Her mood's changed completely.

"Rathlee, I'll be fifty years old!"

"Oh, to hell with it, none of that matters. Nanda, look at me."

"All right, Rathlee. We have our own ceremony, don't we? Much better than theirs. You and I, Golla, in the field. And these clothes! You don't think I wear them because I like them?"

Nanda stood up before him. Rathlee grinned.

"Nanda. You're best without clothes."

Nanda began unbuttoning her padded jacket. The buttons were wooden ones. She ripped them off.

"How I hate the goddamn things. And these pants. Now, don't I have a nice figure, Rathlee?" She stood before him on the corn stubble. "But my hair. My god, look how they cut it all off."

Her face, neck, and shoulders wore the blue moon marks.

"You look beautiful," Rathlee Golla said, a lump in his throat.

Nanda began to cry.

THE ANCESTOR SOCIETY

Old Harditt complained: "I can't eat. Everything tastes like cardboard." His skin had become stretched as parchment. The family watched him waste away. Cancer of the stomach, they were told. Occasionally the patriarch rallied and for short periods appeared to regain his energies. His duties as bank examiner for the bisacauga took him traveling through the countryside and even as far as Puth. The decisions came heavy. Sometimes his great-grandchildren would accompany him on these trips, riding in a bullock cart to which had been strapped a parasol to shelter the old man from the sun.

Venu saw little of the clan head. He was now a panchayat member. He had his own duties to the Commune and would return to the compound short-tempered and exhausted. Every week brought some difficulty to be resolved, to somebody's disappointment. He had reached the age when he could not walk down the street without meeting past opponents in some dispute and with whom, for this reason, he shared some bond.

His relations with his son had become increasingly irritating. The young husband returned from Gonwonda, where he had become a junior partner in the Baniya enterprises. Venu stared balefully across the table at this person who had adopted the habits of the Filtheaters, picking his teeth like his wife's uncle and wearing Zamindar's business clothes.

Even Sathan said of the bridgegroom, "The Moon has gone out of him."

A chieftan of the Singhs' died, and there was a funeral in the adjacent tholla. Various Red Willow men got drunk at it. A heavy bean soup, meat pie, and wine had been served. Venu making an address presented as a gift to the deceased a bottle of peach brandy.

The chieftain had been a Jat, and yet the funeral room was full of Karsts. Were these merely business connections of the Singhs'? This did not seem to be the case, because there were a number of children, all with webbed hands, who were said to be related to the Singhs. The candles in the room glowed unpleasantly on the skin of the albinos, and Venu was reminded of his childhood, of being back in Garh during his factory year.

After midnight the band from the Red Willow tholla re turned across town. They split off at their various compounds. Venu, fuddled, found his steps wandering from one side of the narrow lane to the other. Occasionally he bumped up against a wall.

He could still hear the clapping and foot stamping. The fiddles of the "nahn dieu" funeral party scraped in his head.

"This is no good. I'll have to sober up," he told himself.

A light was burning in the sickroom on the roof of the Harditt household. Venu made himself a cup of coffee in the kit chen and went up to have a chat with Gopal Harditt.

As he entered, Sathan's grandfather was up playing check ers with Tattattatha. The Deodar's flute lay at the foot of the bed. The invalid raised his head to be kissed, at the same time he put his hand warningly on Venu's arm.

"Steady. Don't spill the coffee. You're a little tipsy."

Venu, who normally kept his distance from his in-laws, was fond of the old man. He would have liked to unburden himself and share his troubles. Phrases which had a melancholy ring ran through his head, such as: "My son is a disappointment to me" or "What is a man to do? He labors and makes a success, but the sweetness has gone out of it." As he thought this he imag fined his face took on a pathetic expression, and he even began to cry. But instead of this subject, Venu launched into a long description of the nahn dieu ceremony, how everyone was dressed and what they ate.

What strange behavior. He described how the shamans placed a bunch of bananas on the dead man's stomach, to fool the Celestial Dog, and a plate of dry rice at the head of the coffin, in case the corpse tried to get up. In fact the corpse had tried to get up and climb out of the coffin, and everyone had thrown rice at him, and had gone back.

"It was the noise. Old Singh never could stand music," was Harditt's comment. He laughed, and this brought a pain to his chest, and his face went gray. He lay very still for a minute.

"Father, would you like me to get someone to change the sheets? Would you like some Darvan?"

Venu held his hand tight.

Then he left, saying he was going to make himself another cup of coffee, but did not return.

• •

Tattattatha resumed the game of checkers after a while. Harditt asked: "What do you think of the old customs?

"You know I don't approve of them. I find the yellow shamans reactionary as a class. Oh, they're likable enough fellows, and I suppose they have a strengthening influence on the family by encouraging the ancestor rites. But the world is burdened enough with the dead and ghosts."

Harditt thought that the family of the living has its roots in the dead. "It's like a vein of coal: sometimes it flickers on the surface, there's a glow. But to find the seam you have to follow it deep underground. It becomes mysterious."

"No, let us do our wandering here on the surface of the earth." Tattattatha smiled. "You know that the true mysteries are founded in the clear light of science and ecology."

"People are superstitious, one way or another."

The priest also disapproved of the shamans' traveling shows. A recent practice, now almost every county in the Plains had its "unlicensed areas" outside the village limits where American movies were shown, followed by the vaudeville and "individuality freak shows." This was supposed to innoculate the folk against foreign ways, but Tattattatha put this down to pure tribalism.

"Of course, morality is a factor. And naturally moral sanctions are local, that is they depend on the tribe and family. But the Gay Science cuts across all that."

"But then, everything is going bad these days." Tattattatha complained that even among the students at Egwegnu few wished to follow the "Path of the Six Aspects".

"We all see the region in a different way," Harditt ob-served simply. "And that way partly depends on how old a person is."

The visitor had tired Harditt, so he wished Tattattatha would go away. Instead the blue shaman fumbled into the bottle of the sick man's pills, loosening the glass stopper and twirling it, then pushing it back again. He sat slumped in his chair and passed his hand over his own damp face. Though the priest had come to cheer the invalid up it was clear he had only succeeded in making himself melancholy.

Finally Tattattatha stood up, bowed to take the old man's blessing.

Harditt asked: "When will you be going? I suppose you'll be leaving for the encampment soon? With the Wind people."

"Yes. When the geese fly over."

• •

The Deodar had left. There were no sounds in the house. Below, Venu lay with the sleepers. On the deck outside the sandbox was empty except for a few scattered toys.

Gopal Harditt lay dozing.

Members of the Ancestor Society crowded into the room. At first he was scarcely aware of them, in the dim light. They pressed around his bed. One of the Ancestors seized his hand and pulled him upright. Harditt sat on the edge of the bed, his feet in slippers. Some of the men of the

Society he recognized. Some he did not.

The party moved out onto the roof. A wind stirred the olives. The thin moon of Kanagat doubled in the skylights. The newly dead had green mold covering their gray skins. Their eyes were bitter. Shadows deepened their sockets, and their hair hung lank as ropes. But the older Society members—those who had been worshiped in the tocs longer or who had already passed beyond, into the Region World—these appeared sound and brisk. There were also a number of living "Ancestors" whom Harditt recognized. One old man, as decrepit as he, seemed to be enjoying his difficulties.

"Come on, Gopal, old timer. You're walking too stiff. You'll have to move faster." It was the Nai headman, still manager of the neighboring tholla, the ones who had lent the Red Willows the ox.

"All right. But I have this pain."

He was taken into the sweat lodge. The air was thick and so hot it seemed to burn his lungs. Harditt felt his whole body go slack and his pores open. The pain under his rib left him, and he began to sweat. Around him the skin of the naked men glistened.

A single bulb burned overhead. The thickening steam above billowed against the murky ceiling. The emanation of light focused into a cone in which the bathers seemed to become palpable.

"Well, we are still *in* our bodies," Gopal thought. With the heat sinking into the muscles he had some sense of physical relief. But he was frightened.

The lodge members sat on raised benches around the walls or stood in the center on duckboards, opening their mouths in order to breathe deeper and rubbing themselves. Through a window in one wall he could see the exercise room. Here other masked members of the Ancestor Society were present and moving among the shamans. It was a vast room onto which many other doors opened. He had the sense of bathers standing in other sweat lodges focused in the same cone of light.

The exercises appeared to be beginning. Some Ancestors were performing dance steps; shamans were helping others on with their masks. But the great room was vague.

Steam pipes ran around the walls of the sweat lodge. There was a water tap beside which a dark young man squatted. A red-bearded man addressed Gopal.

"Is the heat too much for you, or can you take more?"

Harditt said he could stand it hotter, and the man opened the tap and sluiced water onto the pipes. The steam rose in billows, obscuring the window. It grew hotter very quickly. Harditt gasped, smacked his chest, and the red-bearded man laughed.

"That's good. We Harditts have a thick skin. We can stand anything." The tribesman seemed to be familiar with Gopal.

"They say an elephant will hurry, if you whack it with a shovel—but never a Jat," Harditt replied, joking. The squatting man on the floor opened his mouth in a grin. His front teeth were missing, giving him a droll expression.

"Do you know who he is?"

Harditt looked. The young man's face was pitted with smallpox. He had never seen him; he had died young, but Gopal recognized him as his own grandfather, from the photograph he had seen on the family altar. He supposed there were others of his toc present in the sweat room.

Of the other Ancestor Society members in the bath some were old. With their skin wrinkled and loose over their bones, and thin wispy beards, they were the image of patriarchs. However, most appeared to be of middle age, and there were several young men, some even in their teens. From their rough hands he could tell most of them were farmers. But not all.

A prim young Jat sat on a stool next. His eyes squinting he was looking intently at a sheet of paper; and other sheets of the paper were tucked under his buttocks. He was wearing a bowler hat.

"He's reading a newspaper. We don't have such things now," the red-bearded man explained. He turned to the Jat on the stool and told him to read out loud, "To give us a little entertainment."

The bowler-hatted man read. It was from the financial page of the

Calcutta *Times*. The lines, written down in the long outlawed "fresh" script, sounded curious.

"Read on," said the red-bearded man. "It's intriguing."

"Here is an interesting item." The Jat flipped back a page.

> FAMINE IN BIHAR PROVINCE
> Informed sources in Sringeri, capital of Bihar Province, announced today that there is no end in sight to the famine that has devastated this area. Due to the prolonged drought, crop losses are estimated in the millions of lakhs. Health officials estimate that in this village of Ind with a population of 40,000 a third of the lower caste inhabitants have died and another 15,000 are suffering from beriberi and other deficiency diseases due to eating grass and bark. Stores of grain on hand have been pronounced adequate but have been unable to reach the starving due to transportation breakdowns and wide-scale corruption among provincial officials.

"Yes, yes. You see, "Things don't change so much at all," the red-bearded man said. "There are always too many people for the food."

The room was getting hotter. Old Harditt felt himself drained of strength.

There came the clinking of little bells. There were two doors, the first leading from the steam room into a vestibule. The sound passed in the space beyond. Harditt recognized it. It came from the bells at the end of the leather strings and rags attached to the skirts of the shamans in charge of the exercise room.

Several of the Ancestors rose and left. Harditt saw a strange thing happen. As they moved out of the steam, and beyond the light cone, they became less substantial. As they passed through the door, their skins clouded and grew smokey, like the chimney of a kerosene lamp. "It is the lamp of spirits that I have always believed in," Harditt thought. They went out through the vestibule, out the other door, and he lost them. At intervals there were more bells. Other Ancestors went.

In the sweat room, the light cone had dimmed. Through the window the great room beyond had become illuminated. Now he could see into it clearly. It was thronged with Ancestors, their articles of regalia; the decorative marks and costumes were recognizable. But the figures as they moved vaguely . . . Harditt asked himself who were they? At first he answered: they are simply people who have moved out of their skins—into the tribes.

But neither was that clear. It was evident that there were many tribes. All the phratries were there, but this too became confused. And though Harditt had been able dimly to follow his own tribal people as they went out the door and as they paled, this line too became lost.

A storm shook the great room. It was as though a current moving out from a river's mouth was confounded by other currents. The tide pulled out the Jats, Drybeds, and the Forest tribes toward some distant reef against which the ocean beat and threw up its spray.

All was overwhelmed in the wave of Ancestors.

Now in the exercise room they were beginning to perform the Dance Houses. Some clumsily executed the first steps encumbered by their regalia. The great masks and costumes were heavy, so they had to be assisted into them; the gestures were awkward. Tutored by the shamans the ancestors began to perform stiffly the steps of the first rites.

Harditt watched them move dreamily into myth . . .

He had been left alone with his own toc.

He looked around him and saw them. They were his father and his grandfather, the pockmarked man. There were three others seated on the warm benches, their skin glistening. The lineage marks were the same.

One of the men left.

For a long time the five remaining toc members sat there and said nothing. Harditt gripped the bench, looking to them for some signal whether he were alive or dead. But they were indifferent.

Then he remembered: "There are no individuals. It is only . . . motes dancing in the light cone."

Finally Harditt turned to his father, who had gone before him, and asked:

"How am I to conduct himself?"

"You'll get the hang of it soon. There are decisions that have to be made, for the folk. It's a question of dissolving your own skin, to embrace Holy Region."

The pain had lodged under Harditt's gut. He asked, moving his lips with difficulty, "But how am I to judge—seeing that I am that corrupt official?"

"Shall we have more steam? Shall I make the room hotter?" the red-bearded man asked.

Harditt felt his lungs burn.

"Are you all right? Are you in pain?" the leader of his toc asked him. "What you are feeling now is the spirit flame coming."

Harditt said, twisting his lips: "No pain. Ah, it is only that one part of my soul clings to earth."

"Don't worry about it. You have passed through the last phase. In a way, this is only the beginning. The Wheel of the Age Sets turns. It cycles into the darkness and comes up again. One day there will be another Gopal Harditt."

HARVESTING THE WIND

1 HARVESTING THE WIND

When he was forty-five years old and after he had worked as a wind technician for ten years, Venu had been chosen to represent his group on the Regional Power Federation. The Kansu Hardan region manufactures electricity from the wind during the late fall through the early winter months, the dry monsoon season. Each group of sixteen villages contributes its cadres. These set up the encampment at Goose Gap and organize work on the generator sites.

One afternoon soon after his arrival, Venu received a call to come to the board room. The Power Federation offices were located on a hillside high up above the plateau. Dry grass covered the upper valley. Below lay the plains of Kansu Hardan, dry in autumn with the late afternoon sun touching brown fields, over which high tension lines marched to the Rift cities.

The Chairman of the Praesidium, a Karst by the name of Wen Fang, was gazing out of the window.

"Eight megawatts of electricity. It's astonishing how much you can get out of a few hundred windmills—that is, if they're all connected in parallel. Ah! The Collective Effort . . . " The Chairman, his face beaming, released his grip on Venu's hand. Venu recognized some of the other commissioners, including the Praesidium Vice-Chairman, a distinguished Plainsman whose face he had seen on wall posters. There were five other Jat representatives and as many Forest Men. The rest were Karsts, old trade-union leaders and anarchosyndicalists—hard bargainers who had made their way up through the Rift factories and represented a large urban membership.

Venu thought: They're a tough bunch. I've got to watch my step with these boys.

He was sweating profusely under the armpits and wondered if this showed. The gathering was extremely friendly. The welcoming ceremony over, the Praesidium members crowded around Venu and another freshman and gave the traditional greeting of autumn:

"Health, brother. May there be power, May the geese fly high."

"Yes. And may the region be holy."

A huge map from floor to ceiling of the board room showed the districts of the Kansu Hardan region in multiple colored inks. Industrial was indicated in a deep purple; commercial in red; various densities of residential—high, medium, and low—in shades of orange and yellow; agriculture in green; the Forest Cantonments black. The spindly Nghsi River, bounded by the Grand Canyon, wandered in a dotted line, as the stream was intermittent. Water cachement areas were shown in diagonal broken lines—the subterranean "quanats," reservoirs for the twin cities of Garh and Puth Majra, which also furnished local electrical power by a system of pumps and hydroturbines.

Now the briefing occurred, an explanation of the Next Year's Plan. This was given by the committee Chairman standing before the wall map. Venu saw a video machine running and had the idea that the proceedings were being taped—but was not sure.

The Chairman concluded:

"Naturally an organization of this sort deals in large blocs of power. Of course, there are small blocs: the village refrigeration and heating requirements, the communes' farm machinery in the summer months, and so forth. But we have consolidated all these in a single bloc, for the sake of efficiency. I don't have to remind you, we are a regionalwide organization and some sort of subordination is necessary. So we have to pull together."

"Well, what do you think of the Plan?" A Deodar priest stood by Venu. It was Hupe--Boinville, an elderly Blueface dressed for the occasion in a monkey skin.

"I don't know, it's too early to say. I'll have to take it back to the men."

"Good. The answer of a true anarchosyndicalist."

The Chairman and the Vice-Chairman, Siddahavanah, took Venu and the other freshman by the elbow and steered them into the adjoining room. The priest followed.

This was the control room. It was square, with no windows. One stainless steel wall housed the instruments. The other three walls were in mahogany veneer, which glowed under cove lighting. In one corner stood a bar, furnished with club chairs.

Venu examined the instrument panel. The top row high up on the wall was mostly gauges and sensor screens for monitoring the operations of the power production plant. At shoulder height was a bank of switches. These were labeled and numbered in order of priority from right to left.

The Vice-Chairman said: "Of course it's not working now, because the monsoon hasn't come. When it does, you can actually *hear* the system in operation, the sound of the various loads pulling the generator down."

"And all the colored lights come on, it's very pretty," added the priest.

Wen Fang explained the function of the system to the freshmen. It was to regulate the current coming from the wind chargers into the energy accumulator, and break it down into loads. It was essentially a switching device consisting of a coil relay which energized the circuit in an ascending or descending order depending on the demand for power, the number of mills in operation, and the wind velocity.

"This is what we call a 'load selector.' It's only an ingenious device, a machine," the Chairman winked at Siddahavannah. "The important thing is, who controls the machine."

2 THE SKY SERMON

Venu passed down to the encampment through Steep Wood. In a glade the young men and women who that fall were to join the Sky Phratry were being instructed by Tattattatha. Venu found them sitting in a circle under a teak tree and stopped to listen. The lesson began with a brief homily, one of the "Creation Stories."

"What was the beginning of the sky? We cannot ask the question. Our ears are not profound enough, our eyes are not wide enough to take in the universe. But we extend them with our instruments. The spectroscope shows a trace.

"A star condenses. It is collapsing in the furnace of the primal elements, hydrogen and helium. Two forces are at work. As it collapses it consumes itself. It gets denser and hotter. At the same time there is an increase in magnetism, the magnetic core strengthens in a fluid of incompressable electrons.

"The supernova explodes. As it does so it goes in two directions. The core moves in. By a process that we call rotational mechanics, it keeps shrinking and becomes a neutron star, a little sun compressed to the density of a hundred thousand tons per cubic millimeter. Conceptually it may go further. It may keep going and disappear altogether into what is called a "black hole," a condition of rotational energy or pure force, a magnet rotating in the field of its cosmic debris.

"What happens to the debris? At the same time as the shell is exploding outward, matter is thrown out, the ejecta, which is a plasma of high-energy electrons. In the first phases this acts as a piston, driving into space the interstellar a medium. Rotational energy is translated into kinetic energy.

"In the second phase this kinetic energy is translated into wave energy. The shock wave, traveling slightly ahead of the ejecta, interacts with the charged particles in the magnetic field and emits thermal radiation and the flux of X-rays.

"In the final phases of the exploding star there is a cooling and slowing, along with an increase in mass. In this process the translational energy has been carried away, in what we call the law of angular momentum. Radiation is emitted at longer and longer wave lengths, and we get readings within the visible light spectra and radio emissions. With further slowing and cooling we are in the realm of ultraviolet light.

"We pass beyond the thresholds of our instruments. And here in a darkness we cannot see and by a process of creation we can barely know, a new cosmos is formed, new galaxies conceived out of the congeries of interstellar dust."

So ended the Sky Sermon by the Blue Priest. However, he was not a member of the Sky Fraternity. Tattattatha belonged to the Forest sign, and his specialty was not astronomy but music.

And yet the musical rhythms of his discourse had made the subject more impressive, Venu thought. The catechumens sat at the instructor's feet. His leopard lay beside him, sleepily gazing at the students.

Tattattatha had taken out his flute. Now would come the question and answer period called "Koans." He sounded a single soft note.

"We must talk of our home—which is a hexagon of many houses.

"Now my catechumens, a few questions: you may answer singly or together. Is it possible we can know the heavens, but be ignorant of this earth and ourselves?"

One of the catechumens replied: "We can know it, but barely. On earth as with the stars, being is a miraculous process."

Q. In an ocean without salt, an earth without soil, and an atmosphere without air, the first proto-organism split the water molecule. That was the primal event. How does life develop?

A. Life organizes its own site. Life multiplies and evolves into what we call the habitats of the ecosystem.

Q. An ecosystem is a stable, complex, resistant, self-regulating community of users that expands the site. To the mountainside the salmon returns from the sea with the world in her belly. What are the Two Chains?

A. There is the grazing chain, and the decay chain. Each gives up ten per cent, the producer to the user, and retains his own, which is built into its own structure.

The grass / the seaweed / the swamp / give up ten per cent
the sheep / the fish / the browsing deer
                the mouse give up ten per cent
the toad / the dragonfly / the fox
the lynx / the hawk / the mackerel give up ten per cent.
Man the hunter.

Q. That's the grazing chain. What is the decay chain?

A. The eagle and the weasel
the carp / the crab
the bacteria / the fungi
the decaying leaf mold
city harbor / the sludge
the well of nutrients.
All give it up   they give up the tissue of their bodies
to the others   and it is recycled.

Q. Is the circle of the biome closed?

A. No, it is open. It is Open-Steady-State   a membrane.
The process of Dynamic Equilibrium.

Q. Where is our home?

A. Our home is the Region, with its six sides in tension. At the center is the balance, the coupling of the Two Energies.

Q. What are the Two Energies?

A. Photosynthesis/Growing—Respiration/Burning. One is blue, green, and orange, the other black and red. Burning is pure force energy. When man simplifies species he wastes life and burns it. When he extends species man moves in the direction of creation. As the supernova explodes.

3

Venu passed through Steep Wood. In a few minutes he was at the river. Several housekeepers, their kamiz rolled up to their knees, were washing clothes. The encampment spread out before him.

Each autumn, when the first chill winds heralded the dry monsoon season, the clans comprising the Sky Phratry gathered here from all over Nghsi. They came from every city and village to the sacred site. The journey over the Plains was made by canal. At the landing stage the great spidery Le Tourneau cranes unloaded the gear, backing into the water with their shining tires and swinging the steel longhouse frames and utility cores ashore. The frames were covered by polyethylene skins to make "yurts."

The place was called simply the Gathering Grounds. From the old days, the clans had come here during the dry season, originally to fish and gather berries, and now to make electricity. Over the great meadow, bounded by a loop of the river, towered the twin scraggy heights of the West Scarp. Between them was the Wind Gap.

Venu crossed the river at a shallow place and, wet up to his knees, approached the meadow. The further settlements were those of the Drybeds and Forest Windmen. Nearest the river were the Plains compounds or "villages," each formed of its circle of yurts. As he made his way across the meadow the first village he came to was that of the "Scraggly Feathers." He passed by two others set up by the "Herring Catchers" and the "Little Cucumbers." Between these sites and that of his own clan, the "Swallows," in an open space they were playing a game of lacrosse.

He recognized the Dhabar Jat team. Golgo plunged by, then his own younger brother, Prakash, charging and brandishing his stick. Prakash called to Venu: "Come on, First Brother, join us! They're giving us a drubbing." Another brother, Neelam, whom Venu had not seen in several years, stopped beside him, panting.

"What's the trouble? Have you gotten too old and fat?"

"I'm afraid I'll get my head cracked."

Neelam himself had put on weight and looked incongruous on the playing field. He had a large family and a business of his own in Puth Majra.

Venu walked on, then turned back to look. The team, made up of men and women clansmen, had their shirts off, and their skins glistened. The sun on the field was golden. Grasshoppers were in the edgy weeds. And the big hares, their ears already beginning to turn white, followed the game from the tall grass, their noses twitching.

A bunch of small-fry nephews and nieces were engaged in flying a model airplane. Their plane had been clumsily constructed with a double wing and was powered by a miniature thermionic converter. At a distance stood the girl pilot. A little boy knelt on the ground lighting a lump of cow dung in the ignition chamber.

"Watch out, Uncle!"

The contraption burst from the grass like a scared partridge, and Venu ducked. At the center of the arc a small girl turned, on her face a look of solemnity and enchantment. She revolved slowly, her arm taut with the cable as the plane whirled. Venu called to his niece: "Candy! You're becoming a real Sky person!"

"May the region be holy."

"Home! Home!" His heart sung within him.

The pennants of his own Dhabar village fluttered from the masts of the yurts. His sister stood on the top step. Venu went up to her and worshipped her, pressing his fingers together, then touching her on the shoulder. For the first time Rahira was wearing the Middles uniform. Other sisters embraced him.

Soon lunch would be ready. The solar cooker had been set out, and the stew pot was simmering. Helpers moved back and forth bringing bowls. At the start of the meal Venu's sister would give the blessing—as the ranking lineage member present from the home village.

The home village . . . the mother village. Since the last encampment the blood had been divided, the tribe scattered. Now within the circle of the Swallows they would be together in harmony.

Venu noticed with a pang that his sister's face had grown graver and her eyes harder.

The lacrosse game was over. Venu's brother came up. Nee-lam filched a bit of stew from the pot. It burned him. He blew his lips out. A boy, Ramdas from Rampur village, put his arm across his first uncle's shoulder.

The men waited for the soup, talking about life in the villages they had been bound to: wives, farming, and the weather.

4

Above the slopes of Goose Gap, over the struts and gleaming cowls of a thousand windmills, lay the bright October sky. The windmills were raised in clusters of a dozen, a common stabilizer equalizing the flow of electricity from each turbine. These mills were mounted on a concrete pad, each managed by a different clan. The pads themselves were linked across the slopes by long runs of wires atop pylons, which flashed in the sun.

On the Dhabar Jat site the last of the turbines was being hoisted up. The team of riggers was directed by Neelam. Steadied by guide ropes, the big turbine was lifted slowly with the chain hoist. The housing with its tapered cone level in the air looked like a hornet's tail.

An apprentice clung to the hub frame thirty-five meters up. When the turbine reached their level, the team grappled it, swung it against the shaft head, and bolted it into place.

Neelam yelled up: "OK. Now you better get down here, before you break your ass."

Nearby, a group of apprentices was working under Venu's cousin, Garg. They had assembled an armature and were rewinding it. Garg stood by silently, chewing a stem of witch hazel. Parts were everywhere. The apprentices were smeared with grease. They wound and fastened the last coil. It was done.

Garg's lip curled. "Now you're sure you ain't got it on backward?"

The apprentices checked again, not sure of themselves. Squatting in the dirt, the workman made a diagram with his stick. He drew the field magnet and core, next the armature, with wires going to the commutator ring and thence to the brushes, and finally the carbon pile regulator which controlled the frequency.

Golgo whistled.

"That's it, the regulator." The master explained that the wind varied, so there was voltage swing of plus or minus ten to twenty volts, and this had to be balanced with the frequency. "You have to keep flux density constant in the magnet, otherwise you'll burn out the induction motor."

On the windmill frames and stabilizers already erected, the giant rotors were being attached. These would support the sails. Each village favored a different type of rotor: some plastic, some cast aluminum, depending on the specialty of their machine bank. The Dhabar mens' were of steel with sails of reed mat. Already the apprentices were painting these mats with appropriate signs and totems.

From the Dhabar Jat site other installations could be seen, a hundred of them dotting the slopes of the Divide. Most of the clusters were complete: wired up together in parallel and already hooked up to the main grid. The sky was empty. A hawk coasted in the cold blue.

Some of the cadre men had strung up bamboo mats. These served as wind breakers and formed a kind of sun trap. Inside this shelter the Swallows sat around talking and smoking.

A group of apprentices stood around Prakash. He was making his medicine bundle. In his hair was a snipe feather. He cut a stem of poplar, carefully hollowing it out to make a whistle.

These medicine bundles were "for sale"; that is, on the night of Diorthra, after the apprentices had passed through their rites, they would be entitled to buy them from the master cadremen. The bundles themselves represented the franchise extended by the region to these Wind tribesmen because of their special knowledge and skills.

In this sense a tribe had a patent on their wind-chargers and sites, even though they did not own them. A new passage meant that the license—to produce electricity—was being extended to a further group.

Ramdas had pulled on his sweater. He had been watching his uncle shape the whistle. "Can it call the wind?", the young man asked with some irony.

Prakash nodded. Playfully Ramdas grabbed it from him and blew a short note. Prakash looked at him in alarm. The apprentice crimsoned.

Others came over. They were cadremen who had been sunning themselves and apprentices who had been painting the mats. They stood by the two with grave faces.

One of the men said: "Now we've taken all the trouble to put up the equipment, but maybe it'll be useless."

"Brother, don't you know it's bad luck for a bareskin to whistle for the wind? One must be marked by the rites."

5

A panchayat of the Windmen was meeting under the council tree. The frost had disappeared which had whitened the field earlier. The clans stood under the leaves, netted in shadow. Beyond, the grass was a burnished yellow. The clash of lacrosse sticks was borne on the crisp air.

Represented on the panchayat were the various clans of the Plains Phratry—Swallows, Dirty Feathers, Coots, the Streamers, Busted Clouds. This assembly conducted its seasonal affairs at Goose Gap. During the rest of the year, everyone was a farmer.

Other phratries of the Windmen also met under the council tree.

Venu as the leader of the Right agricultural faction had just presented the plan prepared by the power commissioners. In the center the older counselors, turbaned and in their padded service uniforms, smoked their hookah in silence. Around the edges stood the younger members. Some of them were wearing parkas.

A herd of goats browsed on the turf beyond the council circle.

The feeling of the assembly was that the plan did not sufficiently represent the agricultural interests. However, there was to be more debate. Perhaps a consensus could be reached. If not the various points would be thrashed out and brought to a vote between the Right and Left factions.

A mild-mannered older counselor had expressed some confusion over the plan. He put his questions innocently and yet in such a manner, Venu noted, as to prejudice any answers that might be forthcoming. The speaker, called Uncle Ho, had a thin wispy beard and deep eyefolds, which gave him a sleepy and at the same time sagacious look. He wore "old-fashioned" clothes; that is, a tunic of faded black silk with frogs instead of buttonholes.

The counselor appealed to tradition. Peering at Venu from under his eyefolds, the uncle reviewed the history of the original settlement. Their forebears had been herdsmen, and it had been convenient for the women to mix cow droppings with straw and knead them into bricks for cooking fuel.

That pastoral age had gone by. The modern woman of the Plains heated and electrified her house with earth-energy wafers, the bitauras. And in recent times the tribe had had the sagacity—not to mention the political influence—to arrange for a system of subsidiary power lines direct from Wind Gap.

The speaker reminded his hearers that the first windmills had been invented in Kansu Hardan. Most assuredly the Jats had been a forceful and independent people. If a challenge were to be made, surely they could make an appropriate response?

This rambling and platitudinous speech concluded to applause, and someone shouted at the top of his lungs, "We did it then, we can do it now!" But what this referred to Venu could not tell.

There were Left faction toughs at the edge of the crowd. Venu heard another of them call, "Uncle is right! Uncle is right! The farmers have had a bad year. We need all the power we can get!"

"Let the Left faction speak!"

As the leader of the Left or Naxalite faction stood up, Garg whispered to Venu, "Now we're in for it."

The man was Haakon, of the Clown Fraternity. These were not technical cadremen but dancers responsible for the Wind rites.

But first Haakon made a great show of being reluctant to speak. He was urged. With a solemn and melancholy air, his duck feathers drooping, he began to back into the center. As he did so, he took elaborate care not to step on the pipes of the counselors, trailing from the hookah. This provoked laughter.

Once arrived, the clown scratched his head and plucked out an imaginary flea, or perhaps it was a real one. He held it over the bubbling hookah.

"He's cooking it. He's going to eat it."

"He's seeing which way the wind blows. Haakon's a smart one."

The Naxalite clown made a deep and somewhat mocking obeisance before the elder counselors, including Venu. Suddenly he dashed out of the council circle toward the meadow. In the field he ran at top speed, then stopped. He knelt down and scooped something into his hat, dashed back, and dumped a hatful of goat dung at the counselors' feet. He dashed out again and returned. The action was repeated several times until a substantial pile of goat dung had accumulated. He patted this into a pile. With his foot the clown pushed this toward the uneasy counselors. Then he took out a ten-rupee coin, spat on it, and polished it on his sleeve. Flipping the coin high in the air, he caught it and thrust it into Venu's hand.

Haakon returned to his place.

"That's it," said one of the toughs. "The Power Commission gets the money and the farmers get shit."

Venu stood with his blood. His two brothers, Neelam and Prakash, and his friend Garg were beside him. There were other supporters from the Dhabar site.

The Commissioners' plan was argued further among the Right and Left factions of the Plains tribesmen. Then it was brought to a vote, and rejected. The final decision was that they should cut loose from the grid.

But during the course of the debate and the Naxalite clown's pantomime, Venu's position seemed to have undergone a change. He was no longer the responsible though somewhat wearied representative of the agricultural interests, but had been cast in some darker role.

6

Venu was having his second discussion with Fang.

"I hear your bisacauga has voted to withhold power," the Praesidium Chairman was saying affably. "OK. OK. So we don't try to impose the plan from above, do we? After all, there's no question of coercion."

Venu said, "They're hard to persuade."

"And quite proper too. We are an anarchist federation. That's not to say the decision is not *wrong*. Mistakes that are made now, though they seem trivial, may cost heavily in the future. You'll have to learn, my young friend, that a leader has to keep a certain distance from the folk. The role of a leader is a lonely one."

They were driving in Fang's car. The car was a Mercedes. Fang's chauffeur and a deep-chested matron, his personal secretary, were in the front. Fang, Venu, and the old dignitary HupeBoinville occupied the rear seat. The Deodar slumped under a lap robe. Occasionally the party stopped, and Fang would send off a telegram or confer energetically with some local body of officials that had gathered around the car while the Thai chauffeur checked the oil.

The sightseeing tour had been suggested by Fang. First they visited the rice terraces which were nearby on the east slope below Wind Gap. The highway ran on top of a dyke and followed the winding hill contours between the terraces. These were now dry and cracked. During the wet monsoon they would fill. They would be planted and harvested in early summer by the Water Brotherhood.

In the distance the dykes converged into a mountainous landscape. Forest climbed the scarp. The tips of the logging booms cut the mountain blue.

They did not visit the Drune but instead descended to the Salt Flats. This was the fourth regional production sector, sacred to the Fire Brotherhood. This was wasteland, sunk below the canyon walls in the place where the upper Rift begins. Steam from geysers rose and drifted over them. They looked down and saw far below the pipelines and storage beakers and the heads capping the geothermal energy. At their backs were the great pylons with their high-tension lines running to the Rift cities.

At noon they returned to Goose Gap. A dedication ceremony had been scheduled, the opening of one of the commission's processing plants. The officials participated briefly and Hupe-Boinville read a few prayers. After the ceremony they dropped the old fellow off and drove on for lunch.

Fang turned to his secretary and the Thai, at the same time pressing Venu's arm:

"Why don't we have a picnic, the four of us? I've brought along a hamper of fried chicken and strawberries. We can have it with a bottle of schnapps. These dedications are fatiguing." Fang appeared exhausted. He said: "It's all nonsense anyway, and these priests are a sham." He seemed glad to be rid of Hupe-Boinville. "It's true, we have a state religion, and certain approved character traits—which are supposed to foster the preservation of the region in a state of balance with nature. But that has nothing to do with the facts . . ."

They had gotten out at a picnic spot overlooking the encampment. The chauffeur was spreading the robe on the grass, and the secretary unpacked the hamper.

Veru asked: "What are the facts?"

"The facts." Fang explained: "Well, the facts are, there is no such thing as a natural balance. You have to fight for it; a scrimmage among the competing factions. Not nature, my dear boy; but politics red in tooth and claw!"

"But there are several kinds of politics."

"No. Only one kind. Politics is the carrot and the stick. To appease interest and drive by force human nature, which is naturally sluggish and brutish. There *are* real rewards and punishments, that will show up on the balance sheet sooner or later. And as for us, as for you and I. . ." With a wave of his chicken bone he included Venu. "We've reached the top of the greasy pole. Our business is to stay there. Of course, for the good of the Collective."

The Chairman washed down his strawberries with a gulp of schnapps and prepared to take a nap. He reclined, his feet held by the chauffeur and his head on his secretary's lap.

"I take it," Venu said, "we went on this tour for a purpose. Why did you show me the Golden Quadrant?"

Fang cocked a drooping eye at him. "My dear boy, in the end the centralization of technology is irreversible—whatever the political system."

7

Venu had come out of his yurt that morning and had seen the scorn pole. It had been placed in the council circle near the loudspeaker array, a bare bloody pole stuck in the ground with a severed horse's head on top of it. The "curse" which was directed at him was composed in the traditional short couplets:

A child of the earth was born/
    between his mother's legs
He developed good soccer muscles/
    and a sweet tongue on the flute
to call the sheep
    on the hillside above Dhabar
But we Jats are not sheep
    Who will follow a leader
with his head two feet/
    up a Karst/s asshole?

It was signed "Naxalite." Below it was scrawled another mordant verse.

When you see a stray dog
  hanging around the council fire
throw a stick at it.

All day the crowd had gathered to the drum beats. It was the last day of Niortha-Dasahra when the initiates would join the phratry. There would be the rites. Then power production would begin. All day the people of the Wind tendency had come from their compounds, gravitating toward the council circle. The cadremen were in full regalia. They wore necklaces and headbands of wild bird feathers, depending on their clans, with small photos of the windmills sewn in them and the charms which were mathematical formulae.

Now it was night. Haakon was dancing in the center of the circle in a bearskin. A band of children, hardier than the others, stood out in front baiting the masked clown. The bear made a rush at them, and the kids, screaming, dove between the crowd's legs. Someone threw a flaming brand over Venu's head.

"When you see a stray dog hanging around the council fire throw a stick at it."

Venu moved back from the edge of the crowd. Then he turned away. He walked along the shadows between the yurts, the sounds of the loudspeakers following him into the darkness.

He came to the river and crossed the ford. He went barefoot, feeling his way across the stones, reached the side opposite, grabbed a willow branch, and swung himself up the bank. The path led uphill toward the wind pads. It was well tracked by the goats and by the gangs of Wind cadremen. On a hilltop he looked back and saw the bonfires gleaming between the compounds. The path wound further away. He climbed a bare hillock, then down into a draw with a scattering of thorntrees. Finally the lights and sounds of the camp disappeared.

He was in a pasture flooded by the moon. The woods lay further up.

Venu had been walking painfully, dragging his leg. There was swamp nearby opening to a shallow pool. He noticed he had cut his foot crossing the ford. He sat at the edge of the swamp and cleaned the wound with a handful of grass, then stuck his foot in the water, pressing the edges of the cut to clean it, to make the blood come.

One side of the swamp was open. Around the rest of the margin were cattails and a tangle of high reeds. Everything was still. Some fireflies wavered, their bodies aglow. There was a swirl in the water below, and the jaws of a fish broke the surface. A frog jumped, others began to croak. As if at a sign, the swamp and the teeming meadow behind him woke to life.

Venu lay listening, his foot bleeding into the pool.

The sky was mirrored there. He thought of the Sky Sermon. But the placid mirror did not show the fiery creation and destruction of stars. It reflected rather the glow of fireflies.

An owl shrieked in the wood. In his mind's eye he could see the plunging wings and the prey caught in the ripping claws. But the night was quiet. And yet there was the great wheel, as Tattattatha had described it, the passing and repassing of the chains of life. All suspended in the balance.

The array, the multiplicity of species—like the fireflies of the night—pulsated around him.

"And I am part of the balance. Painful . . ." He felt himself sucked into Being, gradually dissolved into it—as the blood from his foot oozed out in a thick stain and mingled with the swamp.

The reeds parted on the far side. A raccoon appeared. The creature bent to drink, first washing its paws and face methodically. After a while the rushes parted again. Two deer lapped at the water but started away suddenly.

His body was numb. Venu moved back and rested against a stump. Tearing a strip from his shirt, he bandaged his foot; then he took out his tobacco pouch and began to smoke, leaning back on the stump with his eyes closed. A dark shape had come. He felt its warmth next to him. The animal pressed against his coat, its head on its paws. It was Tattattatha's leopard.

He followed the leopard inside the wood, walking gingerly. The way up was steep. There was a sound of chanting high up. The leopard padded ahead noiselessly. The path was packed hard over a ledge, then moist and resilient as they crossed a stretch of fallen leaves. The large trees stood further and further apart. They came to an open space where the dark roof of the forest gave way and the moonlight flooded through, crossed with branches.

A woven structure hung in the air, swaying slightly. The shelter was suspended from a branch of a great tree with cords, like an oriole's nest. Pinpoints of light scintillated through the reed walls. Outside there was a cantilevered deck on which figures were standing. The catechumens were naked. The others, the instructors, he could but dimly see. They were masked and covered in bulky raffia.

It was here on the last night of Niorthra that the Wind initiates made their meditations. It was here they came seeking the proper spirit and the moment when the Wind would tell them their names. They would have just returned, Venu guessed, from the upper slope, where they had taken their final observations at the instrument mast. At different heights on the mast were the temperature and air-pressure gauges, the anemometers with their spinning chrome cups where each hundred meters of wind was measured and marked by a solenoid device on a recording drum. On the mast too were the prayer platforms.

"Our ears are not profound enough, our eyes are not deep enough to take in the universe. We extend them with the holy instruments . . ." Tattattatha had said. And are we not too, the instruments? But instruments of what? Venu asked himself. We are not the masters. But who is the master?

Against the dark backdrop of woods and hanging in space below the light-pinpointed shelter, he seemed to be able to see Fang's Golden Quadrant. *But as if in the past.*

Yes. And is not the process of instrument-reading sacred?—the passage, *outward* into the world, of souls. Let us go out, then. Venu remembered his own apprenticeship years ago, when he had been of this age and had gone (with another of the Blue priests) to the Sky observatory to read the wind-rose and to learn to make sky charts and to take star observations.

"Reading the wind-rose, one finds out one's own name. . ." From the Sky, one finds it. As if in a whisper. And whose voice is it?

Venu rested his back against a tree trunk. He saw before him the stages of his own life. The chanting had stopped. And suddenly he remembered his own secret name—whispered long ago in the sky-hanging nest and since forgotten—"The Limping Man."

His pain seemed to drop away from him.

On the moonlit deck the figures of the initiates sat or stood quietly. Now the catechumens would be at rest, their minds prayerful and empty, waiting to receive the name. And the emblem which they would then be entitled to bear as Sky members would be tattooed on their backs by the older cadremen. Now they sat dreaming under moonlight.

Venu thought, Sathan's moon. My wife is the moon. The universe filters through us all.

Inside the litany resumed, the sacred song of initiation. First a single voice giving the line, Tattattatha's, then the others, the sweet boys' and girls' voices joining in. Venu recognized it. It was St. Francis's canticle to the sun, written in another place and language long ago. A version of one of the lauds called "Praises to the Creatures." The words drifted down softly, through space and time.

> O wide wordless limitless sweet lord God
> we praise thee Nameless One
> our rites science and our sacred songs
> emanate from thee   Shining One
>
> We praise thee for the radiant and splendid Sun
> power source
> for moons/stars without number

and for all galaxies flung in space

We praise thee for our own Language
and for the mysterious grammar of relationships
the miraculous metaphor
by which we pray to thee: "Father"
and reach out to the earth: "Mother"

We praise thee for the mantle and topsoil of the earth
which is gentle and mellow and serviceable
and can be ploughed
for Fire and all metals and elements
and for oxygen that moves our lungs

We praise thee for the lovely molecule Water
transparent and changeable
a light airy vapor which condenses into a lake
cool under the sands of Altai
We praise thee for Wind our brother

Praise be to thee Lord for all tools and technologies
for that special artifact of our hands
                                        City
and for the Countryside half made
                                        where we go in and out
and for Wildnerness   un-made

We praise thee for All Species/varieties/
                                        contradictions
for the bridegroom who goes out and becomes Alien
for the Strangers   our brothers   peace-makers
and for our merciful Sister Death

O brief   brief   the   life

of the individual in the Commune
like a dew drop on a blade of grass in the morning
it concentrates the light
from the six directions
then evaporates into weather

The chanting stopped. Venu was alone. The leopard had left him. It had climbed up and was now lying on the deck, its head on its paws outside Tattattatha's hut.

The sky deepened.

That night the wild geese passed over.

END OF BOOK III

EXILE

To my grandparents, Rose and Lavenus Lalone, immigrants from Three Rivers, Quebec Province, and others unknown.

HIGH MASS / ENERGY CANTICLES AND SACRED FORMULAE

WEATHER PATTERNS

1

The geese fly over

Early September (the month of Asauj)   thru mid-November
(Katik)   The poles tip.   Transit of the Autumnal
Equinox setting into motion the dry monsoon season

The weight of air   the subsidence
A polar wind pinched out of the air pressure differential
                    streams from the Siberian uplands
atmosphere of the Earth/   dragged by celestial mechanics

And rays of light broken/   from the upper sky
                    reflected from the clouds
The rest penetrate through   to Earth

And are convected back as heat

The radiation budget
The immense heat engine The thermocouple
at work
reversal of sky currents over Asia/ whole oceans
of atmosphere moving another way
Winter/Summer oscillations

And the Sea of Air
The majestic sweep and swap
of the continental air masses
with a shift of a few isobars
1030 to 1028 to 1020 to 15 to 10
the polar front slides out of the mountain slopes off
Heliunkiang
ice on the Yellow River

the fishing fleet off the jetty at Haiphon
trims its sails
I touch you my brother/Wind

The hills as aerofoil on the mountain above Nghsi-Altai
accelerate the current sluicing it into the propeller blades
of the windmills
set at an elevation of 35 meters with a swept area of
2500 sq. meters
the wind is picking up speed/ at a threshold of
3/m/sec the rotors begin to turn
Energy yield at 12.4/m/sec max./according to the formula
k $(Tv^3\text{-}d)$
Praise the Altgaier wind charger

Praise him the Danish inventor
They said of him the farmers of that area
Askov Denmark 1887
about Poul la Cour that he could
"transform the rain and wind into electricity and heat"

Venu harvests the wind

2 The Operating Procedure

We watched the weather anvil
the cold layer settling in over the Great Plain
High up the alto-cumulus
bruised storm masses/ lightning flashes between
tattered dark cloud then sleet
outriders of the wind
catch the geese wings
Over the brown fields the march of the power lines to Garh

That day the team of twelve or so Windmen were on the slab. Snow dusted our parkas. At the edge of the slab a rabbit hole partly covered and a scattering of dry leaves. The grip of cold iron under the gloved fingers. A bright clinking of the chain echoes on the ribs of the hills.

And the endless political meetings
"Up all night the interminable discussions and countless cups of coffee"
Getting the line straight. The ache of leadership goes through my bones.

3

The blades spinning/   not icing up yet
and the directional servomechanism working quite
                    nicely thank you

Winter
It's a hard gig

But in a couple of months and I'll be out of all this
back home fucking my wife

The march of the power lines to Garh

An hour after sundown
          stamped up and down in our felt boots
As we pulled the straw cloaks over our shoulders

we heard the geese bark
                    navigating by the moon

The Rose of Winds favors us

THE MEANING OF FESTIVALS

1

A ray of sun breaks thru the clouds & illuminates
a field   And I am surrounded by light as if coming
from the white birches   or the snow on the ground/
thru which stalks of goldenrod lift up

weeds & the flowering crowns of ferns

touched with radiance
It is the meaning of the festivals revealed
so long hidden . . .

the brown skeletons of the ferns the flute sounds
her cheek smeared with turmeric paste shines
yellow yellow
As the dancer raises her eyes to me
the river of time stops

2

The swirling street Animals
crowds of people in costumes, masks
the dream spirals with the drum beat in the heat
the revelers are throwing colored powder at each other
By the bank of the sacred river
the throng bathes wedged against itself

As in the old story: A shout
"The bulls have been stolen the royal doors
to the cattle shed have been broken into." We must follow
the thieves thru the suburbs under the banner of
the "Right Communists"
thru the mists of time

Firecrackers explode the marchers have broken into a run
in front of the governor's mansion in Calcutta. My eyes swim. We're backed to the curb. A procession of lanterns the crowd separates & a cart is pulled thru slowly decorated with flowers the bride proceeded by a limousine

her veil is the mystery.

The bulls are loose on the street
The crush deepens. The radio blares out
that the municipal power plant has been sabotaged

3

This is the way DEIR is performed:
on the day before: fast
    wash away the chaff from the threshing floor
    sweep the shrine Women leave the lights on
    and go to the rooftop with your pitchers
    and pour out water to the moon

On the morning of DEIR:
    by this time the fireplace has been replastered
    the house machinery has been oiled and the tools put away
    The children may go around in groups begging for toys
    The Ganji Figure (tantra) has been incised on the wall
        in fresh plaster

At 2 p.m. or an appropriate time:
    The Household gathers and the story of Ganji is told
        Ganji—the Speedy One
    Each time a part of the story is completed one of
        the family shouts
    and the storyteller drops in a bean
    When the pot is full of beans   the story is ended.

The complete mantra for Ganji-Devi:

    devi   devi   devi   Ga
                                        sa bu   thanoi
    devi   devi   Ga

DEvi devi ga
OM sabu thanoi om ga
WEE HA
WEE HA
OOO ri ai GAI bha
WEE HA
WEE HA
OOO ri ai GAI SABU THANOI
GA OO OM SABU SABU THANOI BA
WEE BA
WEE BA
DEvi devi ga
RAmi devi ga
RAmi RAmi Ba
DEvi ba

"BE IN GOOD HEALTH!"
(or a better translation:
may there be good public health)

4

The meaning of the festivals is revealed
as the snow melts from the hill
bare patches of the earth
the stiff heads of weeds still up and flying
their pennants
leftovers of the year
the Festival
And the long line of cars going out bumper to bumper
"City traffic it's awful but it'll ease soon
as we reach the pike"

Headlights of the cars sweep the nite
the children asleep in the back seat
in their best clothes
"Going to visit grandmother
for the Holidays"

Wheels
the whole country on the move
worshiping the GOD

Sing it!
"a poem is no more than a pair of tight pants"
Frank ("Francis") O'Hara
killed Fire Island Atlantic sands
June 1961
by jeep taxi
ebb tide of the breath
Death among the seashells

GODDESS MOTHER MATTA PROTECT US FROM
CHOLERA
PROTECT US FROM SMALLPOX
PROTECT US FROM POWER FAILURES
PROTECT US FROM BACTERIA MUTATIONS
GODDESS MOTHER MATTA PROTECT US FROM
SNAKE BITE
PROTECT US FROM TRAFFIC ACCIDENTS
BLOOD ON THE HIGHWAY
SIV-RATTRI OF THE MIRACULOUS MEDAL
PROTECT US FROM THE WEATHER
PROTECT US SIV-RATTRI MOTHER OF SULPHUR

5

"On Amavas day the cattle are not yoked but decorated with reddish paste made of red oxide and oil. Spots are daubed on animals sides and faces, their horns painted red, green, or blue.Peacock feathers may be attached to their heads, while their necks are hung about with beads, necklaces, and leathery bands clinking little bells."

The tools "worshiped" and put away
        & the "bitauras"
the concentrated energy-packets blessed
        high energy phosphate bonds

The flux of the year organizes itself
                                        on the occasions of the Festivals
just as the stream of a man's life is organized
around the events of the age-grade societies
the growth stages

6 *Mensas—A Calendar*

PHAGUN (Feb. March)	SIV RATTRI	Weather changes Worship of the refrigerator
CAIT (May)	KRI KARALI	Ghi lamps are lit The child gets his first haircut
SAVAN (July)	TIJ	Swings hung from the trees Wrestling & menstruating

		exercises
ASAUJ (Oct.)	KANAGAT	Allhallows eve When the dead come back
POH (Nov. Dec.)	GOBARDAN MAKAR- SANKRANT	Regional Planning Festivities Quarrels are patched up Policemen's motorcycles are decorated
MAGH (Feb.)	BASANT PANCHAMI	Grandfather Frost's day Last bags of rice are given away

"Tij comes and sows the seeds of the festivals
Holi takes them away and wraps the Festivals in her shawl"

and so the year passes

and so the year passes

7

In the heat of the courtyard   we are gathered this Amavas day

my brothers have swept the ground bare
                    in the newness of this holiday

& made the effigy on the wall
on the matrix of the bright whitewashed wall
on this fifth day

Pour buttermilk into Ganji's mouth
Our hands fashioning the picture out of cowdung:
MANKIND'S head and mouth

Sing the festival song:
on this the fifth day
"GRANDMOTHER
COWDUNG WEALTH
BE WITH US!"
from the neck the four walls of our house extended into
the landscape

contains us and the sacred animals
blessed be this Easter of the year
We fashion it out of straw
the model of the Celestial City
Weeds flame
the head of goldenrod burns

FEAST MY BROTHERS

A DAY IN THE LIFE OF SATHAN

1

Now that my husband is crew chief I am able to be at ease a little. I lie back in the hammock. On the roof with its blue tile is a lemon tree and from the administration office below comes the clack-clack-clack of machines.

Bring me the report   I want to look at it. And bring me the computation sheets   I want to see the figures. The scene of the collective spreads out below. The shade of the glossy leaves of the lemons falls on my arms.

"Raking up the Bitterness Sessions." The web of ties are like the locust branches in winter   their thorny spikes. How they cut the chest

My sons are going out. In a few hours you will hear the call of the men with the ox team. And the call of the cadre on the truck loading bay of the cannery. And my daughter Maddi will go out with her electrician's tools and repair the wires.

How blue the sky sparkles!

2

Husbands   am I attractive to you   Or do you find me plain in my padded coat? Is my hair hidden from you braided in a coil under my canvas cap? Can you judge how my legs move?

Husbands   do you find my daughter beautiful   with her shawl woven of bright plaid   thrown over her shoulders? Would you like to strip it off? Does her blouse please you   spangled with silver mirrors?

The wash house is full of people. Billows of steam rise under the rafters. The woman bends over the pile of clothes beside the bathers   her buttocks gleaming. The door opens   from the cold. As the laborers take off their frosty parkas   a breath of winter steals out. And my flesh tingles

My flesh   my nipples washed with grass. It is sunset. Bring the child to me here   and bring the brass tray with bunches of striped kami grass to cleanse the breasts and to sweeten them. I squeeze the first milk onto the tray and throw down a wrist bangle

In honor of my first-born

3

A shrill blast. The loudspeaker is calling from the top of the command post. And the people with the hard faces are streaming across the snow

In the sweaty meeting room   the bowl is passed around. It has been broken and mended, and broken and mended again. Drink the bitterness from it   women with eyes hard as slate.

That history is over   the bad days are past. But sisters we have elected to remember it.

The chairperson begins: I remember the sky dark with dust   we thought it was a locust plague   The fence posts were buried in sand. A field of corn sailed over the barn

Then the secretary remembers: there was no hay. We beat the donkey but he was too weak to   get up.

The treasurer of the marketing section   we kept going down the road. Grandfather and Varya were pulling the cart. It had all our belongings in itthe sink and a crate of chickens. The army was like a river   we kept pushing against the stream of soldiers

Fill the bowl with the bitter herbs   drink from it, you have only remembered half of it

A woman says: that summer we were on the Delta. The ground dried up it was baked. A corpse lay on it

And another says: then the flood waters went away. We came down out of the trees.

Another says: That winter the city was without coal

No I can't eat the elm leaves they make my stomach sick. But the roots can be chewed

I would walk. Yes I would gladly sell the child for 5 annas. I would take her and carry her to the crossroads where the helicopter is hovering and the officials are giving out medicines. But my feet are bound

"Raking up the Bitterness Sessions." The fire is down. But if there is a coal of hatred among the ashes blow on it

4

The scene spreads out to view. Sometimes the road is lost between the narrow walls a maze of alleys open from the bazaar. At the edge of town it emerges again a white stroke baked onto the fields. The High Road

Through the region the rivers run down, melting under the ice of Altai. There is a river running beside Watermeadow, where the council meets. There is a river running through the Lake Sections, through the forest cantonments where the universities are located. There is a river running under the Rift Cities. And in the dry Plains it runs under the windmills

Clouds gather in the sky. And in the market place they have set up a speakers platform. In the dust in front of the platform children are playing.

A woman has pushed forward from the crowd. She has lifted one child up on her shoulders so the speakers can see him. Another child held by the hand presses close to her

And I ask the sky: Will you be luminous enough? Will you have enough
warmth? And I ask the earth: Will you be full enough
Earth will you have enough milk to nourish this woman's breasts?

Woman with the hard face and rough hands I draw you aside
I push the rough cloth from your breasts and kiss them.
Sister I embrace you

And your children whose are they?

5

It is the Festival of Girdi-Divali marking time of the new year. It is necessary to distribute the new rice. The trucks of the Buyers' Co-operative have arrived. We will distribute the radios.

I raise my arms over the tiles washed by the blue sky. The lemon tree is a storehouse the flesh is full of oil of the fruit glistens

Open the cupboard. It is enough if I say to you: the sun is drying he clothes.

Now it is necessary to make an inventory. For instance there are beehives. In the garden a hummingbird is going back and forth over the petals. It is enough if I say to you: the sea is making salt

In the planning room of the commune the officials have gathered. We have maps and production estimates. We have the models for the next year's development which the computer has organized. Let us choose the options:

For instance
there is the nutrient budget. For instance there is a heat budget. There is an energy budget. For instance a man with his bare hands on a hectare of ground will perform in a day 600 calories of work. And with an investment of capital in a machine he will perform 1800 calories.

There is the population budget. This is the array of facts   and these are the limits. It is necessary for us to calculate.

On the roof   I lie back on the hammock. The scene of the collective spreads out to view. The breeze lifts the leaves of the lemons and strokes my arms.

Sisters   in our hands

    the abundance.

THE COMING OF NEW MAN

1

Across the veld   the coming of New Man
The distances divide   A thorn tree is on fire against the azure
a glass jar at the base   tells us half the truth

Leaves plummet   It is *as if*
the world were burning up in autumn

a smoky haze   strips the hills bare / and evaporates

Oh   I am dazed with seeing / his house   down to the
  smallest detail
You too, traveler, will taste the salt on his skin
as the caravan appears through the dust / cluttering the
  horizon

Across the dunes & shuttling oases the great distances over the desert—
Tashkent   Sinkiang   Lop Nor   Ama Attu —
are covered by the light leap of a gazelle
                    my song to you
                    Venu: New Man

2

Woman of a 1000 years hence   I don't know you
Man of a 1000 years hence   I don't recognize you

And the cities of the airy dawn

  Solieri's City of Light/   & concrete nodes
              spun out like vertebrae

  Kikutate's Perforated Cylinders/ sunk under the sea
      with their great shopping centers & apartments
        powered by algae and phosphorus

  Isamov's Modulors with their etherealized machines
      suspended between Spitzbergen & mainland Russia

Chicago of the double helix
                    lifts   on the next tide

Tear down the walls. It's imprisoning us this pyramid
this ziggurat
heaps of scrap & tangled conduit the Eagle/ the
Fasces

We will need dynamite bulldozers to clear a path
The obstruction is in our midst
a thin door of steel/
seals the backs of our eyes

3

Bride GO to meet the bridegroom
It is the Time of trembling & fear but GO OUT
to meet him holding your lamp high
against your face
When he touches you you will be changed
beyond recognition

Blind one your eyes Oh the pain of opening them
how difficult it is for you
Reluctant one your flushed skin

Bride go to meet the bridegroom/ When we touch
I see I have repelled you
the flesh turns away

4

The leaves plummet an autumn fire
strips the hills bare
Visions of the New World of Albion

After the War decades   the smoke lifts

over the valley of broken wagons

by the river bank   the curve of houses
it is the same roofs   the same TOWN
                                that we always knew
        but hidden   from   us

Oh   cityscape   how I have longed for you
The bolts at the back of eyes   drawn
        the freshness of prima verde
Fra Angelica's colors
        the blue the umber   the yellow cinquefoil
Going   back to him   thru the fields
        this spring day!

5

By the thorn tree we came upon his camp
But he'd gone   leaving noting but a direction signal
                                & a broken bottle

The immense distances over the veld
over the horizons   of time
                                Is there some formula we can use
a sine curve or projection showing
how the electrons stream out of the rocks shown by an
    absorption spectra?
            the genetic drift

Scratchings on the cave wall in Lascaux
and I the artist

draw tomorrow's Sun
& the game we have to catch
the hunter draws on the wall in red oxide
it is the ikon /
New Man: the quarry
the solar wind

Mother of Animals
from your navel a cord winds across the picture
to the arrow
my canticle to you
New Man

In the sky with its jets/ the vapor stream condenses
my song to you/
New Man

6

Night evaporates On the hill the first spark
The light strikes New Man's porch
the prophecy
and falls on a chair a table
Window of this poem I want you to frame
every utensil that he uses
The day flames
he raises porridge to his lips

AMULETS OF THE BLUE SHAMANS

The sign on the forehead: the hexagon
(a double circle intersected by triangles)

Color: .35 - 45 microns (between blue and ultraviolet)

Sound: speech
Ornaments/decorations:
on the wrist an ear of corn/ welded
about the neck feathers
middle technology totems
about the ankles poplar leaves twisting
little propellers

Meaning of the hexagon:
The Spaces

THE CITY
THE PLAINS
WILDERNESS

FREE MARKET
THE PLANNED
THE HOLY

The corresponding images

FIRE
TOPSOIL
WATER

THE CURRENT
THE RULER/THE FULL MOON

SUN/SKY

The tribes or tendencies

THE STEELERS
TRACTOR OPERATORS
SLIDING FISH OR RAIN PEOPLE

FILTHEATERS
SOREHEADS
STUNNED/BY/BRIGHTNESS PEOPLE

Formula: $E = hv$ (h = Planck's constant)

Degree or mode
of operation: photo-chemistry or/alternately the
Fibonacci series

The Blue Shamans move with the wind
uphill
and release the thistle

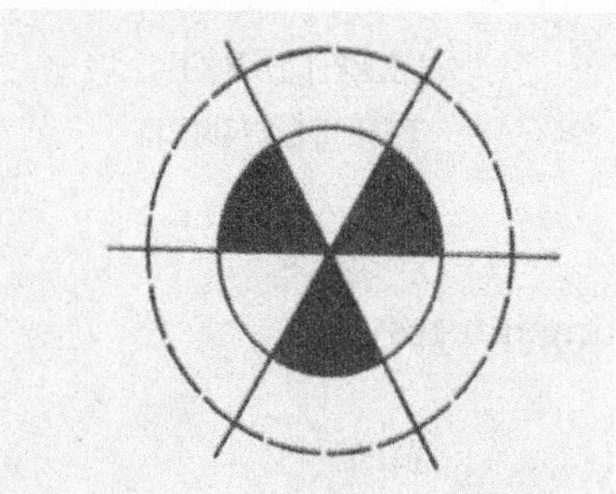

BLUE SHAMAN'S EMBLEM

AMULETS OF THE YELLOW SHAMANS

The sign on the forehead: two superimposed triangles

black to black to black
the outer dark
streaked with fire
where the earth has cracked open

Direction: downward & inward

Mode: force/cataclysm

the boat of the Yellow Shamans
navigates the cataract
by banging against the rocks

Their dress:
Frayed sleeves yellow robes
Priests/
of the rotting grain sacks
The line grows thinner and thinner
beyond my Fifth Ancestor
till it breaks into mist
(his breath on the window?)

Ornaments/decorations/masks:
a man's forehead and behind
a little furnace or box
where the magnet revolves

Sound: replication/
the printing press

To the fringes of the garments of the Yellow Shamans
everything is attached
thongs
strings
radiation particles
threads
bits of atomic debris
wire
keys
strands of dirty raffia
newsprint

Formula: $E = mc^2$

Their world an explosion between
the teeth

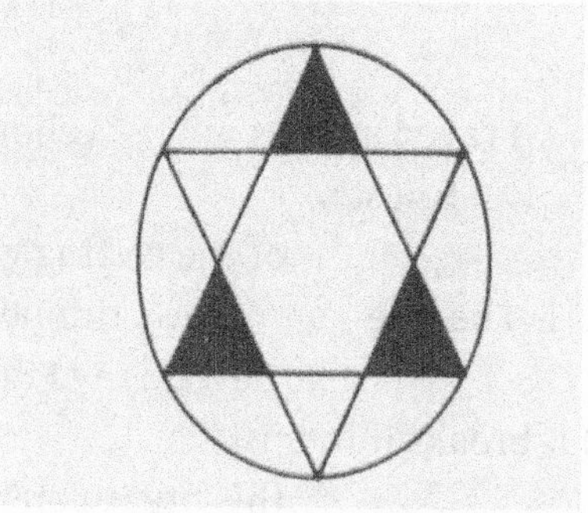

YELLOW SHAMAN'S EMBLEM

SAINT FRANCIS' CANTICLE

(Translated from the Italian by William Blake)

Most high encompassing good lord god
Breath of Being

Hear our praises they belong to you
along with the glories and the sacred songs
They are all thine Shining One

Praise be to you and to ALL CREATURES
especially to my worshipful Brother SUN
thru whom you bring heat and brightness
He is beautiful and radiant with a very great splendor
Our Source
but he is only a pale signal from you

Praise to God for our most graceful Sister MOON and for
all stars
and galaxies by the millions
The heaven is full of them lost in space. In the darkness
you have found them. The intensity amplified.

Praise be Javeh for our blustering Brother WIND
This region's clan emblem
and for air and clouds and all weather
for our counsin the Wet Monsoon out of the east
and the Dry Monsoon out of the west
Windy lineage brother

Praise be my lord for our radiant Sister WATER
who is pure and transparent
and very precious in the dry season
and lies at the bottom of the quanats
who is raised thru the pipes

Praise be to thee for Holi Region
which we perceive with our five senses extended by X-rays
All praises be for all

earth/aircosmos infinite membrane
and for the wave of process   from which ocean escapes

While walking in paradise I saw Altai
which is common
also its mirror image Albion—now called
America—which is extraordinary

God of the Double Shamans
in your energy you have created them both
From the rags of your coat
hang an infinity of worlds

Praise be to thee for Francis' festivals
who named the days of the world
and who walked out of the devil's city in yellow and blue
Umbria
as out of a cave
and stripped off his clothes
for Giotto to paint him in future flesh

SAINT FRANCIS' CANTICLE

(Adapted by William Morris)

O wide wordless limitless sweet lord God
we praise thee Nameless One
our rites science and our sacred songs
emanate from thee   Shining One

We praise thee for the radiant and splendid Sun
power source
for moons/stars without number

and for all galaxies   flung in space

We praise thee for our own language
and for the mysterious grammar of relationships
the miraculous metaphor
by which we pray to thee: "Father".
and reach out to the earth: "Mother"

We praise thee for the mantle and Topsoil of the earth
which is gentle and mellow and serviceable
and can be ploughed
for Fire and all metals and elements
and for the oxygen that moves our lungs

We praise thee for the lovely molecule Water
transparent and changeable
a light airy vapor which condenses into a lake
cool under the sands of Altai
We praise thee for Wind   our brother

Praise be to thee Lord for all tools and technologies
for that special artifact of our hands
                                        City
and for the Countryside half made
                                where we go in and out
and for Wilderness   unmade

We praise thee for all species/varieties/contradictions
which together make up Open Steady State
        which is our state   stateless
In Francis' name I walked into Trafalgar and Haymarket
to protest the war   And looking for Other World
        in their eyes   and my eyes

The rattle of machine guns.

SONG

Civilization thieves the flowers
and weaves them into Elizabeth's coronal
I will be the singer mild
who unravels those ceremonies
and returns stolen properties

But how can I give them back to old hands
                    ploughed   underground?
the Chams watched the locomotive smoke cut thru the vines
Malraux saw them and he told me so
in a book made of bones

So I won't go after Queen Elizabeth's coronal
but with Blake love the chimney sweeps
I will will them my forgeries
and for their sake invent fantastic technologies

SACRED FORMULAE FOR EARTH/SPACE SHIP

The rose of winds   favors us
if we are not already   annihilated
we will die into it   the windstream on my face
tide of cold air off Heliankiung
                         tips the propeller blades
Power floodgate opens   my mouth in praise
        for Earth/Space ship
red rose petal set spinning in space

Every direction of the current tosses our boat
the terrestrial magnet   Out   to all points
vacancies   force fields
streams of lumens in between space
our necks cricked to look up
no other way   the taste in the mouth
my cheek red   registers the cold
isobars
fall of sky pressure   on earth
My eye reading the instrument gauge is Thine

Chrome cups of the anemometer spin at night   prayer wheel
anchored in basalt rock   iron earth core
also the geotherm gives up its steam   prayer
Sun's radiance caught on the roof
where the children are singing their morning school
biology anthem
sacred/

the array of mirrors reflected onto the steam boiler
Maddi is taking a public bath
her skin   red rose   earth petal   sky atmospheres
condensed
flowers around the milkhouse
the cows browse and allow us to steal milk
for solar processing

Pasteur's lovely spirit presides
the saint in the ikon   212 degree holiness
Yes thank you Pasteur is alive and well for the future
in his white coat   boiling off microbes

Earth/air science   wind/rose   space   ship

infinite accumulations
as the leaves fall
they yield in a million years 3 or 4 inches topsoil
our precious knowledge and store
we're stored there in earth/space cupboard
I saw in a museum near Uppsala
the boat dug out of the bog
wood black and hard as coal
the stem and ribs remain
a few gold bracelets and eye sockets of the wayfarers
lost in soil
moving thru earth/time
we stumble thru the corn shucks
this song on our lips for the new commune

Every direction of the current orders our boat
from the terrestrial magnet out
to all points
of the wind/rose star/space miraculous commune journey
the sun's rays gathered into our hands
as the old food-gatherers brought back wild rice in their canoes
baskets of seeds/energies
fantastic blackberry furnaces burn on each bush
hand steel computerized instruments
bloom
sacred technology smoke around the temple swallowed in
palms
each day the Chams watched the locomotive smoke out cut
thru the woods
carrying International Harvester tools
the topsoil
so easy to break easy to renew
compañeros the Rome Plow broken at last

Brothers I come to prophesy
Open the doors of the boxcar and let me out
you standing along the forlorn rails
        the hammers on yr shoulders
                in the Polands with the blue railway stations
I come to bring you the good news
                    State's withered
            old sticks/rags/ magics transmuted
Bakunin in his fat anarchist pajamas   old foolishness
                        but the wand flowers

heat latent in the song   bangs the pipes
                        Oh sweet weather hammer
                                        sleet   slants
and every drop of rain fires the forge

THE HISTORY OF NGHSI-ALTAI

We have been given the following brief history of the country of Nghsi-Altai. It seems curiously like our own —with some features reversed, as if seen in a mirror. It is impossible to fix any correspondence in dates. Presumably "present time" refers to something like our own present, extended forward somewhat. It should also be noted that our informant has given a biased account, being one of the Blue fraternity.

Prehistory: Forest covered the world, according to old legend. It was the era of the so-called "Walking Trees." For a long time the trees with their dense tops were able to keep out Sky, so the story goes. One day the trees weakened. Sky punched a hole in and entered accompanied by her brother, a monkey called Weather.

The southern half of the world was flooded and drowned in lakes. The north half received no water at all; it became dry steppe. The sun turned all the steppe-dwellers (men, ostriches, goats, and camels) as brown as dung. The rain falling in twilight turned the skin of the forest dwellers blue as lichen.

A wall was built between the West and the Dry by Monkey, which he called "The Divider." All elements of the world were separated: the Sky,

Earth, and Forest, the west sacred men and the dry men. They conspired to punish Monkey. The wall was thrown down into a ditch, the present Rift Valley, and the Karsts (Monkey's descendants) were given no skin color at all: they are albinos.

From the "three skins" and the "three weathers" (or types of environment) the fields of knowledge are supposed to have been elaborated: agriculture, the ecological sciences, and trade.

FROM THE FIRST THROUGH FOURTH MILLENIUM/ A PLAINS TRIBAL CULTURE

This period begins with neolithic village culture already established.

Grave diggings deep under the loessal soil show that there were three tribes living in the plains simultaneously. Archaeologists call these the "gray pottery" people – Yang Shao. The "black pottery" people – Lung Shan. And the "painted pottery" people: the Jats.

The Jats appear to have migrated from northern India via the Khyber Pass through Turkestan and Iran, where they learned bronze age techniques: metal-smithing, the wheel (for chariots), and writing. From the plateau they migrated eastward, a ferocious cavalry, across the desert, hopping from one oasis to the next and intermarrying with the local folk.

However, they finally reached the plains in a state of exhaustion, not as conquerors but as a conquered people. They were absorbed in part by the other two tribes, and the bronze age discoveries appear to have been suppressed during the first millenium. (Bronze war axes have been found in the graves buried *below* neolithic pottery.)

This is the period of village high culture (neolithic). From a number of epicenters the population spread through the plains. The pattern of movement operated in this way:

First there was the "mother village": a hundred or so pit dwellings surrounding a longhouse. This was attached to a cemetery presided over by the shaman (ancestor worship). All the great neolithic discoveries are in evidence here: house-building (posts with wattle-and-daub construction), pottery molds and kilns, spindle whorls and needles, stone polishers, the tools of agriculture, and the bones of domesticated animals: the dog, the sheep, pigs, horses, and cattle. There were also extensive cattle herds and the beginnings of rice agriculture.

This improved food supply increased the number of inhabitants in the "mother village." Several "daughter villages" would be established still using the same cemetery and under the authority of the original priesthood. In this way the plains were populated.

High village culture seems to have prevailed during the first three millenia — the settlements in much the same form as they are today. However, at the end of the third millenium there was a decline.

Bad agricultural practices. Overgrazing by cattle, the ploughing of unsuitable land for crops, and a prolonged drought brought an end to this early period. Much of the plains became dust bowl. Productivity declined in the pasture lands. The burning of cow dung for fuel removed it from re-use on the fields as fertilizer. On the little arable land that remained, the crop rotation system was abandoned.

Destruction of the irrigation system by rabbits.

Starvation threatened, with a rising population now divided into rich and poor. Under pressure of population the regular food chain was broken. It was no longer plant (grains and legumes) →to animal (protein) → to man, the original sequence. But simplified to the direct chain: Plant →to human. The property owners ate only black millet. While the tenants and a landless proletariat subsisted on rice gruel and during famine grubbed for roots.

This was also a period of the grossest sexual exploitation, the males becoming the chattels of the matriarchs.

Fortunately, this period ended with the discovery by Jats of fossil fuel. A fragment of "painted pottery" of the fourth millenium depicts what seems to have been a natural gas strike. With the development of this substitute fuel (that is, substitute for cow dung), it was possible to reverse the above cycle and restore productivity. The Jats also developed a primitive textile industry using synthetic fibres.

Thus they gained an advantage over the other plains tribes. Gradual extension of Jat hegemony in the latter half of the fourth millenium. Main features of the present-day culture are established; that is, the matriarchy, limited polygyny, and village exogamous marriage, conservative economic planning performed by the guilds, and government under the panchayat system.

Present calendar of holidays is set. Inauguration of the Great Festivals.

FOURTH THROUGH FIFTH MILLENIUM/ A KARST COMMERCIAL EMPIRE

It is thought that the Karsts were originally lake dwellers. With geological transformation of the plateau, dessication due to weather changes, and the gradual subsidence of the great Rift Valley, the area became the present Drybeds. The tribe continued to live there, inhabiting the beaks and dolomitic caves. From cave dwellers they became miners, excavating the subsurface for minerals. This was the source of their wealth.

The Karsts are a naturally egalitarian people, with a strong aptitude for mechanics. A corporation of free citizens developed the mines. Special machinery was adopted for digging, and for ventilating and pumping water. Through pumps the properties of air (also a vacuum) were discovered. This led rapidly to the discovery of other gases, and laid the foundation for their future chemical industry.

Thus hydraulics led to science, science to trade, and trade to the evolution of money and a competitive market system. Domination of the other territories followed. The earlier portion of the fifth millenium was the great trading period of the Karsts, with their merchants spreading over the plains and Drunes regions. The great city-based merchant houses joined with the local overlords in a profitable alliance. Usually one of the members of a Jat family was assigned to handle the Karsts' commercial affairs. These enterprising young men often became tax collectors.

The Rift Canyon was now completely urbanized. As trade developed there was further rationalization of industry, particularly metals and chemicals. With the spread of the industrial corporation and further capital accumulation, finally the entire Rift had been organized into a national industrial system centered upon the steel industry. The government was one of nominal parliamentary democracy, with two parties. One of these, the Managers, were in firm control. Opposed to them was a weak Decentralist Party.

Certain tendencies, however, favored the Decentralists. One of these was the rigidity of the economic system itself. Its very success hampered it. Inventions were held off the market by the monopolists. There was little adaptation of machines to changing circumstances, due to heavy capitalization and vested marketing arrangements. Ingenuity flagged. In pursuit of profit they aban-doned productivity and even the laws of capitalist dynamics. In its partnership with business the state subsidized an inflated "public sector" which absorbed unemployables and bankrupt industries. However, this resulted in increased inefficiency and inflation. A large advertising and transportation sector, once a stimulus, now became a drag on the economy. Agriculture was depressed.

Opposed to all this, the Decentralists stood for flexibility and free application of current inventions, and also for the freeing of the satellite "countryside" from the metropolis.

At this juncture, there appeared on the scene two inventions of special consequence: one was the small and compact hydrogen furnace, to substitute for the huge blast furnace of the classical steel industry, and along with it the small planetary mill. At the same time, certain new processes (called "pugging") made it economical to work outlying low-grade ore deposits in the plains. This was done by certain native capitalists (Jats)—who became convinced Decentralists. Advances in computerization and micro-circuitry also favored small units. Thus, it became possible to have a regionally based, rather than national, metals industry. All these methods were outlawed by the Managers.

A state of siege was declared.

A black market developed, in which there was extensive bootlegging of the new techniques. Outlaw capitalist groups in the plains were soon to organize the machinery banks. They were allied in an underground network with urban squatters' groups and with workers of certain Karst industries who were beginning to call themselves "syndicalists" or "anarcho-syndicalists."

A split developed among the Decentralists — a part of whom became the "Decembrists." Relying on armed force and financing themselves by kidnapping and extortion, this faction went underground to develop "subregions." Their slogans were "Every village its own steel mill" and "Factories in the caves." However, the movement was so deeply infiltrated as to be rendered ineffectual. The other side pushed for a parliamentary solution. A revived Decentralist party won the next parliamentary contest and swept the elections.

They had not reckoned on the perfidy of the Managers. A counterrevolutionary coup soon followed. All the Decentralist officials (representing a majority of the people) were either killed or exiled.

The Mangers were more firmly in control than ever. By now they had adopted many of the technical innovations promoted by the Decentralists and absorbed the best ideas of the opposition. Thus, under the slogan: "Abolish the state," the state was able to perpetuate itself for a thousand years.

At the end of the fourth millenium there was a civil war in which the state fell and was replaced by authentic popular institutions. These are the urban factory "syndicates" and the farm collectives (run jointly with the machine banks) that survive to this day.

Golden Age of the Popular Decentralists.

SIXTH MILLENIUM TO THE PRESENT/ THE EXPLOSION OF A THEOCRACY

The original Thays and Deodars lived in the forest undisturbed. The Thays are a slight, fair-skinned people probably of Indonesian origin. The stately and blue-skinned Deodars are of Tibetan stock, deeply mystical practitioners of a nature animism. From the beginning the two peoples lived together amicably in the forest under a confederacy of tribes or "genies." They were hunters and herb gatherers. The Deodars, in particular, were skilled in medicine. An early woodland Deodar, Orpheo, is supposed to have invented music, while listening to the sighing of boughs.

At the dawn of historical time the confederacy had no center, merely shifted in the woods. Its members practiced "swidden agriculture," that is slash and burn: planting their seeds in a clearing made by stone axes, then moving on. Their shelters were of bamboo and leaves caked with mud — pitched in places selected by the shamans.

With the penetration of the Drune by the Karsts in the middle of the third millenium, the confederacy dissolved. There was intense trade exploitation. The forest sellers widened their clearings to trade tea, tung oil, and indigo, also skins and the feathers of birds, in exchange of trinkets from the Karsts, and metals. They also took up basket-weaving for cash.

As there was a limit to the size of clearings but not to the rising productivity of the Karsts, whose manufactured products increased each year, the foresters ran into debt. They were also divided among themselves. The basket-makers became enriched. Gradually the consumption of luxury goods from the Rift gave rise to a privileged class of traders, landowners, and moneylenders.

This led to more intense exploitation of the Drune. Ponds were drained and the forest cleared to underwrite the establishment of native manufactures, including a large plywood industry using the complaisant Thays as captive labor. The Thay tribes became completely colonized by the Karsts, and today speak only the Karst language.

The Deodars retreated further into the woods. It was now necessary for them to survive in a world that had diminished to the smallest compass. They first lived in holes. From a sack slung over their backs they planted seedlings to restore their natural protective cover. Hunting in the shade, they survived on a diet of snails and the smallest birds. Their appetites dwindled.

Meanwhile their shamans had become smiths. They set up forges in the deep woods, operated by skin bellows decorated with feathers. There they worked the metal stolen or traded from the Karsts. They learned to draw wire: copper, for which there was only an ornamental use at the time, for jewelry. And steel wire, which replaced catgut for musical instrument strings.

It was at this time that the famous Deodar teaching institutions began. These had originally been "hospices," or hospitals. Diseases had infected the Drune from the Rift, among the most serious being syphilis. For some reason the highest incidence of this was among the former shamans. The disease was cured by herbal medicines. It has been said the practice of celibacy among the Drune priesthood originated at this time.

What had been at first hospitals over the course of time evolved into universities. As their herbal cures became known they attracted the sick; and their musical and decorative arts, preserved from an earlier age, brought wanderers and collectors of folklore from the more developed portions of the country. There were also serious students.

There is some irony in this. It is possible that the students, many of whom came from the ranks of the richest colonizers, were attracted on spurious grounds. Certain aspects of the teaching—those which seemed to give the most weight—were in fact incidental. One of these was the color of the instructors' skins. Originally blue had been considered a mark of laziness and inferiority by the Karst industrialists. Now it began to be thought beautiful, even mystifying.

Their Deodar practice of celibacy gave them a reputation for holiness which was little deserved. The priesthood was intensely secular. Animals were still their sexual partners. And they depended for maintenance of the population level on recruits from other parts of the country, whom though they instructed they often abused.

In any case the Blue Doctrine expanded.

It was natural that the first studies were of forestry, natural history, and public medicine—which were to become later the nucleus of the ecological sciences. Cultivators of the small and the complex, the sciences of the Deodars developed in the direction of microbiology. The first environmental testing devices were originated in the Drunes. Using their medical knowledge and their resonating wires, instruments of all kinds were elaborated, which gave precise ratios and measured the most minute differences among natural phenomena. There were also advanced studies of insects.

When communication was later reopened with the rest of the country, knowledge of these Deodar sciences spread throughout the plains and Drybeds. This period saw also the hiring of the first Sensors—to man testing laboratories associated with the early machinery banks and factory syndicates.

Towards the end of the sixth millenium there was renewed trouble in the Rift. The Decentralist technology had been consolidated after the Civil War and the anarchosyndicalist political system was relatively humane. But the economy was overproductive. Intensive development led to depletion of the natural resources of the country. Waste recycling was merely token; and schemes for the conservation of energy, through the exploitation of alternate resources, were abused by the bureaucracy.

The riches of the soil and subsoil were squandered in an orgy of materialistic consumption. Monoagriculture was ravaged by bugs, despite inspection stations at every border. Lakes and reservoirs were poisoned by manufacturers of chemicals who were, with characteristic hypocrisy, members of decentralized regulatory commissions. Atmospheric pollution increased. This was due primarily to the Jat gas engine which—though scrapped centuries before—had left poisonous residues and in some cases even affected the genes. With wasting of resources came unemployment, and with unemployment, poverty. There was general social unrest and violence; and the regional governments, which had originally been libertarian, grew increasingly harsh and repressive. Persecutions of students and intellectuals followed, and these fled to the Drune.

It is not surprising that the next period, which has lasted about four hundred years from the end of the sixth millenium, has been the most fruitful in Deodar history. It has been marked by two main developments: an intensive effort to extend theoretical ecology to regulate actual economic production throughout the country. And a radical transformation of the Deodar priesthood.

This latter point requires explanation. During the previous millenium the priesthood had been by philosophy and belief, quietist; by character retiring, and by diet somewhat debilitated. But it was revived by the persecutions. At the onset of the environmental crisis in the plains and Drybeds, political dissenters were granted asylum by the Deodars. With the worsening of the crisis, the regional police—organized into companies of "berserks"—actually pursued the dissenters into the Drune, and in the end the Drune was invaded and occupied completely. The Deodar priesthood committed by religion to nonviolence could now not help but put that doctrine into practice. Total nonresistance to force, at the same time total noncooperation was followed. Orders given by the conquerors were received but never carried out, and the invading bands were at first neutralized and later completely absorbed—not without a number of martyrdoms on the part of Deodar high officials. The theocracy was decimated —and transformed.

The country was now divided into two worlds. In both the environment was equally threatened. This challenge was tackled directly — principally by the scientist-exiles (from the plains and Rift) now associated with the Drune universities. A new conservation and resource technology came into being, directed toward maintaining population and resources in dynamic balance in what came to be called the "open steady state planning." For this a new "embryology computer" became a chief instrument.

A key element in all this were the microtechnologies and sciences. Developed centuries before the Blue priests, purely to celebrate their own mysteries and out of a sense of the playful, these aptitudes of the Deodars became suddenly useful. And their practicioners, who had by temperament and historical development been at the margin of history—

now moved to its center, as everything else failed.

The Deodar priesthood came to govern the country by accident, and as it were in spite of themselves, with the breakdown of all other institutions.

Religion revived based on the "Six Tendencies," which had survived from the ancient animism. The cult radiated outward, borne both by the squatters who had repopulated the devastated cities and by the Sensors who migrated in ever-increasing numbers back into the Rift and plains. As the authority of the Managers declined, that of the young Sensors attached to the Weather and Soils stations was strengthened. With the worsening of the ecological crisis the Sensor stations tended to take over certain functions of the local administration, until finally the state was absorbed completely.

Thus what came to be called the "Blue Revolution" and the "Magical Hexagon-in-balance" radiated outward from its many centers.

At this juncture a decisive and quite fortuitous event tipped the balance: the discovery of electricity in one of the forest universities by a Drune named Mazdo. This discovery was quickly applied, and grafted onto the traditional solar and wind technology, bringing universal benefits and enhancing immeasurably the authority of the new class.

Thus, under its double slogan: "Electrification/Conservation" and "A Blue World," the microscientific revolution was achieved, and the confederacy of Nghsi-Altai established in its present outline.

THE EMBRIOLOGY COMPUTER

The confederacy of Nghsi-Altai is an open steady state. An open steady state in nature maintains itself over varying periods of time. There is the water cycle, the carbon cycle. There is the geo-chemical cycle: the formation and weathering of rocks, the movement of the earth's crust, the laying down of ocean floors, the return through volcanoes of deep-core elements to the atmosphere. We say a "balance is kept" over a million years. Meaning: there is a grand swing and return. A cycle.

But in human society the dynamic balance—a state which is open and can take in new elements, yet is constant and self-sustaining —must be maintained by design. That is, by planning.

• •

We are designing a machine. (Actually the machine is in use in Altai. But we must reinvent it.) The first requirement: to calculate numbers and organize data on the model of an electronic computer. Also it must parallel living organisms, in that it must be capable of development.

Mechanical Requirements (simple computer model): typical nonlinear electric circuits in juxtaposition, with resistances, capacitors, inductances. Relays will be an electromechanical system with two alternative positions of equilibrium. The main synthetic functions will be:

ARITHMETIC & LOGIC OPERATIONS, MEMORY (information storage), PROGRAMMING & FEEDBACK.

Diagram of typical relay and circuit:

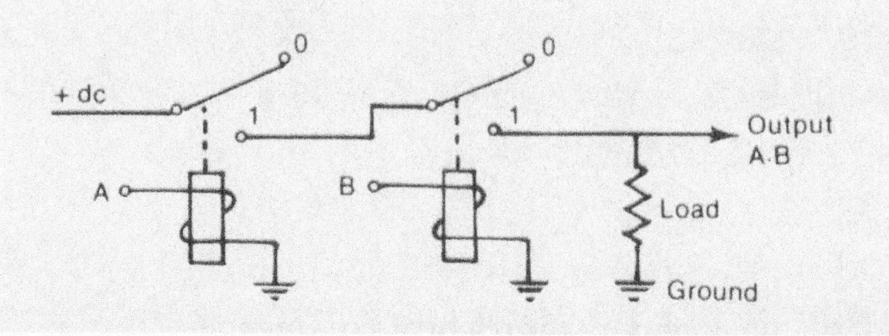

WIENER ON THE HUMAN BRAIN

This perceptive man (incidentally a real anarchist) makes a comparison between the human brain and a calculating machine. Both use the binary system. "The data are presented by a set of choices among a number of contingencies and the accuracy is determined by the sharpness with which the contingencies are distinguished, the number of contingencies presented at every choice, and the number of choices given." Rules for combining this data follow Boolean algebra: that is, a Yes-No system of notation.

Elements of the computer are like neurons. The nerve cell may be taken to be a relay with the message fed in from free endings or sensory organs, through points of contact, the synapses. These synapses are either at rest or they "fire" when the action threshold is reached.

The memory is similar in both structures. The firing of the synapses may be "clocked"; that is, the impulses retained and held up until some future time. Thus memory is a loop. The manner in which the loop is closed determines how long and how deeply the information is stored, storage taking place either by the opening of new paths or the closure of old ones. Apparently, in biological development no new neurons are formed in the brain after birth.

Weiner quotes from Balzac's novel *La Peau de Chagrin* and speculates that perhaps our whole life is on this pattern and "the very process of learning and remembering exhausts our power of learning and remembering until life itself squanders our capital stock of power to live."

Finally, there is the matter of self-regulation. The brain and the computer both regulate themselves. This is done by a feedback device which in biology is called "Effective Tone."

Our computer has its conditioned reflex. It has become in effect a "learning machine."

(From Norbert Weiner, *The Human Use of Human Beings: Cybernetics and Society*.)

A METAPHOR FROM BIOLOGY

How are we to enter upon the terrain of biological science? The first rule is not to consider this realm conceptually closed. Though it contains, it is like a torn fishnet. One must look at the grid for what it contains and for what it does not contain.

Thus we regard the biological sciences not as a map to follow with all its roads and connections, but as a field to pick flowers. Here "flowers" are images.

TIME SCALES

"Not only must we study the hour-to-hour or minute-to-minute operations of living things as going concerns (the chemistry), but we cannot leave out of account the slower processes in the period . . . of a lifetime, by which the egg develops into the grown-up adult and finally towards senescence and death. On a longer time scale there are phenomena which must be measured in terms of a small number of lifetimes; they are the processes of heredity by which characteristics of organisms are passed from parent to offspring. Finally on a time scale of many hundreds of generations there are the slow processes of evolution." (From C. H. Waddington: *Nature and Life*)

We use the passage as metaphor. It provides us with an image: Time which like a wave of the sea or current of air extends the range.

THE CROEDOES

An organism begins life with certain hereditary materials which define how it will develop. These paths of development are stable; i.e., the direction in which the cell develops is, in Waddington's term, "canalized." It is inflexible in the sense that it has a tendency to reach the normal end result in spite of abnormal condiions. But it also has a measure of flexibility and a tendency to be modified in response to circumstances.

The organism develops through steps, phases of the biological continuum. At certain points, pathways branch off, and the individual can go either way. Embrionic development though "canalized" is a sequence of moving through these branching paths (creodes). Through feedback there is a balance between this inflexibility and this flexibility.

The growing organism pursues its "developmental fate." The fate is not just its materials, its building blocks. It is a set of potentialities depending on the larger relationships. There is an architecture. As Waddington says, "The architecture of the body can be defined as a probability function spread through the whole of its space."

So the body politic has its architecture. It too has its probability functions, determined by planning.

AN EMBRIOLOGY COMPUTER FOR COMMUNITY PLANNING

Requirements:

I Must exploit all above elements of computer/human brain model.

II Must accommodate growth in the biological model (also solving the dilemma of control vs. flexibility).

III Must be non-technological; i.e. politically useful.

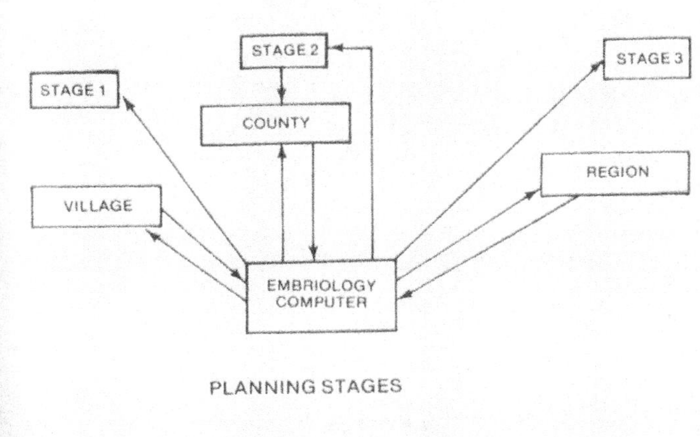

PLANNING STAGES

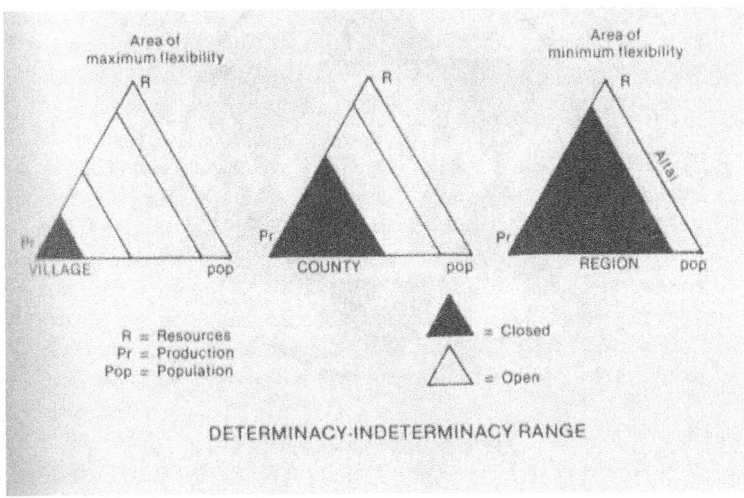

DETERMINACY-INDETERMINACY RANGE

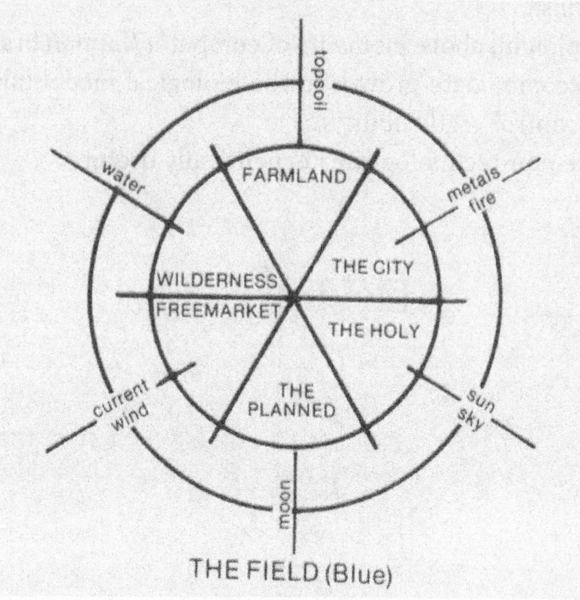

THE FIELD (Blue)

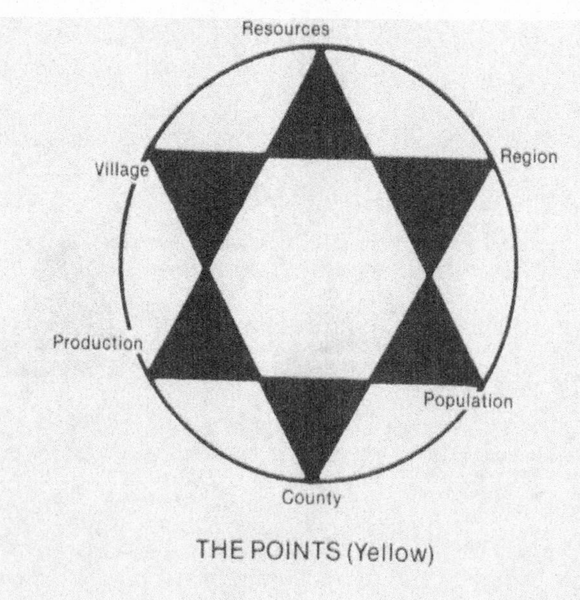

THE POINTS (Yellow)

A PROJECTED FILM

Alvarez would like to do a film on regional planning in Altai. But he has no time for it. He, Blake, and Morris are engaged by the Yellow shamans in their vaudeville show, which tours country fairs.

Still—Alvarez thinks about the film. How could such a film be made, taking into account the difficulties? (The complexity of the Embriology Computer, the feedback/feed-forward method of planning in Altai, etc.)

The Cuban sees two possibilities. The first would be a documentary approach: to show how the process actually works. It would be made up of interviews between the agents at the various levels explaining their roles: the matriarchs who operate the village consoles; the cauga or county planners collaborating with the village to put together the five-year plan; state and regional review boards, etc.

These nets would be concerned with examining the three basic terms of planning: agricultural and industrial production, the availability of natural resources, and population demands, and bringing them into balance. The entire *range* of subject matter would be indicated in a kind of cinematic shorthand: a film sequence of pastureland to denote resources. A scene from a steel mill or a Machine Bank. Population problems suggested by a shot of a teeming neighborhood, undernourished children, etc. But this would hardly make an absorbing film.

The second possibility would be to dramatize the personal element. A series of portraits showing the process as it intersects individual lives. For instance: the matriarchs in the Masters' Studio, they are making the plan with representatives of the farmers' collective—a freshness, a rough authenticity to this . . . the plan is sent up to the county planners at a higher level. These are more professional, pride themselves on a more objective view, as they evaluate it with the other village plans . . . conflicts of interests, attitudes?

But would this be sufficiently comprehensive? Would it not emphasize personalities at the expense of the clarity of the whole?

Finally, is it possible to treat the subject of planning at all in terms of art (even a popular art like the cinema)? One might illustrate the procedure as a conceptual scheme (the bones). And dramatize the agents and protagonists (the flesh and blood). But neither get at the interesting question about planning— whether in real life its direction runs from the top down, or from the bottom up. Who is the plan *for*?

In this regard Alvarez might film *two* possible ideal models for the country of Nghsi-Altai. One would be: maximum participation at the workplace and maximum local autonomy, within the framework of a central and binding macroeconomic plan (socialist model). The other that of overall production and distribution regulated by the play of global market forces; while at the same time brakes are applied to counter uneven development: the stunting of those areas which have nothing or little to offer in exchange (capitalist model).

But both models might be false. Could the art of the film show whether the plan were truth or fabrication?

But art is itself a fabrication.

• •

How to get below the surface?

One of the shamans suggests how Alvarez might solve the difficulty. Why not simply film the sequence of "Planning Dances" that are performed in Altai on Gobardan, during the Festival of Planners?

REGIONAL PLANNING DANCES: A SHAMAN'S DESCRIPTION

On the first day of Gobardan when the wheat yellows, the dances begin on the threshing floor of Sawna village. The yearend inventory has been made up by the Guild of Planners and a draft plan for the coming year forwarded to the county or cauga. It is the response of the county that initiates the dance series.

A CALENDAR

FIRST DANCE HOUSE October 1

Village asking plan sent/answering plan received.

A.M. March of the guild masters from the Studio of Planners.

P.M. First Dance House by the villagers. Village dances. Reception of The Other.

That evening the panchayat in full assembly debates the options presented. Return to the Planners' Studio. Submission of second asking plan.

SECOND DANCE HOUSE October 10

A.M. March. Reception by the guild masters of the village—county answering plan.

P.M. Barley threshing and bagging. Second Dance House by villagers. County dances. Reception of The Other. Sequence of events morning afternoon, and evening, as described above.

THIRD DANCE HOUSE October 24

A.M. March, etc. Guild masters present the village-countyregion answering plan.

P.M. Wheat threshing and bagging. Third Dance House, Regional dances. Reception of The Other.

Sequence of events as before.

FOURTH DANCE HOUSE November 10

A.M. March. Presentation of village-county-region-confederacy answering plan.

P.M. Wheat threshing. The Fate Dances. Fourth Dance House. In the evening, panchayat debates and final plan is decided. Coded by the planners and fed into Embriology Computer.

NOVEMBER 11 FIRST DAY OF THE NEW YEAR

Afternoon: Transformation dances by the villagers: Fate dances continued. The Mysteries.

Evening: Announcement of confederacy-wide results.

SUGGESTED FILM SHOTS/TYPICAL START OF THE DAY

Note: during the course of each holiday all the villagers become "planners," that is, they move away from the personal realm. Perhaps a film sequence should show a typical family rising in the morning. They wander around the house lazily. Perhaps one is playing a flute; the clan is having breakfast . . . In a desultory way they pull on their regalia, attach their tribal decorations and feathers. And are *drawn* gradually out . . . first by the music of the other villagers, the flutes the drums, heard in the lane. The sound of the dancing in the lanes ... very gradually swells . . . the excitement builds. The pull toward the threshing floor . . .

HEXAGON DANCES/GAMES

The threshing floor has become a hexagon, the space divided roughly into six segments. On receiving the plan options, the participants dance as members of their phratries or brotherhoods.

For instance, the Filtheater clans try to pull in the direction of "Free Market"; the Soreheads toward "The Ruler/Full Moon," etc. (Suggested film shot number 2.)

This is called "Moving the plan into one's corner." Thus the saying in Altai: "The plan is pulled apart by the Six Tendencies."

MUSIC

Informal or random. Instruments of the participants, guitar, bagpipes, etc.

Formal, antiphonal. Two brass ensembles, one on each side of the threshing floor. Loud, brassy. Each band is under the direction of a shaman society.

MODES

Each Dance House is performed in two modes or moods. Mode of the dance is first comic, gross, ribald. The *low* planning or "kyogen dances."

At the appearance of The Other, the mode is satirical; then changes to grave and solemn. *High* planning style or "hinoh dances."

The participant is transformed through the modes.

MASKS/COSTUMES/REGALIA

First day: Rustic figures, lampoons, caricatures.
Second day: Animals and birds.
Third day: Insects and Regional Beings—rivers, mountains, etc.
Fourth day: Personification of weathers (confederacy-wide).

MEANING OF THE OTHER

In the middle of each festival dance, dividing the low and high nodes, appears the Beggar. The figure is at first alien, in a different mask from the dancers. But at the start of the next Dance House, all wear this mask.

The Beggar does not represent the plan on a higher level (which would be merely an abstraction) but some other *place* or group that has hitherto been excluded. The Beggar dances as "Appalachia," for example.

The Beggar is at first jeered at but later is "worshipped."

Sometimes the Beggar is not a representational figure but real.

(Suggested film shot number 3.)

TRANSFORMATION DANCES/FATE DANCES

The dance houses essentially are the process by which the individual citizen transforms himself, that is, goes to meet his "developmental fate." This he does not do willingly, but neither is it unwilling either.

"I respond in order that I may change, and in order that I nu be changed," is the saying in Altai.

The Beggar stands at the creode, or branching pathway. Sometimes one avoids him (goes around him). Sometimes one annihilates him. Sometimes one becomes him. In any case, one closes a door as one moves forward. This is why the last Dance Houses are called Fate Dances.

• •

After the planning dances are over, the panchayat decides the plan options in the full assembly of the people. Decision is by cot sensus. After that the plan is coded and submitted to the Embrio I-ogy Computer. Thus it is said: "The village votes by countin g heads and seeing faces. The confederacy votes by algebra."

Another one of our sayings in Altai: "The professional pre pares/the dancer indicates/the panchayat acts."

However, the acts are not always virtuous. In deciding option the panchayat may chose either the "high" or the "low" mode.

• •

With the final mysteries and exchange of masks between the shaman societies — called the "marriage of shamans" — the New Year begins.

NEW YEAR'S NIGHT

A crew of shamans is filming the village New Year festivities. The scene is commonplace; and after six weeks of activities, during which many of the citizens have been dancing and arguing almost continually, the pace is slow. Therefore it is not an important film. Still, the film involves documenting and recording what is there; that is, replicating. It is only the Yellow shamans who are allowed to make films in Nghsi-Altai.

It is evening, but there is a full moon. There is sufficient moonlight to shoot the film. Besides, lights shine over the threshing floor. The screen of the Embriology Computer, set up at the edge of the field against the wall of the cannery, is also a source of light.

The same projection on similar screens is being shown in a thousand villages through Altai. The last deliberations have been taken simultaneously throughout the country, the choices made and programmed for the computer by the planners. The final returns are beginning to appear on the screen. In this village, as in a thousand other villages and city quarters as well, is being shown in flickering light the shape of the New Year.

The options have narrowed to one. The points or nodes of the branching pathways —once opened almost to infinity—have been danced through. Now the doors are closed. Flickering on the screen, in a pattern of shifting and changing equations and symbols: the cold light of the real.

This is the "blue light of balance" focused in a single finality by the planning process.

"We are awaiting our fate."

It is this mood that the shaman filmmakers are capturing.

A great heap of grain as high as the cannery roof stands under a lamp. The threshers and electric winnowing fans have been put away and the ground swept. There are some boys of the Squirrel or Naming Society sitting on a pile of pumpkins beside a parked truck. Others of the folk are sitting around eating New Year black millet and mung beans and drinking corn liquor.

On the threshing floor there is only a scattering of dancers. There are some musicians also. These are the hardiest and most perservering dances. Their faces gleam with sweat and their arms and legs are white with chaff.

Two old sendi drinkers are weaving among the dancers. It is not clear whether they are trying merely to cross the space or to perform on it. One has a limp bagpipe under his arm which he blows fornlornly.

Voices call: "Sit down, Harelip. What are you trying to do?"

"Time to go home, Uncle Desai. You haven't any breath left."

A wind has sprung up, whirling the chaff. Beyond the granary bins and over the shoulder of the windmill, the moon is sailing. Heads are turned upward. From the great screen there is a wash of light turning the faces of the onlookers blue.

A family of a dozen or so —the Harditt family, perhaps —is sitting near the film crew around a picnic hamper. A small girl is on her mother's lap. As the figures on the screen move and flicker, she tries to keep her eyes open, fighting sleep.

Is this Lucia's child?

THE POPULATION LOTTERY

The final returns are known. The plan is made, through the network of communication and consultation and through the Embriology Computer. Now it must be acted upon.

"Technology is a tool. But the tool is iron."

Each commune must live within its "force triangle" composed of the three vectors:

PRODUCTION/RESOURCES/POPULATION

In some distant sections of Nghsi-Altai there has been drought. The monsoon rains have not come in season. And this burden must be distributed through every part. To keep the balance, the Sawna families will be diminished.

In Sawna it was the Nai headsman (the rites master) who presided over the population lottery. This was held in the square in front of the baithak a week after New Year. The actual drawing took place on the baithak porch. On the dusty ground below stood the folk. Families had come in from the other cauga villages, from Rampur and Dabar Jat. Clansmen from the "daughter villages," that is, those with blood ties, had also returned to Sawna for the lottery drawing.

On a table on the porch was a large jar full of dried yellow beans.

There was also a scattering of black beans. The lottery drawing was no different from any other lottery drawing —for instance, the choosing of officials, or factory managers in the machine banks of the cauga. Blue shamans' weeds decorated the railing of the baithak porch.

It was the old women—the heads of each family—that reached into the jar and pulled out a bean. They came out of the crowd with dark reluctance—it was almost as if they were being pulled out of it, like turnips out of the ground—while the knots of relatives that surrounded them pulled at their shawls making a great show of refusing to let them go forward. Finally they did so and were escorted with great dignity up the steps to the platform by the rites master.

However, it was not the matriarch herself who would be sent away if her selection were unlucky. In a ritual sense the whole clan was marked, but in practice it was only "second generation's households" that would be forced to leave Sawna. Not the family community— only a part torn out and sent into exile beyond the borders —like the thinning of forest trees.

At the bottom of the baithak steps, members of the Dog Society lounged and played dominos. In the small shade of a banana plantation, a hookah smoking group was in progress, the old men occasionally shifting their places to avoid the sun.

It was Helvetia Harditt who picked the black bean.

FAREWELL TO SAWNA VILLAGE

The sun shone on a white wall. Venu was wakened by a cart clattering over the cobbles. Sathan lay against him.

A pot banged in the kitchen. He heard someone cry: "You there, get me those eggs." Helvetia's voice continued: "I'm letting them sleep. The packing is mostly done anyway."

And another voice: "Yes, they have a long day ahead of them. Let them rest."

Most of the other occupants at the sleeproom had already gotten up. Venu noted that his son, Dhillon, who had spent the night with his extended family, was gone. Maddi and her husband lay still asleep. But Lucia's children were up already, their bedrolls piled neatly against the wall.

Where were they? Dhillon may have taken the boy and girl to the pasture on a last visit, Venu thought. Someone would have to be sent to fetch them or they might be left behind.

Venu pictured Harelip with his load of pumpkins bound for the freeze locker and the little mare on a lead trotting beside its mother as she pulled the cart. As the cart turned a corner, the clattering diminished but the light twinkling bell attached to the mare's harness continued clear.

Yes, for the last time, Venu thought.

The sleeping gallery was almost empty. The part of the floor where they lay was still in shadow. An oblong of light washed across the wall where a lacrosse racket hung twisted with a knot of dry grass from Watermeadow.

Again, voices from the kitchen.

He could hear Nanda's and Motteram's voices arguing sharply.

Sathan's face was blurred as she lay resting on her husband's brown arm. Venu had thought she was asleep, but she was not. As he pushed her hair aside, gently so as not to waken her, he could see that she was awake. The daily sounds of the house floated up. And Sathan lay without moving listening to them, her eyes filled with tears.

Lucia's children, Bhungi and Lal, accompanied by two uncles, were going on a walk outside the village. They were going to say good-bye to the herdsmen.

The uncles, Dhillon and one of the city-dwelling Harditts, would also be bidding the children good-bye.

Dhillon, who had arrived from his in-law village the day before, was explaining the mysteries of the Motor and Metals Pool tothe city relative. Leaving the village outskirts they struck out across the fields. The older men had set out on their walk in a somber mood, each holding a child by the hand. Now however, lost in conversation, they had forgotten them.

The uncles walked ahead rapidly. Dhillon occasionally stopped to point out something remembered from his herdsman's days, then resumed the climb with long strides. The pylons of the power lines marching up the middle of the pasture had been decorated with tantras during Dasahra, he recalled. By that stone wall the cowherds had built their fire in winter. The children struggled to keep up.

A truck loaded with its clanking field kitchen climbed by them slowly along the road which marked the edge of the canefield. The field was now stubble, stretching as far as the eye could see.

Over a rise they came on a band of young herders. Around the margin of the water hole the grass was green, but beyond it was straw. The mild-eyed cattle, the color of coffee, grazed at a distance. A herdsman was playing an accordion.

At the bottom on the gently sloping hill lay the village, and on this side of the village the wash pond.

After a while one of the men stood up and came over to the children, who were occupying themselves catching grasshoppers. Then another man came over. Lal had a grasshopper cupped in his fist. Struggling to get out, it tickled.

"So. You'll be going away from us?"

Bhungi nodded with an air of importance. "Yes. Today." The smaller Lal also nodded.

"Where will you be going?"

Bhungi swung her arm vaguely. "To America."

Through the windbreak of locust trees they could see where the women were washing clothes at the edge of the pond.

By mid-morning their travel guides had come. The two households leaving to go on the long trip through Kansu Hardan had packed, and the children had been collected. They said good-bye to the others, left the house where they had lived as long as they could remember, and closed the gate.

Neighbors stood in the doorways of the lane watching them as they passed. The robing ceremony had been the day before, and the formal family farewell at the Ancestor shrine. Helvetia Harditt representing the Lineage, the line of the family through time, had said the prayer and given them mementos from the altar to carry with them. Jeth Harditt on behalf of each of the "in-law" villages throughout the district had also said a few words.

The Blue priest Tattattatha had also taken part in the melancholy ceremony.

Now they walked through the lane of the tholla in their exile robes. The children had been given yucca blossoms, which they held tightly in their fists. The procession was quiet, accompanied only by the shamans' rattles. In the doorway a woman with a child leaning against her took it onto her lap and clutched it tightly. The pair, mother and child, watched the procession pass with cold eyes. Already a shadow seemed to have passed over them.

Several other exile families had gathered in the square. The collection crossed Maker's Square and went up the ramp onto the vegetable gardens. The sun was shining on the pale aster flowers below the hedges. The stucco wall of a cottage was covered with red henna hand marks, for a wedding. In fact, at the village gate a bridegroom, his head capped with silver bells and his ankles jangling, passed them on a motorcycle.

He slowed down and waved.

A small crowd of villagers had followed the exile families as far as the common orchards. Then they went through the gate and were crossing the fields alone, accompanied only by the Yellow shamans.

• •

In the villages adjacent to Sawna there had been no additions to the caravans of lottery losers. However, out of the four-village cluster comprising the next cauga they had picked up three families, and in the next shire several more.

For some days the exile caravan continued over the plain. They would stop every night and pitch camp outside a village. These villages, dug into the loess earth, were the same as their own. The wayfarers were seldom more than three miles from a village. Yet only the roofs with their warm colors and a few guild halls and windmills could be seen. In front of these the heat shimmered, heightening the atmosphere of impermanence and distance.

The Sawna people were drifting. And it was an unsettling thought that even the soil in which the Jat villages were anchored had drifted in from the desert millenia ago. Was the landscape again shifting? However, life within the villages continued as normal, heedless of the border-bound travelers.

To the Harditt contingent it seemed strange that for years there had been these moving caravans of exiles and they had hardly , noticed them.

They had passed outside the walls, shepherded by the shamans. Perhaps it was the influence of the Yellow shamans that erased the fact of their passing.

Though there was no formal organization, the sections of the caravan tended to correspond to the "bisa cauga," the twenty-village unit or cluster of the plains region. The Sawna pilgrims marched with others, were part of the same slow-moving baggage train, and often shared the same vehicle, a tractor or lumbering bullock cart. These were generally overloaded. Indeed, some of the "second-generation" families had taken along household equipment and even their draft animals.

The Harditts watched one family approach over the fields—a truck piled high with bundles, on top of which rode a grandmother and a crate of chickens.

"It's as if they think they're going to a new settlement. And can start all over again, planting their own yam patch," Nanda remarked humorously to Golla.

Maddi, who was pregnant, took turns with a young woman from Sawna with an infant, riding on a cart and walking. Ramdas, Maddi's husband, walked beside them.

• •

One afternoon the Sawna people had pitched camp. The children had scampered off with friends they had made in the caravan.

After a short while Lal and Bhungi were back. Bhungi tugged at her father's sleeve excitedly.

"Come. There's a dead animal."

Since they had arrived a sickly sweet smell had pervaded the campsite. The clan people were setting up yurts. As they approached the village ditch they could see birds settling on the trees. The stench increased. The pasture, cropped close, was stippled with splotches of pink thistles.

On the flat ground at about a hundred yards distant lay a dead bullock. The animal was on its side, its body against the earth stiff, its four legs sticking straight out. The head was wedged back. A single kite perched between the horns. They were too far away to see whether the eyes had been eaten yet by the birds.

Other birds stood in a dignified pose or stepped slowly over the body. The glossy black hide was distended but still intact. The birds were mostly kites, with one or two white long-necked egrets.

There was a tranquility about the birds, particularly the egrets. They simply stood pruning their feathers or bent down to pick for skin parasites as they had before on the live ox. Perhaps they did not realize yet that the animal was really dead and not merely lying down resting.

At the rear, heavily, a carrion hawk dropped down and began ripping at once at the bullock's anus. There was a stir among the birds on the body. As if with a shock, they too began to pull violently at the carcass.

A sober assembly of egrets and kites watched at a short distance from the corpse. The trees at the edge of the field were now thick with birds.

Lal almost overcome with nausea put his sleeve over his nose and clung to his father. Bhungi wanted to get closer.

Shamans came onto the pasture. The travelers could not tell whether they were from the village or were the same shamans as those in charge of the caravan, as they also were muffled against the stench. Their heads were covered. They were wearing heavy gloves. They stepped through the parliament of birds.

One of the shamans knocked the strutting birds away with his stick. They poured gasoline over the corpse.

These shamans were knackers, Motterman told Bhungi. In the old days their task had been to prepare leather. Their customers had been the villagers, but because the task was unclean they were not allowed inside the village.

The sky was still white as the Sawna folk went down the road and after they had returned to camp. They could see the smoke from the burning corpse a long time, and in the distance other wavering columns of smoke where the shamans were probably burning other dead cattle.

• •

Venu's daughter was having trouble balancing on top of the weaving baggage. Articles from the ancestor shrine were also loaded onto the truck. From a pole decorated with photographs, a black streamer drifted against Maddi's face.

Both Maddi and her father had been on this same route before with the old councilor, Gopal Harditt. Since they had left the village and had been taken from the compound, Venu had felt intensely the presence of the former panchayat head.

Venu and Ramdas were plodding along beside the truck. Every so often Maddi's young husband would reach up and touch the pregnant woman's leg or hand. A shaman walked a few steps in front of the group.

From the fringes of the Yellow shaman's shirt hung all manner of clinking charms and trinkets. Had the shaman also known Gopal Harditt? Venu wondered. The Yellow shamans were connected to the Ancestor societies. Did not the shamans guide the "most recent dead," just as they were the travel guides of the exiles?

The caravan route was through a familiar landscape. Nor was traveling with the caravan strange, as it swelled with new additions from the provincial villages. The dress and articles of regalia showing the Age Grades were alike throughout Kansu. The elders were accorded their proper rank. The brotherhoods with their characteristic tattoos could also be distinguished easily.

The Harditt men struck up an acquaintance with members of Wind clan from the village of Ladpur and with several Firemen. During the intermittent halts they would sit and smoke together in the shade of a truck. Sometimes they would play bowls.

The treeless road continued. The caravan generally halted early at a watering place outside some village bounds. The creak and sway of the loads ceased. The riders clambered down stiffly. Soon over the open field one could see the circles of the yurts going up and the smoke rising from the first cooking fires.

WITH THE TRAVELING SHOW

For a stretch of the journey they fell in with the traveling show. It had been performing on a riverbank on the outskirts of Puth Majra where a fair was being held. The shamans' troupe, which projected movies and gave dramatic entertainment, was also traveling through the villages of the Kansu district.

Toward the end of each day the members of the exile caravan would pick their campsite and be busy setting up their shelters. Nearby on the same pasture they would see the players erecting their bamboo platform and hanging up their ragged screen.

The platform for the performance was set outside the limits of the village, and the villagers came out to it, often bringing their campstools. Because it was beyond the village bounds the exiles also were permitted to attend the showings.

The shaman troupe practiced their dance steps on the grass beside the parked trucks. The shamans took different "voices." Sometimes in the evenings the campers could hear them practicing with their voices on the hill or under the orchard trees. They could project their voices so that they seemed to come from another place or out of another person's mouth.

The three foreigners attached to the troupe also practiced. They specialized in acrobatics and juggling feats and performed their "individuality freak shows." These took place during the intermission and were in the nature of a comic, relief to the more sober spirit dramas.

The Sawna folk had seen many Yellow shamans' shows. In the performance an ordinary villager, called simply "Man" or "Person," goes on a journey, is captured and taken to the land of the dead, or Under world. There one of the spirit animals befriends him and becomes his Spirit Helper, giving him its own powers. The person then returns to the village and shows his magic.

There are a number of demonstrations of skill. One of the shaman dancers reaches with his fingers into a boiling kettle and cats a piece of meat out of it. A cornstalk is made to sprout before the eyes of spectators and produce a fully ripened ear of corn.

The shamans contain inside them the spirit animals, whose presence may be manifested by kicks and other signs. Once a horse was inside one shaman's body, and whenever a certain song was sung the horse tried to get out and the audience could see the horse's tail protruding from the dancer's mouth.

The Sawna spectators enjoyed these "demonstrations of powers." Some were less impressed. Motteram described them as "cheap conjurer's tricks." Generally it was the younger men who were inclined to be skeptical of the shamans' exhibitions, which they found grotesque. They preferred the more civilized Dance Houses of the Blue shamans.

It was true that the magic of the Yellow shamans shows tended to wear off. The Sawna householders had seen them many times. They had somewhat lost their effect.

Several days before someone had lost a wallet. One of the shaman guides had helped find it. The shamans guiding the caravan also it seemed had special powers —like their cousins the performers in the shows.

The wallet, belonging to a family from the bisa cauga, had been lost en route several days before. People had looked for it everywhere, and the shaman, through his "third eye," had located it under a certain bush in a previous camp. They had gone back and found it. This shaman had been traveling with their section, and the Harditts had walked with him often. How was it possible to see things that were not there?

The shaman explained that the third eye was a three-foot-long tube he imagined protruding from his head, formed of rays of light which he was able to focus on the lost object.

Now a circle of campers was gathered around the same shaman, whose name was Elwood. The group included Nanda and two grandchildren.

This time the shaman was giving a "spirit reading" for a dog. The dog belonged to a friend of Lal's. The owner sat holding the dog, and the shaman sat across from the two of them chewing betel nut.

As the dog was present in the flesh it was not necessary for the shaman to use his "third eye." He was in direct communication with the spirit, and the dog spoke through his mouth.

Like all shamans this one had poor eyesight. He complained that the light bothered him. Shielding his eyes he squinted into the faces of the persons questioning him without seeming to see them. He seemed to be seeing the small child and her dog only vaguely.

After the seance Elwood was asked about the dog's "aura." He explained that the aura was not very strong, not like the aura of a person, because the colors are not as bright. There is a lemon yellow which in the aura of an animal denotes affection. And a blue color which shows the energy flow of all spirits.

Did he see other colors in these astral emanations?

Yes, a wide band of green. That is the healing force that animals give out, particularly when a child has been sick.

Nanda asked the shaman whether he could see also the auras of trees and stones? Sathan and Lucia were beside her.

"Of course. Everything in nature."

"Even small things? A flea's aura?"

The shaman nodded. "And you will see them too."

• •

The rawhide costumes were a product of the shamans' "knacker" activity. They would sew onto it beads, hammered pieces of metal, bird feathers, and bits of shell in the old manner. The leather was caked with grime. The raffia costumes of the theatrical performers were less durable but cleaner. Occasionally they had to be completely remade; then the caravan people would be sent out into the field to cut straw and to bring it in in bundles. The children brought feathers.

Most entrancing were the rattles. These were called "thunder sticks" and were made out of gourds filled with pebbles. The fringes of the shamans' garments also sounded: with the rattling of claws, deer hooves, the beaks of owls and clapper rails, etc.

The masks were of animals and birds, even fish and insects, which represented the clan totems. Made of hides and carved wood, they were double and triple masks, with the feat ares painted inside and out so that they could be seen also when the masks were open.

Once Lal was taken over to the performers' camp by his gra ndfather and permitted to sit on the lap of one of the shamans. The double mask was held up and the little boy taught how to o pen and close it by pulling the thong.

The Westerners, Blake, Morris, and Alvarez, who were practicing nearby, had stopped to watch the demonstration.

• •

One evening the Sawna households had been watching the flickering movie screen from a distance. In order to see better the children stood on a wagon.

Then the shaman dances began. Motteram suggested they get closer.

"Not in front," Ramdas warned. They were under an array of generator poles. An eerie light fell from above in the direction of the dancers.

The men made their way across the slope at the backs of the spectators and came in toward the corner of the stage to the side. From this vantage the Sawna people could see both the stage and the backstage performers readying themselves to go on and pulling on their costumes. The Shaman musicians, three on each side, squatted at the edge of the stage before their instruments, which were drums and rattles. There was also a storyteller.

A man appeared, walking. Perhaps he was going off from the village to fish.

A creature bounded on. This was the cannibal bird, Bakbakwalanusiwa, the storyteller announced in his whining voice. The body of the actor was partly hidden under straw thatch. The ferocious head was mounted on top of his own. With his hands he operated the long beak decorated with eye and nose holes.

The villager was taken to the land of the dead, to Under world. But where is the land of the dead? Is it below ground or above it? Voices come to us from Under world, but from where?

Stretching out its wings the being threw a larger and even more menacing shadow against the canvas. The whining voice rose. The Sawna men leaning against the edge of the stage could feel against their chests and hands the pounding of the dancing feet. The bird's bony ankles rattled. The figure loomed over them with its hooked beak.

There were in fact three creatures. The spotted muzzle of Hyena opened, the jaws swung apart. Bear's faced showed below, lazy and crafty. The dance tempo increased. Finally this mask was pulled sideways. With a shiver the spectators perceived Spirit Being appear, with his beak of bone and eyes gleaming, made out of scintillating blue shells.

Though there were only two actors, there appeared to be many, and it was awesome. It was as if the shaky bamboo platform, so plain and unimpressive looking during the day, had become at night a field of force. The dancers were possessed by the animal and spirit beings —and at same time were the animal and spirit beings.

However, when the dance was over, and when the performer stepped from the side of the stage and took off his mask—the Sawna men saw he was the familiar shaman. He was the same person, now somewhat exhausted, that had been standing next to them as he adjusted his costume only a few minutes before.

It was not the same with the three foreigners, who performed next.

They did not dance using the generalized animal or bird masks, but as individuals. In fact they wore the masks of their own faces. The masks were perhaps exaggerated. The pallor of the skin, the prominent noses, and deeply recessed eye sockets of the Westerners gave them a ghostly quality. As the figures danced there seemed to be *only* the masks and costumes. Through the eyeholes of the masks the Sawna men, from their vantage point at the edge of the stage, were astonished to see nothing, only a kind of smokey vagueness.

Were the Westerners' spirits entangled in the shamans' coat fringes? If so, where had they come form? From Under world, storehouse of souls?

The Sawna men watched closely.

When the Morris and Blake figures came off the stage the performers had actually dematerialized. It took several minutes for their bodies to reappear.

• •

Venu, Rathlee Golla, and Motteram, coming to pay their friends a last visit, found the foreigners behind a tent. The battered truck, with the name of the troupe painted on the side, was parked nearby. Theatrical paraphernalia spilled out of it. The Westerners had been doing their washing. Articles of clothing, mostly old socks and underwear, were strung on a line.

This was the lottery losers' last stop in Kansu. After that, the caravan was scheduled to go on into another province, while the players continued to tour the villages.

The stopover at this campsite had been for several days—longer than usual—enabling the foreigners to catch up on their housekeeping.

The Sawna men squatted. Between the truck and the tent, the ground was worn bare where the players had been practicing. Morris, his arms covered with suds, bent over a basin.

Motteram, though he had been afraid of him at first, had grown particularly fond of Alvarez. All the Westerners were pink, but Alvarez was the pinkest and most flamboyant. His hair stuck out angrily from his head like a hive of bees. The missing ears with their patches of scar tissue heightened this effect of ferocity.

However, at the moment it seemed the fire had gone out of him. The filmmaker sat disconsolately on the ground mending his socks.

In the vaudeville skit the Cuban socialist gives a long and pathetic description of how he came to the country as an explorer, married, and worked in a noodle factory. He is asked by one of the shamans how he lost his ears. Alvarez replies:

I am lucky I did not lose my hand
    meddling in the economy of this country
I would have had all of you stamping out machine products
    and tied to a production line
With no room to breathe.

This is said so penitently and with such an air of injured innocence—the eyes rolled up and the hand held over his head in a gesture of surprise —it makes the audience laugh.

In fact, the confession was false. As Alvarez himself had been at pains to point out to Motteram and to anyone else who would listen, he had been misunderstood. He had not been interested in the assembly line but rather in increasing the country's general abundance and well-being. But such was his sinister role in the theatrical performance, whenever he appeared he was hissed—proof of his guilt being his mutilated ears.

Unlike Alvarez, Morris's routine was not set. He composed the songs himself and generally went over them late in the afternoon before each performance. He had finished rinsing and running his articles through the wringer. As he hung them on the clothesline, Morris sang to himself softly:

I who have loved old things
    old craftsold trappings
looked for them in a new land
    with no routes   no mappings

I did not seek them in art —the dyer's color
                    the fine line
    incised by the smith on his silver
but in the product's wholeness   a sense of measure
    that joined maker and user

I found them best in the songs
                the ancient artifacts of this place
                    and your deepest treasure
And you have called me a thief of songs
            and put me in shackles.

He paused. Inadvertently Morris reached down and rubbed his ankle where he had been held in the stocks.

Rathlee asked with sympathy, "Do you still suffer pain?"

The poet-artist, a bluff, forthright man, had struck Venu and Golla as the most approachable of the three. And perhaps he had suffered most. He had committed one of the gravest crimes, to have taken down music sung by the folk, on a tape-recorder — thus pre-empting the right of the Yellow shamans to replicate.

"Well, I've learned my lesson at any rate. Nothing is set. One must compose extempore, in life as in art, depending on one's mood and circumstance."

He sang again—in a revision of the last stanza:

In your foreign land
        how we are marked!
How strange
        that our deepest passions
should be for you
        mere eccentricities.

"Yes, things alter," Rathlee Golla said. "Perhaps everything . . . The song, the man, the landscape, it's all a trick of perspective.

Venu was sitting on the ground. The others watched him in silence as he finished weaving a figure out of blades of kana grass He finished the bird. He attached a handle to the bird's neck, made out of the same spiky grass, pulled at it with the back of his knife, and curled it. He presented it to Morris.

"And what about him?" Rathlee asked, pointing to a figure on the stage.

Morris laughed. "Oh him. He has a madman's role to play!'

It was still an hour before the performance. Blake had mounted the platform and was practicing some of his stage business.

Blake's shirtfront was open, showing a flowing cravat. He wore high boots and an American cavalry hat. His suit was composed of pantaloons and a knee-length coat, both of loud black-and-white striped worsted. The large nose and closely set eyes with deep eyefolds were the only features visible in a bloom of wiry white hair.

Some shamans in the field were putting up the loudspeaker equipment. Already the performer had a few impromptu spectators among the campers. There was a scattering of applause as Blake stepped forward and adjusted the microphone. "Can you hear me back there?" He struck a bardic pose.

"I shall begin with a little warmup. What I call my inflationary verses."

He took a deep breath and began:

"I celebrate myself....
I loaf and write my soul,
I lean and loaf at my ease observing a spear
of summer grass."

"My god, it's not his own poem!" Alvarez exclaimed. He and Morris had stepped over to watch. "He's expropriating another's verses!"

"And misquoting at that. No matter," Morris reassured him. "So long as he sticks to the repertory of Egotism."

"... the smoke of my own breath
echoes, ripples and buzzed whispers ...
my respiration and inspiration ...
... the passing of blood and air through my lungs,
the songs of ME rising from bed and meeting the sun."

There were cries of encouragement from the audience. The poet continued more volubly.

"Swift wind! Space! My soul!
Divine I am inside and out, I make holy whatever
I touch or am touched from
The scent of these arm-pits is an aroma finer
than prayer ....
Seeing, hearing and feeling are miracles, and each
part and tag of me is a miracle."

A dreamy look of contentment settled on the poet's face.

"I dote on myself ....
I sing the body electric
I have instant conductors all over me whether I
pass or stop
They seize every object ....

I hear you whispering there O stars of heaven
perpetual transfers ....
I ascend from the moon, I ascend from the night ....
Wrenched and sweaty ....
The spotted hawk swoops by ....
I am not a bit tamed, I too am unstranslatable,
I SOUND MY BARBARIC YAWP OVER THE ROOFS OF THE WORLD."

There was by this time a swell of prolonged applause and hand-clapping from the handful of camp followers at the foot of the stage, as

Blake had continued to the end with mounting fervor.

They clamored for another.

"I hope it will be his —but I wouldn't count on it," Morris said to Alvarei in an aside.

"Here's one of my more recent compositions, in a darker mood." Blake threw his head back. His forehead had grown purple. He started off the text, shouting, at top speed.

MOLOCH THE INCOMPREHENSIBLE PRISON! . . . MOLOCH THE VAST STONE OF WAR! MOLOCH OF STUNNED GOVERNMENTS!

MOLOCH WHOSE EYES ARE A THOUSAND BLIND WINDOWS! MOLOCH WHOSE SKYSCRAPERS STAND IN THE LONG STREETS LIKE ENDLESS JEHOVAHS! MOLOCH WHOSE FACTORIES DREAM AND CROAK IN THE FOG! MOLOCH WHOSE SMOKESTACKS AND ANTENNAE CROWN THE CITIES!

MOLOCH IN WHOM I SIT LONELY! MOLOCH IN WHOM I DREAM ANGELS. CRAZY IN MOLOCH! COCKSUCKER IN MOLOCH! LACKLOVE AND MANLESS IN MOLOCH!

MOLOCH! MOLOCH! ROBOT APARTMENTS! INVISIBLE SUBURBS! SKELETON TREASURIES! BLIND CAPITALS! DEMONIC INDUSTRIES! SPECTRAL NATIONS! INVINCIBLE MADHOUSES! GRANITE COCKS! MONSTROUS BOMBS!

"He dearly loves to howl," Morris remarked to the Sawna men. "And this is only the warmup. Can you imagine how he's going to take off on the night session!"

Blake was introducing his next offering, which he called "A Vision."

"Ah, the authentic Blake! But no doubt to be badly mangled."

The poet began:

"A new heaven is begun. And as it is now thirty-three years since its advent, the Eternal Hell revives.

"The prophets Isaiah and Ezekiel dined with me amid the fires of hell. Both roundly asserted —and in this I concur—that the ancient tradition that the world will be consumed in fire at the end of six thousand years is true.

"Already the fountain of fire overflows and the secret world—chinked by our senses five—is exposed.

"Rintrah roars and swags on the angry deep.

"Shadow of prophecy, Albion's coast is sick; the American meadows faint!

"France, rend down thy dungeon! Golden Spain; burst the barriers of old Rome!

"The fire, the fire is falling! Look up, look up! O citizen of London, enlarge thy countenance! O Jew, leave counting gold! Return to thy oil and wine. O African, go winged thought, widen his forehead!

"The fierce limbs, the flaming hair, shot like the sinking sun into the western sea.

"The Eternal Female groans."

Blake was weeping at the end of these stanzas, and the audience was in a trance state.

Venu commented, "We find it strange, this vision of the future . . . when here there is only present time."

Already Alvarez had wandered off. Morris returned to his washing. The fire under the wash tub was low. The older man sent the children to fetch sticks.

Blake descended from the stage, spent. He was going among the spectators. He was coming toward them, his hands, loose, chewing a blade of grass.

But the audience was still in a state of excitement, warmed by fires that were in their own country illicit, of egotism, romantic challenge and scrappiness, and apocalyptic prophecy.

THE PICNIC WITH TATTATTATHA

The caravan passed the Great Sandy and Little Sandy rivers. Crossing over into Shao province, there had been behind them over the plain a last glimpse of the tall buildings and factories of Puth Majra. To the west there was a line of tawny mountains. These lay in the direction in which the Wind clansmen had once traveled on the way to Goose Gap and the tribal encampment at Watermeadow.

The caravan slowly crossed over a high gorge. They looked over into an abyss which was almost dry. The bridge, under repair, was supported by a tenuous bamboo scaffolding on which a team of roustabouts were at work. The Harditt men thought they recognized Dhillon's old companion, Rawilpindi.

Here the land was more arid. It was flatter, and there were irrigated sections. The route of the caravan paralleled a line of blue hills which neither receded nor came any closer. In this district the village clusters were more widely spaced. Each cluster yielded its lottery losers.

These new pilgrims were Luns. Their language was only partly comprehensible to the Jats, their gestures brusquer. But in build and color they were similar.

With the filling of the exile quotas from the rest of the plains districts, the caravan stretched out in a thin file along the road for several miles. It moved slowly.

Now, when in the late afternoon the Sawna group arrived at the outskirts of some village, the long caravan still moved up behind, the loaded trucks swung into view, and it would be almost night before the last yurts were pitched.

There were no more traveling shows. Sometimes in the dusk outside these villages a gathering of peasants stood watching the arrivals, beside a tractor.

• •

Venu found himself annoyed with Sathan. His wife and daughter, who had been responsible for the Harditt packing, had each taken along an extra shawl but had neglected to bring his favorite mug for coffee.

Meanwhile Nanda was having a feud with Motteram. In the early stages of the journey, betel nut had been plentiful. One could walk up and down the caravan and see the old women chewing it, a look of relaxed contentment on their faces. Now the gums of the matriarchs were no longer stained purplish black. When Nanda stuck out her tongue, it was like a child's.

In the normal course of things she would have sent her son-in-law out to bargain or trade for the nuts. When Nanda ordered Motteram, he refused. As they no longer lived in the village he was free of his apprenticeship obligation.

Lucia sided with Motteram. The dispute was carried on vociferously for some nights —not in the bosom of the family but around the campfire with everybody watching. Indeed, the audience of outsiders made the controversy more ugly.

• •

The travels through Shao province continued. Lal and Bhungi roamed the caravan and the adjacent fields with the other children. The contingent from the Ladpur sixteen-villages or bisacauga tended to stick together on the road. At night they pitched camp, helping each other put up the yurts. Meals were shared and decisions of the improvised panchayat were taken around a com mon fire.

The cauga campsite was ordinarily laid out in the shape of an ellipse, with the sites occupied by the families around the peri phery. If possible these were grouped according to tribe or ten dency. Thus on one side of the Ladpur ellipse were the Tractor Operators and the Sliding Fish people and opposite them the Filtheaters and Soreheads. The Harditts were of this latter cate gory (under the Moon sign) and regularly pitched their tent next to another family of Moons.

• •

Not far from the dusty road, Lal and Ramdas came across the skeleton of a bullock. The skull lay porous on the field. Only above the hooves were there meager tufts of hide. The bones had been plucked clean. Lal stood twisting on his finger a ring of sweet fern.

The whiteness and the cleanness were startling. There were only the light curving bones. The child's uncle would not let him touch the skeleton.

"Now it must be reclothed."

Lal's nose puckered. Ramdas explained that were was a storehouse under the ground for souls and that the species of beings in the world were constant and did not diminish.

When the child looked at him puzzled, Ramdas merely said: "You will see another ox walking."

Still, the matter continued to puzzle the child's youngest uncle. Did the teachings mean that in the Underworld storehouse, there was always the same *number* of souls? Or did it refer only to species—which remained constant though the numbers of individuals grew or diminished?

He discussed the question over glasses of sendi with his father-in-law and Rathlee Golla, and several other Fifth Age Set men. Ramdas was astonished to discover that each held a different opinion on the matter. Perhaps the question could have been resolved had there been a member of the Ancestor Society present.

• •

Tattattatha joined the Harditt group. The Blue Sensor, who had traveled without his leopard, relayed a number of messages from the Sawna compound. A Harditt cousin of Rathlee, of the Third Age Grade, was enrolled in the Weather and Soils Station. Sathan and Lucia were informed of progress at the Master's Studio. A new synthesizer had been installed, and they were preparing the printout of the autumn plan.

Sathan said, "Well, I guess they're getting along well enough without me."

"Does that surprise you?" Maddi countered.

After giving his news, Tattattatha made a tour of inspection around the campsite with the reigning matriarch, a Topsoil tribeswoman. The two walked with great dignity along the six boundaries dividing the space. Each segment was blessed with one of the "blue wilderness weeds."

• •

The hills were lower and had changed from smoky blue to slate. They had reached the last border settlement before the swamp country. There was a grove of palm trees fronting an immense field where pineapples were grown. Along the side was a row of bright aluminum-clad cannery buildings. These were backed by a low dyke. Beyond, stretching as far as the eye could see, was a feathery wall of bamboo.

There had been canneries connected with the machine bank in Sawna, but these were larger. The line of bitaura-driven truck-carts, which shuttled back and forth from the fields to the processing shed, was also a familiar sight in Sawna.

Yet this was perhaps the last time they would be seeing the carts—and the fields and the agricultural settlement too. In fact these days, the Harditts reminded themselves, all sights were "for the last time."

• •

Tattattatha had spent the evening before at the encampment. After breakfasting with the others on millet cakes seasoned with catni and a cup of sit, he remarked that he would like to stretch his legs. Together with a number of county folk, he set out on a walk through the palm grove. The group included Sathan.

The sun had just risen and was barely over the horizon. The sandy ground under the coconut palms was a bright glitter. The trunks were dark, they strolled over the violet shadows.

The exile caravan from the plains biome was now complete. A thousand yurts—in clusters of half dozen to twenty—filled the grove which extended for half a mile along the edge of the pineapple plantation.

The yurt clusters or caugas were named after the counties from which the wayfarers had come. The encampment was thus a miniature region of the plains in exile. The clusters had been pitched the night before in the cool sand and would soon be taken down. In fact, the trucks and other vehicles which had transported the pilgrims thus far were being assembled preparatory to the trip back. Baggage was piled among the palm tree trunks, also to be returned. They passed several caugas where a Yellow shaman squatted on top the the piles, lazily smoking bhang.

A steady stream of strollers moved the length of tented grove viewing the assembly. Tattattatha passing another Blue shaman that he knew would exchange greetings, and they would make the "balancing" sign, touching each other first on both palms, then on the forearms.

Returning to the Ladpur cauga, they found their own folk already packing. A crowd gathered around Tattattatha. The priest, making the round of the yurts, appeared to be displeased. He pointed out that the sacred circle was incomplete. Two of the brotherhoods were missing.

Sathan, next to him, replied that among the lottery losers in their own county, there had been no Fire people or Sky clans chosen. "So naturally," Sathan added, "we set up the tents as we could. It is not our fault there are empty spaces."

Tattattatha, frowning, looked at the faces of the group crowded around him.

"I can see lots of masters, and people of the First, Third, Fourth, and Fifth Age Grades. But there are no Seconds, or any old people either. How can you make the journey without a commune?"

He selected people to fill the missing age grades and brotherhoods and coached them in their roles. The Blue priest spent the rest of the day, as he told them, reconstituting civil society.

• •

The region of the plains was assembled by its caugas or counties. Each county, gathered around its Blue priest, was having its picnic in the immense pineapple field. This was the "passover" meal being celebrated.

The mood was set by the brilliant blue sky, the brash silver of the cannery sheds against the dusty green of the swamp woods, and by the elegance and smartness of the pineapple plants themselves, which extended in endless straight rows. The children had made pineapple cutouts of colored papers.

Between these rows sat the cauga remnants. On a plaid blanket were a freshly baked bread and piles of fruit. The wine was a fiery palm wine, not the familiar sendi.

Tattattatha's talk to the folk was "On Agriculture." As always the words were accompanied by his flute and by the musing of his "breath spaces," and so seemed to have only a rambling continuity. In the years to come, members of the households were to remember only certain parts of the homily, or to remember it differently.

TATTATTATHA'S SAYINGS

With this wine and this bread we offer ourselves. The baking oven and the wine press are not the work of our hands only.

•

We are sitting at a common table, even though we are not all of us here. If this is our last meal and we are leaving—then for those who are staying it is also the last meal.

•

The "cauga" is not real. It is only a symbol of the real. That is what makes it sacred.

•

In the candle's smoke the Ancestors became myth figures. But you are moving into myth, merely by stepping beyond this field.

•

These lovely dances are being performed by the animals for us. The hyena still laughs and steals. The hornbill is shrewd. The anteater resists. But the antelope no longer plows the soil with its hooves. How alienated we have become!

•

We live in a diminished totality. What we think now, and the system in which we think it, merely catalogues what remains. With the original paradise in fragments, what can we remember? And who do we become as we remember it?

•

Individuality is merely a stage in process of social breakdown.

•

Because man originally felt himself identical to the animals, his mind feeds on metaphor.

•

The amazing bird flies, the fish leaps, the reptile sheds his skin.

•

Without transcendence, the world of fact would choke us.

•

How shall I orient myself in the three regions? In the landscape where I go, under every bush, some god or spirit animal has left a footprint.

•

The Blue shaman weaves. The Yellow shaman unweaves.

•

The Blue shaman: growth, joy.
The Yellow shaman: compression, power.

•

The veil hides. The web knits together.

•

Society recycles itself through the age grades. Nature recycles itself through the swamp.

•

If there were a kingdom of Decay, its highways would be the great tides and its signposts the empty shells left by the migrants on the way.

•

The salmon leaps and spawns. The body is reclothed easily.

•

The process of recycling is the swamp. The reclothing and re-embodiment of souls is accomplished elsewhere.

•

Communards, you are not dying, you are only emigrating. Your guides will suffer the loss for you.

•

Be of good cheer. As you leave this place you are carrying the Ancestors with you. You are only looking for your bodies.

•

Two oceans were crossed over. The Atlantic was a Lethian stream in which we forgot Europe. The Pacific was a Lethian stream in which we forgot America. And now you are going back there with your eyes opened.

•

Inside the mountain: the storehouse of souls. The Lake Outside and beyond the mountain: the tumbling River.

•

In the spinning cataract the ferryman goes through light years.

SWAMP INHABITANTS

They had been traveling in the swamp for some days. The bamboo continued. The enormously tall canes in clumps stood straight up overhead on patches of higher ground. These were called hammocks. Between these the flats were covered with saw grass. Here the ground was relatively hard and the grass matted with tracks. Runnels of watery mud extended up into the grass, and into these the swamp drained.

The bands voyaged mostly in shade. Was it the feathery gloom that affected vision, or had the atmosphere altered in some way? The overtopping bamboo shaded the flats with their deep, dark grass. Sometimes there was an opening. The grass lightened in color, and the runnels with their oily film of decaying vegetation gave off a rainbow hue.

The route skirted the hammocks and was built up with logs over wet spots. There were increasing stretches traversing the open. The tree-topped hammocks would recede, and appear in the distance like islands over the horizon of grass. The grass was waist high.

Then they plunged into the woods again. The bamboo which bordered the swamp had given way to hardwoods, live oaks, and mahogany. They were on higher ground. Perhaps these were islands in the swamp with their own climates. Or perhaps they were the end of some wandering peninsula, attached somewhere to the mainland of Nghsi-Altai.

• •

The sacred "cauga"—so constituted by Tattattatha—had been walking together in a band since the beginning of the swamp journey.

A troupe of monkeys raced overhead. "Why, listen to them scream! How nimble they are," remarked one of the women from the Fire phratry who had been walking beside Sathan and Maddi. "They're like birds."

Indeed the monkeys, swinging from branch to overhanging branch, seemed to spend as much time in the air as birds. And when they lighted, the branch was barely weighted down.

The woman's children, who were called Pulin and Mukh, had made friends with the Harditt children since the pilgrims had entered the swamp.

The monkeys had descended. It seemed the monkey band was now directing the caravan, leading the way down the road. A monkey family was walking with Lucia and Maddi. The rest of the households were laughing at their antics, which seemed to mimic the walkers. When they left, Maddi's purse was gone.

• •

One of the new Sky clansmen was the first to notice the bear. The man had been making the journey that day with Venu and Rathlee Golla.

The column was at the edge of a wood and had been skirting a creek. The man pointed, and there in the middle of the creek was a bear, unconcernedly fishing. The big animal had a simple, somewhat droll expression on his face and looked almost human. They noted he had slyly chosen a shady spot in the creek so as not to show his reflection.

The cover had gotten denser, the trunks vine-covered and the ground wetter. It had been some time since the caravan had been in an open section of the swamp.

With only several of the bands visible, and with the track wandering aimlessly among the dim woods, the Sawna folk felt they had lost all sense of time.

In the middle of the path sat a lion. The lion did not move. He sat upright over his kill, the tail feather of a peacock sticking out the side of his mouth. The formal amber-colored mane made him look as if carved. The lion's eyes were closed.

The wall of the wood was steamy and stippled. Vines twisted around the trees. It was all leaves and stripes. Leopards moved liquidly against the camouflage, and creatures who seemed to be nothing more than some furtive and fleeting presence coalesced into eyes. These eyes of tigers burned like fires.

The column of pilgrims were standing with their feet in the water. They had been marching since early morning under a ban k along the edge of a creek.

Pelicans rose squawking. They were apparently at the mouth of a larger creek or river. The reedy bank had been dug away, further up a waterfall sounded, though it could not be seen. Through a lip of grasses higher up there was a sheen of light on some wider open space.

In the foreground a pair of long-necked eland browsed among the leaves. The color of their hides was dark chocolate and tan, and their horns, though coming to a sharp point, were turned as on a lathe. On the sun-drenched plain behind them a herd of antelope grazed.

Then the animals were running away. They were slowly moving off into the distance in straight lines. With their heads down they seemed to be ploughing the savanna grass—or showing the art of plowing.

Were the animals real? Venu discussed the question with the newly substituted Sky man and with Rathlee Golla.

Rathlee was of the opinion that they were "spirit animals," brought here by the shamans for their inspection. Probably the shamans merely wished to display them to the exiles of Nghsi at this point in their journey. But they were undoubtedly there. In any case, the members of the caravan together had seen the animals.

But they had seen them as aesthetic objects. These animals on the tranquil plain were splendid, and those in the dreaming shade also seemed to have been placed there as in a painting.

What was perhaps most strange: everyone had recognized the animals. They were species which the plainsmen had never seen in real life. Nevertheless they had seen them accurately portrayed, in a characteristic pose or gesture, in the shaman dances. Some of them were clan "Ancestors." The animals had long since vanished from their familiar habitat, but were still remembered in the dances.

Now, with the appearance of the totem animals, the onlookers seemed to have been thrown back into another period of time. In fact, to the time of the Ancestors.

• •

They had been traveling for a week through cypress and mangrove woods. The mangroves were raised; the roots were the perches of birds and small animal nests. The trunk of the trees sent out props, and the lower branches of the red mangrove reached down stilts into the mud. Thus the woods were actually lifted. They appeared to be suspended in air.

Late one day the column left behind the mangroves and struck out through swampy pools. It was after sundown, and they could actually see the sky through the trees' roots.

They were in a wide half-submerged bog with islands of grass on the far side. The sky was glowing. In the bog the "swamp lavender" flowers burned in the lurid light, and looking back it seemed that the black water under the trees was rising.

During the first days of exile, after the lottery losers had left Sawna, traveling through the other villages of the county they had had the illusion that the very soil was drifting away in the wind. And now in the twilight it seemed the mangrove forest had floated off.

After that everything was saw grass. The terrain through which the caravan passed was more level and also lower. It seemed as if now, with nothing but the grass, the landscape had become simplifed.

One of their shaman guides told them that having left the woods behind and having witnessed the ancestral animals, the band was entering the second stage of their swamp journey.

"From now on," he said, "you will begin to see objects as water."

• •

The drainage channels increased. After a while the caravan took to the channels. The only skyline was the feathery tips of the spartina grass. The bank also was held by the tough, deep-delving grass.

A moisture hung in the air, and seemed to wash up into the air. It seemed that the bank itself was no longer composed of solid earth. In the spaces between the soil grains there was water, and in the binding roots there was also water being pulled up through the stems and capillaries. Air and earth interfaced through the wet membrane. Water pressed to the top and evaporated into air, and through the membranes below, the water of the swamp, slightly salty, was sucked in.

Even the structure of the Spartina was water-bound. The water coalesced into these shapes of stems and spiky blades. It was as if the travelers were seeing, like an aura, the watery shapes of the plants.

After traveling long days in this way under the banks, they began to develop eyes for small things. In the week before, passing beneath mangroves they had hardly noticed the roots crusted with coon oysters. Now they felt, through the smallest life, the processes of the swamp. At the cool base of the spartina, the melampus snail fed on the detritus made by the decayed grass. The snail would rest and hide from the sun at midday, then climb the stem of the plant in the afternoon, along with the periwinkle. A beetle foraged among the roots. Nearby a clam worm left a trail of mucus on the mud. Transparent lice sucked the plant stems. The kernels of the seed stalks were cracked by frit larvae; and above, swarms of small flies hung like wisps of smoke over the marsh.

In the water too there were the countless small creatures and larvae that fed the fish. Water boatmen and whirligigs. The mosquito wriggler hung head down, pulling particles into its mouth and breathing through its tail from a tube. Anemones withdrew into the mud. They began seeing the ghostly shrimp.

• •

The Harditt band had had a number of shaman guides since the plains region. A guide would accompany the column for a certain stage, then be replaced by another. There was no attempt to assign one guide permanently to a group of lottery losers.

During the nights the shaman guides preferred not to stay in the camp but returned to one of the swamp islands. Possibly there were shaman settlements on the islands, which were used as bases for rest and to resupply the pilots of the caravan as it advanced in stages through the swamp country toward the border.

One late afternoon some Sawna women went down to the creek. The camp was pitched not far from a decaying pier. Here they found the shamans "looking at microorganisms."

They were using their third eye, their own guide explained to Nanda, to extend the visual spectrum so they could see objects of only a few microns' width.

"What is the third eye?" another of the Fourth Grade women asked Nanda. Nanda, who had seen the shaman on the trip find the lost handkerchief, also with his third eye, was at a loss to explain.

"And what do the shapes look like?"

The shamans only smiled.

What the shamans were experiencing seemed to be mostly an aesthetic pleasure. Their eyes almost closed, they were lying on the docks face down, squinting between the boards.

The shamans left soon after for one of their swamp islands.

That night it was hot. The women were having trouble sleeping. Sathan got out from under her mosquito net. Nanda and Bhungi, her granddaughter, joined her. The child trailed around the grass in her bare feet, holding her nightgown up so that it would not get wet from the dew.

They decided to wake the Fire woman and Bhungi's friend, Pulin, and go down to the creek again for a swim before dawn.

They slipped out of their clothes and left them on the bank. Stepping into the pool, they felt the softness. Though the creek was deep at this point, still the women could touch bottom. Sathan slowly paddled as her sister held up Bhungi. The child lay on the water trailing her hair.

The world was quiet. Sathan pushed her arms forward, then pulled them gently back. As she did so, her body seemed to lighten. In the great stillness of the swamp, she seemed to be the only thing moving.

When they returned to the bank their mosquito lamps had gone out. It was lighter. In the air somewhere birds were chorusing.

The stars had faded. Imperceptibly the sky had lost its transparency and grown milky. Above their heads, the outline of the swamp grasses began to appear.

A hazy light hung over the swamp, and now they could begin to see their own bodies, yet these were part of the milky dawn light. At the same time the stalks and leaves of the spartina became palpable.

The three women and the two children sat on the bank watching and feeling the first warmth.

There was a quickening flush over the sky, then the first sun struck the tops of the spartina.

The sun's rays struck the bank, and as the sun rose, its rays moved further and further down into the pool.

"Look!" exclaimed the Fire woman. "Can you see them?"

There was a line. On one side the pool was darkly still. And on the other side there was an active kinetic zone. During the night the energy-giving sediments had filtered down the underwater slope. The photoplankton were becoming active.

Light struck the minute silica skeletons of the diatoms and turned the mud gold. Where the bathers had stepped and scraped the bottom, there were purple ribbons and splotches. It was the hue of the exposed sulphur photosynthetic bacteria. Heat quickened the organisms. Sheets of blue-green algae shone from within the saw grass litter.

Above stretched the leaves of the grass that would die down to litter. Through the leaves the flower stalks were thrust up. On their threadlike stems pollen chambers were open and trembling, loosing pollen grains into the air in an invisible cloud.

The women also seemed to be dissolving and loosening in the first light of morning.

• •

Even the saw grass had been left behind. The ground rose and fell, but it could not be called a landscape, alternating between sun-heated pools and higher muddy flats baked by the sun.

During the early stages of the journey the shaman Elwood had given a dog's spirit reading for a child. Because of his bad eyesight he could hardly see the child or the dog. Nevertheless he had seen their "auras." During the swamp journey the shaman's eyesight had declined further. Leading the exile column along the marsh trails, their guides proceeded mostly "by feel." They seemed almost blind to their visual surroundings.

Were they then seeing the auras of the swamp, in particular the plants' and insects' auras? Were there to be other auras? Or were they using some other mode of perception?

One day the marchers were pursuing a muddy channel when Elwood, who had been leading the Ladpur "cauga," held up his hand. Before them stretched an alligator. She had laid her eggs and covered them in a heap of mud and decaying vegetable matter. This compost as it rotted produced heat, and the heat incubated the eggs.

The immobile female alligator, herself covered and caked with mud, seemed barely alive. Vapors of steam rose above the incubating mounds.

What the marchers noticed was that the shaman had not seen the animal. His eyes, caked with mud, were not even open. It was the heat that he had sensed, and that had caused him to stop and have them detour around the alligator.

Just as the Blue shamans were Weather and Soil sensors, were the Yellow shamans then heat sensors? Not oriented toward to track of the visible, nor following a compass direction, they seemed to be pursuing some other mode. Their response was to something felt through the pores and membranes like an osmotic pull, the lessening of a pressure gradient.

• •

The folk had continued their practice of telling their dreams and the myth stories. But the myths—whose origins were with the Blue shamans and which signified obscurely the Daily Lives in Nghsi-Altai—had become barely relevant. As to the Yellow shaman myth cycle, was it to be played out here in some manner?

They had now reached the "Kingdom of Decay," their shaman pilot had told them. The Sawna folk, who had come already through several stages, guessed that this must be one of the last stages of the exile voyage.

In past days the water in the marsh had grown brackish. But there were no tides. The salt, they conjectured, must be leached from the agricultural lands from which the wastes and sediments drained off, through the muddy channels into the swamp basin.

After the encounter with the alligator, their track lay along a section of swamp where on one side was bog or peaty muck. On the other side was a sheet of black water out of which rose a wood of dead trees. Hardly any branches remained, only the gray-green trunks were standing. On one of these a fisher hawk perched.

Beyond the flooded wood were more low flatlands covered with swamp lavender. And beyond that they could see open water, a stretch of pale steamy white that had no bounds or features and that seemed like the sea.

The shaman said: "All Nghsi drains into this. Toward the other side it is mostly salt. And there is the canal that leads to the cataract."

The day before the Yellow shaman had led them around the alligator, yet he was blind. The shamans were heat sensors. The band were in the place now where life decomposed, where all things burned with the slow combustion of decay.

"Wandering in the fields of hell, I came upon the realm Infrared"—one of Blake's songs had described.

The life processes burned—that is they passed energy on through the membranes activating one process after another. The sun and the atmosphere were one heat engine, but the internal processes of sentient and growing life were another. Here the energy gradient was always downward. Organized through the sun, as they burned the structures broke down through decay into their micro-elements, which were again recycled.

All of Altai, the biomes of the Plain, the Forest and Rift, drained into the swamp and were renewed.

The band had witnessed the shaman's knacker activities outside the villages, where they had burned the corpses. Now in the swamp, where everything was fluid and where plants and animals dissolved, they presided over the Decay Chains—just as the Blue shamans had presided over the growth chains, that is the building of structures and species.

In this way the exiles of Nghsi were being guided to the border, and perhaps were already experiencing what lay beyond the border.

MADDI'S CHILD

They were in open water, but the steamy mist had shut down around them. The liquid surface was light brown, streaked with yellow, and at intervals mottled with plants. Yet the channel or the several channels where they had been drifting must be deeper. Here the water was darker.

The landscape had vanished in steam—both the sky and the element on which they were being carried. Still, the "cauga" remnant on the raft seemed to have been brought closer.

The children floated gaily beside them. First Bhungi and Pulin, then Lal and Mukh, took turns riding on the back of a huge turtle.

Except for the sluggish underwater pull there was no movement. However, at intervals the steamy air would eddy and part. They could see they were passing between islands. Their banks rose distinctly from the swamp, but the places had no features. They were only mud. They were told that these were the islands of the Mud men.

Passing by one of these islands they were surprised to see naked figures. They were on the beach cooking. Near them were mid-dens, piles of shells and bones where they had previously eaten, and what appeared to be a totem pole. The Mud men were making their supper in a huge pot from which steam rose, but there was no fire under it.

There were about twenty. Their bodies were completely encased in mud, and their genitals were covered by a branch also mud-smeared. It appeared that they were wearing masks and that these were made of the same light gray or whitish blue mud, stiffened into clay. But it was hard to tell because the faces were unformed and without features.

It was possible, too, that some of these figures were shamans. The islands, like the hammocks earlier, were the resting places of the guides during the steamy trip through the swamp. Perhaps they were their permanent abode. The mud islands were the place from which, perhaps, the Yellow shamans appearing at intervals in the country to escort the lottery losers had always come.

The steam was lifting. They were passing by other islands without figures, only the piles of shells to indicate that the Mud men had been there. There were the totem poles, as many as three or four on a single island. On one the Sawna folk passed so close that they could see the great wooden totem in detail. At the base was a terrapin or broad land turtle. On the back of that was a mullet with a wide-open mouth. On top of these two were a crab and then a beetle. Then there were carved shapes which were not recognizable, but which might have represented May fly larvae or bacteria of some kind.

The topmost figure was a kite.

It was appropriate that the Mud men, who were residents of the swamp and who presided over the cycles of decay, should erect such a symbol.

Some of the carvings were of the Mud men themselves. And some of them seemed to be of the shamans.

• •

They had come to a place that was called Last Island. There the shamans made Maddi a but under one of the totem poles. Her labor began on the next day.

The hut was constructed of reeds. Reeds and straw were spread on the floor.

Sathan and her aunt Nanda encouraged her. Maddi gritted her teeth and concentrated. Between the contractions she sipped juice and enjoyed the company gathered around her. Maddi, with her knees bent and her back resting against a board, was very much the center of attention.

A family of white-footed mice were already making use of the shelter. Perhaps they had been living on this same spot before. They seemed almost tame. A mouse scampered along the pole, stopped, and twitched its ears at Maddi.

Her stomach was enormously stretched. Ramdas kept rubbing powder on the taut skin. She felt her hair lank and damp but did not lift her hand to smooth it.

Maddi lay panting with her mouth open. When the pains came she moved her head from side to side. Ramdas thought her eyes were large. The envelope had broken, and the blanket under her legs was wet.

Her father, Venu, was bending over to give her juice, and for a moment she had him confused with her great-grandfather, Gopal Harditt. And Ramdas she mixed up with Reddi. The light was behind their heads, and it seemed to be coming through them.

Maddi smiled at the animals. The rest of the animals of the place had come, summoned no doubt by the mouse. As Maddi lay they looked at her. There was a muskrat and a racoon sitting on its haunches. Two muddy gray birds stared solemnly down at Maddi. One of them kept twisting his neck to peck at fleas.

Finally the contractions sharpened. Her stomach, as the muscles tensed and the pressure mounted against the cervix, was hard as a stone. Her fist was clenched around Sathan's. During the last stage she could feel the creature adjusting its head, and there was a deep sexual feeling in her vagina as the baby was pushed forward.

• •

Maddi woke with the baby cradled on her arm. The morning light stole through the cracks in the reed mat, stippling Maddi's breast and the baby.

During the evening before the Ancestors had come. She remembered seeing Reddi, one of the "last gones," and the old councilor. They also had been present with the animals.

And so this was Last Island. The but was located on the shore, and the animals had come out of their holes and perches where they had been living. These were not the legendary beasts that the caravan had glimpsed when first entering the swamp, but the actual animals of the place—the residents. The thought made Maddi want to cry.

Yes. This is the last *place*. After this it will not be a place at all. It will be something different.

The Ancestors had come through the swamp to attend the childbirth. They had come from the Kansu region and had returned. As the pollen grains of the swamp grasses, lifted in the air, floated back over the plains, so the Ancestors had floated back. Like the pollen grains the members of the cauga band too had been loosened from their earthly soil and were now being dispersed toward America.

The visit of the Ancestors had been strengthening. She felt the strength, the pull of the line going back through time. The great-grandfather had been here, leaning beside the bed with his thin fingers and the veins bunched over the knuckles. He had reached down and smoothed Maddi's hair.

But for the Harditt toc, was this not also the last island? They could accompany the exiles only so far, and now they had reached the border. Were not they too "tied to earth?"

• •

The next day the "cauga" celebrated Kanagat. Also the Harditts had their child-naming.

During the swamp passage all the baggage had been relinquished except for the fragile family shrines made of bamboo and rice paper. After the last "ghost meal" even these were to be left behind. The cameos would dim, the burned joss sticks grow damp, and the colored streamers rot and unravel in the wind on the island shingle.

The new baby was called Gopal Harditt.

THE CITY OF BAKBAKWALANUSIWA

Already the waters surrounding Last Island were salt. The salt increased. Over the wide marsh, which extended back to the mainland, the bottom of the reeds and cattails were crusted with salt. As they reached to shore over the flats even the flowers were saltcaked.

The many "caugas" of lottery losers of the plains abandoned their rafts as they reached the shallows. Struggling toward the shore through the stiff reeds, there was a moment when the entire caravan seemed to disappear and become lost from each other.

The shore and the hills rising from the shore were a coarse naked sand.

Bunghi and Lal found themselves running up a line of dunes. There was in fact a wave of children running along the entire length of the beach, clambering up the dunes, calling and shouting to each other, and using their arms and legs in the loose sand. It was as if they had escaped and were impelled up after the long confinement on the rafts.

The two Harditt children had started out with Mukh and Pulin of the Fire woman's clan but had left them behind in the mad scramble up the beach. The sand grew looser and the flank of the dune steeper. The adults, far below on the shore, were coming ahead, but very slowly, as if unable to move out of the salt landscape.

They had reached the top. Here the dunes flattened to form a dyke. From the top of this, looking backward to the north over the wide basin of reeds, they could just see, barely visible on the horizon, the faint line of the mud islands.

On the opposite side was desert. The desert was flat sand at a level far lower than the inland sea. It was a grayish wan color and trackless, extending as far as the eye could see. Running straight along the bottom of the dyke was a canal, sunk in the stained sand.

The plane of the desert rose imperceptibly to the west. Here the surface was modeled into shifting hills.

Then they saw in the distance, struggling over the sand in a wavering line like ants, another of the exile caravans. And along the road, a third caravan of exiles was advancing.

The canal which lay along the bottom of the dyke was a continuation of the Nghsi River. The river passed through the Rift valley draining the Karst cities. The lakes and cantonments of the wilderness region were also drained by a tributary of the river which, circling in a wide arc, traced the western margin of the Drune. Then the wall of the forest ended and the land dwindled, first to low hills and then became dry scraggly mesa. At the point where the branches of the river joined, the desert began.

The wayfarers who had passed through the swamp struck out toward the east along the top of the dyke, above the others. For some days the march of the caravans from the Rift and the Drune was parallel.

Swarming up the dunes, the children had left behind Mukh and Pulin. And during the march along the dyke, the Harditts had become separated from several of the other clans which had composed the swamp-traveling "cauga."

Looking down one morning, the Sawna folk saw that the other two exile columns had joined. The next day all three caravans came together at a place where the dunes ended.

First the Sawna pilgrims had seen the shamans' skins stippled in the bamboo woods. Then they had become dirty and disfigured with brown streaks, passing through the mud islands, and had been blinded. And finally, on the water stretch of the journey, over the Sea of Reeds, the shamans' skin had become salt caked.

The long trek through the swamp had been as arduous for the shamans as for the pilgrims. And perhaps it was the shamans who were suffering the process of breakdown and recycling through the swamp. And now they were at the city which marked the end of the swamp journey.

The "cauga" remnant stood looking down at a lagoon. And on the other side of the lagoon was a city, constructed of reeds and cemented shells, but many of the buildings were vast. They appeared to be mostly warehouses. Behind the warehouses was a power station.

There were no compounds or point houses, as there were in the Rift cities of Altai. In front of the windowless warehouses stretched a long quay.

An array of boats ran out from the quayside. They were flat scows or sampans. The first rank was tied to the dock at the prow, and the rest extended back, lashed together side by side along the gunwales. The packed mass of boats extended out into the middle of the lagoon, cluttering it like a floating mat of lillies.

It was a city without inhabitants, an empty city. The Sawna families had been told it was a transhipment depot for souls. Was it, Motteram and Rathlee Golla wondered, a transhipment depot for the shamans as well?

• •

The caravan people had been gathered into the boats. Nanda and Rathlee's family were seated by the gunwale of one of the scows, crowded in with other families. It seemed to Nanda they were completely disoriented.

There was no order. Everyone had started clambering onto the boats at once. Nanda and Rathlee, together with Lucia and her family, stepped gingerly from the deck of one tipping sampan to the next. In the confusion they had almost lost Bunghi. The little girl, who had been clinging to her grandmother's hand, became separated from them only for a moment. They retrieved her, bawling. Motteram was carrying Lal on his shoulders.

These scows had flat open decks which rose slightly toward the bow and stern. They were sturdy and very battered and had evidently made the trip through the cataract many times. Along the gunwale, the deck was worn in a narrow track where the oarsmen or pilots had propelled the vessel with their long poles.

Night had settled over the lagoon. On top of the mast of Nanda's and Rathlee's boat was a lighted oil lantern. As the minutes passed, more lanterns were lighted.

Nanda Harditt, looking around the crowd, could see no sign of her sister's family.

There were no shamans within the boats. However, they had been at the quayside that afternoon. It had been at the command of the guides that the crowd of wayfarers had filled the boats.

The wide space in front of the warehouses was empty, and it appeared that the buildings were empty. Suddenly the quayside lighted up.

From the inside of the warehouses, from the roofs and basements, even—it seemed—from under their own boats, voices began to call. It was the high nasal calls of the Yellow shaman storytellers, their voices eerily projected.

The last one of the "earth leave-taking" or "capturing" dances of the Yellow Shaman Society was about to take place. Bunghi's arms tightened around her grandmother's neck. And Lal, clutching Motteram, began to whimper.

Though the unfamiliar setting heightened the drama's effect, the dances were the same ones that the Sawna folk had seen performed many times outside the villages of Kansu by the traveling troupes. A horde of terrifying and ferociously howling animals and birds erupted from the warehouses into the square. Among these was the cannibal bird, Bakbakwalanusiwa. But it was not one hapless villager being pounced on and eaten. In this case it was the shaman guides themselves. The entire length of the quay, before each section of the floating audience, performances were going on at once. Deafened by shrieks and assaulted by claws and beating wings and the tearing of beaks, the hapless victims were "captured." The former guides, surrounded by the Spirit Beings, were dragged bound into the boats.

Were these boats then destined for the "Under world"? Had the shaman guides, having been eaten by the cannibal bird Bakbakwalanusiwa and the other Spirit Beings, now acquired their potency and magical power to guide the boats during the descent through the cataract?

They were only ceremonial, these "earth leave-taking" dances. Yet there was no doubt that the travelers had gone through another step which approached the underground. And soon they would be traversing the world of spirits.

THROUGH THE CATARACT

The next day the flotilla left behind the empty city and proceeded through a series of locks to the canal, with the Spirit Beings "piloting" the boats. In their extravagant masks and regalia of feathers and skins, the Ancestral beings stood by the bows. Other shamans, now unshackled, manned the oars and sweeps.

Now at the level of the canal, they were at the back side of, and below, the city where the capturing dances had taken place. Looking up, the pilgrims could see an immense hydroelectric power station.

At a point below this was the outfall where the water, after passing from the lagoons to turn the turbines of the plant, gushed out in a torrent into the canal.

Standing high at the bow of each boat, with claws for hands and the visages of bears and hawks, their new pilots presented a fearsome sight. For the first time, the impending trip seemed terrifying.

"They have been eaten themselves. And now they are the eating ones," Rathlee Golla remarked to Motteram. It was clear that he felt himself victimized.

However, beyond the power outfall the flotilla halted. After guiding the boats for a short stretch, the old pilots disembarked and were replaced by new ones.

The journey toward the border continued.

• •

The water route had been wandering. Now they could see only a dozen or so of the other boats. The convoy had been separated. Though the river current moved rather slowly, many of the boats had evidently been carried on ahead.

The power outfall was behind. After the stage where they had let the pilots off, the deck of the river boat seemed even more crowded. The second branch of the Harditts sat close together. The Sawna folk were no longer with their plains clansmen. There were ten families on the deck. Several were Rift and Wilderness families.

Venu and Ramdas, their backs against some grain sacks, were discussing with Sathan the meaning of the capturing ceremony. Most of it was clear. They were forced to emigrate. Was it not an advantage, or at least a consolation, to have this event ratified by the power-giving birds?

Sathan said wryly, but with some puzzlement: "Yes. We are being exiled, and they are showing the way for us. But they are also forcing us."

Sathan thought that these guides were not like the others. They must be some kind of specialized shamans.

The faces of the new shaman pilots were those of young men and were quite plain. They had no special markings. They had come aboard with long poles, but these were not now in use. They had also carried some rotting grain sacks on board. A third pilot sat in the stern, guiding the boat with a long sweep.

The sturdy bamboo poles which were now lying on the deck were each about twenty feet long and capped with a steel tip.

The stream meandering between its banks flowed evenly. What had before been only a stagnant canal had now—with the added volume from the hydroelectrical plant outfall—become a sizeable river.

Gradually the sound of the tumbling water spewing from under the plant receded, and its place was taken by another distant roaring, that of the Falls. Beyond the last city, the great basin of reeds also came to an end. This was the last border and the terminus of the inland sea as well. Here, over a basalt ledge and combed by cypress roots, the water concentrated at the lip of the hanging plateau of Altai and plunged over the Falls.

As the sound of the outfall diminished, that of the Falls, high overhead and to the left, kept getting louder.

Venu asked Sathan if she were thirsty. One of the Karst families had managed to bring a container of water on board and a Coleman stove. Otherwise, there were no belongings of the wayfarers on the river boat.

The river in a wide sweep was taking them in a direction away from the border. They were passing between banks of overhanging trees through which some farmland could be glimpsed. One of the pilgrims took out a harmonica.

The rough spritely tune and the glimpse of the plowed fields through the willows made Venu think of home. Instinctively he looked around for Motteram and the other Harditt family. But they were not to be located in the boat convoy.

The river wandered in great sweeps and sometimes deepened. And sometimes they rode over shallows where the pace quickened and the guides worked the poles. Then the placid drifting resumed.

The empty city and the power plant were behind. The squadron, taken along by a current which was sometimes barely perceptible, had nevertheless descended a good distance. They were now far below the level at which they had set out early that morning from the lagoons connecting to the Sea of Reeds.

The river had swung back toward the border. To their left and right the low hills which they had been passing through steepened abruptly.

The hillside had now become a ravine. Above were misty crags. Venu stared up at terraces built into the slope where there were tiny figures, and which he took to be corn or tobacco plots perhaps. Then it was only crags and trees. A high-tension line marched by over the firs. There was no further sign of life.

The gorge widened and straightened, and for an interval they could see ahead. The wall of mountains they had been approaching was now directly in front of them. The face was scarred as if by stone quarries and partly obscured, by mist. The river had widened and grown faster. It seemed that the river was entering the mountain through an enormous hole.

• •

There had been a strong current earlier, but now the gliding waters were almost smooth. The flotilla was reassembled again and could be made out by a long line of lights.

They were in a cavern. From the entrace through which they had come, light still diffused over the immense milky roof. Ramdas looking back could make out the outlines of the vast roof. Ahead there was only darkness. And the line of the lights and masts growing progressively smaller and dimmer.

• •

They were still under the mountain. Their own boat was in a roofed-over channel sliding between walls of black rock. Again they could hear the stunning roar of the falls above somewhere. The two shamans at the sides had moved apart. Every once in a while they would lean out and exert pressure against the rock with their poles. The shaman at the back had taken in his sweep and was also using his pole to fend off the boat from the wet walls.

The pull of the sluiceway was steady below them, it seemed as if they were racing. The other families, perhaps because they were crouching on the deck, could barely be seen. Ramdas could see Maddi, who was holding the small Gopal tight to her breast. Her back was wedged against Ramdas's leg.

Passing under these low places, where the limestone buttresses of the cavern stood close, the light on the mast of their small boat grew sharper and yellower. Ramdas could almost reach out and touch the wet face of the rock as it moved by.

• •

The squadron had taken a turning. Here there were no openings to the light and no current. There seemed to be no will to move in the stillness of this underground lake or series of lakes. It seemed not to be a place they had come to or would ever leave.

The clear air was laden with cold.

Ramdas watched the shamans, who were sitting idly. Wavering patterns and oscillations of light came from the water itself and played against the roof of the cavern and against the ship's sides.

The shamans had stopped poling and were sitting along the gunwale with their feet in the water. Moving their feet playfully, they stirred streams of luminescence. Their poles which now lay on the deck seemed also to be a source of illumination.

He stood watching the play of light-shapes over the vast roof. There seemed to be an infinity of shapes.

"We are in the storehouse of souls."

Ramdas also remembered the phrase, "shapes are changed."

The play of light appeared to come from the surface only of the underground lake. Below it was cold and dark. No doubt, on the floor of the cavern also the illuminations played.

A coldness gripped him. Though there were other figures on the deck, he seemed to be the only one living. In any case, he was alone.

Was it on this lake that the dead were recycled after being dissolved in the chemistry of the swamp? It was possible that, for all the others of the land of Altai who had come this way through the timeless cave, piloted by the shamans, it had been to undergo death and re-creation.

The lake and perhaps the mountain were beyond time. But they were moving out of it. Still living, they were passing through Under world. But to where?

He remembered what Tattattatha had said: "Remember, in the new place you carry your souls with you. You are only looking for your bodies."

• •

The last sluiceway was behind them. The rock walls had rushed apart. The sampan, plunging and sliding, rode on an expanse of foam. They were riding down the center of the cataract at tremendous speed.

The boat was in a kind of trough, as if there were a river within a river —depressed and constrained at the lower level by the element of sheer speed, by its rushing load. Washing back against the shore, there was another river which seemed to be held there in suspension, or even moving backward.

Beneath them the boat plunged and slid. It veered among mounds of water which excploded over the rocks. The current boiled around the Yellow shaman's poles as the shamans themselves leaned out over it tilting and lunging.

In the hands of the plunging shamans, the poles seemed to lengthen and grow taller. The figures, moving at such speed, seemed to be pure concentrations of force. And the cataract itself like some spinning black hole.

Then quickly it became lighter. The two rivers had subsided into one again. The walls at the sides became clearly visible. Then they were out and into the sunlight.

• •

They were through and in the sunlight.

High overhead the mist drifted from the lip of the Falls over the forest. It was a white silky mist, but even so it partly obscured the high falls. The sound of the falls was partly muted.

The river, white and glassy, flowed between banks below which the green of the forest was reflected. The obscure forest green was also partly clouded as the mist at the bottom of the Falls boiled up and settled back.

Evidently some fish had leaped into the boat as they had passed the cataract. On the deck one of the Karst families was collecting them and putting them in a pail.

On the deck still lay the grain sacks. Evidently these were meant for them to exchange in the coastal cities, for their passage perhaps.

The shamans' poles were gone. However, the sweep was lashed to the stern where the shaman had left it. One of the passengers took this up and began to move the river boat through the gorges.

END OF BOOK IV

A SHORT BIOGRAPHY OF ROBERT NICHOLS

An American writer, Robert Nichols was born on July 15, 1919 in Worcester, Massachusetts. As his paternal grandfather was a homeopathic doctor, he was probably born at home. His father, Charles L. Nichols, struggled with schizophrenia and paranoia throughout his life, and this illness profoundly affected the family. He hoped that his only son, Robert, would have nothing to do with the family banking and insurance business and would, instead, become a painter. Perhaps because of his need to escape being institutionalized, Nichols' father developed a passion for railroad trains and the rights of railroad workers (this informs Nichols' first book of poetry, *Slow Newsreel of Man Riding Train*). He was an important, albeit fraught, influence who gave Nichols a deep appreciation for art. Nichols, however, identified more closely with his mother, Clara Lalonde, and with her French Canadian family who had migrated to New England to work in the textile mills at the turn of the twentieth century. He memorialized Clara and her family in *Clara Remembered*, a work of poetry and prose recounting his mother's early years.

Nichols completed his undergraduate work at Harvard, where he studied Philosophy and spent his free time acting in and directing plays. He then served as a Navy officer in the Pacific Theatre during World War II. Based in the Philippines, he saw no direct action. After the war, Nichols moved to New York City where he worked as a welder in Brooklyn and on a tugboat until he returned to Harvard to pursue his graduate degree in Landscape Architecture from the Harvard School of Design where he studied with Bauhaus' Walter Gropius, and where he graduated in 1948. While in Cambridge, he became part of the Harvard poetry scene, becoming friends with the poet and publisher James Laughlin, who went on to found New Directions Books, the first publisher of the *Nghsi-Altai* series. "Nichols was one of a select group of poets that Laughlin sent his poetry to for comments," poet Geoffrey Gardner remembers. "The others included Kenneth Rexroth, Denise Levertov and Hayden Carruth." Nichols also became associated with the Cambridge Poets Theatre, which included Frank O'Hara, Gregory Corso and Richard Eberhart.

By 1950, Nichols was designing playgrounds and parks in Gothenburg, Sweden; Philadelphia, PA; and New York City, which was his home up until the 1970s. He began designing playground equipment for the pioneering mid-century company Creative Playthings, which employed sculptors Isamu Noguchi and Henry Moore, as well as architect Louis Kahn. A firm believer in the creative play movement, Nichols went on to found his own not-for-profit playground company, Playground Associates, to further the development of abstract sculpture for playgrounds. He worked with sculptor Mitzi Solomon Cunliffe, landscape architect Hideo Sasaki, and American architects Shepard Schreiber and Edward Larabee Barnes to produce easily reproducible and affordable pieces of equipment. Playground Associates' best-known piece was called Saddle Slide. Cast in stone that was formed in fiber glass molds, children could happily slide down its curves and climbed through the varied, child-sized holes. As a father, he encouraged his young children to help develop the forms for his playground equipment incorporating them into his numerous park projects.

In 1952 he married Mary Perot. The couple had three children. Dan Wolf, co-founder and publisher of *The Village Voice,* hired her, and she became the founding City Editor, and her weekly column, *Runnin' Scared*, covered local politics, the Italian Mafia and exposed corruption in New York government. Perot later became the President of WNYC, the New York public radio and television stations. Her marriage to Nichols ended in divorce in 1968. Perot, introduced Nichols to community activist Jane Jacobs, and they joined the 1958 campaign to stop New York Parks Commissioner Robert Moses from destroying Washington Square and part of Greenwich Village with an automobile expressway. Moses' plan would have cut through Washington Square Park, the South Village and would have decimated Chinatown, Little Italy and what now includes the SOHO and Tribeca neighborhoods.

Moses had been plotting a dramatic intervention in Washington Square since 1935, and it eventually became a critical piece of his broader plan to route traffic to a massive freeway he proposed to connect the Williamsburg and Manhattan bridges across Manhattan to the Holland Tunnel, dubbed the Lower Manhattan Expressway, or LOMEX. Washington Square Park, the center of Greenwich Village, was free of traffic for the first time since the Parks Department had taken it over in 1870. With roads closed (except for a bus turn-around operating near the Arch until 1963), the central area around the fountain began to flourish as a performance space. Folksingers and poets gathered around the fountain and the lawns to perform and listen. Led by Jacobs, Washington Square became both the rallying site and cry against Moses' scheme, which was finally defeated. The victory had great significance for Nichols and Perot. Ed Fancher, the *Village Voice*'s co-founder, credited Perot's articles on the campaign against Moses with increasing the *Voice*'s circulation and saving the nascent publication from bankruptcy.

For Nichols the experience would lead to one of his best known plays, *Expressway*, which was produced as street theatre by the Public Theatre's Joseph Papp in 1968. Yet the saved Washington Square Park would become one of Nichols' most prominent architectural accomplishments. He was chosen to lead a team of nine local architects who volunteered to redesign the park pro bono for public and pedestrian use. With the promise of an uninterrupted car-free expanse came the opportunity to rethink what the Square should be.

Over a period of years, Nichols worked with representatives of local organizations to reach some consensus about the Square's future. Nichols reconciled divided community preferences from as many people as possible, and from all ages. These included his idea for three small hills where young children could run up and down in unstructured free-play;

curved seating nooks where people could meet and talk; a wooden adventure playground for older children; a stage where local artists could perform, and a pétanque court for older members of the neighborhood. Perhaps the greatest invention of the 1970 renovation was the opening up of the central area around the fountain to create a large sunken plaza ringed by shade trees. This plaza again became the heart of Greenwich Village, attracting performers, orators, and audience alike to participate in free and open public expression.

In the midst of becoming one of the political leaders of Greenwich Village, Nichols returned to one of his passions: the theatre. Other than acting during his undergrad years, he began writing plays during the war, and continued to do so. His arrival in Greenwich Village coincided with a theatrical renaissance that was occurring on side streets away from Broadway, particularly in what had become known as the Off-Broadway movement. But the rise in property taxes and the demands of unions had forced the more experimental theatre companies to move downtown to the Village, creating an entirely new revolution in American drama that would be named the "Off-Off Broadway" movement, and which operated in basements, lofts, in streets and, most famously, in cafés. Nichols became the co-founder of the Judson Poet's Theater, within the sanctuary of the Judson Memorial Church, which became one of the movement's cornerstones. The theatre (which was separate from but worked closely with the Judson Dance Company) would premiere work by Rosalyn Drexler, Maria Irene Fornes, Sam Shepard, and Robert Nichols. While the notion of a church fostering experimental and frequently irreligious theatre may be hard to fathom today, it was not in the early '60s for a liberal congregation bordering Washington Square Park. Nichols and the pastor and composer Al Carmines were given only two guidelines: no religious drama and no censorship. The first theater season started in 1961with poet Joel Oppenheimer's *The Great American Desert* and Nichols' production of Guillaume Apollinaire's *The Breasts of Tiresias* (the first production in the Anglophone world in English). In 1963, the company produced Nichols' finest early play, the prophetic *Wax Engine*. Nichols also maintained a connection with the Hardware Poets theatre, which premiered two of his plays, and performed behind a hardware store in the village.

After three years with Judson, and with the rise in America's involvement in Vietnam, Nichols decided to take art to the streets on a flatbed truck that travelled around the city and performed his political plays for the public, influencing Papp and his outdoor theater. Many of these early plays took aim at the Vietnam War, racism and discrimination, and corporate exploitation of the urban poor. Nichols had already begun an association with Peter Schumann and the Bread and Puppet Theater, which lasted a lifetime.

Through his experience with the Washington Square Park campaign, Nichols' interest in and commitment to the "parks for people" movement grew, and he invented the term "vest-pocket playgrounds" and fought to reclaim sections of the East Village and the South Bronx, neighborhoods where landlords were paying arsonists to burn down buildings as part of a long-range speculation scheme. From his involvement in poor and underserved communities through his street plays and collaboration with the Bread and Puppet Theater, Nichols applied his environmental sustainability, playground and public space ideas to these neighborhoods. In 1972 Nichols founded a construction company and basketball team, Avanza, which grew out of his concern that teenagers needed skills and community. With the neighborhood teenagers, most of whom were either Puerto Rican or African-American, Nichols designed and built "junk" playgrounds made out of found and recycled materials (railroad ties, old tires, etc.). Nichols was also part of the movement to occupy abandoned buildings and make them livable. His construction company and basketball team put up some of the first windmills and solar collectors in New York City.

In the mid-1970's Robert moved to Vermont with his second wife, the author and activist Grace Paley, whose life and work have been well-documented. They remained married from 1972 until Paley's death in 2007 and shared a passion for literature, social justice, and environmental action. In Thetford, Vermont, Nichols began to farm while continuing to write fiction, literary criticism, and essays on economics; he also created serialized comics for three collective communities for his own Penny Each Press. During these years, other than his journalism, Nichols wrote two collections of poetry, *Red Shift* and *Address to the Smaller Animals* (both published by his own Penny Each Press); *Daily Lives in Nghsi-Altai* in four volumes (New Directions Press, 1977-1979); the long biographical poem about his mother, *Clara Remembered* (A Musty Bone, 1991); a collection of short stories, *In the Air* (Johns Hopkins University Press, 1991), and a comic novel, *From the Steam Room* (Tilbury House, 1993). Much of his work remains unpublished, including two novels, Early American Communist Utopias, and Simple Gifts.

Readers of Robert Nichols short stories will find his United States of America to be a place that is at once familiar and yet strangely different. In the story 'The Meter Reader', for example, a Mr. Gross discovers his monthly utility bill includes a $31 surcharge to pay for the murder of four Nicaraguan villagers ("That seemed low," he muses). Throughout his writing, Nichols' moral outrage is the more eloquent for being muted. His characters continually confront the intrusion of the grotesque and absurd into everyday life with an understated puzzlement reminiscent of Kafka's Joseph K or Gregor Samsa. Depicting a world in which the comfortable and well-off are denied the luxury of isolation from those who suffer, "where the invisible and hidden is measured." During his early years in Vermont, Nichols, who saw economic pressures on small farms as a crisis, worked with local dairy farmers. He regularly participated in town meetings with Paley and became active in the community. He donated a part of his land to the Thetford Fire Department, which recognized him with a service award in 1988.

For over fifty years, Nichols was an activist in the antiwar movement and antinuclear movements and a proponent of the Social Ecology movement. He took part in many non-violent direct actions around stopping the Vietnam War and, later, the Vermont Yankee and Seabrook nuclear power plants. His work with decentralist, anti-war, anti-nuclear, and conservation organizations in New England, such as the Northeast Organic Farmers Association, the Institute for Social Ecology, the Ompompanoosuc Affinity Group, and Clamshell Alliance was a passion he shared with Paley. Nichols and Paley also had a publishing company, Glad Day Publishing Collaborative, which published the work of nearly a dozen authors during the late '90s. Nichols said that the "aim of Glad Day is the restoration of a political literature." Nichols was also on the faculty of the Joiner Center Writing Workshops for many years, a center in Boston that studies war and social consequences through literature.

As for his position in American literature, Nichols, the consummate rebel, never could be pegged. While friends with his first publisher, Lawrence Ferlinghetti, and poet Allen Ginsberg, Nichols resisted being associated with the Beat Movement despite having been published in Elias Wilentz's 1960 anthology *The Beat Scene* and Ferlinghetti's "Pocket Poet Series." And although Nichols drafts Jack Kerouac as an important character in the *Nghsi-Altai* series, he was not a fan of the writer of *On the Road.*

Robert Nichols died on October 14, 2010, in Thetford, Vermont, at the age of 91.

CPSIA information can be obtained
at www.ICGtesting.com
Printed in the USA
BVOW09s0853120318
510169BV00001B/69/P